MW01088134

10 MARCHFIELD SQUARE

10 MARCHFIELD SQUARE

NICOLA WHYTE

UNION
SQUARE
&CO.

NEW YORK

**UNION
SQUARE
&CO.**

NEW YORK

UNION SQUARE & CO. and the distinctive Union Square & Co. logo
are trademarks of Sterling Publishing Co., Inc.

Union Square & Co., LLC, is a subsidiary of Sterling Publishing Co., Inc.

Text © 2025 Nicola Whyte

All rights reserved. No part of this publication may be reproduced,
stored in a retrieval system, or transmitted in any form or by any means
(including electronic, mechanical, photocopying, recording, or otherwise)
without prior written permission from the publisher.

All trademarks are the property of their respective owners, are used
for editorial purposes only, and the publisher makes no claim of
ownership and shall acquire no right, title, or interest in such
trademarks by virtue of this publication.

This is a work of fiction. Names, characters, businesses, events, and incidents
are the products of the author's imagination. Any resemblance to actual
persons, living or dead, or actual events is purely coincidental.

ISBN 978-1-4549-5841-3
ISBN 978-1-4549-5842-0 (e-book)

For information about custom editions, special sales, and
premium purchases, please contact specialsales@unionsquareandco.com.

Printed in Canada

2 4 6 8 10 9 7 5 3 1

unionsquareandco.com

Cover design by Patrick Sullivan
Cover images: Shutterstock.com: Con_Texture (intruder);
Anastasiia Gevko (type); LadadikaArt (binoculars); sergio34 (wood texture);
Nadia Snopek (woman at window)
Interior image: ahmad agung/iStock/Getty Images Plus (binoculars)
Interior design by Kevin Ullrich

For my father, Andrew Gordon Whyte.
1952–2020
You always believed this day would come.
I wish you could have seen it.

10 MARCHFIELD SQUARE

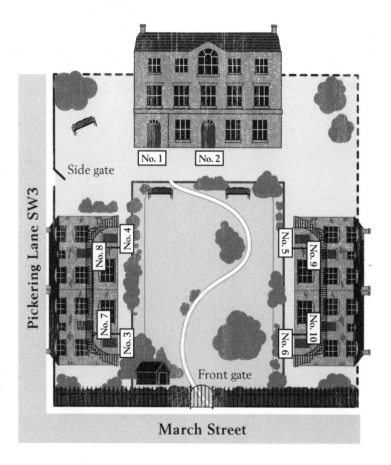

Side gate

Pickering Lane SW3

No. 1   No. 2

No. 8   No. 4

No. 5   No. 9

No. 7   No. 3

No. 10   No. 6

Front gate

March Street

1

Celeste

Celeste van Duren shifted in her armchair, trying to stop herself from dozing off. The late-afternoon sun was setting, bathing her carefully positioned chair in golden autumnal light and creating the perfect conditions for a very pleasant nap. But she mustn't nap today. She was waiting for someone to find the body.

The body of Richard Glead had lain on the kitchen floor of 10 Marchfield Square for almost a day. Initially, Celeste hadn't been sure that he was dead. Injured, certainly, if the blood on his shirt was anything to go by, but perhaps he was just unconscious. There were also a number of beer bottles on the table, so it wasn't outside the realm of possibility that the man was both injured *and* dead drunk.

As it turned out, he was just dead.

Celeste had considered calling the police but decided, on the whole, it would be better not to draw attention to her habit of spying on her tenants. Richard Glead had been the worst kind of human being. Barely human at all, in Celeste's opinion. The only mystery, as far as she was concerned, was why no one had killed him before.

But after many hours of watching, waiting for Richard's unfortunate wife to discover the body, Celeste was starting to worry that perhaps she wasn't coming. Perhaps Linda Glead had finally got up the courage to leave her awful husband, and taken her tears and her bruises off to somewhere or someone else. Not that Celeste wouldn't be happy with such an outcome, but she couldn't help thinking that if anyone deserved to see Mr. Glead dead, it was Mrs. Glead.

She lifted her binoculars.

The bright red bloom of blood on the front of Richard's shirt had darkened considerably over the hours, but as far as Celeste could see, there was no blood on the kitchen floor. She was glad. She'd watched Linda scrubbing that floor as if her life depended on it, which, on some days, it had. The silver coin on the table glinted one last time as the sun dipped behind the London skyline.

Maybe she *should* call the police. She wasn't keen to be known as the kind of busybody who spent hours at her window, watching her neighbours, but then, how else was an eighty-two-year-old with an artificial hip and a lot of dead friends supposed to fill her days?

She swung her binoculars around the square. From the picture window in the upper room of the town house—Celeste would never call it a maisonette—she could see the windows of the flats to the right and to the left. On the second floor of the right-hand block, her cleaner, Audrey, had just arrived home to Flat 7, and Celeste watched as she stood at the kitchen window, perhaps making herself a cup of tea.

Mr. Hetherington sat in his wheelchair in the courtyard, sketching, but here came Mrs. Hetherington to call him back inside the studio of their ground-floor flat, directly beneath Celeste's apartments. It never ceased to amaze her how little they seemed to argue, in spite of spending almost every waking moment together. The late Mr. van Duren had been the very best of men and Celeste had adored him, but post-retirement, even they had needed to spend some time apart to preserve their equanimity.

Her binoculars continued their sweep. Captain Gordon from number 4 was sitting on his usual bench with *The Times*, although the fading light would surely send him inside soon, while Brigitte Hildebrandt from number 6 was just entering the square, her latest beau laden with expensive shopping bags. No one else in the left-hand block seemed to be home, their windows dull with a flat, grey emptiness.

A discreet clank signalled the entrance of Dixon, Celeste's valet, and in a moment, he was at her elbow, setting the tea tray down on the small table.

"Anything?" he asked.

She lowered the binoculars and sighed.

"No."

"Not like her to stay out all night," said Dixon, and Celeste suppressed a smile. Dixon disapproved of her people-watching habit, rarely commenting on her observations and giving the impression he thought it beneath him. Occasionally, however, he betrayed himself.

"It was quite a knock he gave her this time," she said. "Perhaps it was the final straw."

"Won't look good though, will it?" He handed her a cup of tea. "To the police."

"No, I suppose not."

Dixon sat down in the other armchair while Celeste reached for a Viennese finger.

"Tomorrow night is poker night," she said, dunking it in her tea. "They'll find him eventually."

"When they do, they'll question everyone in the square and realise you can see number ten from here. They'll wonder why we didn't call it in."

Celeste nibbled her biscuit.

"You're right," she said eventually. "Being unobservant is worse than being nosy—to the police, anyway. We'll call them after tea."

As it transpired, they didn't have to call anyone after all. As Dixon stood to help Celeste out of her armchair, movement caught his eye.

"Ey up," he said, straightening for a better look. "She's back."

Celeste reached at once for her binoculars and saw that "she" was indeed back and crossing the courtyard. She watched as the hunched figure of Linda Glead, mousy hair hanging over her face, let herself into Flat 10. Celeste waited, breath held, glasses trained on the kitchen window, and then Linda appeared, standing in the doorway, looking down at the body of her husband on the floor.

One Mississippi, counted Celeste, two Mississippi, three Mississippi . . .

Linda unfroze and crept forward, as if unsure what she was looking at. Perhaps death had changed the face of Richard Glead, or perhaps she thought he might be asleep and that waking him would earn her a second black eye.

But as Celeste watched newly widowed Linda Glead stand over her husband's cold and lifeless body, she wondered if perhaps her slow reaction was down to something else entirely.

Perhaps, quite simply, she just couldn't believe her luck.

2

Audrey

As she did every day after getting home from work, Audrey Brooks drank her tea on the window seat in the lounge. She enjoyed this peaceful half hour, having the flat all to herself, before she did whatever chore she could find to soothe her conscience. Mei insisted that her constant cleaning was unnecessary, that she was happy to pay more of the rent because of her bigger salary (and bigger bedroom), but Audrey could never shake the feeling of being beholden. Mei was an incredible best friend, and their move to Marchfield Square had been entirely down to her, but the inequality when it came to the rent weighed heavily on Audrey, so she tried to earn her keep the only way she could.

She looked out over the square to where Roshan Jones, the caretaker and gardener, was sweeping fallen leaves from the flagstones in front of the big house. Once a double-fronted Georgian town house but now split into two large flats, the house made up almost one entire side of the square, and Roshan always kept the paving free of debris for both Celeste and the Hetheringtons.

A movement caught her eye and she turned her head, scanning the small central garden that lay beyond the courtyard to the wrought-iron gates at the end. There was Mrs. Hildebrandt, entering the square with her new boyfriend and looking like the film star she used to be, her camel-coloured wool coat and fur hat lending her an air of autumnal glamour.

Down in the garden, Captain Gordon sat on his bench, doing the sudoku in an actual newspaper with the silver pen he kept in the breast pocket of his blazer. From time to time he'd pause, tap the pen against the end of his grey moustache, then return it to the paper. The Captain could be a little pompous at times, but Audrey was fond of him. She was fond of everyone here, except Richard Glead and the strange guy in Flat 5, who acted like the other residents didn't exist.

The old coach houses and the servants' quarters above, now converted into flats, ran along both sides of the garden, between the gates and the big house. Audrey watched as Mrs. H and her friend walked down the path toward number 6, the ground-floor flat at the far end of the mews on the opposite side of the square. Audrey and Mei shared Flat 7, a two-bed maisonette with the entrance on the first floor, on the other side of the square. The unusual numbering system ran a clockwise loop around first the lower flats, then the uppers, with the exception of the big house, which was, naturally, 1 Marchfield Square.

She sipped her tea, glancing up at the top floor of Celeste's apartments. The pink light of the setting sun reflected off the picture window of the big room, but there was movement beyond. Dixon, maybe, bringing Celeste her afternoon tea. A flash glinted behind the glass, but Audrey was already turning to look at the city skyline. She and the other residents had been out late last night, watching the fireworks in Battersea Park from the shared balcony outside her and Mei's flat. She'd felt so warm and safe, standing near her own front door with a mug of hot chocolate, watching the display with Mei and their neighbours.

Audrey wondered how long she'd be able to keep living here, in Celeste's carefully manicured safe haven, cocooned from the world. And what would happen to it once Celeste had passed on. She shook her head to banish the thought. She never wanted to leave. And with the exception of her bad hip, Celeste was in perfect health. Nothing to worry about for a long while yet.

Her phone pinged and she reached for it, steeling herself. There it was, another alert from her bank. Another debit from her account, which was once again dangerously close to the limit of her overdraft. She swiped the message away but the pressure in her chest remained, so she took a deep breath and let it out in a series of short puffs. She was at Celeste's tomorrow, and Celeste always paid in cash, the money waiting for her on the hall table in a little brown envelope. She'd go to the bank straight after. That should keep the wolves at bay for a few days.

She needed more clients, but she worked a full week as it was, and no one wanted the cleaner in on evenings or weekends. Only the office-cleaning agencies did that, and she avoided them. Her options had become extremely limited.

She took another deep breath and let it out. Then another. And another.

She gulped her tea, which was already growing cold. Maybe she'd steam-clean the tiles in the bathroom. That was always soothing, and then Mei would be home and they could plan dinner and go through Mei's dating apps. She liked doing that. All the fun, none of the risk.

She'd just stood up when she heard it.

Screaming. Someone outside was screaming.

3

Lewis

Lewis McLennon swiped his electronic key fob against the side gate with a sigh, and shouldered his way through, thinking about dinner. He fancied Thai food tonight, or maybe pizza. Or maybe both. Did anywhere do a Thai pizza? He'd have to go through the menus on his app, see if he could find one. That'd take up the first part of his evening. Then there'd be the eating part and then, well . . . same old same old.

He went through the courtyard with a nod to the Captain, sat on a bench as usual, then let himself into his flat, shutting the door and dropping his keys into the bowl with another sigh.

"Right," he said out loud, to no one at all. He'd ducked out of work early, telling his boss that he'd finished his calls for the day and had a terrible headache. Of course, what he'd actually said was that his head was "bangin'," and his boss had nodded and said, "All right, mate," and that had been that.

God, he hated his job.

Suit off, quick shower, and then he didn't need to think about his horrible job until tomorrow.

Lewis hadn't even taken off his coat when he heard the scream. It was loud, very loud, and sounded close. Maybe one of the upstairs flats? He grabbed his keys and headed back outside.

Captain Gordon was standing up, newspaper loose in his hand, while the gardener hastened down the path toward them.

Lewis opened his mouth to ask if they'd heard it too, but it was patently obvious they had.

"Up there," said the Captain, pointing.

Lewis turned and saw the woman from one of the flats above him—Linda something?—standing on the balcony, looking back through the open door of her flat.

"Are you all right?" he called up to her. Again, this was a stupid question. Of course she wasn't all right, she'd just screamed at the top of her lungs. No wonder his editor said his dialogue needed work.

Linda Whatever-Her-Name-Was turned around but didn't speak, at which point Lewis heard footsteps. A woman—young, reddish hair, pink cheeks—was running across the courtyard. She took the stairs to the first floor two at a time, heading toward Linda and the open door of Flat 10. Lewis and the Captain exchanged a look, and Lewis realised perhaps he should have thought of that, although he consoled himself with the knowledge that evolution would soon filter out the majority of people who ran toward screams rather than away.

Shamed into action however, he did likewise, hurrying up the stairs.

"What happened?" he asked Linda, touching her shoulder. She flinched away.

"I . . . he . . ."

She pointed to the open door, so he followed the young woman inside.

The hall was devoid of furniture and spotlessly clean. He glanced through the door on his right, into the living room, but nothing seemed amiss. The door on the left was to the kitchen, and here he found the girl standing, staring at something on the floor.

"What is it?" he asked, and she jumped, looking at him in alarm, her eyes wide and startlingly green in her now-ashen face. She stepped aside so he could enter the room and he saw, lying on the linoleum floor, a man.

He took a few steps closer. It was Linda's husband, his chest covered in blood and his face a waxy shade of grey. Lewis could see at once that he was dead. Gunshot wound, by the look of it.

He walked around the body to get a better view. The man's mouth was twisted into a grimace, as if in his last moments he'd been trying to say something. Whatever made a person alive was definitely no longer inside Whatever-His-Name-Was. Robert? Richard? Some *R*-name, anyway.

Lewis had never seen a dead body before. He wanted to get his phone out, take pictures, make some notes, but common decency—or at least, the girl observing his common decency—wouldn't allow it. He needed to remember the weird sheen across the man's head, and the way the colour of his skin changed near his ears.

"What are you doing?" asked the girl. Woman. Probably in her late twenties. Definitely not a girl. She was now looking at him, not the body, and frowning.

"Just making sure."

"We need to leave," she said. "Call the police. And an ambulance. Or something."

Lewis nodded.

"Or something."

The woman made no move, either to leave or to call anyone. Perhaps she'd gone into shock? He walked around the body toward her, but she immediately took a step back.

He held his hands up.

"Sorry. I thought you'd frozen. I'll call, shall I?"

She nodded, then turned abruptly and left the room. Lewis took out his phone and, after a minute, dialled 999.

"Emergency services operator. What service do you require?"

"Police," said Lewis firmly. "Someone's been murdered."

4

Audrey

Audrey sat beside Linda Glead on the Captain's bench. Mrs. Hildebrandt had brought out a cup of strong sweet tea, which Linda sipped only when Audrey reminded her to, and every now and then she'd give a little shake of the head, as if struggling to compute what was happening. Roshan Jones sat silently on her other side, his expression still and unreadable.

It was dark now, and the Victorian street lamps lit the courtyard in circles of orange light. The Captain stood beside the side gate, chatting to the police officer stationed there, while another two officers stood beside the main gate, directing personnel in and out of the square. The man from Flat 5, meanwhile, hovered around outside Linda's flat. Today was the first time she'd ever seen Flat 5 Guy up close, and he was behaving oddly. Taller than average, with dark curly hair and brown eyes, she'd have put him in his mid-thirties, yet he was behaving like a child at a theme park. He seemed interested to the point of excitement in everything going on, and kept his phone in his hands the entire time, typing furiously the minute the police weren't looking. Probably posting about it on social media, or acting the big man on some lads' text group. He looked the type, in his junior-stockbroker suit and too-shiny shoes.

A female uniformed police officer stood beside the bench. Occasionally she glanced down at Linda and smiled reassuringly, but Audrey saw her gaze lingering on Linda's black eye, visible beneath her makeup, and the livid purple bruises on her wrists.

Audrey could tell what she was thinking, and had to resist the urge to tell Linda to pull her sleeves down.

It was impossible to live in Marchfield and not know the situation with the Gleads. There'd even been a visit from the police once, but nothing had changed, and every time the husband's friends slunk through the square on their way to Flat 10, the other residents muttered under their breath and exchanged knowing looks. Audrey would be the last person to blame Linda if she'd finally taken matters into her own hands.

But if Linda was pretending to be shocked by her husband's death, she was doing a very good job of it.

"Audrey, hey," said Mei, emerging from the darkness and giving her a start. She was carrying her briefcase, and her work suit barely had a wrinkle, in spite of having just done a nine-hour day. "I left as soon as I got your message. What's going on?"

With a quick glance at Linda, Audrey rose from the bench and pulled Mei to one side.

"Richard Glead's dead. He was shot."

Mei raised her eyebrows and peered round Audrey to Linda. "Did she do it?" she murmured.

"I don't think so. She seems genuinely shocked."

"Not upset though," Mei observed.

"Would you be?"

They stood quietly, watching Mrs. Hildebrandt fuss around Linda, tucking a blanket around her shoulders with trembling hands. Mei scanned the square, her gaze taking in the police on the balcony before shifting across to the gates.

"Oh, shit," she said, abruptly turning away. Audrey looked up to see a man and a woman walking toward them. They were an odd pair, the man short and rough-looking, in spite of his suit, which strained at the buttons under a touch of middle-aged spread, while the woman was younger, maybe around thirty, tall and willowy with beachy blonde waves, and somehow making her suit look like it was fresh off the catwalk.

"What?"

"Sofia," muttered Mei.

"Who?"

"Sofia Larssen. We had a date last year."

"The detective who hated defence lawyers and Phil Collins?"

"That's the one. How could I be with anyone who didn't like Phil?"

The detectives reached the bench and looked down at Linda.

"Mrs. Glead?" asked the man, a small black notebook in his hand. "I'm Detective Inspector Banham, and this is Detective Sergeant Larssen. How are you doing?"

Linda lifted her head but didn't speak.

"How do you think she's doing?" growled Roshan, and Audrey glanced at him in surprise. She'd never heard him speak like that.

DS Larssen sat down beside Linda.

"Linda, is it?" she asked gently. Linda nodded. "Can you tell us when you found your husband?"

"When I got home," said Linda, her voice low. It was the first she'd spoken since Audrey had emerged from the flat.

"And what time was that?"

"I don't know." Linda looked around, as if hoping to find a clock somewhere.

"I heard her scream at around four forty-five," said Audrey, stepping forward. DS Larssen turned, and as Mei moved to stand beside her, Audrey saw the detective's eyes flicker with recognition. She nodded once, although whether that was in response to Audrey's comment or in greeting to Mei, she couldn't tell. Banham was still focused on Linda.

"Did you go into the kitchen immediately after arriving home?" he asked.

Linda nodded.

"And when you found your husband's body, what did you do?"

"I didn't do anything."

"What DI Banham means," interjected DS Larssen, "is did you touch your husband at all? Check if he was breathing or try to revive him?"

Now Linda frowned, seeming to wake up a bit.

"He was dead," she said firmly. "Blood all over him. I didn't touch him. I didn't need to."

The detectives exchanged the briefest of glances, then DI Banham turned to Audrey.

"And you? Are you the one Mr. McLennon said was next in the flat after Mrs. Glead?"

"McLennon?"

DI Banham consulted his notebook.

"Lewis McLennon. Flat Five. What's your name, please?"

"Audrey Brooks," said Audrey. He wrote that down. "Flat Seven. I heard the scream and ran over. Like Linda said, it was obvious he was dead. I didn't touch anything either."

Mei reached for her hand and squeezed it. She'd be worried about her, Audrey knew, but she felt strangely unaffected.

"Then what did you do?"

"The guy from Flat Five said he'd call the police, so I went back outside. Brought Linda down here."

DI Banham nodded and turned back to Linda.

"Mrs. Glead, I think it would be best if you came back to the station with us. We have a number of questions, and this isn't the right place to ask them. Is there someone who can come with you, or who you'd like to call? Do you have any-where you can stay tonight?"

"My sister, Jane." Linda's hand automatically went to her side. "Oh! My phone. It's in my bag. I left it . . ." She looked helplessly up to the open door of her flat, the light within glow-ing faintly in the darkness.

DI Banham turned to DS Larssen.

"Would you take Mrs. Glead back to the flat? Help her find her bag and pack a few things."

"Of course," said DS Larssen. She put her hand under Lin-da's elbow and they rose from the bench together.

Mei broke away from Audrey and hurried over to Linda.

"Linda, I don't know if you have a solicitor," she began, her eyes flicking to DS Larssen, "and you might not need one, but just in case, here's my card." She pressed her business card into Linda's hand. "Call me any time."

Linda looked bemused, but nodded and pocketed the card. Audrey watched as DS Larssen escorted her away.

"You can head home now, Ms. Brooks," said DI Banham. "I'm sure your friend is keen to make sure you're all right. It can be a shock, finding a body. We'll call on you in due course if we need more information. You too, Mr. Jones."

The caretaker ignored him, still staring after Linda. Audrey opened her mouth to protest, but Mei took her arm.

"Thank you," she said to the detective, pulling Audrey away. "Come on, let's get home. We have a *lot* to talk about."

As they reached their landing and Mei opened the door, Audrey glanced across to the opposite balcony, where Lewis McLennon was chatting to the uniformed officer standing sen-try outside the Gleads' flat. She couldn't help but notice that while she'd been dismissed, his presence was being amiably tolerated. She'd ask Celeste about him tomorrow, find out what the deal was.

Celeste. She must have noticed the commotion by now. What must she be thinking? Horrified at a murder in Marchfield Square? Or delighted by the excitement? Knowing Celeste, it was probably the latter, but you never could tell.

"Audrey?"

Mei stood in the doorway, looking concerned.

"Sorry, I was just thinking about Celeste. I hope she's okay."

Mei laughed.

"Are you kidding? Celeste will be loving this. Finally, some infamy! Now come inside, I need to know every last detail. What the hell happened to Richard Glead?"

5

Lewis

Lewis was hungry. It was almost eleven and, he now realised, he'd completely forgotten to eat dinner. He got up from his desk in the corner of the lounge and went to open every cupboard in his kitchen on the off chance he'd bought some real food and forgotten about it.

He hadn't, so he made a bowl of Crunchy Nut cornflakes and ate them over the sink.

He went back to his computer, sitting down in the expensive leather desk chair that had helped him produce precisely zero good ideas since he'd bought it, and rubbed his hands together.

Harding surveyed the scene, the paper hood of his forensic suit rustling as he moved. The body of Ricky Speen lay face up on the kitchen floor, the front of his shirt crisp with dried blood. Harding's experienced eye took in the lividity of the skin, and the cold, blue-grey changes around his ears, where the blood had gradually drained downwards. He noticed the position of the arms, the sneer of the lips and determined that Speen hadn't fought his killer, but had been standing in front of them when he was shot.

He looked at the victim's slippered feet, the remains of a pie on the plate on the table, and decided the man had likely died between six and ten the previous evening. There was no second plate anywhere, so unless the killer had washed up, Speen had been interrupted during dinner.

"Probably died between six and ten last night," he told the waiting Detective Sergeant, a young woman whose name he hadn't yet learned. "Pathologist will analyse the stomach contents and confirm."

"That fits," she said, looking down at her notebook. "A witness saw him coming home just before six."

It felt good to be writing again. Not that he hadn't written, of course he had. But to write with this urgency, compelled by all the information in his brain trying to get out through his fingers, confident that it was *something* . . . that'd been a long time.

He'd spent the last two hours typing up notes. First, about the body, about the colour of the skin, the twist of the mouth, the position of the hands, the shape of the bloodstain. Even how it felt to be in a room with it—an odd combination of tense and peaceful, the corpse somehow commanding attention with its complete absence of life. He'd written down every question the police had asked him, and every question he'd asked PC Singh, who'd been happy to talk to him even before he'd said he was a writer.

Then he'd written an opening scene. The description of the body and the crime scene, including the plate, the beer bottles, and the strange, old-fashioned-looking coin. Not much to start with, but it was already growing into something, he knew. The kernel of an idea had wormed its way up through the compacted soil of dead ideas that had been his brain for the last five years. Just the tiniest flash of green, not even real leaves yet, but he treasured its possibilities. He needed to water it, to let it see some sunshine.

Characters. He should write out a list of everyone at the crime scene today and invent new characters to fill the roles. All the police and witnesses, and of course, the victim and his wife. On balance, it was most likely the wife who'd killed

Richard Glead—he must write the name down before he forgot it again—but fiction had to be more complicated than real life. More interesting.

He nodded at the words on the screen in front of him.

God, it felt good.

6

Audrey

"I'm glad you're at Celeste's today," said Mei the next morning, watching the toaster. "I don't want you to be alone."

"I'm fine. Honestly," said Audrey, her nose inside the kettle. "But I'm glad too. I'd like to make sure she's okay."

The toast jumped up.

"Celeste will be fine," said Mei, flicking it onto the bread-board. "More than fine, I expect. That holiday in Switzerland did her the power of good. What in God's name are you doing?"

"Sniffing the kettle. I descaled it earlier but I think it still smells of vinegar." She held the kettle out toward Mei. "Does it?"

Mei gave it a sniff.

"No. And it's not even eight. How much earlier is there?"

"I was up at six." Audrey sat down at the counter. "Don't you think it should bother us? That someone in the square's been murdered? Just because he was an abusive shithead doesn't mean we shouldn't care."

Mei looked as sympathetic as she could with a mouthful of toast.

"This won't be a random crime of opportunity," she said. "Most likely it was Linda, and who could blame her? If I was her solicitor, I'd be pleading a clear case of self-defence." Mei reconsidered. "Although the gun complicates things. Shows premeditation. But either way, Marchfield is just as safe it was yesterday, but minus the abusive shithead."

Aggrieved at having her moral quandary interpreted as self-interest, Audrey dropped the subject, and after breakfast they hugged goodbye and left for their respective works: Mei with her leather briefcase, Audrey with her bag of cleaning supplies.

She carried it down the stairs and across the courtyard to the entrance of 1 Marchfield Square. Celeste had never explained why she and Leonard had split the big house as well as the coach houses, putting in a lift and moving into the top two floors. They were richer than Croesus, so couldn't have needed the money, but then it was a very big house and they didn't have children, so perhaps it had just felt like a waste. One of many little mysteries about the van Duren family.

Audrey used her key and let herself in, heading for the stairs. The lift was kept in good working order because of Celeste's bad hip, but it took her less than thirty seconds to jog up the two flights of stairs to reach Celeste's landing. She checked her watch before ringing the bell. Eight thirty, on the nose.

Dixon opened the door.

"Morning," he said, standing back to let her in. Instead of his usual suit, he was wearing jeans and a T-shirt, and she smiled as she passed. Dixon was somewhere in his forties and from Yorkshire, and handsome in a rough-around-the-edges sort of way, but his formality and bearing meant that although she liked him very much, she could never quite relax when he was around.

"Audrey, dear!" called Celeste, waving at her from her armchair by the picture window. Audrey dropped her bag by the door and crossed the palatial space to reach her.

"Morning, Celeste." She perched on the arm of the second chair. "How are you holding up?"

"I'm perfectly well," said Celeste, smiling. A neatly folded newspaper lay across her lap. "Isn't it thrilling?"

"Thrilling?"

"So exciting, all the comings and goings. The police were at it all night, you know, taking all sorts of things in and out. I thought it would have made the papers, but there's nothing."

Of course Mei had been right. Celeste was loving this.

"Aren't you worried? About security?"

Celeste patted Audrey's knee.

"No, my dear. Mr. Glead had all sorts of unsavoury visitors; most likely he invited his killer in himself. But as soon as the police uncover what happened, I shall make whatever changes may be necessary to improve security. You have my word."

"You don't think it was Linda, then?"

"Good heavens, no." Celeste sounded shocked. "She came home and discovered the body. We all heard her scream."

"She came home and screamed," Audrey pointed out. "That's not the same as discovering the body."

The old lady's eyes narrowed for a moment.

"I suppose it isn't. What a sharp mind you have. Do *you* think she did it, Audrey?"

Audrey bit her lip.

"I don't want her to have done it, but . . . well, I don't know if you know this, Celeste, but Mr. Glead . . ."

"No need to beat around the bush, dear. We've all heard the noises and seen the bruises. You're saying the logical explanation is that she snapped. Well, I'm sure the police will work it all out. They have ways of knowing things like time of death, don't they? Hopefully Linda can prove she was elsewhere at the time."

"Yes. Yes, of course." Audrey looked out of the big window, down to the Gleads' flat. The blinds had been drawn but someone might see an awful lot from this position, if the light conditions were right. She glanced across to her own flat, realising for the first time that her landlady had a pretty good view of her and Mei, too. She couldn't make out the small details, like the plant on the living room windowsill for example, and Celeste's eyesight was bound to be worse than that of a twenty-eight-year-old with twenty-twenty vision, but she'd certainly be able to see if someone was moving about.

"I'm off," said Dixon from the door. "Do you need owt before I go?"

"No, thank you, Dixon," said Celeste, smiling at him fondly. "Audrey and I will be just fine. Have a good day."

Dixon nodded to Audrey and she rose, following him out to the hall to see him off.

"Anything I need to know?" she asked.

"This Glead business has upset her more than she's letting on," he said, keeping his voice low. "And when she's upset, she gets confused, so maybe don't let her talk about it too much. I'd rather stay, if I'm honest, but I've got some business to take care of. I expect the police'll start canvassing the building, but I'd prefer to be with her when they talk to her. See if you can get them to come back tomorrow."

Audrey nodded. Celeste seemed no different to her, but Dixon knew best.

"Of course."

"Thanks. I'll be back usual time. Call me if there's anything."

She closed the door behind him and returned to Celeste, who had put her glasses back on and was studying the murder-less front page of the newspaper with disdain.

"Journalists aren't what they used to be, are they?"

"It's probably online," said Audrey, returning to the arm of the chair. Celeste looked so crestfallen at the lack of sensation that, in spite of Dixon's warning, she couldn't stop herself. "Do you want me to look?"

Celeste perked up.

"Would you? I wouldn't know what to googly."

"Google," said Audrey, suppressing a smile as she pulled her phone out of her pocket. "'Googly' is cricket."

"Do they have cricket on the Google? That would be fun, wouldn't it? A googly on the Google?"

"They have everything on the Google, Celeste," said Audrey, tapping into the search. "Including googlies."

"You'll have to teach me how to use it. I did ask Dixon once, but he said the text setting on my telephone was too big to read, which seemed odd to me. The bigger the better, I always say. I learned that from the late Mr. van Duren."

Audrey paused. Celeste's eyes were twinkling at her over the rims of her glasses.

"Mrs. van Duren," said Audrey reprovingly, and the old lady giggled. "Okay, it's made the local BBC news."

"The BBC? How marvellous. What are they saying?"

"'A forty-year-old woman is being questioned in connection with a murder in Pickering Lane, Chelsea,'" Audrey read aloud. "'A forty-five-year-old man was found dead of gunshot wounds at a property in Marchfield Square. Detective Inspector Dean Banham of the Metropolitan Police asks anyone with information on the crime, or who may have witnessed anything unusual in the area of Pickering Lane on the day in question, to get in touch.'"

"Is that all?"

"Yep. From yesterday evening. Nothing from today that I can see."

Celeste snorted.

"And that's modern journalism, is it? Pfft."

"I should get to work," said Audrey, putting her phone away. "Do you need anything?"

"No, dear," said Celeste, opening her newspaper again. "You get on. Then we can have a nice lunch. I'll call if I need you."

Audrey collected her bag and headed for the cloakroom. Top floor first—the cloakroom, the big room, and then, after lunch, the kitchen. Then downstairs to do the main bathroom, the library, and Celeste's bedroom. The only room she wouldn't touch was Dixon's, who maintained that a man must be allowed a little privacy, especially one living with Celeste van Duren.

The cloakroom was, as ever, perfectly clean and tidy, but she opened the window and took Dixon's carefully chosen cleaning products out from under the sink. Then she put on her rubber gloves and got to work.

7

Lewis

"Yeah, mate," croaked Lewis. "I feel awful. Must be that flu you had the other week."

He was sat in his expensive office chair, in front of his expensive computer, where he'd been all night. The words were pouring out of him, and he hadn't dared go to bed in case they dried up while he was asleep. He even resented the time he was wasting right now, calling in sick to his hateful job, putting on this charade for his infant boss, who was at least ten years younger than him. It was all just bullshit getting in the way of what he was actually meant to do with his life.

"Cheers, mate. Will do. Bye."

He jabbed the disconnect button and tossed his phone back onto the desk. Where was he?

He wrote until his stomach growled in a way he could no longer ignore, so he got up and made himself another bowl of cereal. He ate at his desk, absently spooning cornflakes into his mouth while planning the next page.

A sharp knock on the flat door made him jump, and he cursed, milk dribbling down his chin. He wiped his sleeve across his mouth and hurled himself at the front door, ready to give whoever it was a piece of his mind for knocking so loudly at—he checked his watch—nine thirty in the morning.

Standing outside was the detective sergeant from yesterday, and a uniformed police constable. The fury died on his lips.

"Hello, Mr. McLennon," said the detective. "Nice to see you again."

"Good morning, DS . . ." Shit, what was it? Hanson? Flarson?

"DS Larssen," she finished for him, smiling so politely that he winced. "And PC Edwards."

"Sorry, yes. DS Larssen. Terrible with names."

"We're canvassing the neighbours, building a picture of what happened yesterday, what people saw and heard. Is now a good time?"

"Yes. Yes, of course. Please, come in." He stood back, pressing himself against the wall to make room in the little hallway, then ushered them through to the lounge. "Can I get you something? Tea? Coffee?"

"No, thank you."

The constable remained standing by the door, while Larssen looked around the room which, now there were guests in it, suddenly seemed grimy and unkempt. Lewis sniffed. When had he last opened a window?

"May I?" said Larssen, gesturing to the sofa, and he nodded.

"Sorry, yes. Please sit down."

Lewis sat down in the armchair while Larssen got out her notebook. PC Edwards remained standing.

"We'd like to go over your statement from yesterday," she began.

"Yes. Sure." It was all material, after all. Invaluable research.

"Let's start with you arriving home. What time was that?"

"Uh . . . about four forty? Give or take five minutes."

"Was that usual for you? To get home at that time?"

"No. I normally leave work at five and am home by six, but I left early. Wasn't feeling well."

"And what is it that you do, Mr. McLennon?"

"Recruitment. It's very boring."

Larssen flipped back a page in her notebook.

"You said yesterday you were a writer? You were asking lots of questions, I remember."

She asked it innocently enough, but he thought he heard a dig in there somewhere.

"Am a writer, yes. But most writers need a day job." No need to mention that for two glorious years, writing *had* been his day job. Until he'd run first out of ideas, then money.

"I see. So you got home at four forty, and then what?"

"I crossed the courtyard. Said hello to Captain Gordon. I'd just got in when I heard the scream. It sounded close, so I ran outside and the Captain was standing up, looking at Flat Ten. Then the girl from over the way went running and I followed."

Larssen consulted her book.

"That would be Audrey Brooks? Flat Seven?"

"I suppose so. I didn't get her name."

"You'd not met before?"

"No."

"So you and Miss Brooks went up to the first-floor balcony to see Mrs. Glead. Then what?"

"The door to the flat was open. The girl—Miss Brooks—went inside. Mrs. Glead was pointing down the hallway so I went in too, and found him in the kitchen. The husband, I mean. Mr. Glead. On the kitchen floor. Hole in his chest."

"And where was Miss Brooks?"

"Oh. She was also there. In the kitchen. Looking at the body. Then she went outside again and I called the police."

A note was made in the book.

"Apart from Mr. Glead's body, did you notice anything unusual about the flat? A mess? Signs of a disturbance?"

Lewis didn't need to think back. He'd made copious notes when he got home and had consulted them many times since.

"No. It was all very clean and very tidy. Bit empty though, like a holiday let."

Larssen nodded.

"We noticed that too. What did you think of the Gleads?"

Now he paused. Truth be told, Lewis hadn't thought about the Gleads ever.

"Erm, they were okay? I met them when they moved in but we never really spoke. He was all right. Friendly. Said hello when we passed. She was quiet. Didn't speak to anyone that I saw."

"And how did they seem as a couple?"

"No idea, I'm afraid."

"No rows, that you heard? Anything of that nature?"

"Don't think so. I'm out in the day though, and I've got surround sound for the television, and noise-canceling headphones for when I'm writing." Another, more cursory nod from the detective. For the first time, it occurred to Lewis that he might not be the excellent witness he'd expected to be. "Why? What's everyone else said?"

"The other neighbours were under the impression the marriage wasn't a happy one. We were just wondering if you'd support that conclusion, but obviously nothing had struck you in that way."

"No, sorry."

He felt disappointed not to be more helpful. With the exception of Celeste, Lewis never spoke to anyone in the square if he could help it, rarely listening when she gossiped about the other tenants. He'd always been rather proud of the distance he'd kept. Until now.

"After you called the police," said Larssen, "what did you do then?"

"I went back outside and then stayed there while the girl took Mrs. Glead away. Didn't want anyone to go in and touch anything, mess with the scene." He smiled, waiting for them to be impressed by his knowledge of procedure.

"One last thing, then we'll let you get to your day. Were you home between four p.m. on Wednesday and two a.m. Thursday morning? If so, did you hear anything unusual?"

The smiled faded.

"I was home, yes. From about six, anyway. But no, I didn't hear anything. Is that when you think he was killed?"

"You didn't go out to watch the fireworks?"

"Fireworks?"

"Your neighbour said the residents watched the fireworks together on the other side of the square. You didn't join them?"

Lewis frowned. He vaguely remembered one of the guys from upstairs inviting him to something but he'd declined automatically and forgotten all about it.

"No. I write in the evenings, and have my headphones on . . ."

"Anyone to confirm that?"

"My boss can confirm when I left, and the Captain saw me get home. I had a video call later, if that helps? Lasted about an hour." He unlocked his phone and held it out for her to see the call log. Larssen peered at the screen, then glanced at him before jotting down the details.

"So nothing seen or heard?"

"No. Sorry."

"Okay, then."

Lewis watched as Larssen scribbled a last few notes.

"Can I ask what kind of gun it was? I didn't see any casings at the scene." She looked up, eyebrows raised, and he smiled sheepishly. "Professional interest."

"We don't know yet, but the bullet was a twenty-five calibre, so the gun was a small one." The detective closed her notebook and stood up. "I think that's all. Thank you, Mr. McLennon."

"Oh." He tried to hide his disappointment. "Nothing else?"

"No, but if you think of anything . . ." She fished a card out of her pocket. "Do let us know."

"Sure."

"Don't worry about seeing us out," she said. "I'm sure you have to get ready for work. Thanks very much for your time."

Lewis nodded.

"No problem."

He stayed seated as they left, closing the front door quietly behind them. He was annoyed with himself. He was perfectly capable of writing nosy neighbours and observant detectives, and had fictional motives for a fictional murder coming out of his ears, but here was a murder right under his nose and he hadn't the faintest idea why it might have happened.

He'd have to do better in future. No more playing the reclusive writer. And no more headphones. He needed to start paying attention.

8

Audrey

As Audrey wiped, polished, waxed, and vacuumed the big room, Celeste gave her a running commentary on what was happening in the square.

"They've been in with Brigitte for some time. Gossiping, do we think? Or perhaps she made some of her chocolate cake.

"Now Lewis. He'll be an important witness, I'm sure.

"The boys in number nine have already left for work. What a shame.

"They didn't get much out of Captain Gordon by the looks of it. Only ten minutes.

"Oh, now they're calling on you, Audrey dear. They're making very good progress."

Celeste sat in her armchair in what she inexplicably called the gallery nook. Audrey didn't know what it should actually be called. It was just a couple of armchairs and some low bookshelves in front of the big window. With the exception of the kitchen, the cloakroom, and the hallway, the top floor of Celeste's apartment was one big open-plan space, like a New York loft, and zoned with furniture. The dining area, with its mahogany table, green velvet cushions, and silver-laden sideboard, was at one end, while the silver and blue suite and gilt-framed pictures made the living area at the other. The weird little viewing station Celeste had created for herself in the middle of the room wasn't the sort of thing featured in *Country Living* or any of the other design magazines Audrey's clients left lying around.

"Do you suppose the police are leaving me until last?" Celeste called over.

"Probably," said Audrey, buffing the last of the polish off the dining table. "I expect they'll want to hear what you think of your tenants."

"I suppose I should tell them?" said Celeste. "About Mr. Glead, I mean. Beating his wife."

"Everyone else will," said Audrey, going over to her.

"Oh, yes." She sighed. "Poor Mrs. Glead. She's finally been relieved of that awful man but now she might be suspected of murder. That's not the way things should go at all."

"Depends on whether she had any other options," said Audrey. "If not, then it's the only way it could go, isn't it?"

Standing by the window, Audrey could see straight down into the courtyard, where a blonde in a grey jacket, whom she recognised as DS Larssen, and a uniformed male officer were exiting the Hetherington studio. She cocked an ear, waiting for them to ring Celeste's doorbell, but instead they turned and walked away, heading for the gates at the other end of the square.

"Who's the guy in Flat Five?" Audrey asked Celeste, watching as they stopped by the railings. They were inspecting the entry system, she realised. "I'd never spoken to him until yesterday."

"Lewis McLennon," said Celeste. "Nice boy. Writes crime novels, or at least he used to. He hasn't published much lately."

"Ah."

DS Larssen and her colleague left the front gate, heading back across the square.

"I think your time has come, Celeste."

"Oh, goody," said Celeste, reaching for her stick.

"Dixon said I should ask them to come back later. He wanted to be with you when you were interviewed."

"Phooey," said Celeste, waving her concern away. "Dixon can be quite the old woman. You show them in, dear."

Audrey had just reached the hall when the bell went, an electronic impression of an old-fashioned doorbell.

"DS Larssen and PC Edwards to see Celeste van Duren," said Larssen, holding a badge up to the intercom camera. Audrey pressed the buzzer to release the door.

"Come on up," she said into the speaker. "The lift comes up to the top floor, just hit the button."

She opened the front door and waited.

"Miss Brooks, isn't it?" said Larssen, as they exited the lift. "We called on you earlier."

"I clean for Mrs. van Duren on Fridays," she said. "I'm here all day. Come in, please."

She led them through the hall to the big room, where Celeste was standing, leaning heavily on her cane.

"Good morning, officers," she said, smiling. "Won't you sit down? Would you like a cup of tea? Coffee?"

"No, thank you," said Larssen, looking around the room. "We've had a lot to eat and drink already."

Celeste waved the officers over to the sofa while she sat down in the silver and blue armchair, a queen holding court. Audrey stood awkwardly behind the sofa, unsure whether to make herself scarce or not.

"Lovely place, this," said Larssen, taking out her notebook. "You own the whole square?"

"It's just a small one," said Celeste, as if it were a garden shed and not a residential complex worth millions. "My great-great-grandfather had a big house here with a garden and stables. Then my grandfather converted the stables and built this little enclave, which passed to my father, and then to me. Leonard and I turned the house into flats."

"Leonard is your husband?"

"Was, yes. He passed a few years ago."

"I'm sorry," said Larssen. "Do you live alone now?"

"No, I have Dixon, my man."

"Your . . . man?"

Audrey pressed down a smile.

"My valet."

"Sort of like a butler," Audrey put in, "but does a bit of everything."

"Like a carer?" asked Constable Edwards, and Celeste's eyes widened in indignation.

"Certainly not!"

"Is Dixon here?" asked Larssen. "We'll need to speak to him, too."

"It's his day off," said Celeste shortly.

Larssen glanced back up at Audrey.

"Shall I go and finish in the kitchen?" asked Audrey, taking the hint. "Give you some privacy?"

"No need, my dear," said Celeste. "A woman has no secrets from her cleaner."

Larssen looked unhappy but said nothing, so Audrey sat down in the other armchair and tried to make herself as small as possible.

"So," began the detective, "how well did you know the Gleads?"

"Not that well," said Celeste. "They've lived here for about two years."

"Did you interview them before they signed the lease?"

"Yes, I did. They were very charming, or at least Mr. Glead was. They appeared very much in love."

"Appeared?"

"As I'm sure you've already been told, things changed quite rapidly in that respect."

Larssen nodded.

"They argued a lot?"

"At first it was arguments, yes, but then he became—What's the term? Handy with his fists. Mrs. Glead became very quiet. Stopped chatting. Stopped having visitors."

"I see. And Mr. Glead? Did he stop having visitors?"

"No, he quite often had people over. Men."

"The same men?"

"I think so," said Celeste. "Although my eyesight isn't what it was." She scowled at Constable Edwards, as if he was personally responsible for her failing vision.

"You said Mr. Glead used his fists," said Larssen. "Did you ever see him hit Mrs. Glead?"

Celeste paused.

"Once," she said eventually. "A few months ago. On the balcony. I called the police on that occasion. The rest of the time it was merely bruises. A plaster cast once, on her arm."

Larssen nodded again, and made a note in her book.

"When you called the police . . . that would have been the twenty-eighth of September?"

"Goodness," said Celeste, raising an eyebrow. "However did you know that? I couldn't swear to the exact date, but sometime around then, yes. It was unexpectedly hot, I remember."

"We have a record of calls to this address," said the detective, flipping back through her notebook. "Mrs. Glead refused to press charges, it seems. Several times. Did you ever see Mr. Glead with bruises? Any sign that Mrs. Glead was defending herself?"

"Never."

"All right. Let's talk about the day before yesterday. Wednesday. Did you see or hear from the Gleads at all that day?"

"Oh, yes," said Celeste at once. "There was an almighty row. About seven o'clock. Dixon was in the kitchen, cleaning up after dinner, and I was in my armchair by the window. I heard a man shouting and then there was a crash. I looked down into the square and saw some of the neighbours out. Presumably they'd heard the ruckus too."

Larssen frowned at her notebook and mouthed the word "ruckus."

"Then Mrs. Glead came running out, down the steps and across the courtyard, Mr. Glead shouting after her from the balcony. She didn't come back until yesterday afternoon."

Celeste folded her hands in her lap and sat back, looking pleased with herself.

"And how do you know Mrs. Glead didn't come back until yesterday afternoon?" asked Larssen, scribbling in her book. "Is it possible she came back later and left again without you seeing her?"

Now it was Celeste's turn to frown.

"Well, it's possible I suppose. But she was wearing the same clothes."

"The same clothes? Are you sure? You did say your eyes weren't what they were," said Larssen.

"That's as may be," said Celeste, "but it seems unlikely that any woman would have more than one lilac skirt."

"Did you find a gun?" asked Audrey, unable to stop herself. "And have you already checked Linda's clothes for gunshot residue? That's what you do, right?"

Both police officers looked at her in surprise.

"Yes," said Larssen after a beat. "That's what we do. And no, no gun yet. What about you, Miss Brooks? What did you see yesterday?"

"Oh. Right, well, I got home about half past four and I was having a cup of tea when I heard Linda scream. I ran outside and she was just standing there, on the balcony, pointing back inside the flat. So I went in and there he was."

"Did you also know about their marital problems?"

"Everyone knew."

"Not quite everyone," Larssen muttered as she made a note. "You're directly opposite Flat Ten, aren't you, in Flat Seven?"

"Yes."

"So you'd have had a pretty good view of the Gleads. Did you see much happening over there?"

Audrey shrugged.

"I work all day and we watch the TV at night, so . . ."

"'We' being yourself and your girlfriend? Mei Chen?"

Audrey wasn't sure if she was imagining Larssen looking extra hard at her notebook, but she decided to be kind anyway.

"Mei and I are just friends. We're not a couple."

A nod.

"And you're a cleaner?"

"Yes."

"If you don't mind me asking, how can you afford to live in a place like this? A private square, good security, two-floor flat. That must set you back a bit."

"Is that relevant?" she asked, startled.

"It might be," said Larssen. "Access to the square appears to be fairly secure, which means this is most likely an inside job. We're looking closely at all the tenants."

Celeste coughed politely.

"Leonard and I always played fair with the rents," she said. "We'd rather have good people than rich people. I can assure you, the killer is not one of my tenants."

"You rent these properties out below market rate?" said Larssen, her eyebrows disappearing under her blonde fringe in astonishment.

"That's right."

"As you know, my flatmate's a lawyer," said Audrey, becoming less kind in the hope of ending the conversation as swiftly as possible. "She earns more and pays a bigger share. It's not that cheap."

"I see." Larssen scribbled something else in the notebook Audrey was starting to resent. "Back to the Gleads. Did anyone ever try to intercede? Talk to either of them?"

"We all did, at different times," said Audrey, now well and truly on the defensive. "Joe and Manny next door went round a few times, I think, but Linda always refused to report him. Mei and I went over once, when Richard was out. Mei offered to help her, but Linda didn't want it."

"Why do you think that was?"

"I suppose because she loved him."

Larssen turned back to Celeste.

"Mrs. van Duren, you said you wanted 'good people' living here. How did you feel about the Glead situation?"

Celeste pressed her lips together.

"Terrible, of course, but what could I do? If I'd evicted them, Mrs. Glead would still have been in trouble, I just wouldn't have had to see it. At least this way I could keep an eye on her."

"And did you? Keep an eye on her? What did you see from your nice big window on Wednesday evening?"

Larssen smiled, but it was clear she thought Celeste knew more than she was letting on.

"I saw Mrs. Glead leave close to seven, as I said. I saw Mr. Glead moving around inside his flat just before the fireworks started, at eight o'clock, after which I saw nothing else from my 'nice big window,' as you put it."

"And the following morning?"

"On Thursday morning, I breakfasted in bed at eight, as usual, and was doing the crossword in my armchair by half past nine. I spent the day in my usual way, doing bits and bobs and keeping busy. All was quiet until Mrs. Glead screamed at four forty-five."

"I see. Thank you."

Larssen stood up and crossed over to the picture window.

"You can see the front windows quite clearly, can't you?" she remarked, scanning the square. "Of all the flats."

"If I had your young eyes, perhaps," said Celeste, sighing with what Audrey felt to be rather performative resignation. Larssen merely nodded.

"There are no security cameras in the square. Why is that?"

"We never felt the need," said Celeste. "The two electronic gates provide security, and if people can't have privacy in their own home, then where can they? No one can get in without buzzing a resident. Mr. Glead must have let the killer in himself."

Larssen arched an eyebrow but said nothing. She turned away from the window.

"Well, thank you both for your time. We'll still need to speak to Mr. Dixon but we'll call again another day. Edwards?"

Constable Edwards rose and Celeste also got to her feet.

"You should look into those friends of Richard's," said Celeste, leaning on her cane again. "Criminals to a man, if I'm any judge. When will Linda be allowed home?"

"The crime scene should be released this evening," said Larssen. "But Mrs. Glead is still being questioned."

Audrey saw them to the door, where Larssen stopped and pulled a business card out of her pocket.

"If you think of anything else," she said, "give me a call. And let Mr. Dixon know we'd like to speak to him. This is an unusual setup here. We've not quite got our bearings yet."

As she watched them get into the lift, Audrey's phone dinged with a message from Mei.

> Linda called. Heading over to the station now.
> Wish me luck.

Shit, she replied. Good luck x

Unusual setup. Understatement of the year.

9

Lewis

As the bells of St. Luke's chimed two o'clock in the distance, Lewis sat down on a bench in the square and began to sketch a map in his notebook. After living in Marchfield for nearly five years, he'd been annoyed to find he couldn't map the square properly in his mind, and had eventually resorted to going outside and actually looking at stuff.

It was an odd place, really, he thought as he drew. Technically, it should have been a mews, as the original buildings had been stables, but the enormous van Duren residence at the far end, and the garden in front of it, had made it just as much a square as any of the bigger parks in London. Although even more technically, it was very much a rectangle.

He drew and rubbed out, then drew some more and rubbed out some more. He'd never been good at art and his sketch was abysmal, but he only needed it to plot out the possible movements of his fictional killer. It didn't need to be pretty, but somehow it didn't seem to reflect reality at all.

"Your proportions are all wrong."

Lewis looked up to find the man in the wheelchair from number 2 peering over at his drawing. He couldn't stop himself from looking down at the path, wondering how he'd managed to sneak up on him. He was older but not old, with silvering blond hair and piercing blue eyes, and was wearing a thick woollen jumper over a striped shirt and moss-green corduroy trousers.

"Hah, took you by surprise, did I?" said the man, spinning around to park his chair beside the bench. He had a sketchbook of his own and a canvas pencil case on his lap. "Need a hand?"

"Uh, no thanks," said Lewis. "It doesn't need to be good, I just need a sort of plan."

"You're the writer chap, yes?" said the man, unzipping the case and taking a few seconds to select a pencil that looked to Lewis like all the other pencils in it. "I'm Philip Hetherington. Live in number two with my wife, Mekhala. Don't think we've ever met."

"Lewis McLennon. Flat Five."

He felt embarrassed saying that, given their homes were only a few metres apart, but Philip merely nodded and opened his sketchbook.

"Reclusive writer sort. Totally understand." He swept a hand over the paper. "Good to finally meet, though."

Lewis went back to his drawing, but now he was distracted. He wasn't intentionally reclusive, just not particularly interested in other people. Or their lives. And what was wrong with the proportions of his drawing?

"Terrible, all this murder business, eh?" Philip said, his eyes on his own paper. "Terrible man, but a bad job to have it happen here."

"Was he a terrible man?"

"I wouldn't call a wife-beater a good man, would you? And those friends of his. Crooked, every one."

Lewis opened his mouth to ask how Philip knew all this when he heard someone approaching and looked up to find the gardener walking toward them, a bin bag in one hand and a plastic green rake in the other.

"Afternoon, Roshan," said Philip cheerily, without looking up. "Garden's looking fine."

"Thank you, Philip. Getting things ready for winter, and keeping the paths clear for you all."

"And we appreciate it enormously," said Philip. "I hope the police haven't messed anything up with all their tramping about?"

"They've been very respectful, considering. Terrible business, though."

"I was just saying to young Lewis here. Terrible man but terrible business."

"You've got that exactly right, Philip," said Jones, putting down his bin bag full of leaves. "In poor Mrs. van Duren's home. Terrible."

Lewis scowled. How did everyone but him know that Richard Glead was a terrible man?

Jones began to rake the leaves from the grass around the bench, filling the air with the peaty scent of damp earth. Then came more footsteps, the unmistakeable sharp taps of Captain Gordon.

"What's going on here then?" asked the Captain, eyeing them all suspiciously. He had a newspaper tucked under his arm. "Mothers' meeting? Don't often see you out here, McLennon."

"How are you, Gordon?" said Philip, before Lewis could respond. The Captain was the one resident Lewis did notice often, possibly because of his cartoonish military bearing and clipped, plummy accent.

"Fine, fine," replied the Captain. "Bit of excitement. Good for the heart."

"You have taken your pills though?" asked Jones. "Just in case?"

"Yes, Roshan, I've taken my pills." The Captain sat down on the bench opposite and shook out his newspaper, frowning at Lewis as he did so. "Don't you worry about me. How's your mother? Is she back from India yet?"

"Much better, thank you," said Jones, returning to his raking. "And no, not yet. Having too much fun with her family. She'll be back in a week or two."

Bloody hell, thought Lewis. He'd had no idea how very into each other's business the other residents were.

"How is Linda, does anyone know?" asked Philip, his pencil flying across the paper with an ease Lewis envied.

"Happy as a pig in clover, I expect," snorted the Captain.

"No, no, Captain," said Roshan, scooping up more leaves and putting them in the bag. "Linda isn't like that. She'll be grieving."

"She should have left him years ago," said Philip.

"Yes," agreed Roshan. "But I believe it didn't sit well with her faith."

"Ah, faith," said the Captain, nodding with what Lewis strongly suspected was faux wisdom. "What can you do, eh? Good thing someone saw off the blighter."

There were murmurings of protest from Philip and Roshan, but no one seemed to put much feeling into it. It was suddenly a bit much for Lewis.

"I think I'll go in," he said, standing up. "Nice to see you all."

"One sec," said Philip, holding up a finger. He made a few more pencil strokes, then tore the page out of his sketchbook. "There. That should do you."

He handed Lewis a perfectly drawn picture of the square, as seen from the main gate, facing the big house. The garden was drawn in simple but clear lines, with the trees, paths, and benches all sketched in. It was accurate and beautiful.

"Thank you," was all Lewis could think to say.

"Any time," said Philip. "I've drawn this place so many times, I could do it with my eyes shut."

Lewis smiled, then, with a nod to the gardener and the Captain, beat a hasty retreat to his hermitage.

10

Audrey

Audrey shoved her hands into her pockets as she left the bank on Cromwell Street. One of the downsides of living in a well-to-do area of London was that all the nearby businesses catered for a much wealthier type of customer, so by the time she'd left Celeste's, she'd had to half run the mile to the bank to get there before they closed.

It was dark and the air crisp, and she enjoyed the walk back, bundled up against the cold and invisible to the people she passed. Black cabs moved slowly down the street, queuing to join the Fulham Road, their For Hire signs darkened as they carried passengers home or to their dinner plans.

The shops were already lit up for Christmas, with windows full of twinkling lights and Christmas trees outside on the pavement. Audrey loved London at this time of year, when the fairy lights gave the city a magical quality and the darkness hid its uglier side.

She joined the crowd at the crossing, waiting for the lights to change. The traffic was already crawling, buses, cabs, and town cars inching along, while cyclists wove through the near-stationary vehicles. Maybe she'd do something nice when she got home, like polishing. There was nothing like polishing for soothing the nerves.

They crossed the road en masse, and as Audrey turned onto Sydney Street, heading away from the noise and the crowds, a black cab pulled up to the kerb ahead of her and she heard someone call her name.

She stopped at once, glancing behind to check that her escape route was clear, but then the door of the cab opened and Mei tumbled out, followed by Linda Glead. Linda looked flushed and wrung out, her face pink and her hair limp and greasy. She was still wearing the same clothes but seemed different. She stood close beside Mei but was less hunched than usual, and Audrey could tell from her eyes that the shock had worn off.

"We were on our way home when we spotted you," said Mei breathlessly. "Thought we'd get a bit of fresh air. It's been an exhausting day, especially for Linda."

"I can't even imagine," said Audrey. "How are you holding up?"

Linda smiled wanly.

"I'm okay," she said. "Took the police a while to confirm my alibi."

"Which was rock solid, thankfully," added Mei.

"Oh, really?" Audrey smiled. "That's a relief."

They started walking. Sydney Street was lined with white-rendered, iron-railed houses, and the pavements were wide. It ran for half a mile between the Fulham Road and the King's Road, broken up by the imposing grounds of St. Luke's Church in the middle.

"I was at the Dogs' Home," said Linda, either sensing Audrey's burning curiosity or feeling the need to clear herself. "For Bonfire Night. I help out a few times a week and they asked for volunteers to stay late with the animals because of the fireworks. I was there until two, then got an Uber to my sister's in Streatham. Richard and me . . . well, we'd had a row."

"So they know what time he was . . ." Audrey hesitated. "What time he died?"

Linda looked away.

"They don't like to pin it down that precisely," said Mei. "But they think he died between eight p.m. on Wednesday and eight a.m. Thursday morning. Most likely shot during the fireworks, which were going on all night all over, explaining why nobody heard anything. It's not cut-and-dried, but it makes sense. The police have confirmed with the Dogs' Home and Uber, so it's just a question of checking the traffic cameras outside Linda's sister's place, which might take a while. They're snowed under with gang-related activity at the moment."

By Audrey's reckoning, that only accounted for Linda until three on Thursday morning, at the very latest, but she nodded anyway.

"I'm glad. Are you sure it's a good idea to go home so soon though? Would it not be better to go to your sister's?"

"Oh, I am," said Linda. "But I need to pack some things and . . ."

She stopped.

"And what?" prompted Mei.

"Nothing. I just need my things. I'll pack my bags and then I won't be back."

They walked in silence for a few minutes, until Audrey began to sense Linda slowing down. Perhaps she was reluctant to return to Marchfield?

"How long have you worked at the shelter?" she asked, trying to keep her tone light. "Do you like animals?"

"I love them," gushed Linda at once. "All animals. Ever since childhood. Jane and I didn't have the easiest of times. Our parents died when we were young and my aunt brought us up, but we had our dog, Bobby, and he just made everything better. That unconditional love you only get from an animal. I'd love to have a dog or a cat, or any sort of pet really, but Richard's very allergic."

The mention of her husband's name made Linda fall silent, and Audrey noticed her use of the present tense. Then Linda lifted her chin.

"There's this scrappy little mongrel at the shelter. Ugly as anything, frightened of everything, and no one wants him. We named him Muffin—you know, like ragamuffin?—but he's very gentle and he seems to like me. I could give him a home now, couldn't I?"

They crossed the road at the corner of St. Luke's, and as they neared, Linda stopped.

"I think I'll go in, if you don't mind?" she said, looking up at the church. "I'd like to see Reverend Fitzbride. I can make my own way back."

Mei frowned.

"Are you sure? I'm happy to wait and walk back with you. Help you pack."

"You're very kind," said Linda, looking from Mei to Audrey. "You've both been very kind, but I'll be all right. I just need a bit of quiet."

"All right," Mei said, then reached out and gripped Linda's arm. "It's going to be all right, Linda. The police will find who did this."

Linda nodded.

"I hope so. I don't want there to be any doubt, you know? It's awful having everyone looking at you, talking behind your back. I'm sick of being looked at. I want to leave that behind."

They watched as she walked down the path to the church, climbing the steps slowly before disappearing inside.

"Well," said Mei with a sigh. "That was a day and a half, and it's not over yet. I need a drink."

As they headed home, Audrey couldn't stop thinking about Linda and the soon-to-be-adopted Muffin. The small and simple dream of a lonely woman now free to please herself.

About time.

11

Lewis

Lewis woke, confused, his head slumped against the executive headrest of his desk chair. A few hours earlier, he'd watched Linda Glead walk home through the square, looking somehow taller and less frightened than he'd expect for someone returning to the scene of her husband's murder. Barely twenty-four hours since Richard Glead had been found shot, and the police had already released their prime suspect!

The plot twist had inspired him, and he'd written furiously for several hours before somehow dropping off. He wiped drool from his mouth and blinked, wondering why he'd woken.

His computer had gone dark but the clock on his phone said it was midnight. The light from the Victorian street lamps in the square backlit his kitchen window in orange and he yawned. He needed to sleep but that was fine. He had the whole weekend to write.

He'd just got up to head to bed when he heard a noise. Several noises. Footsteps on the stairs to the second floor. The guys upstairs coming home, perhaps.

Except someone was coming *down* the stairs. The guys upstairs going out? Surely not at this hour. And now that he thought about it, the footsteps were quieter than usual on the stone steps. Someone being considerate? Or someone creeping about?

Lewis unlocked his front door as quietly as he could and opened it a crack, the draught making him shiver. The courtyard was quiet, the air damp and hazy beneath the lamplight. Was that someone on the lawn near the tree, or just a shadow? He opened the door wider. The trees in the garden swished gently in the darkness but there was no other movement. There was no one out there.

He looked at the stairs going up to the next floor. Perhaps the police had left something. Or maybe Mrs. Glead had decided to make a midnight flit and get away while she still could.

He took his keys out of the door and stepped outside, still in his slippers. It wouldn't cost him anything to check. He closed the door softly and began to climb the stairs, careful not to disturb Mrs. Hilde-thingy next door.

He stepped onto the balcony as lightly as he could and crept along to number 10. The kitchen was dark, so he looked past the front door to the living room window. Inside, beyond the closed curtains, there was a warmth that suggested a light was on. Perhaps Mrs. Glead had a visitor?

He hesitated. An unexpected knock at the door at midnight would probably freak her out, not least because her husband had just been murdered in their home. He definitely shouldn't knock.

He made to go back down the stairs, which was when he heard the creak.

Lewis froze, heart in his throat. He slowly turned back to the door.

There was no one there. The door was still shut. He relaxed. It must have been his feet on the landing.

Except there it was again. The creak. He hadn't moved and there was no one in front of him.

He took a step back toward the front door, which creaked again.

The door wasn't closed, as he'd first thought. It had been pushed but not latched and was responding to his movements.

Mrs. Glead should not be leaving her door open.

He knocked softly on the door, and called through the crack. "Hello? Mrs. Glead? Linda?"

No sound from within. He knocked again, a little louder.

"Linda? It's Lewis from downstairs. Your door's open. Hello?"

Still nothing. This time, Lewis pushed the gently creaking door open until he could see down the darkened hall. Orange light spilled out from an open door on the right. The living room, he remembered.

"Linda? Is everything all right?"

There was nothing for it. He'd have to go in. Please don't let her be in bed, he thought. Or sitting in the lounge with earphones in or something.

"I'm coming in, Linda!" he called, loudly this time, and stepped into the hallway. He took a few steps and glanced through the living room door, finding it much as he had the day before—with one notable exception.

The dead body of Linda Glead.

12

Audrey

Audrey had only just fallen asleep when she was woken by the sound of knocking. She'd barely opened her eyes when Mei entered the room.

"There's police in the square again!"

"What?"

"Look out the window."

Audrey opened her curtains and Mei went to stand beside her in the darkness. They looked out over the square, the warm orange light from the iron lamp posts illuminating the bulky black shapes of police officers moving about below.

Audrey's breath hissed over her teeth and her heart started thudding. *Breathe*, she told herself, *breathe*.

"What's going on?"

"I don't know. I didn't hear a sound, just noticed some movement when I went to close my curtains. Perhaps they're arresting someone."

They watched the police spread out around the garden, not seeming to make for any particular place. Blue lights flashed intermittently across the square from the direction of the front gates.

"What are they doing? Who are they arresting?"

"I don't know," said Mei, and Audrey could hear the frown in her voice. "Maybe this is how they secure the area? I called Linda to make sure she'd gone to her sister's but she hasn't answered. I hope they're not here for her."

Audrey counted in her head, trying to get her breathing under control.

She looked at the windows opposite. There was a light on inside the Glead place, but the curtains were closed. Joe and Emmanuel's place was similarly illuminated, while Mrs. Hildebrandt's windows were dark. Flat 5 was also dark, but Audrey fancied she saw movement inside. Lewis McLennon was no doubt watching too. She glanced up at the big house, and Celeste's many windows. They were all dark except one—Dixon's room.

"There's a light on in Linda's," said Audrey. "And Dixon's still up. I should text him."

She grabbed her phone from the bedside table and rejoined Mei at the window, the light from the screen blinding in the darkness.

> **Police in the square again,** she typed. **Don't know why.**

She'd just hit send when Mei grabbed her wrist.

"Look."

Police officers had begun to climb the stairs to the Glead place.

"They're going to arrest Linda," said Mei, gripping her phone. "They're going to frighten the life out of her, doing it at this time of night."

"Wait. The door's open!"

"What?"

"Linda's front door. I think it's open."

A sudden movement from the big house made them turn, and the silhouetted figure of Dixon appeared, backlit, at his bedroom window. A second later and the light behind him was extinguished, and Audrey felt reassured to know that he was there, watching with them.

The officers arrived at Flat 10 and the one in front reached out a hand and touched the door. It swung open, revealing soft light within, and after a beat, they went inside. As they passed beneath the light outside the flat, Audrey realised that two of the officers were in fact paramedics.

"Shit," murmured Mei. "Shit shit shit. What the fuck's happened?"

Barely a minute later, two of the officers reemerged, one of them waving down into the square, before positioning themselves on either side of the open door. Down in the courtyard, the remaining police fanned out.

"What do we do?" asked Audrey. "Should we go over?"

Mei looked grim.

"I honestly don't know. The first team cleared the flat, and the paramedics are inside, which suggests it's safe but that someone is hurt."

"Someone who's not being brought out on a stretcher and rushed to hospital," observed Audrey.

"Which means either they're not badly hurt, or they're so badly hurt, it's too late."

As they gazed across the darkened square at the open door of Flat 10, Audrey was pretty sure she knew which one it was.

13

Lewis

Lewis sat by his kitchen window all night, watching the drama as it unfolded beyond the dirty glass, making notes in the darkness so as not to interfere with his night vision. As the police were operating under nothing brighter than the twee iron lamps around the square, he needed to be able to see them in the dark.

He watched as the paramedics came and vanished into Flat 10, followed by more police, including DI Banham and DS Larssen, who all put on white forensic suits before going inside. At around seven in the morning, as the light was becoming grey with the approaching dawn, the coroner arrived, and shortly after that, an empty stretcher went up the steps to the flat and came down loaded, a white body bag strapped to it.

He was pretty sure the police hadn't apprehended anyone. He'd been so worried the murderer was still in the square that he'd scurried down the stairs and locked himself in his flat before calling the police. He regretted that now. The call handler had told him to stay inside until further notice and so he had, watching and waiting as the police secured the square. He'd expected shouts, a scuffle, and, at the very least, a knock at the door, but after several hours, nothing of any kind had happened and he was still shut inside, away from the action. He'd eventually come to the conclusion that either the murderer had escaped before the police had arrived or there had been no murderer in the first place.

He made notes the entire time, paper illuminated by the light from his phone as he scrawled and scribbled, hoping it would still be intelligible in the light of day. He'd described—in as much detail as he could while it was still fresh in his mind— the scene as he'd found it. Unlike with her husband, it hadn't been immediately obvious how Linda had died. There was no blood, no wound that he could see, and if it hadn't been for the fixed glass-eyed stare, he wouldn't even have known she was dead. She'd been sitting on the sofa, slumped against the black leather, her head lolling to one side, eyes wide open. An empty plate and a glass of water were on the coffee table in front of her, and when Lewis had touched her neck to check for a pulse, the body was cool, but not cold.

He'd expected the police to call on him as soon as the coroner had arrived to take the body away. Instead, he'd watched all manner of people come and go, in and out of the white overalls, in and out of the crime scene, and not one of them had come to make enquiries yet.

What kind of shoddy investigation was this?

He checked the time on his phone. Nearly eight. He was flagging. The initial adrenaline had long worn off, and the feverish drive to capture every detail was also gone. All he felt now was tired. He could see the police clearly now, standing around one of the benches, talking. What were the odds they'd knock on his door the minute he went to bed?

A yawn cracked his jaw so wide it made his eyes water and he decided to risk it. He got up from the stool on which he'd been hunched for hours and stretched, groaning as he did so. When had everything started hurting? He should have got up and walked around a bit. He'd been sat right by his espresso machine too, and hadn't even thought to make himself a coffee. Idiot.

He went into his bedroom and lay down on the bed, not bothering to remove his clothes. A few hours' sleep, that was what he needed. Linda's death—so neat and silent—was a plot twist that baffled him. Not just baffled, disturbed. He'd learned more about the Gleads in the past thirty-six hours than in the last two years of living in the same place, and felt ashamed that he hadn't noticed Linda's situation.

And now this. That was twice he'd misjudged her.

A knock at the door made him sit up. Of course.

He dragged himself off the bed and went to answer it, his head heavy with exhaustion. He opened the door to find the two detectives from the other day standing on his doorstep.

"Mr. McLennon?" said the woman. "DS Larssen and DI Banham. Sorry to call so early, but we noticed you at your window all night. You appeared to be watching us very closely. Can we come in?"

"Sure."

He ushered them through to the lounge, where DS Larssen immediately sat down. DI Banham, however, moved about the room, his eyes roving over Lewis's possessions as if searching for something. He reminded Lewis of a bulldog, with a thick neck and flattish nose, his hair clipped short and receding at the front. His face seemed to be set in a permanent frown. Or maybe he just didn't like Lewis's flat.

"It was you who found Mrs. Glead," said DS Larssen. It was a statement, not a question, but Lewis nodded anyway. "What made you go round at that time of night?"

Her notebook was already in her hands, pencil already on the page.

"I heard footsteps," said Lewis. "On the stairs. At first, I thought someone was going up but then I realised they were coming down. I looked out the window but couldn't see anyone. It was midnight and seemed a bit weird, and after what had happened . . . I just thought I'd check everything was okay."

"And what did you find? Take us through it."

Luckily for DI Banham and DS Larssen, Lewis was able to consult the extensive notes he'd made to ensure he didn't leave anything out. The only sticking point was that he couldn't remember whether or not he'd touched anything besides the front door. And Linda's neck.

"Would you be prepared to have your fingerprints scanned?" asked Banham, who'd declined to sit down. "So Forensics can eliminate your prints from the crime scene?"

"No," said Lewis, folding his arms. "No, I don't consent to that."

The detectives exchanged a look.

"I see," Banham said in response. He stood by the living room window, looking out onto the street beyond the square. "Any particular reason?"

"Do I need one?" asked Lewis. Why would anyone want to be on a police database if they didn't have to be?

"Is there access onto the street here?" said Banham, ignoring the question. "From this side of the building?"

"Not from the ground floor, no," said Lewis. "But the upstairs flats have fire escapes at the back. Not sure what rooms they go to."

"The second-floor landing," said Banham absently.

"Did you have your headphones on last night, Mr. McLennon?" asked Larssen.

"Lewis," said Lewis irritably. The formality was getting on his nerves. "And no. I didn't."

"Why not?"

Did he need a reason?

"Because I was the only one who didn't know about the Gleads and I didn't want to miss anything else. Why do you ask?"

"Nobody else heard anything," said Larssen. "Other than the footsteps you said you heard, was there anything else that suggested Mrs. Glead had had a visitor?"

"Well, the fact that her front door wasn't closed properly." Lewis reached for his phone automatically. "That immediately made me think someone else was inside or had been inside."

"We're considering that, but it's not unheard of in cases of suicide. People want to make sure they're found. What are you doing?"

Lewis looked up, his face heating as he realised both detectives were staring at him.

"Oh. Uh, making notes. Sorry. Force of habit." He locked the phone and put it away, then registered what she'd said. "Wait, you think it was suicide? Was there a note? I didn't see one."

"No, but people don't always leave one."

"You're not considering murder?"

Larssen sighed.

"We're not ruling anything out but in spite of what you said when you called it in, there are no signs of anyone else having been present. No evidence of a struggle, no defence wounds. There's also no obvious motive or suspect. A quiet person with a very small circle of contacts. Suicide fits the profile."

"What about the footsteps? Someone *was* there."

"But you didn't actually see anyone, did you? Perhaps it was a noise from the other flat?"

"I don't think so. And her husband was just murdered. That seems a pretty solid reason to think she was also killed. Oh." Realisation dawned. "You still think she did it."

Larssen glanced over at Banham, who was inspecting the mess on Lewis's desk.

"That's one possibility. Or else she was grief-stricken and just didn't want to go on."

"You write crime novels, so they tell me," said Banham, turning around.

"Uh, yes."

"Including a bestseller."

"Yes." Lewis didn't feel the need to explain that the other two had sunk without trace.

Banham nodded, staring at the bland abstract print on the wall.

"And is this your first involvement in an actual crime?"

"Yes. Why?"

"To be blunt, Mr. McLennon . . ." said Banham, and Lewis heard the emphasis on "Mister." "I hope you're not going to get in our way. Hobbyists and true crime fans are par for the course when we're talking about cold cases, but for an active investigation, they can be a significant problem."

"I'm not a hobbyist," said Lewis, in disgust. Had he not just told them about his books? He stood up. "And I'm not a 'fan' either. I'm a writer, and writers do research. If the opportunity to learn something about one of your cases dropped into your lap, you'd be making notes too."

"I would indeed, Mr. McLennon. On account of them being *my* cases. So unless you're planning on getting your PI licence, I recommend you keep your note-taking to a minimum."

"Actually," said Lewis, "you don't need a licence to operate as a private investigator in the UK. I could set up as a PI tomorrow, if I wanted."

Larssen winced.

"There are training courses you can go on," Lewis went on, wondering why Banham's eyes were starting to bulge, "but really all you need is a half-decent methodology and some common sense."

"Half-decent?" repeated Banham. "Is that all?"

"I don't think it pays much though, and I expect a lot of it is pretty boring. You guys would get all the good cases."

"The good cases?"

"The murders and suchlike. But there's probably less paperwork than you guys get. Being a detective in the force is practically a desk job now, right?"

Banham took a step toward him, eyes now narrowed. "A what?"

"DI Banham," said Larssen sharply, and Lewis stepped back. It was possible he'd said the wrong thing.

"I mean, not entirely, obviously, or you wouldn't be here now, but you know what I mean."

"Not sure I—"

"Thanks for your time, Mr. McLennon," said Larssen, abruptly, standing up and flipping her notebook shut in one movement. "We'll see ourselves out. We'll be in touch if we need anything else." She began to steer Banham out of the room.

"No problem," said Lewis, watching as she almost pushed Banham into the hall. "Anything I can do, let me know."

The front door slammed behind them and Lewis relaxed. That hadn't gone too badly, all things considered.

No longer tired, he went back to bed anyway, and lay on top of the covers, thinking.

Suicide? He supposed it wasn't outside the realm of possibility, especially if Linda had killed her husband, but what about the footsteps? Someone had been moving about. Someone who'd vanished when he'd gone to look. Another resident? Or an intruder?

But if it was a double murder, then who on earth would want to kill Linda? She'd been so quiet, so meek. How could she possibly have been a threat to anyone? Was it something she'd done? Or something she knew? Something about her husband's killer, perhaps?

Either way, there'd clearly been more to the woman than he'd realised.

Poor Linda Glead, he thought, as he closed his eyes. Poor, sad Linda Glead.

14

Celeste

"We're not ruling anything out at the moment," said DS Larssen, perched on the edge of Celeste's silver and blue sofa at half past eight that morning. She'd brought DI Banham this time, but he turned out to be just as rude as PC Edwards. After refusing a seat, he'd walked around the space as if it were an art gallery, peering and sneering at everything, before standing in front of her picture window. He now gazed out over the square, twisting his wedding ring round and round his finger.

Celeste was furious and scared, in equal measure. She'd gone to bed satisfied that Linda was no longer suspected of shooting her husband and so would be free to enjoy the rest of her life, but when Dixon had woken her to tell her what had happened, all her hopes had come crashing down around her. After everything Linda had endured, and now she'd been denied what should have been her happy ending. Who could have done such a thing to that poor, innocent girl?

"What does that mean, exactly?" she asked. "'Not ruling anything out'?"

"It means that we're still not sure how Mrs. Glead died but that the circumstances don't currently appear to be suspicious. We're not ruling out foul play, but at the moment, it looks like either natural causes or a sad case of death by suicide."

Dixon, who was standing behind Celeste's chair like a soldier on sentry duty, cleared his throat.

"You think Linda Glead took her own life?" he asked, with just the right note of contempt.

"We're not ruling anything out," repeated DS Larssen.

"That's preposterous," said Celeste impatiently. "Why on earth would she have done that?"

"Grief?" suggested DS Larssen. "Fear?"

"Guilty conscience," said DI Banham from over at the window.

Celeste snorted.

"You surely don't still believe she killed her husband?"

"We can't rule it out," said DS Larssen again, but at least had the decency to look embarrassed about it.

"When will the postmortem be held?" asked Dixon.

"Soon," said DS Larssen. "The coroner always has a backlog, so we can't say how long it'll take, but we'll be holding the property as an unprocessed crime scene until the coroner tells us otherwise. And of course, we'll be talking to anyone who saw or spoke to Linda before she died."

"That's all very well," said Celeste, "but time is rather of the essence, don't you think? You're giving the killer time to get away."

DI Banham turned, fixing her with his watery blue eyes.

"Why are you so sure there *is* a killer, Mrs. van Duren?" His accent suggested better breeding than his behaviour. "You said you didn't see or hear anything last night, and the security logs from the gates show no one entering the square except residents. Is there anyone you know with a motive to hurt Linda Glead?"

"Inspector," said Celeste, using her stick to heave herself out of her armchair, "Linda Glead was a dear, sweet girl and I cannot imagine her having any enemies. Everyone here felt sorry for her. I'm sure there are more than a few people who would wish to murder Mr. Glead, but not one who would wish to murder Linda."

"Yet you're convinced it *was* murder. Explain that to me."

"Mrs. Glead was a healthy young woman with her whole life ahead of her, a chance to start again." She emphasised her next words with thumps of her cane. "This. Makes. No. Sense."

DI Banham simply stared at her, unblinking, and a silence descended that might have been uncomfortable had Celeste's thoughts not been elsewhere. It was clear to her now that the police had no intention of investigating the case properly. At least, not until some chap in the coroner's office told them to.

"Very well," she said at last. She turned to DS Larssen, who got to her feet. "Will you let me know when you release the apartment? I'll need to talk to Mrs. Glead's sister about arrangements."

"Of course," said DS Larssen. "Thank you for talking to us, Mrs. van Duren."

Celeste didn't so much as glance at DI Banham as they left, letting Dixon show the detectives out to the lift. It had been a long time since she'd felt this angry, and while she found the emotion stimulating, she was out of practice suppressing it. She took a deep breath to centre herself.

"It *could* have been suicide, you know," said Dixon, when he returned. "Or natural causes, like they said."

"You know as well as I do that Linda had no reason to do that," she said, settling herself back in her armchair in the gallery.

"They were right about the gate logs. Only residents in or out all day yesterday. If it was murder . . ."

"I don't care what the gate logs say. No one here would hurt a hair on Linda's head."

Celeste knew that Linda had been murdered. Knew it in her gut and in her bones. But if the killer didn't live in the square, then they must have gained access to it, and that wasn't easy to do. She and Leonard had made sure of that.

"I won't stand for it."

"What do you think you can do?"

"Do you have your mobile telephone?"

"Yes," said Dixon. "Why? Who do you want me to call?"

Celeste shook her head and lifted the binoculars again.

"My cleaner, Dixon. I'd like you to call my cleaner."

If the police weren't going to solve the case properly, then Celeste would just have to do it herself.

15

Audrey

"Morning," mumbled Mei as she clattered into the kitchen at nine thirty, eyes still half closed.

Audrey sat at the kitchen island, staring blearily into her cup of tea. When the paramedics had exited Linda's apartment without a patient, Mei had gone out to talk to the police. All they would tell her was that Linda was dead, so she and Audrey had stayed up, watching from the window, until the coroner had arrived. Then, too exhausted to stay awake any longer, they'd lain down on Audrey's bed and fallen asleep, still fully dressed.

She'd woken to the sound of Mei swearing and had dragged herself off the bed and down to the kitchen to put the kettle on. In the same time it had taken Mei to shower, change, and, from the looks of things, do her skincare, all Audrey had managed was to make two hot drinks and reply to a message from Dixon.

"You've got moisturiser on your chin," she said, pushing a mug of coffee across the counter. With the exception of the white streak under her lip and the dark circles under her eyes, Mei looked pretty well put together given the circumstances, her black hair neat and shining like she'd spent a lot more than eleven minutes getting ready. Instead of her usual Saturday morning yoga outfit, though, she was wearing another work suit, ready to go and talk to the police and Linda's sister.

Mei reached for the coffee, wiping her other hand across her chin.

"You're a lifesaver," she said, taking a gulp.

"Are you okay?" Audrey asked, and Mei was silent for a moment, thinking seriously about the question.

"Not really," she said at last. "I was so busy being relieved that Linda had an alibi for Richard's death, I didn't stop to think she might be a target for the real killer. I feel responsible. I should have got her out of here, got her somewhere safe. And to have it happen right across from me . . ."

"You think she was murdered then?"

"What else could it be? She wasn't ill, and in spite of everything, she didn't seem depressed, did she? Talking about that little dog and moving back in with her sister. But who would want to kill her? She seemed so . . ."

She stopped, trying to think of the word.

"Gentle," finished Audrey. She knew how Mei felt. When she'd finally slept, her dreams had been full of sad women and scruffy dogs and black-clad men watching her from the shadows. Unlike Mei, Audrey had thought it possible Linda *had* killed Richard, so it hadn't occurred to her that she might be in danger. It obviously hadn't occurred to Linda either.

"It must have been the same person who killed Richard," went on Mei. "Maybe they thought she knew something."

Audrey shivered, not wanting to think of how frightened poor Linda must have felt in her last moments.

"If you'd been in Linda's shoes, knowing that someone had killed your husband in your home, would you have come back here? Wouldn't you have been scared the killer might come after you too?"

Mei sighed. "I've been wondering about that. She said she didn't know who'd killed Richard, but she didn't seem scared.

"She might have had an accident. Or a heart attack?"

Mei looked up from her coffee, looking hopeful.

"It would be a hell of a coincidence."

"But it is possible. Young people die all the time of undiagnosed health problems."

"Is it awful that I hope that's what it was?"

"Of course not. I hope so too." Audrey turned her phone around for Mei to read the screen. "Check this out. From Dixon."

"'Please drop in on Celeste at your *earliest* convenience,'" Mei read aloud, emphasising the word Dixon had put in capitals. "Bit stroppy."

"You have to imagine it in Celeste's voice."

"A royal command? When is your earliest convenience?"

"Whenever," said Audrey with a shrug. "I've got nothing on."

Audrey took a shower to wake herself up and by the time she headed out the door, it was nearly ten thirty. As her footsteps echoed down the steps into the courtyard, the police in the square turned their heads toward her. Besides the two officers stationed outside the Glead place, there were people in white paper suits standing near the door, talking. She did her best to ignore them, studiously keeping her gaze away from Flat 10, although the entire scene seemed designed to attract attention.

Audrey let herself into the big house and took the stairs two at a time. She rang the bell and fidgeted as she waited for Dixon to open the door.

"You're late" was all he said as he moved to let her inside, and she bristled at once, patience already frayed by anxiety and lack of sleep.

"How can I be late? This is as soon as I could get here."

"You're normally here by eight thirty."

"That's on a Friday. A normal Friday. When I'm supposed to be here, working. This is Saturday. A very unnormal Saturday, when I was up half the night watching the police deal with another death in the square. I think ten thirty is very reasonable under the circumstances."

"Quite right," called Celeste, waving at her from the armchair. "Dixon, be nice."

Dixon opened his mouth to protest but then shut it again, and Audrey sighed, aware that it would have been Celeste complaining about her tardiness. She went over to the gallery nook and sat down in the second armchair. Celeste leaned forward, peering at her with concern.

"How are you, dear?" she asked. "I hope this hasn't upset you girls too much."

"It has a bit," she admitted. "We spoke to Linda late yesterday afternoon. But what about you? How are you?"

"Distressed, Audrey, I'm distressed. That's the only word for it."

"Of course you are." Audrey reached for her hands, soft and crêpey beneath her own. "Is there anything I can do?"

The doorbell went again.

"Ah, good," said Celeste. "He's here."

Confused, Audrey turned toward the front door, then frowned as Lewis McLennon walked in from the hall.

"Morning," he said. He looked tired and unkempt, as if he'd also slept in his clothes, and his curly black hair was sticking up on one side. As he spotted Celeste, leaning around from her armchair, he started toward her, pulling up short when he noticed Audrey. "Oh, sorry. I didn't know you had company."

Celeste waved him over.

"Lewis, come and join us. Do you know Audrey? She lives in Flat Seven."

"We met the other day," he said, nodding. "Hi."

"Hello," she said.

She expected Celeste to suggest relocating to the living area or the dining table, to accommodate the extra guest, but she didn't, and Lewis sank down onto the footstool in front of Celeste's chair without hesitation. How many times had he been here?

Dixon stood to the side of the picture window, leaning against the wall, and Audrey recognised the attitude. Whatever Celeste was about to say, Dixon was not in agreement.

"I'm sure you both suspect why I've called you here," began Celeste. "Dixon woke me this morning"—she eyed her valet with disapproval—"much later than he should have. A ghastly thing has happened and something must be done."

"But we don't know what happened," said Audrey. "They wouldn't tell us any specifics, only that Linda was dead."

"Because they don't know yet," said Lewis, smiling as everyone turned to look at him. "I found her," he added. "It was me that called the police."

"When did you find her?" asked Dixon. "What time?"

"Just after midnight. I thought I heard someone on the stairs and when I went out to check, Linda's door was open. I went up. Found her in the lounge."

"And?" demanded Celeste, but Lewis shook his head.

"And nothing. She was sitting on her sofa, eyes wide open, stone dead. Not a mark on her."

There was silence as they took this in and Audrey noticed Lewis had the same haunted expression Mei had had.

"I'm so sorry," said Audrey, and he frowned. "That must have been horrible."

Celeste drew herself up.

"The police are not currently treating Linda's death as suspicious. They think she may have taken her own life."

"Suicide?" Audrey spluttered. "But . . . when we saw her, she was making plans, looking to the future. Why would she?"

"They think she was racked with grief, or guilt, or some such nonsense. Which is why something must be done."

"What do you mean?" said Lewis. "Just let the police do their job."

Dixon snorted.

"I have lost confidence in their ability to conduct this investigation," said Celeste haughtily.

Lewis looked baffled but another glance at Dixon confirmed to Audrey that Celeste was up to something.

"What are you planning, Celeste?" she asked. "Why are we here?"

Celeste cleared her throat.

"I want the two of you to look into it for me." She paused, possibly for effect. "You're clever, both of you, and I trust you implicitly. I'd like you to investigate on my behalf and find out who killed Linda Glead."

16

Lewis

Lewis couldn't believe what he'd just heard.

"Celeste . . ." began Audrey, after a lengthy pause. "Don't be ridiculous. I'm a cleaner, not a private detective. I wouldn't know where to begin."

"That's where Lewis comes in," said Celeste. "He knows all about criminal investigation. Between the two of you, I'm sure you'll do a fine job."

Lewis felt his mouth drop open.

"Sorry, you've drafted me in as an assistant to your *cleaner*?" he said. "Are you out of your mind?"

Audrey narrowed her eyes.

"What's that supposed to mean?"

"Not assistant, Lewis, partner," Celeste interjected. "You're both highly intelligent. Audrey is sharp as a tack, while you have experience in these matters, albeit theoretical. And I'll pay you both, of course," she added. "For your time."

"Celeste, I have clients," said Audrey.

"And I have a full-time job," said Lewis, which earned him another filthy look from Audrey for some reason.

"I know, dear, but you could juggle things around? And, Audrey, you could drop some clients? I know you're a simply wonderful cleaner, but I'm sure your clients could find someone to replace you, temporarily. And I'd pay you well, I assure you. More than enough to cover any losses."

Lewis was about to huff that he didn't have the option of dropping some clients, and besides, he had his writing to think about, when it all came together in his head.

This was his chance to get on the other side of things. To interview real people, to get answers. To follow real evidence rather than stuff he'd made up. To go on stakeouts and follow suspects. And get paid for doing it. Plus, there was a safety net. The police were doing it too. If he uncovered something, he could assist their investigation, and if they got there first, then no harm no foul. He could only help, right?

"I can't rearrange things," he said, speaking slowly. "It's a nine-to-five job. There's no time for anything else. Unless . . ."

"Unless what?"

"Depending on the salary you're offering, then I could possibly take a sabbatical. How long are you expecting this investigation to take?"

Celeste looked thoughtful.

"We could say a fortnight? No more than a month, at the outside. How would that sound?"

A month. A month off from his horrible job, which he hated with every fibre of his being. A month in which to get firsthand experience and useful on-the-ground research for his novel. It would doubtless leave loads of time for writing, too. Could he write a book in a month? He bet he could, without the shackles of the nine-to-five. Then he could spend as long as he liked editing it. That's what they said, right? Write hot, edit cold.

Audrey bit her lip and he was sure he could see a flicker of excitement in her eyes. Her gaze fixed on him.

"You'd really take a month off work for this?" she asked. "With no experience or expertise? What on earth do you do for a living?"

"Recruitment," he said at once. "In which I also have no expertise. I would take a month off work for literally any reason, if I could afford to. Recruitment is the worst job in the world, probably even worse than cleaning!"

Her face hardened again.

"I like cleaning."

"What?"

"I *like* cleaning."

"Really? Wow. That's . . . great. For you, I mean. It must make it easier." He tried not to pull a face. "My boss likes recruitment. Takes all sorts. But it's not my calling."

"And this is?"

"Yes! Well, not this exactly, but writing about this. I might not have field experience, but I've researched investigative procedure for years."

"But then what?" she asked. "I can't drop clients for a month, then expect them to take me back on."

"Tell them you're on holiday?" suggested Lewis. This was surely not as hard as she was making it look. "Everyone's entitled to a holiday."

Audrey looked at him for a moment, her expression one of incredulity and contempt.

"Look, this is all very exciting and everything, but real people have died," she said. "This isn't a game. We're not remotely qualified! Why not just trust that the police will get it right in the end?"

"I told you what the police are thinking, Audrey," said Celeste. "The police think Linda killed Richard, and so now they think she took her own life. They're not even going to investigate until the pathologist finds something, which may be too late. The killer will be long gone. I need someone to consider all possibilities."

"If there even is a killer! You want someone to find what you want them to find!"

Dixon coughed but didn't speak. Lewis wondered if he was as annoyed by Audrey as he was.

"I don't see how it could have been suicide," said Lewis, thinking back to the scene in Linda's living room. "Unless she ate or drank poison. There wasn't a mark on her that I could see. But she could have had a heart attack, or an aneurysm. Something like that."

"Exactly," agreed Audrey. "Tragic and desperately sad, but not murder. Surely the police know when a death is suspicious?"

"Usually, yes," he said. "Even when cause of death isn't known, they look at the scene and see if there's anything out of the ordinary, anything that suggests foul play. But there *were* footsteps and her door *was* open. That should bother them."

"You see?" said Celeste triumphantly. "You're already ahead of the police."

"The way I see it," he said, "we can't do any harm. If we look into it and find nothing, then we find nothing. If the pathologist comes back and says it's natural causes, then case closed. But if we do find something, something the police would have missed because they were holding back, then we've helped."

"Audrey, dear, the thing is . . . if and when the police eventually come to their senses, the trail will have gone cold. I'd like to have our bases covered, by someone who'll look outside as well as in, and who can see what the police can't."

"Namely us."

"Namely you."

Audrey looked from Celeste to Dixon, but something in what Celeste had said seemed to chime with her.

"This is silly," she said. "Isn't it?"

"Silly or not, I'm in," said Lewis, folding his arms. He could handle this without the cleaner. He wasn't really seeing why Celeste thought she was so clever anyway. "I can't promise I won't come to the same conclusion the police have, but at least it'll put your mind at rest."

Now everyone was frowning at him.

"Now, Lewis," said Celeste, her voice holding a warning, "I really think we need both of you."

"Why?" he demanded. "I'm the one with the know-how."

"Yes, but . . . dear, you must see. Audrey's a people person. People respond to her. You're . . ."

"I'm what?"

"You're not . . ." Celeste paused, evidently picking her words carefully.

"You're rude," finished Audrey. "It makes you unlikeable."

He felt himself gape, and Dixon made a strange choking noise.

"Unlikeable? And *I'm* rude?!"

They glared at each other.

"Tsk, Audrey," chided Celeste, "I wouldn't say unlikeable. But, Lewis, you do have a habit of saying slightly the wrong thing, dear, which is a disadvantage. Plus, I need Audrey for a specific task."

"What task?"

"Cleaning the crime scene."

"What?" Audrey sat up straighter and a spark came into her eyes. "How?"

Celeste gave a knowing smile.

"I thought that might interest you. As the crime scene is my property, I can decide who cleans it. Once the police have vacated, of course. I'd like you two to be first on the scene, and I just know, Audrey, given how thorough you are, that you'll find something the police have missed."

To Lewis's astonishment, the idea of cleaning the crime scene appeared to seal the deal. Audrey let out an audible puff of air and shook her head.

"I can't believe I'm saying this," she began, and Celeste clapped her hands, "but all right, I'm in." She looked at Lewis and her nose wrinkled. "A cleaner and a crime writer. What could possibly go wrong?"

17

Audrey

They walked down the stairs together, the silence not exactly hostile but not entirely friendly either. Audrey couldn't believe she'd agreed to work with this idiot, and she was pretty sure he was thinking the same thing.

"I have to know," said Lewis, when they reached the door leading back to the square. She stopped and turned to face him. "Why was it the crime scene that swung it? The cleaning, I mean."

She shrugged.

"I like a challenge. Half the places I clean are already clean. Like Celeste's. Her apartment is never dirty, but I clean it once a week anyway. I love seeing her but it's not exactly satisfying work."

"I don't think this will be that satisfying," he said. "The Gleads' flat was pretty clean when I was in there."

"But the police will have made a mess, right? Traipsing in and out? I'd like to have something I can get my teeth into."

"You should see my place," he said, with no trace of humour. "You really like cleaning that much?"

She studied his face, wondering if there was another insult in there. He wasn't bad-looking, really, tall and broad-shouldered, with curly black hair, decent cheekbones, and dark brown eyes. Shame about the personality.

"Yes," she said eventually, deciding no offence was meant. "I do."

He appeared baffled by her answer, but nodded anyway. "Okay."

"Anyway, it wasn't just the cleaning. Linda . . . she'd been through a lot and she deserved better. Better than Richard, better than this, and now the police using her death as a convenient way to tie everything up? She had an alibi for Richard's murder. Pinning it on her just because she's dead feels like . . ."

She stopped, trying to find the right word.

"Cheating," finished Lewis.

"Yes." She sighed. "So . . . we should probably exchange numbers, right? I expect we'll need to make a plan?"

"A plan, yes, good idea." He pulled out his phone. "Erm, right. New contact. Where's that app gone?"

She watched as he fumbled his way through the address book on his phone, resisting the urge to take it from him and put it in herself. He obviously hadn't added a new number in quite some time.

"Thanks," he said eventually, repocketing his phone and opening the door. "So what next?"

"Good question," she said, following him back outside into the square, which was still teeming with police. "Do you want to come over to mine?" she asked, feeling that it would be polite to offer. "We can talk through this idea."

She glanced over at his front door, on the other side of the courtyard, hoping he'd suggest his place instead. He'd made it sound intriguingly squalid.

"Uh, sure. Yes, good idea."

Feeling awkward, Audrey led Lewis across the courtyard and down the path to the opposite block, passing the Captain's flat on her way to the end of the row, where the little staircase leading up to Flat 7 went up and over the entrance to Flat 3, the other ground-floor flat where Victor DeFlore lived.

As they climbed the steps, their feet tapping on the stone, Audrey considered what she'd just agreed to. A month of being a private detective. And working with the rude guy from Flat 5, no less. The whole thing was absurd. She should back out while she still could. Tell Celeste she'd changed her mind.

But as they reached the top of the steps, she paused, keys in hand, and looked across the garden toward Flat 10, where the yellow crime scene tape looping across the balcony flapped in the wind. Poor Linda. She'd wanted so little, but now the best she could hope for was truth. And justice, if it came to it.

Would she get that from the police? Audrey was no longer sure.

18

Lewis

"I've never been in one of the upstairs flats before," said Lewis, standing at the counter while Audrey made coffee with what looked like the last of a bag of grounds. "Gives you lots of room, having the bedrooms on another floor. What did you say your flatmate did again?"

Audrey got two mugs out of a cupboard. She seemed nervous, although maybe it was just awkwardness. He'd feel the same in her shoes, or at least he imagined he would. He hadn't had a friend over in years.

Not that he and Audrey were friends.

"Mei's a lawyer," she said, her back still to him.

"Mei, right." He nodded to himself. "Explains it."

"Explains what?"

"How you can afford it."

She paused, the milk in her hand, and turned around.

"What?"

"This place." He gestured at the kitchen to illustrate his point. "On a cleaner's salary. What's wrong?"

She was glaring at him again.

"Is recruitment well paid?" she demanded. Why was she being so hostile?

"Not too bad." He peered at a landscape on the wall of the dining area. Lots of green, rolling hills. "Pays the bills."

Audrey put the drinks down in front of him and hopped up onto one of the stools. He did the same on the other side and then they were sitting opposite each other, Audrey looking just as awkward as he felt.

She pushed the sugar bowl toward him and he put two teaspoons into his coffee, then added a further careful half spoon. He looked up as he stirred and saw her staring at him.

"Did you know that only three in ten people take sugar in their coffee?" she said. "I bet not many have two and a half teaspoons, though."

"I wouldn't normally, but I need it," he said, aghast that she might think of him as a sugar-taker. "I was up all night and then the police came early. I only got about an hour's sleep before I was summoned by Dixon." He took a sip, expecting the worst, but in spite of the sugar, he was pleasantly surprised. "Hey, nice coffee."

"Thanks."

"Celeste is right that they're considering suicide for Linda." He took his phone out of his pocket and read back through his notes. "No signs of a struggle, or any defence wounds. They said, and I quote: 'A quiet person with a very small circle of contacts. Suicide fits the profile.'"

She looked at him, aghast.

"So because she didn't have many friends, no one would bother to murder her?"

"No one saw or heard anything," Lewis went on, wondering why she looked like she was going to cry. "And apparently people do sometimes leave their doors open, to make sure their bodies are found."

"God, that's sad. Did she leave a note?"

"Nope."

"I just don't buy it," she said, shaking her head. "Mei and I spoke to Linda yesterday and she was looking to the future. This just doesn't seem right."

Lewis looked at her curiously. It didn't seem right to him either, but then, he'd been there. Heard the footsteps, seen the body. Why was Audrey so sure?

"Did you know her well?"

"No, not at all. I knew Richard was knocking her about, but everyone knew that."

He squirmed a little. Everyone except him, apparently.

"Whenever Mei or I tried to talk to her about it," she went on, "Linda changed the subject and scuttled off. The longest conversation I ever had with her was yesterday."

"Did she say anything interesting?"

Audrey went quiet for a moment, head tipped to the side as if trying to remember.

"For starters, she was going to get a dog. She'd been volunteering at the Dog's Home for ages but Richard was allergic, so she couldn't have one. That was her alibi, actually, for Richard's murder. She'd been helping out during the fireworks, then went to her sister's in Streatham. They sounded close. It seems odd that she wouldn't leave a note for her, at least. And then, after we finished speaking, she went to church. St. Luke's. Said she wanted to speak to the priest."

"A churchgoing animal-lover," said Lewis, tapping a finger against his mug. "Doesn't rule out the possibility of her being a murderer, but it does seem unlikely. And given that she had an alibi . . ."

"Exactly," agreed Audrey. "Although depending on when Richard was killed, her alibi might leave her with enough time to do the deed. Logically, there are only two reasons for Linda to end her own life: grief or guilt. And she didn't seem that heartbroken . . ."

"So that's where we start," he said. "The church and the sister. See if Linda Glead had anything to feel guilty about, and if not, just how much she really loved her husband."

19

Audrey

Audrey was surprised at how reasonable Lewis made it sound, going to interview people to find out if poor Linda Glead had a guilty conscience or a broken heart.

"Then what?" she asked.

"Then we talk to the other Marchfield residents." He sounded confident. "Even if it doesn't seem like they have motive, they'll all have had opportunity, to kill either Richard or Linda."

"All right. That shouldn't be too hard."

"What about the gardener?" asked Lewis. "Where does he live? Do you know his home address?"

"Why would I know his home address? You think the gardener and the cleaner must automatically be friends?"

He shrugged.

"I don't know. Why would the gardener know about the Captain's heart pills? Why would the artist know about Richard's friends? Who knows why people know what they know?" Her contempt must have shown on her face, because he frowned. "What?"

"Captain Gordon's lived here for thirty years," she said, "and the Hetheringtons for sixteen years. Mrs. Hildebrandt's been here nearly a decade, and Roshan's worked here since he was twenty, which has got to be—what?—fifteen, twenty years? It would be weird if they *didn't* know stuff about each other."

Lewis appeared to consider this.

"Well, I've not been here that long, I suppose," he said eventually. "You've been here a few years, right? What do you know about our neighbours?"

She inhaled before launching.

"Flat Three, Victor DeFlore. Born in Jamaica and was an officer in the Merchant Navy before losing his wife and teenage son in a car accident. Retired ten years ago and has never married again. He likes the horses. Captain Gordon in number four was a sniper in the Coldstream Guards for twenty years. He moved here when he was discharged, after having a heart attack during an exercise. He's fine but keeps an eye on it. Next door to me and Mei in Flat Eight is Sarah Scott and her son, Tom. She's a teacher. She moved to London from Yorkshire to be with her husband, who left when Tom was a baby. Tom goes to school a five-minute walk from here and plays football every Thursday at the club by St. Luke's. They're away at the moment, visiting her parents, because her mother's not been well.

"Philip and Mekhala Hetherington have lived in the flat below Celeste since she and Leonard split the big house. They call it a studio but it's huge inside. Philip's an artist. He was a scholarship boy, as he calls it, and used to be an advertising draughtsman. Mekhala is also an artist, but exhibits under the name Michaela, because when she first came here from Thailand, no one could pronounce her real name. She's sixty-three, and he turns seventy next year.

"Flat Six, Mrs. Hildebrandt. She was an actress, back in the eighties. Her name was Bridget originally, but she changed it to Brigitte to sound more glamorous. She met her husband, Walter, while filming in Austria—he was a producer, I think— and they moved over here. When he died, she discovered he'd financed one too many bad horror movies and left her with nothing. Leonard van Duren met her sobbing outside an estate agent's on the Fulham Road, looking for somewhere she could afford on her pension. She's had at least three boyfriends in the last three years that I know of, each one richer than the last. The latest is Fraser, who has a silver Rolls and sends her pink roses every week.

"Then there's Joe and Emmanuel in Flat Nine, who've been together for seven years and lived here for three. They met at Joe's cousin's wedding. Joe's a chef, like his dad, and Manny's a software developer. Both his parents are doctors. His sister's some sort of social media influencer and does a lot of traveling. Their fridge is covered in postcards from her." She stopped. "What? Why is your mouth open? This is a perfectly normal amount to know about people who basically live next door!"

"I'm not sure it is normal," he said. "And I thought Celeste was nosy."

"I'm not nosy! I've been here four years!"

"Well, I've been here five and I know nothing about any of them. Nor do I want to," he added firmly when she opened her mouth again. "Do you know Linda's sister's name? We need an address."

"I can get that," said Audrey, figuring she could persuade Mei to share that with her. "And St. Luke's is only up the road. We can call in, see if we can talk to anyone who knew Linda."

"Great," said Lewis, grinning at her over the top of his mug. "Time to see if this investigation has legs. If it does, I'll talk to my boss on Monday and see if I can get my sabbatical sorted."

Easy for some, thought Audrey, as she watched him finish his syrupy coffee. She'd have to work out how to rearrange her clients to ensure she didn't lose any. She could see that Celeste's suspicions weren't entirely unfounded, and if the police really did take a step back, then they wouldn't be treading on anyone's toes.

At least, not yet.

Once Lewis had gone, Audrey returned to the kitchen to wash up. She'd just put the mugs in the sink when her phone pinged.

Another alert from the bank, and now the message was in CAPITAL LETTERS, as if shouting at her would result in the immediate materialisation of cash. Where had the money she'd paid in yesterday gone?

Heart pounding, she logged in to her banking app.

Damn it. Charges. The charges for her overdraft had gone out—on a Saturday, no less—and put her over her agreed limit. If she didn't transfer money in by the end of the day, the charges would quickly spiral out of control. She placed the phone, screen down, on the counter and put her head in her hands, pressing her palms to her eye sockets.

Breathe, she told herself, and inhaled deeply.

She let the breath out in little puffs, counting each one.

She couldn't keep doing this. She had to move out, find somewhere cheaper. The stress of paying her share, even the smaller share, was getting too much. Or perhaps she could get another job. How much *did* recruitment pay? It had to be more than cleaning, right?

She'd have to ask Mei for another loan. Humiliating and shameful, and with no idea of when she'd be able to pay it back.

Another deep breath.

Celeste. Celeste and her crazy job.

She found herself a piece of paper to do some calculations on. Celeste had said she'd pay them well. A few weeks of a good income, and she could get herself back on track, maybe even back in the black. Stop living hand-to-mouth all the time, or from whatever level was below hand-to-mouth, anyway.

She could still fit in some of her regular clients, and then she wouldn't have to use the holiday excuse on anyone more than once. A fortnight off would allow her to keep her clients, whereas a month would almost certainly result in her losing some of them. Even the Channings could clean their own bathroom for a fortnight. Probably.

Could she and Lewis really find out what had happened to Linda? Audrey couldn't bear the thought that Linda would never get to experience happiness, and the idea that her killer—if there was one—might get away with it made her feel sick. Watching every episode of *CSI* and *Inspector Morse* did not a detective make, although Lewis seemed confident he knew how to run an investigation. At least when it came to cleaning the crime scene, she would know what to do.

Oh, *God*, she was going to have to explain all this to Mei. Mei was going to freak. She was going to go all lawyery and explain exactly how and why the whole thing was insane, like Audrey didn't already know.

She couldn't say no to the money though, even if she wanted to. Mei would understand that, as long as they didn't do anything to damage the police investigation. She'd never forgive herself if their interference meant Linda's killer got away.

Never.

20

Celeste

"What's been happening?" asked Dixon as he laid the table for dinner that evening. He'd been in the kitchen for several hours while Celeste had remained in her gallery nook, observing the square.

"Not much," said Celeste, walking over to him. "The police have all gone now. Lewis went home and Mei returned not long after. All's been quiet since. I expect she gave Audrey a lecture. Mei can be a little overprotective."

"I still think it's ridiculous. What's wrong with doing it ourselves?"

"Your objections have been well and truly noted, Dixon," said Celeste, allowing him to pull a chair out for her. "But one has to delegate eventually. I think you'll find my instincts are correct."

"I hope not," he said, pouring her a small glass of white wine. "If the police discover Linda did die of natural causes, you'll call this investigation off, yes?"

Celeste shook out her napkin and laid it across her lap.

"Yes, of course." She sighed. "I hope it *was* natural causes. But the alternative . . . that dear Linda was killed right under my nose and the perpetrator might get away with it . . . It's intolerable."

"I know."

There was a pause as Dixon went back to the kitchen and returned with two bowls of homemade soup. Celeste took a slice of soft brown bread from the basket on the table and waited for Dixon to settle himself before lifting her spoon.

"Carrot and tomato," she said after a sip. "Very good."

"You have to tell them about the logs for the gates," said Dixon. "It might help them."

Celeste said nothing.

"You either want justice or you don't," he went on. "Withholding them achieves nothing."

"Audrey and Lewis are going to talk to everyone in the square eventually," she said. "I don't see what me putting entirely meaningless gate logs in front of them will achieve, except to create suspicion amongst innocent residents. No sense in pointing them in the wrong direction."

"And if it's the right direction?" said Dixon, looking at her across the table.

"It won't be," said Celeste firmly. "I know that it won't be."

21

Lewis

"Was everything okay with your flatmate?" Lewis asked Audrey as they sat together on the 319 bus the next morning. It was a damp and grey day, and as they crossed Chelsea Bridge, the mist was still visible through the grubby bus windows, clinging to the river while the weak November sun struggled to break through the clouds. "Did you tell her?"

He'd returned home yesterday for a few hours' sleep before getting back to his computer. He'd written all evening, fleshing out his mystery with new characters and a second murder, then gone to bed early, ready for his first day on the case.

They'd met in the courtyard that morning and walked to the bus stop together, dropping in at a supermarket on the way at Audrey's insistence, to pick up some flowers. She'd seemed despondent, although he didn't know her well enough to know whether the downcast eyes and quiet voice were normal.

"Yes, I told Mei," said Audrey. "And no, not really. She started lecturing me about safety, saying we should leave it to the police. She said Celeste was taking busybodyness to a new level."

"She's not wrong there."

"She wasn't happy about handing over Linda's sister's address either, but she gave in when I said I'd ask Celeste to get it instead. She wants justice for Linda, just like we do."

Lewis said nothing, momentarily ashamed that hadn't been foremost in his mind when agreeing to take the job. All he'd been able to think about were the twin joys of spending a month out of the office and investigating an actual real-life crime.

"Did she tell you anything else useful?"

Audrey hesitated before answering.

"She said she was going to speak to the coroner's office, see if she could get the postmortem moved up."

While Lewis had been initially convinced that he didn't need the cleaner to solve the case, he had to admit it was useful her being friends with Linda's lawyer.

"And?" he prompted.

"And what?"

"What else?"

She turned to look out the bus window.

"She fundamentally disagreed with us getting involved," she said at last. "She was concerned we might end up charged with obstructing a police investigation."

Lewis shrugged.

"We can't obstruct it if it's not happening. All we're doing is giving our condolences to Linda's family." He looked at her pained expression. "I'm sure Maia will come round."

She sighed.

"Mei."

"Mei, yes. Sorry." He tried a different tack. "Look, maybe we'll uncover something the police can use. Then she'll see that we're not only doing the right thing, but that we're helping."

The bus had already crossed the river but it would take another half hour to reach Streatham, so he pulled out his phone and started writing. Once inspiration had caught him, Lewis could write anywhere, using his commute time to flesh out plots and characters, the only hindrance his thumbs on the small touchscreen keyboard. The last few years had brought him nothing but miserable, empty journeys, scrolling endlessly through social media, where his old literary feeds tortured him with news of book deals and book launches, but today his mind was on his story within seconds, and he was surprised when Audrey nudged him.

"Next stop."

They got off at Streatham Hill and started walking. Linda's sister lived only a few streets away, and as they passed row after row of Edwardian terraces, Lewis admired the bay windows, the clean paintwork, and neat, well-tended driveways. Everything was very . . . was "kempt" a word? Whatever the opposite of "unkempt" was, these houses were it.

"Just down here," said Audrey, as they turned onto Waldorf Road. "Number forty-eight-A."

The house was a good size, with a portico in the Arts and Crafts style over the entrance. Two doors stood side by side, one red and one blue, bearing the numbers 48A and 48B, respectively.

Lewis unlatched the little wooden gate and Audrey led the way up the gravel path. She rang the bell on the red door, and it was almost a minute before they heard the sound of footsteps.

Keys rattled in the lock and the door opened on a chain to reveal a short woman with red eyes peering at them through the gap. Even with such a restricted view, Lewis could see at once that it was Linda Glead's sister, from the pale brown hair set in the fluffy curled style of a much older woman, to the pinched look and the downturned mouth, although this last could be due to her recent bereavement.

Audrey held the flowers in front of her.

"Jane Brown?" she asked, and the woman nodded. "I'm Audrey, and this is Lewis. We were Linda's neighbours in March-field Square. We wanted to come by and let you know how sorry we all are, and to check how you were doing."

Jane looked from Audrey to Lewis and back again, then promptly burst into tears and slammed the door shut.

"Shit," said Lewis, but Audrey held up a hand. They heard the rattle of the chain and the door opened again, revealing Jane to be a stout woman holding a sodden tissue up to her nose with a shaking hand.

"That's so kind of you," she said, standing back to open the door wider. "Come in, won't you? Sorry about the mess but I wasn't expecting visitors. I didn't think Linda had any friends." She sobbed the last few words and waved them in.

Lewis followed Audrey inside, feeling rather at a loss. He hadn't considered the state Linda's sister might be in but now he was here, he was thinking it might have been better to have left it a few days. He doubted they'd get anything useful out of her like this.

But once the sister had ushered them into her shutter-darkened lounge, blown her nose a few times, and cleared the coffee table of a sea of damp tissues, she gradually regained her composure. Lewis took out his phone, checking the questions he'd written down to ask, but when he looked up, Audrey was frowning at him.

What? he mouthed, but she just frowned deeper and shook her head.

"We're so sorry to just drop in," she said to Jane, who had curled up in the armchair opposite them, a box of tissues in her lap. "We didn't know Linda that well, really, but . . . well, we felt we should have, you know? Living so close. She kept herself to herself."

Jane nodded, and wiped her nose again.

"That was Linda," she said, sniffing. "Even before Richard, she was a quiet one."

"Did she really not have many friends?" asked Audrey.

"Not really. Only me and Alf."

"Alf?" asked Lewis.

"My husband." Jane pointed at a wedding picture on the wall, where a much younger version of her stood in a simple white dress beside a portly man with a red face and a buzz cut. "He's at church. He offered to stay home with me, but I sent him off. He's as shocked as I am, but he won't talk about it otherwise. He doesn't have the sort of friend he can talk to about his feelings. Men don't, do they?" She looked at Lewis, her pale eyes red and searching for his agreement.

"I . . . suppose not," he said, realising with a start that if it wasn't true for all men, it was certainly true for him.

"He'll talk to Father Darren though, thank goodness." Jane nodded. "Alf loved Linda like she was his own sister. We both thought that with Richard gone . . ."

Tears sprang again and Jane yanked a fistful of tissues out of the box. Lewis looked at Audrey, wondering what they should do now, but Audrey didn't so much as glance at him. She leaned toward Jane and spoke in the same soft, soothing voice she'd used when he told her he'd found Linda's body.

"Let it out," she said, gazing at Jane with her big green eyes. "You poor thing, I can't imagine what you're going through."

Jane nodded, tears streaming down her face while she held the wad of tissues to her mouth.

"She volunteered at the Dogs' Home, didn't she?" said Audrey.

"That's right." Jane paused to gulp in some air and wipe at her eyes. "She liked animals better 'n people. Only place she was happy was Battersea. Except here with us."

"I can see why," said Audrey, looking around. "You've a lovely home."

A flicker of pride came into Jane's damp eyes.

"Thanks," she said, clearly pleased by the compliment. "We've lived here since we were married, coming up fifteen years."

Lewis was starting to lose the thread of things. At what point could he change the subject without being rude?

"Linda went to church, you know," said Audrey. "The day she . . ."

Jane looked startled.

"Did she?"

"Yes. I share a flat with Mei Chen—Linda's solicitor? I met them coming back from the police station but Linda wanted to call in at the church."

"St. Luke's, was it?" she asked, and Audrey nodded. "Well, that does surprise me. The police think . . . Well, you know, I'm sure. But Linda always felt hopeful after church. That's why she stayed with Richard. Me an' Alf told her, you've tried your best, it's not like the old days, the church'll support you if you leave, but she believed she could change him back to who he was before." Jane shook her head. "I told her, some people can't be saved and some people don't want to be saved, and some people is both. Richard Glead was both."

"I couldn't believe it when I heard," said Audrey. "She was talking about getting a dog."

"I still can't believe it," said Jane, swallowing. "I told the police, she'd never have done that, but they said there's no signs of foul play. There'll have to be an autopsy and an inquest. Linda would have hated that. She hated a fuss."

She started sobbing again, and Lewis, uncomfortable with Jane's distress and keen to expedite things, decided to try a more direct approach.

"There'll be one for her husband too," he said, and they both turned to him. "An inquest. Murder creates a lot of bureaucracy."

"At least she'll be spared that," said Jane, gulping in air and dabbing at her eyes. "They still suspected her you know, even though she was here the whole time. Can you believe it? The nerve."

That was more like it.

"The whole time?" he asked. "She couldn't have gone out in the night?"

"I hope you're not suggesting Linda killed him," said Jane sharply.

"No, I was just . . . That is to say—"

"I thought you was a friend of hers!"

"I didn't mean . . ." Lewis looked to Audrey for assistance.

"No one thought Linda did it," said Audrey, her voice calm and soothing, even while looking daggers at him. "Even before we heard about her alibi. But Marchfield is quite a secure place, not many strangers going in and out. Probably seemed easier to look at her than look outside."

Jane sniffed, and pulled a fresh tissue from the box.

"Well, that's the police all over, isn't it? I told them Linda was here all night. I fell asleep in my chair, waiting up for her, and woke at half two, when she got in. We chatted for over an hour, then went to bed. Alf was up at half six—he's always been an early bird—and I was up at seven and Linda came down at eight." Jane blew her nose ferociously. "The police reckon she could've legged it there and back in three hours, but why would she?"

"It makes no sense," agreed Audrey.

"That's what Miss Chen said," said Jane, warming to her subject. "She was already on that side of town, why make life hard for yourself? Linda was as gentle a person as you'll ever meet, but she wasn't stupid neither. She'd never have used me and Alf like that, never in a million years. She was mortified the police were asking us questions."

Jane shot Lewis another angry look. Sensing that he needed to build some bridges, he shook his head.

"That wasn't her fault," he said, trying to mimic Audrey's soft-voice thing. "They'd have had to speak to you anyway. To find out about Richard."

He found himself glancing at Audrey again, who gave a tiny nod.

"Of course it wasn't her fault," said Jane, but now she was shaking her head too. "I thought whoever'd killed Richard had done us all a favour, but now . . ." Tears filled her eyes again.

"Who do you think might have done it?" asked Lewis, but immediately regretted it.

"No idea," snapped Jane. "Why should I? He wasn't my business. *Linda* was my business. She was my baby sister and now she's gone." She gasped, sobs engulfing her body and breaking up her words. "I just don't know what I'm going to do without her."

22

Audrey

This time, there was no stopping Jane. Her body rocked with great juddering sobs, and even when Audrey put her arms around her, she couldn't get them under control. Audrey cursed herself for not thinking this through. Of course it wouldn't be like the television, where the victim's relatives stoically suppressed their grief while being interviewed by the police. She should have known better.

All Audrey could hear was the sound of Jane's crying and her own murmured reassurances, so she was shocked when she looked up and saw a man standing in the open doorway.

Even with the extra years and the ruddy face now pale and drawn, Audrey recognised him as Alf from the wedding picture. He was looking at her, this strange woman comforting his wife, with confusion and suspicion, but he rallied quickly. As Audrey released Jane from her embrace, Alf was there in a flash and Jane fell into his arms, clinging to him for dear life.

Neither Audrey nor Lewis spoke as Alf held his wife, shushing and repeating "there now" until Jane had calmed down. Without a word to either of them, he steered her out of the room, and they heard him taking her upstairs, his voice just audible over the sound of carpeted footsteps.

Lewis stood uncomfortably by the shutters looking through the angled slats at the front garden. Eventually, he turned to her.

"Did I do that?" he asked quietly.

"No," she said, sinking back down onto the sofa. "You were a bit clumsy, but it wasn't because of that. Her heart's broken."

He nodded but turned back to the window, so Audrey sat and gazed at the collection of pictures on the wall. An old one of Linda and Jane standing in a garden, Linda some years younger than Jane and wearing a school uniform. Another, more recent one, of them both smiling and laughing. Although it was just a head-and-shoulders shot, Linda was wearing white and Jane had feathers in her hair. Linda and Richard's wedding, perhaps? A group shot of both couples, Alf wearing a comedy apron and holding a pair of barbecue tongs, while Richard stood with his arm slung around Linda's neck, head held high. A more formal picture of the sisters when they were young: Linda a small girl of maybe five or six, Jane perhaps in her early teens, standing stiffly beside a much older woman Audrey presumed to be the aunt who raised them.

What struck her the most was how different the two women looked. For as long as Audrey had known her, Linda had always looked folded in, somehow, hiding behind lank hair and eyes that never met yours, while Jane was now an empty shell, crushed with grief. But in these joyful, happy pictures, the sisters looked beautiful and full of life.

"Looked a bit different, then, din't she?"

Audrey jumped to find Alf standing in the doorway, also looking at the pictures. She took a breath before answering, to steady her heartbeat.

"Yes." Audrey stood up and Alf looked from her to Lewis and back again.

"You're friends of Linda's?" He spoke roughly, but didn't seem angry.

"Not friends, really. We were her neighbours." She stuck out her hand. "Audrey."

"Lewis," said Lewis, coming to stand beside her.

"I'm Alf," said Alf, shaking their hands. "It was good of you to come, although a bit soon p'raps."

"I see that now," said Audrey. "We cared about her, being her neighbours and everything, but we shouldn't have come. We only stayed as long as we did because Jane was so upset. I'm so sorry for your loss."

Alf rubbed his eyes with pudgy pink fingers. He nodded.

"Thanks. Under normal circumstances, I'd offer you a cuppa, but if you don't mind . . ."

"Yes, of course," said Audrey, picking up her bag from the sofa at once.

They followed Alf to the front door, and as he opened it to let them out, Lewis suddenly stopped.

"How are you doing?" he asked Alf, surprising Audrey with his gentle tone. "It must've been a terrible shock for you too."

Alf's eyes misted up and he blinked a few times.

"It was that. It was that." He croaked a little, then cleared his throat. "We married young, y'see, and Linda was just a girl. She couldn't wait to leave the aunt, so Jane and me . . . we didn't exactly raise her, but . . ." He cleared his throat again, blinking all the time. "It's been a shock, like you said."

"It was my fault," said Lewis abruptly, surprising Audrey. "About Jane being upset. I mentioned Richard's murder, and she thought I was suggesting . . ."

"Ah, yes. That'd do it," said Alf, nodding wearily. "Although you're a fool if you think Linda did it. She never held a gun in her life. He ran with a bad crowd, did Rich. Something was going to happen sooner or later, and things always happen to people who run with Paulo."

"Paulo?" said Lewis, suddenly excited. "Paulo Ram?"

"That's right. You know 'im?"

"I've heard of him."

Audrey looked at Lewis in surprise. How did he know who this man was?

"Rich always said it was just business, but you know what they say about playing with fire . . ."

Alf opened the door wider, so they took their cue and filed out onto the step.

"Will you let us know about . . . about any service?" asked Audrey.

"Yes." Alf sighed. "There'll be one. Even if it turns out she did . . ." He looked at her then, meeting her eyes. "Why wouldn't she leave a note? That's what I don't understand. Why wouldn't she leave a note for us?"

Audrey shook her head.

"I don't know, Alf. It doesn't make any sense."

"No," he said, and now he was talking to himself. "It doesn't make any sense."

He shut the door behind them before they'd left the front step, and as they walked back down Waldorf Road, Lewis said quietly, "If the husband was involved with Paulo Ram, then that changes things."

"Who is he?"

"A minor gangster. Has a pawnshop off the King's Road. Lives semi-respectably, in a new-money kind of way. Fingers in lots of pies. He also acts as go-between for another player known as the Fixer, who no one's ever seen, but the bigger fish use him to sort out their problems. Ram's the middleman, and you do not want to piss him off."

"How do you know all this?"

Lewis was quiet for a moment, and she looked at him curiously.

"There are groups online," he said finally. "Unofficial news groups. The stories behind the headlines, that kind of thing. People get named, connections explained. It's not exactly dark web, but not exactly *not* dark web."

"That sounds . . . scary as all fuck."

"Yeah," he agreed. "But it's also good source material."

Audrey didn't speak again until they were back on the bus, heading for Battersea. She didn't know how she felt about Lewis being the kind of person who skirted the dark web; it made her uncomfortable. She focused instead on how weird it felt to be traveling with someone who wasn't Mei, and how it had been a long time since she'd had the time or the money to go anywhere that wasn't work. Although technically, she realised, this was her work now.

Lewis pulled out his phone and began typing.

"What are you doing?"

"Making notes."

"Should we discuss our interview plan for the Dogs' Home?" she asked. "It didn't feel like we were on the same page back there."

"No, quite. Good idea. Maybe we could not start with them bursting into tears, and take it from there?"

23

Lewis

"Do you have an appointment?" asked the voice through the crackling intercom on the black iron gates of the Dogs' Home.

"No," said Lewis, leaning in to the speaker. "We're not here about an animal. We wanted to talk to someone about Linda Glead."

"Who?"

"Linda. Glead. She volunteers here."

"One moment please."

The intercom went dead. Lewis and Audrey looked at each other.

"Should have made an appointment," said Audrey. "I'd no idea it was so big. There must be hundreds of volunteers."

It was indeed big. Lewis must have passed it dozens of times without ever noticing it. It was a tall, glass-fronted building on Battersea Park Road, its entrance through a series of iron gates connecting the main building to the brick arches beneath the railway line, which cut across the plot at an angle. Beyond the black gates they could see a large complex, stretching back some distance, with a converted station cottage in the middle. Even the Victorian railway arches had been turned into useable space, each one fronted with walls, doors, and windows.

Behind them, light traffic trundled down the road, the smell of fumes and bitumen mixed into the damp air. Audrey gazed out at the road, her back to the gates, while Lewis hovered beside the intercom, waiting for the receptionist to return.

He was just starting to wonder if they'd been forgotten when the intercom clicked.

"Hello?" came a voice.

"Yes! Hello," said Lewis, crouching to speak into it.

"Buzzing you through. Head to reception and Val will meet you there."

The gate buzzed and Lewis held it open for Audrey. Together, they walked through the courtyard toward another, smaller building.

The foyer was large and painted entirely in magnolia, with a wraparound desk facing the door, and offices lining the corridors either side. A young woman in a headset sat behind the desk and in front of it, an older woman with long black braids and wearing a navy-blue fleece was waiting for them.

"You're here about Linda?" she said, coming toward them. Lewis nodded. "I'm Valerie James, the volunteer coordinator."

"Uh, hi," said Lewis, a bit taken aback. He hadn't expected anyone to be so accommodating. "I'm Lewis McLennon, and this is Audrey . . ." He trailed off when he realised he'd forgotten her surname.

"Brooks," said Audrey, through gritted teeth. "Hi."

"Come into my office," said Valerie. "We can talk in private."

They followed her down one of the magnolia corridors to a small no-nonsense space with a cluttered desk, one office chair, and a collection of uncomfortable-looking guest chairs opposite. The only nod to design was the circular window in the back wall with a bushy trailing plant nestled in front of it.

The chairs were, as expected, hard and uncomfortable. He supposed that was one way of keeping meetings short.

"So, how can I help?" asked Valerie, sitting down in her own chair. "I hope you've not charged Linda?"

Lewis paused. She thought they were the police.

"Uhh . . ."

"We're not the police, Ms. James," said Audrey, without so much as glancing at him. "We're Linda's friends. I'm afraid we've got some bad news."

The woman's brow furrowed.

"Oh? What news? What's happened?"

"I'm afraid Linda's dead. She passed away on Friday night."

The following silence was so profound, Lewis finally understood what it meant to hear a pin drop.

Valerie opened her mouth and shut it again.

"But . . ." she said at last, looking from Audrey to Lewis and back again. "That can't be. I spoke to her Friday night. What happened?"

Lewis's heart skipped a beat. "What time Friday night?"

She was too shocked to ask why he wanted to know.

"About eight, maybe?"

"What did she call about?" He tried to keep it conversational, but she narrowed her eyes at him.

"Who are you again?"

"Neighbours of Linda's," he said, then Audrey nudged him with her foot. "Friends. And neighbours."

The expression on Valerie's face suggested she was not convinced. She glanced at the phone on her desk.

"Was it about Muffin?" asked Audrey inexplicably. Some sort of disruption tactic? Whatever it was, though, it worked, because Valerie's face softened.

"She told you about Muffin? What happened? She was alive and well when I spoke to her."

Lewis frowned. This was not one of their agreed questions. How could he conduct an interview when people were blithering on about muffins?

"We don't really know. She was found dead in her flat just after midnight. The police think . . . Well, they're considering suicide as a possibility."

"Suicide?" Valerie's eyes became distant, as if trying to overlay the idea of suicide onto the Linda she knew. "That doesn't seem . . . I mean, why would she? She said she was going to adopt Muffin. Why would she do that and then . . . ?"

Aha! Muffin was the dog. Stupid name.

"I know," said Audrey, nodding. "It doesn't make sense to us either, but . . . We weren't sure if the police or Linda's sister would have been in touch, and didn't want anyone wondering why Linda didn't turn up for a shift."

Valerie's eyes glistened now, and Lewis steeled himself for another emotional outburst.

"Thank you, that was very thoughtful," she said, managing to keep any tears inside. "We have many volunteers, but Linda was very popular in the kennels. A quiet, gentle person. And a bit sad. Like a lot of our animals, really. She was so good with them. She was always the first person I rang if I had an extra shift."

"She loved it here," said Audrey, sounding like they really had been friends.

"Her sister said it was one of the only places she was happy," Lewis put in, keen not to be left out again. Valerie smiled weakly.

"That's a bit sad too, isn't it? But lovely to hear. We do get that, with our volunteers. They get back twice as much as they put in, emotionally speaking."

"How many shifts did she do?" Audrey asked. "Lewis and I can fill in if you're left with any gaps. Linda would've hated for you to be inconvenienced."

He glared at her. What was she playing at? He didn't have time to look after animals!

"God, that's . . . so kind," Valerie sniffed, now dangerously close to crying. "We try to only use trained volunteers with the animals, but Linda did do a lot of shifts. She had so much free time because of her husband. She'll be missed."

"Because of her husband?" repeated Lewis.

"He didn't like her to work." Valerie opened one of her desk drawers and rooted about, pulling out a packet of tissues. "She was home alone most of the time. Didn't seem healthy to me, but there you go."

"Was there anyone in particular she worked with?" Lewis asked, and when she looked up, added, "Anyone we should let know?"

She blew her nose.

"Only Nathan. Nathan Roper. He worked the same shifts. I don't know if they were close but he'll be in on Wednesday. I'll let him know."

"We should get going," said Audrey, standing up, and Lewis followed suit. They'd agreed, after their visit to the Browns, that it was better not to be thrown out if they could help it.

"Thanks for dropping by," said Valerie, also getting to her feet. "Can't have been easy for you. Do you think the police will need to speak to me again? Only I don't work Mondays or Tuesdays. They're our quiet days."

Audrey looked at Lewis.

"They might," he answered honestly. "Once the postmortem's done. Depending on what they find."

Valerie inhaled sharply at the mention of the postmortem, but nodded. As they went back out into the reception area, Audrey stopped and pulled a grubby-looking business card from her bag.

"Here," she said, handing it to Valerie. "If you do need any help, give me a call. Don't want to leave you shorthanded."

"Thank you so much," she said, sniffing. "And thanks again for letting us know."

They walked back through the courtyard to the iron gates, where they waited for the receptionist to buzz them out.

"I think that went pretty well," Lewis said, as they walked down the road together, facing into the wind. "We now know that Linda was still alive and not considering being otherwise at eight o'clock on Friday, and we've got the name of someone she might have confided in. We can look this Nathan up later, see if we can get an interview with him. Plus, no one broke down. I call that a win."

Audrey turned her cheek against the wind and stuck her hands in her pockets.

"So what now, Sherlock?" she asked. "Who do we talk to next?"

He thought for a moment, suddenly very conscious that he'd claimed to know enough to run the investigation. He grudgingly admitted that Celeste had been right about Audrey being a people person. They'd all opened up to her easily, with her gentle questions and her soft voice. That was a good technique. He'd have to practise.

"You said the husband had regular poker nights, right?"

"First Friday of every month, for the last two years. How do you not know that?"

He shrugged.

"I've been busy." Busy not writing a book, he added silently. "Why do you know that?"

"Manny and Joe." She said it like it was obvious but it took him a few seconds to remember that those were the guys who lived above him, and next to the Gleads. "And Mrs. H, who lives underneath them, of course. Richard was extra horrible and loud on poker nights."

"Oh. Well, I always have my headphones on, so . . ." There it was again, that wormy feeling. "If we are looking at murder, then it'll probably be the same person that killed Richard. The odds of a married couple being killed within forty-eight hours of each other without the deaths being linked have to be vanishingly small, right? If we can work out why Richard was murdered, then it should also tell us why the killer felt they had to get rid of Linda as well. As we've now exhausted Linda's not-so-extensive list of friends, it means we need to start with his."

"Including Paulo Ram?"

"Especially Paulo Ram. We need to find his gangster friends and rattle some cages. See what shakes out."

Audrey bit her lip, but instead of protesting, she let out a short series of little puffs, clouds of warm breath huffing out into the cold air.

"Rattle some gangster cages," she said. "Cool. No problem."

"I didn't say that," he said, then regretted it when he saw the colour drain from her face. "But it's got to be done. We also need to look at everyone with opportunity, which means the Marchfield residents."

"All of them?"

"All of them. No one is above suspicion. Not even you and me."

24

Audrey

That evening, Audrey sat curled up on the chenille-covered sofa Mei had bought when they'd moved in, her ancient laptop open on a Google image search of London gangsters while she texted Lewis.

> AUDREY BROOKS: Bloody hell, Paulo Ram IS one of Richard's poker buddies.

> FLAT 5 GUY: And the other one?

> AUDREY BROOKS: Seems to be a guy called Chaz Shaw? Any cute nicknames for him?

> FLAT 5 GUY: Not that I know of, but he's bad news. Anything on Richard's socials?

> AUDREY BROOKS: They're all locked down. A profile picture change on Facebook last year got a handful of likes, but that's about it.

"Whatcha doing?" asked Mei, walking in holding a glass of wine. She was wearing grey velvet sweatpants and an oversized pink jumper, fresh out of the laundry if the scent of fabric softener was anything to go by.

"Checking the Gleads' social media accounts and googling gangsters."

"Of course you are," said Mei, folding herself into the armchair. "Any particular reason?"

Audrey hesitated. She and Mei had come very close to having their first proper argument yesterday, and she wasn't keen to bring it up again if she could help it. But she didn't lie to Mei.

"Turns out Richard Glead's poker friends are some criminals called Paulo Ram and Chaz Shaw." She heard the hiss of Mei's intake of breath. "Do you know them?"

"I know of them," she said, sitting up straighter in the chair. "They've been coming here?"

Audrey rotated the laptop so Mei could see the images on her screen.

"That's them, right? The ones we saw coming in on poker night?"

"Well, shit . . ." breathed Mei.

Audrey turned the laptop back.

"Yeah."

"The police asked Linda about Richard's friends and she called them Paul and Charles," said Mei. "Said she didn't know their last names."

"Do you think she was telling the truth?"

"I thought so at the time but now . . . I don't know." Mei was quiet for a moment, sipping her wine. "I know I was horrible yesterday. About this whole detective thing, but it's just because I'm worried about you. The police obviously don't know about Ram and Shaw—once they find out, they'll be all over this. You can't mess around with people like that. They'll eat you alive."

"I know," said Audrey, and she did know. They'd been on the case for twenty-four hours and she was already regretting agreeing to work for Celeste. "But the police have got it wrong. Linda called her friend at the Dogs' Home at eight o'clock Friday night to say she was going to adopt Muffin. That was after she got home from church. Even if she had killed Richard, what could possibly have happened in the space of four hours to make her take her own life?"

"And I'll be chasing the coroner tomorrow about the PM and toxicology, but it has to be the police that do the investigating, Auds." Mei's eyes grew wide as she tried to emphasise her point. "Cases have been lost due to interference from the public; you have to take this seriously!"

"What do you think I'm doing?" snapped Audrey, then checked herself. "Sorry. Look, all we're doing at the moment is talking to people about Linda. The woman had no friends, Mei. Just her sister and the people she knew at Battersea. The police think no one would have *bothered* to murder her." She swallowed. "Linda's life may have been small but it still meant something. If she didn't die by suicide, then it was either natural causes or murder, and if it was natural causes, then why did she leave her front door open that night? That's a strange thing for anyone to do, let alone a woman whose husband's just been killed. And if it was murder, then the two deaths have to be connected. The police think Linda did for Richard, then herself—they're barely investigating at all. We're just trying to find something that might point to a person or a motive before the trail goes cold."

Mei considered this, swirling the wine in her glass.

"You promise that's all?" Audrey nodded but Mei held her gaze. "You won't go talking to Ram or the others?"

"I promise," she said, and tried to ignore the tightening in her chest.

"Thank you." Mei sighed. "So what's next on the agenda for Celeste van Duren's private investigators? Who are you talking to tomorrow?"

"I'm working in the morning," said Audrey, "and I have to try and rearrange some cleaning clients for the rest of the week, but Lewis is going to try and track down someone from the Dogs' Home who Linda might have been friends with. If she was murdered, there has to be something in her life to make her a target, and the church and the Dogs' Home were all she had. Unless she was involved in Richard's business somehow, so we'll look into Ram and Shaw too. If the motive isn't in Linda's life, then it has to be in Richard's."

"I don't like the sound of that," said Mei.

"I don't even know what Richard did for a living. Why was he hanging out socially with gangsters?"

"Linda said he was an antiques dealer," said Mei with a shrug. "With a shop on Pimlico Road. Linda knew nothing about it, or so she said. But if Richard was working with Ram, then most likely it was money laundering or leverage trading."

"Leverage trading?"

"People who are high up in criminal organisations like to acquire leverage for negotiating with the authorities. If they ever get caught and it looks like they might be prosecuted, they can bargain for reduced jailtime by offering to return some priceless work of art, or something of national importance."

"You're kidding? 'You've got me bang to rights, guvnor, but if I give back the *Mona Lisa*, we'll call it quits'?"

Mei laughed. "Pretty much. Happened to one of the firm's biggest cases last year. The police spent two years gathering an impeccable chain of evidence; multiple witnesses already in protection programs. Thought they had an airtight case. Then the accused offers up a Renoir in exchange for a plea. They fought with the Met Arts unit for weeks, but he ended up doing a year in minimum security due to time served."

Audrey felt a fizzle of excitement at the potential connection, and picked up her phone.

"That's another line of enquiry to pursue," she said, typing out another text.

"Excuse me?"

"Is what I will say to the police when I hand over the information," she finished, putting her phone down and smiling innocently at Mei. She closed her laptop and reached for the remote. "Shall we watch something? What are you in the mood for?"

Mei sighed and snuggled back into her chair.

"All right. But no crime dramas, please. I've had more than enough of that for one day."

25

Lewis

THE CLEANER: Mei says Richard Glead was an antiques dealer. If he was working with Ram, it might be something to do with using art as leverage?

LEWIS MCLENNON: That makes sense. If the police find out Glead was working for gangsters though, they'll start looking more closely at everything, including Linda. Maybe she knew something about Richard's death that got her killed. These sorts of people don't like loose ends. We have to get in quick before the police block us out.

THE CLEANER: Is that a bad thing? At least it would mean they were investigating properly.

LEWIS MCLENNON: Of course it's a bad thing! Did she say anything else?

THE CLEANER: That Linda knew Richard's friends as Paul and Charles, and didn't know anything about his business.

LEWIS MCLENNON: That's odd, don't you think? How early can you meet tomorrow?

THE CLEANER: I have a job in the morning,
plus some admin. Meet in the courtyard
at 2pm?

LEWIS MCLENNON: See you there.

Admin. How could she be doing admin while they were just beginning their investigation? Although that did remind him, he still hadn't drafted his sabbatical email for his boss.

He began to type.

Dear Steve,

I hate this job and I'm taking a month off, during which time I don't want to hear from you in any capacity whatsoever. See you in December. Unfortunately.

Lewis

He grinned. Wouldn't he just love to send that? Though his boss probably wouldn't understand it. Didn't include the word "mate," for starters. And he knew for a fact that Steve had attended a private school in Somerset, so why his office-lad banter had an estuary accent, he'd never know.

He deleted it and typed a more professional email, albeit one full of lies, spinning a yarn about a very sick relative with no one to look after her who needed round-the-clock care in her final days, which were likely to total no more but also no less than thirty. He apologised for the inconvenience and added several lines about how he completely understood if he needed to be let go and someone else found to fill the position. Huge regrets, obviously, but family was family and no hard feelings. None whatsoever.

Once he'd hit send, he realised he may have overdone it, but he'd signed off asking his boss to call him, so hopefully he could salvage it. His boss wasn't exactly the sharpest or most erudite tool in the box. He might not even have noticed the hidden plea in there.

Except he couldn't afford to lose his job. He needed it. Maybe that was why he hated it so much.

Lewis went back to his writing, making his fictional witnesses more helpful than his actual witnesses. No one they'd spoken to yet had said anything particularly useful, except that Richard Glead was a controlling and abusive husband, and it seemed everyone but Lewis had known that already.

The only real clue so far was the mob connection. Richard Glead and his dodgy friends—Paulo Ram and Chaz Shaw. Shaw was small fry, but Ram was bad news. The gangland rumour forums Lewis haunted online regularly mentioned the work he did for the Fixer.

No one wanted to make themselves a problem to anyone who knew the Fixer, who was brought in to clean up crime scenes, get rid of bodies, and dispose of incriminating evidence. But how had a legitimate antiques dealer ended up in those circles? The simple answer was that he couldn't be legit.

He read back what he'd written earlier.

Harding rubbed at the crease between his eyes, then downed the last of his whisky. None of it made any sense. If Ricky had displeased the mob, it made no sense to kill him first. He knew how gangsters worked. Either they hurt the wife to intimidate the husband, or, if they had principles, they went straight to hurting the husband. They didn't kill the husband then the wife.

Unless.

Harding lifted his head and looked at the whiteboard
again, his eyes running over all the connections, following
the lines, how it all led back to Ricky Speen.

He stared at the last paragraph. The thing about writing was
that you put all the ingredients into a mental pot and let it stew,
and when you sat down to write, you hoped that all the thinking
and all the answers had happened while you weren't looking.

But sometimes they hadn't.

Something about the same—the real case—was off. Lewis
was sure Linda Glead had been murdered. Ninety-nine percent
sure. But the why was tripping him up.

A quiet woman living a quiet life, if you could even call it
that. Richard was a bad guy involved with even worse guys; his
murder was almost to be expected. If Linda had been killed
first, it would suggest that either someone was trying to frighten
Richard or else Linda was the brains of the outfit. If Linda had
been roughed up before she was killed, that might have suggested she wasn't directly involved but knew more than the
bad guys wanted her to, or perhaps didn't know enough. But to
kill her so quietly *after* killing the husband? Leaving virtually no
trace? That smacked of planning, of Linda being a target in her
own right, and Lewis couldn't make sense of that.

Unless.

Harding lifted his head and looked at the whiteboard
again, his eyes running over all the connections, following
the lines, how it all led back to Ricky Speen.
Ricky and Lindsey Speen.

26

Audrey

As Monday mornings went, Audrey reflected when she got home, she couldn't remember when she'd last had such a bad one.

She'd cleaned the Channings' four-storey town house in an efficient three hours, then told Mrs. Channing she'd have to miss her shift next week, at which point the day had gone rapidly downhill. Mrs. Channing had descended into something bordering on hysteria and gone into a ten-minute rant about what was she supposed to do with no cleaner for a fortnight, and didn't Audrey know that she was much too busy to find new staff just so her unreliable cleaner could have a fortnight in the Maldives.

Audrey had then explained, as patiently as her bubbling anger would allow, that she'd already arranged for a replacement cleaner in the form of a former agency colleague, and that she hadn't taken a holiday in over two years and wouldn't be going to the Maldives because she was a single woman paid minimum wage to clean other people's bathrooms. None of which had made any difference to Mrs. Channing's dudgeon.

She'd then had to go through the same rigmarole with three other clients when she rang to tell them she'd be taking time off. More than two years of near-perfect service and not one of them had cut her any slack or even wished her a nice holiday.

She was still hanging up her coat when someone pounded on the flat door. She looked through the peephole and saw Lewis standing outside.

"Hey," she said when she opened the door, suppressing the urge to shout at him for knocking so loudly. He looked sweaty.

"I've been calling you since the end of the street," he said, breathing heavily. "You walk fast!"

"Sorry, I didn't hear you." She stood aside to let him in. "Tea?"

"Coffee, please," he said. "Thanks."

He took his coat off and draped it over a kitchen chair. She resisted the urge to hang it up, and instead turned to fill the kettle, trying to swallow her foul mood.

He pulled out one of the stools and settled himself at the counter. She opened the cupboard and immediately remembered that she'd forgotten to get more ground coffee on her way home. She reached for the emergency jar.

"Instant okay?"

"Oh, uh. Yes, fine," he said, his tone suggesting it wasn't okay at all but he was being polite. She'd put money on Lewis being a coffee snob. Probably had an expensive machine with a tonne of settings at home.

"How did your admin go?" he asked.

Audrey sighed.

"Not great. I told four clients I was taking some holiday, and they all shouted at me. Every single one. And I've got to call the others this afternoon and go through it five more times."

"How many clients do you have?"

"Ten, including Celeste."

"Ten?! Bloody hell."

"How did it go with your boss? Did he agree to your sabbatical?"

Lewis ran a hand through his hair, the curls tumbling about.

"Yeah, it was fine. He rang me this morning and said"—he switched to a terrible Mockney accent—"'No worries, mate, take all the time you need, but you know you won't get paid, yeah?' and that was that."

It was fortunate that Lewis looked embarrassed, because at that moment, Audrey would have gladly slapped him.

"Oh," she said instead, through clenched teeth. "Well . . . good, I guess."

"Sorry yours is such a shitshow."

"Thanks. So, we're off to see Ram this afternoon?"

"That's right. I thought we could come up with some excuse to go in the pawnbrokers. Rather than be honest."

"Good idea." She breathed out. "Stay off their radar."

"Exactly." He sipped his coffee and frowned.

"Sorry," she said. "I meant to get some ground coffee on the way home but I forgot."

"Hmm? Oh, not the coffee. Although it is bad. It's just we don't even know the means yet, let alone the motive or opportunity. That's how she was killed," he added helpfully, "the means."

There was that urge to slap him again.

"I know what it is. Did you make notes the night you found Linda's body? Straight away, like you did before?"

"Of course."

"Can I see them?"

His cheeks turned pink.

"Erm, they're not exactly . . . I mean, they're a bit . . . what's the word? Business-like?"

Oh, *now* he was worried about how he sounded?

"I understand. Please, can I see them?"

He looked uncomfortable but swiped through some pages and turned the phone to face her.

Sitting on sofa, upright, head lolling to the right. Eyes open, bloodshot and glassy. Hair messy. Blue tinge to sides of nose and corners of mouth. Hands in lap, palms down, fingers curled. Knees together, tipping to the right, ankles twisted together. Body cool, not cold. Wearing white blouse (no marks), purple skirt with flowers on, black tights. No shoes (left in hall).

Sofa and chairs—black leather, very clean. One velvet cushion on chair.

Coffee table—mahogany, shiny. Half a glass of water on a silver coaster, china side plate with pink roses and white crumbs.

Handbag on floor next to sofa. Curtains drawn. Lamps on. No sign of robbery in living room. Very clean and tidy. NO COIN.

In spite of the matter-of-fact description, Audrey could see the picture clearly in her mind's eye. Linda, still wearing the clothes from the day she'd found Richard's body, finally come home from being questioned by the police to a place that was now safe for her. A glass of water and maybe a sandwich before bed, but still using a coaster because keeping everything nice was a habit.

"Are you all right?" asked Lewis nervously. "I said it was a bit . . ."

"Cold," she finished for him, and coughed to clear the lump in her throat. "Yes. But it's helpful."

Lewis took his phone back, looking ashamed.

"How so?"

"For figuring out how she died. I can see why the police think she took her own life."

"What do you mean?"

"Her husband's just been murdered. She found the body. She's taken in for questioning and spends the night at the police station, then they question her some more. She leaves the police station, goes to church, and then goes home. She doesn't shower or change her clothes, but decides to relax with a glass of water and a sandwich."

It took him a minute to get it.

"Shit," he said, when he did. "A light meal to get the digestive juices flowing, and a glass of water to swallow a load of pills. They're waiting for the pathologist to confirm an overdose."

"Why did you write 'no coin' at the end?"

"Did you notice the silver coin on the table at the scene of Richard's murder? I thought maybe it was some sort of calling card, or message."

"And?"

He shrugged.

"And nothing. It's a Manx Angel, 2017 issue. I did an internet search, and apart from some Cold War assassin back in the sixties, there isn't anyone on record using one as a calling card. If it's a message, it was personal to Richard."

They nursed their mugs in silence for a few minutes.

"What were your thoughts?" she asked eventually. "You must have had an idea, when you first saw her."

"Well, yes. The bloodshot eyes suggested asphyxiation but there were no signs of a struggle. No ligature marks on the neck, no defence wounds or damage to the face. She could have been poisoned. Some poisons can cause suffocation, or anaphylactic shock, but I sniffed the glass and it was just water. Hard to disguise poison in plain water."

Audrey put her hands to her throat, imagining she couldn't breathe, then let them fall to her lap. They landed palms down, the fingers curled inward.

"Asphyxiation seems most likely," said Audrey, picking up her tea in a bid to ease the tightness in her chest. "If it's not suicide,

I mean. The bloodshot eyes and the blue tinges . . . I'm sure I've seen that on *CSI*, and don't you dare pull that face at me."

"I wasn't!"

"I saw you. Anyway, it's either that or poison. Can you poison a sandwich?"

"Probably. God knows how though. I'll do some research later. It could be she just choked on the damn thing, although I'd expect there to have been more of a disturbance if she'd died accidentally. Thrashing about and so forth."

"Lovely."

"Sorry."

"I don't suppose you can suffocate yourself, can you?"

"Possibly," he said thoughtfully. "But how do you remove the evidence afterward?"

They considered this for a moment, then Audrey downed the rest of her tea. She'd had enough of imagining all the awful ways Linda could have died.

"Come on," she said, getting down off her stool. "Let's talk to the other residents, then we can go back to yours and you can show me your fancy coffee machine."

"How did you know I had a fancy coffee machine?" he asked, draining his own mug and grabbing his coat from the chair.

"Lucky guess."

"And we're not going to mine," he said, following her out to the hall.

"Why not?"

"It's not fit for company. Been a while since I did a big clean."

"Be honest." She pulled on her coat. "Have you ever done a big clean?"

"Erm . . ." He flushed again, and she smiled in anticipation. "No."

"Brilliant."

27

Lewis

Lewis couldn't remember the last time he'd walked through the square and seen it empty. When he left in the morning, there were other people leaving—the lady with the ash-blonde curls and young son, or Audrey's roommate with the impeccable suits and briefcase—and when he arrived home, there were other people getting home too, or else milling about, like the Captain or the gardener. At quarter to three on a Monday afternoon, it was eerily quiet, and as he stood with Audrey in the middle of the empty garden, he found himself seeing the place with new eyes.

"Where is everyone?" he asked. The wind rustled through the trees, scattering more leaves over the lawns.

"Must be at work, or out doing stuff," said Audrey. "Or inside. I'm not usually home until after four. Let's knock on doors."

"And say what?"

"I don't know. We'll wing it."

Unhappy with this approach but with no better ideas, Lewis followed Audrey as she began to work her way around his side of the square. First up, the woman in the fur hat from next door to him in Flat 6, who wasn't home. Then the guys in the flat above his, Joe and Emmanuel, who were home and very happy to talk to Audrey about the Gleads. Emmanuel, a tall man in his early thirties with light brown skin and a neat, close-shaved beard, stood in the doorway and told them both in no uncertain terms that he thought Linda had been murdered.

"Didn't I say?" he said, turning to his partner, Joe, who was shorter and stockier, with ruddy cheeks and slick-backed brown hair. "Not long after you got home, didn't I say I heard voices?" He turned back to Lewis. "Just after eleven. The police said it was most likely you, when you went up and found her."

Lewis shook his head.

"I didn't go up until midnight," he said. "That's when I heard something. Went out, found her front door slightly open. I called out but no one answered."

"You probably just got the time wrong," said Joe to Emmanuel. "And you didn't hear anyone on the stairs, so maybe you imagined the voices. Let's not turn this into something it isn't, Manny. It's tragic enough as it is."

"And *why* didn't I hear someone on the stairs, hmm?" asked Emmanuel, folding his arms. "Because if I heard Lewis talking, I'd have heard him walking. These damn stairs are so loud. But I was asleep at midnight, so I didn't hear him walking and I didn't hear him talking either." He looked round at them triumphantly. "They had her killed because she killed Richard!"

Joe sighed.

"You really need to lay off the True Crime channel."

"Did you hear anything the night Richard was shot?" asked Lewis, and saw Audrey turn her eyes skyward. He didn't see why. The police didn't have to take the scenic approach to questioning, so why should he?

"No, we were all across the square, watching the fireworks on Mei and Audrey's balcony," said Joe. "You were the only one at home, we could see your lights on."

"I forgot about Bonfire Night," he said sheepishly. "I went home, put my headphones on, and didn't hear a thing."

"That's one excuse," said Manny, pursing his lips.

"I wonder who Richard's friends were," said Audrey, apparently determined to take the long way round every question.

"Not a clue," said Joe, then sniffed the air. "Shit, my casserole." He disappeared back into the hall, and Emmanuel shook his head.

"Always with the casseroles," he sighed, then tilted his head, thinking. "One was called Paul, I think. I remember one terrible argument—one of the times I went round—something about Paul getting Richard into trouble, and how Linda thought they were watching her. Or she didn't like the way they were watching her. Whatever it was, Richard got very angry and Linda had a bandage on her wrist the next day." He sighed. "She should have shot him then."

Next, they called on the Hetheringtons. Only Philip was home, and in spite of his polite and cheery demeanour, and Audrey's chatty way of asking questions, insisted that they had seen and heard nothing, and he had no interest in speculating about Linda's sad demise.

"It's a terrible business," he said, hands folded in his lap as he sat in his wheelchair in the doorway. "Richard Glead got what was coming to him, I'm sure, and you could hardly blame Linda if she did it. But it would be best if the police are correct, don't you think? Better for Celeste and all of us here."

They couldn't argue with that.

"That was a total bust," said Lewis as they crossed the garden to Audrey's side of the square. "Who next?"

"Sarah Scott's away at the moment." Audrey glanced up at Flat 8. "They went up to Yorkshire last week, to see her parents, so at least we can rule her out. Flat three next?"

They walked down the path to the end of the row and the flat beneath Audrey's. The wind was cold, even in the relatively sheltered aspect of the square, and Lewis pulled his coat tightly around him as Audrey knocked on the door.

"Who's this again?" Lewis asked. He was pretty sure he'd be able to pick the rest of the residents out of a crowd, but he had a sudden feeling he might never actually have clapped eyes on the occupant of Flat 3.

"Victor," she replied, in the tone of one who couldn't believe she was being asked the question. "DeFlore."

They waited for someone to answer.

No one did.

"Not home," said Audrey. "Let's try the Captain next."

They walked back down the row and knocked on the door of number 4. Captain Gordon opened the door immediately, greeting them with enthusiasm and the scent of Old Spice.

"Hello, hello," he said. "Come to ask me about the Gleads, have you?"

"Uh . . ." began Lewis.

"Yes, actually," said Audrey. "How did you know?"

The Captain chuckled.

"Marchfield comms received," he said. "You think Mrs. Glead was murdered, eh?"

Lewis frowned, and Audrey tensed beside him. Someone had warned Captain Gordon they were coming.

As the Captain stood there, beaming, a noise behind made them both turn, just in time to see a man disappearing into the garden from the direction of Flat 3. Lewis looked at Audrey, who was staring after the figure with her mouth open.

"Victor's running away from us," she said in astonishment. "Why would he do that?"

Lewis was running before he'd thought about it, cutting across the lawn and through the shrubbery to head the guy off before he reached the front gate. The square wasn't large, and

Lewis was a good thirty years younger than the man in front of him. He overtook him easily, skidding to a halt in front of the iron railings and putting his arms out.

The man from Flat 3 pulled up short and stared at him. He was a broad and muscular man with close-cropped salt-and-pepper hair and wearing a black coat and faded brown brogues, and Lewis realised pretty quickly that if Victor DeFlore wanted to leave, he wouldn't be able to stop him.

Audrey appeared beside them, her cheeks flushed.

"Victor!" She sounded shocked. "Why are you running away?"

"I'm not running away," said Victor. "I'm running late." He was breathing heavily, looking from Lewis to Audrey and back again in the shiftiest way possible.

"But we knocked on your door and you didn't answer," said Lewis.

"Because I was running late." He gestured to Lewis, who was still barring the gate. "Now let me through."

Lewis reluctantly moved aside but Audrey took his place, standing in front of Victor.

"Don't be like that," she said, and now her voice was gentle. "We only wanted to—" But Victor cut her off.

"I know what you wanted," he snapped, his Jamaican accent becoming stronger with agitation. "To ask questions. Playing detectives."

Lewis flushed, and Audrey gave an embarrassed laugh.

"Well, yes. A little bit. Celeste asked us to see what we could find out." She shrugged. "You know how she is."

Victor looked at Lewis. "Who is this person?"

She pulled Lewis forward.

"This is Lewis McLennon from Flat Five. He and I met the other day, at the Glead place. We were having a quick catch-up about it all, and he mentioned he didn't know many people in

the square still, so I thought I'd take him round, introduce him."
She said it so easily that even with his angry expression, Victor
nodded, as though stopping by casually with no particular reason was a perfectly natural thing for Audrey to do. "Plus, like
you say, Celeste asked us to talk to everyone. See how they're
all doing. After all the trouble."

Victor looked Lewis up and down, and relaxed a little.

"I thought I didn't recognise you," he said, his tone soften-
ing. "How long ago did you move in?"

"Um . . . a while actually." Lewis floundered. "I'm not good
at . . ." Making friends? Meeting people?

"Making an effort," Audrey finished for him. Lewis glared at
her but then Victor let out a small laugh.

"I hear that, man," said Victor, holding out his hand. "I like
my privacy too. It's nice to meet you."

Lewis shook hands gratefully. He'd been starting to think he
was the only normal person in the square.

"Nice to meet you too."

"Women are always making friends, have you noticed?" said
Victor. "They collect them wherever they go. Men, we don't
need all that busyness."

"Exactly," said Lewis, nodding emphatically. "Exactly!"

"There's strength in numbers," said Audrey, smiling. "Everyone needs friends, even you two. Lucky I'm here, really."

Lewis was startled to hear himself described as Audrey's
friend, but Victor also smiled and the tension evaporated. Did
she know the effect she had on people, or was it accidental?

"But you're doing okay, Victor?" she said. "All this stuff with
Richard and Linda and the police?"

Victor's smile faded at once.

"Awful," he said, shaking his head. "Gordon told me you saw
Richard's body?"

"We both did," said Audrey. "And Lewis found Linda on Friday night."

Victor tutted gravely.

"Damn shame. Poor woman."

"Did you—" began Lewis, but Audrey trod heavily on his foot.

"Around midnight, wasn't it?" she said, looking at him.

"Erm, yes," he said, confused by the interruption to his flow. "I heard footsteps. I went out to check everything was okay, and Linda's door was open."

"Very suspicious," said Audrey. "You can see why Celeste thinks there's more to it."

"Suspicious?" Victor looked from one to the other. "Everyone is saying it was a suicide."

"Maybe, maybe not," she said. "The police will wait for the postmortem results to start questioning people again."

"More questioning?" Victor frowned. "But what else can I tell them? I barely knew the Gleads, and I already told them I saw and heard nothing."

"You were home Friday night then?" Lewis asked, excited to get to the nitty-gritty. "There was nothing unusual? No one you didn't know?"

"No one. I think I noticed the light on in Flat Ten, but that was all."

"Did you go out?" Audrey asked.

"Out? No. Why would I go out?"

"The light . . ."

"We're just trying to get an idea of where everyone was," said Lewis, but he must have said the wrong thing, because Victor's face froze again.

"It's none of your business," he said. "You leave that to the police."

Lewis opened his mouth, but Audrey grabbed his wrist.

"Yes," she said, her voice soft and sympathetic. "We should, but you know what Celeste's like. She wanted to know what to expect, but we'll wait and see what the police say. Sorry to have kept you, Victor. Where are you off to?"

Victor looked bemused by the change in direction.

"Oh. Um. The shops. Yes, I need to get to the butcher." He looked from one to the other. "I hope you're wrong, the pair of you. And Celeste too. We don't need that kind of thing in the square." He wagged his finger at them. "We don't need that at all."

"That was suspicious," said Lewis as they ducked under the trees to cross the lawn back to Audrey's block. "No one needs to urgently go to the butcher's. He was trying to avoid us."

"And the rest."

"What do you mean?"

She drew to a halt in front of Victor's flat.

"Didn't you notice? He said he saw a light on in Flat Ten on Friday night. You can't see Flat Ten from here; it's blocked by the shrubbery. But when I asked if he'd gone out, he said no."

Lewis looked back at Victor's flat, then across to the gardens, behind which stood his own block. She was right. He could see the corner of his flat, and the one above, but Flats 6 and 10 were entirely obscured by the tall bushes. He pulled out his phone.

"That's very good." He made a note. "Well caught."

"It might not mean anything. Maybe he got confused or misremembered. He barely knew the Gleads, I'm sure. It makes no sense for him to kill either of them."

"Even so."

They strolled back down the path to where a delighted-looking Captain Gordon still waited on his doorstep.

"Ran the blighter down, did you?" he said, hands in the pockets of his blazer. "Good show!"

"Sorry about that, Captain," said Audrey. "We just wanted to catch Victor before he left, that's all."

The Captain guffawed, and Lewis couldn't help but smile.

"You did that, all right." He grinned at them both, the oiled bristles of his silver moustache sparkling in the winter sunlight. "I'll enjoy bringing that up at our next film night. So. If I know Celeste van Duren, and I think I do, it's her that's put you up to this. Why don't you come on in and tell me what've you found out, eh?"

28

Audrey

By the time they left the Captain's flat, Audrey felt as if he'd got more information from them than they had from him. Beyond seeing Linda get home on Friday night, the Captain hadn't seen or heard much, just the light in Linda's window and a couple of beeps from the side gate, which wasn't far from his bedroom window. He hadn't noticed the times, but was sure he'd gone to bed at half ten and read for a while before dropping off.

Audrey, meanwhile, had found herself filling in little details for him as he recounted the timeline as he knew it, and Lewis's glare had gradually turned into huffs and then into little growls of frustration as the conversation had continued.

Eventually, he'd hustled her out of there, tea unfinished, and as Captain Gordon shut the door behind them, he rounded on her.

"You're supposed to collect information, not hand it out in spades!"

"I know!" she snapped, angry with herself. "He kept saying slightly the wrong thing and leaving gaps, and it just felt so rude not to fill it in. I don't know how he managed it."

"Next time, leave the talking to me."

"Fat chance," she muttered.

As they walked away, they heard the faint beep of the side gate as someone entered the square.

"Hey," said Audrey, "that's a point. The gates log who goes in and out, right? Do you think Celeste might have a record?"

"It's possible," said Lewis, still sounding annoyed. "But they might just be generic fobs, and not unique to the holder. Dixon didn't mention them, and you'd think he would have if they'd be helpful."

"Worth asking though."

He nodded. "Worth asking."

"Audrey, darling!"

They reached the courtyard at the same time as Mrs. Hildebrandt, who had just entered the square with her boyfriend, Fraser. She was wearing her fur hat again, and the scent of Chanel No. 5 enveloped Audrey as she neared.

"Hi, Mrs. H," said Audrey, trying not to sneeze as the perfume tickled her nose. Lewis stood beside her silently, as if he hadn't lived next door to the woman for five years.

Mrs. Hildebrandt was hanging on to Fraser's arm, as if reluctant to let him go. Audrey could see why. She'd only ever seen Fraser from a distance before, escorting Mrs. Hildebrandt through the courtyard, but he was a tall, silver-haired gentleman who looked to be in his late sixties, with a fading natural tan and a close-shaved silver beard. He wore a black shirt and a tan suede jacket that accentuated an athletic build, and when he smiled, it was the smile of a movie star.

"Lovely to see you, darling," said Mrs. Hildebrandt, kissing her on both cheeks. "Fraser, this is Audrey. She lives in number seven. Audrey, this is Fraser Townsend."

"Nice to meet you," said Audrey, returning his smile. "This is Lewis. He lives in Flat Five."

Lewis held up a hand in greeting.

"Hi."

"What's going on here?" asked Mrs. Hildebrandt. She looked from Audrey to Lewis, one perfect auburn eyebrow raised. "I didn't know you two knew each other." Then she pursed her lips. "I didn't know you knew anyone."

Audrey laughed when she saw Lewis's face.

"You're not wrong, Mrs. H," she said. "We met the other day. We've been hanging out a bit since then."

"Ah," said Fraser, dreamy blue eyes twinkling. "Eyes across a crowded room, was it?"

"Eyes across a dead body, actually," said Audrey, and this time it was Lewis who laughed, a sound she hadn't heard until then.

Fraser's smile fell.

"Sorry, that was in poor taste," she said hurriedly. "We met the day Richard Glead was killed. Well, the day his body was found. And Lewis found Linda too."

Mrs. Hildebrandt's hand fluttered to her throat. Fraser's arm immediately went around her.

"That poor dear girl," she said, eyes filling with tears. "After everything she went through with that awful man. Although I shouldn't speak ill of the dead. If it hadn't been for him, we'd never have met." Fraser frowned at this.

"Really?" said Lewis. "How so?"

"Oh, it's *such* a boring story, I'm sure you'll think it quite soppy," said Mrs. Hildebrandt, in the tone of one who very much hoped to be cajoled into telling it.

"Okay," said Lewis, and Audrey sighed inwardly and tried not to think about kicking him.

"Do tell," she said, smiling. She'd played this game many times with Mrs. Hildebrandt. "I'm sure it's not soppy."

"Well, if you're pressing me," began Mrs. Hildebrandt, with a flitting up-and-under look at Fraser. "I was out one day, doing a little shopping, and I happened to walk past Glead Antiques and saw him inside, sitting at his desk. Suddenly, I felt an urge—positively compelled—to go in and tell him what I thought of him. It was back in September, after he hurt her arm?"

Audrey grimaced. "I remember."

"He seemed surprised to see me but tried to turn on the charm, no doubt thinking I'd come to buy one of his dreadful reproductions. But I told him, in no uncertain terms, that if he didn't stop abusing his wife, then I'd stand outside the shop every day and tell all his customers he was a wife-beater.

"As you can imagine, he didn't like that, not one bit. Got very nasty. Grabbed me by the arm and practically threw me out onto the street, right into the arms of a passing angel." She put a hand on Fraser's chest. "You went inside and gave him a piece of your mind, didn't you?"

"I certainly did," said Fraser, although he seemed a bit uncomfortable about it. "That's no way to treat a lady, I said. I could tell at once you were a woman of class."

Mrs. Hildebrandt simpered and fluffed her hair. Audrey forced a smile, wondering whether a woman who wasn't wearing a fur hat and designer shoes—scuffed and worn though they may be—would have been similarly rescued.

"I insisted on taking him to lunch to say thank you, and it turns out, he remembered my films. We couldn't stop talking and we've been inseparable ever since, haven't we, darling?"

"A lucky day for both of us," said Fraser, gazing down into her adoring brown eyes. Audrey suddenly felt nauseous.

"Did either of you hear anything the night Richard Glead was murdered?" asked Lewis abruptly. "Or the night Linda died?"

The couple exchanged glances.

"Why do you ask?" said Mrs. Hildebrandt after a beat.

"No reason," said Lewis at once. "Just curious."

"The police have been asking everyone," said Audrey, trying to lighten the tone. "But none of us seem to have been much help."

"The police intimated that Richard was killed the night of the fireworks," said Mrs. Hildebrandt. "And of course, we were all out watching them together, weren't we?" She narrowed her eyes. "All except Lewis."

"What about the night Linda died?" pressed Lewis, ignoring, or possibly oblivious to, Audrey's glare. "I thought I heard someone on the steps, but when I looked out, there was no one there."

"I'm a very sound sleeper," said Mrs. Hildebrandt, turning to Fraser. "Did you hear anything, darling?"

"Out like a light that night, I'm afraid," said Fraser, shaking his head. "The police think it was suicide, don't they?"

"Of course it was," said Mrs. Hildebrandt. "No one could blame her. When it came to the crunch, she took the easy way out. Poor lamb."

"I'd hardly say it was easy, Brigitte," Fraser chastised her gently. "But yes, that makes the most sense."

"Did you know the Gleads?" asked Audrey. She thought she'd made the question sound casual, but something in the way Fraser's eyes fixed on her made her think she'd given herself away.

"I may have bought a few pieces from him in the past." He shrugged. "I don't really remember. And I'd seen them both around the square, when visiting Brigitte, of course."

"Fraser has a town house in Mayfair," said Mrs. Hildebrandt. "It simply eats furniture, it's so big. And a place in the country, where he keeps his car collection."

"We should be going, darling," said Fraser, looking embarrassed. "We're at the theatre this evening, remember?"

"Yes, of course. Nice to catch up, Audrey. And, Lewis, I hope we'll see you around the square more, now you're socialising."

Lewis glowered, but Mrs. Hildebrandt flapped her hand at them and walked off, gripping Fraser's arm, her heels clicking on the flagstones.

"What a ghastly woman," said Lewis, glaring after her.

"She's not that bad, really," said Audrey. "She acts the diva but she's fragile, not to mention flat broke. She wears the same Chanel pumps every day but they're almost as old as me. She has some great stories from her acting days, and she makes the best chocolate cake you'll ever eat in your life. Her last boy-friend turned out to be a bit of a scoundrel, but Fraser seems like a catch, don't you think?"

Lewis turned to look at Audrey, eyebrows raised.

"Anyway, I'm glad we ran into her," she went on, "because now we can tick her off the list. Is that everyone?"

"I think so. No one was very helpful, were they?"

"No, not really." She suppressed a yawn. "We'll figure it out though. I'll head home now, and text Dixon about the gate logs. Meet you back here in the morning."

Later, as Audrey lay stretched out on the sofa in front of the television, waiting for Dixon to reply to her message, she began to type some notes into her phone, the way Lewis had. A Tom Hanks film played in the background but her attention was on her phone, hoping that some detail she hadn't considered would jump out of her memory and unlock the mystery.

10 Marchfield Square

Richard Glead—White shirt, large bloodstain spreading from the middle. Jeans. Brown belt. Hair messed up at the back. Eyes open. Mouth twisted. Hands on the floor beside him.

>   Kitchen—Light on. Blind partly down. Looked and
> smelled clean. No blood spatter on floor. No footprints or
> other marks.
>   Kitchen table—Side plate with crumbs. 3–4 beer
> bottles. Splashes of beer. Money.

Money. Except it wasn't really money, it was a single silver coin. She edited her note.

> Silver coin.

What had Lewis said it was? A Manx Angel? Richard Glead was an antiques dealer, but the coin wasn't an antique. Why was it on his kitchen table?

Her phone vibrated with a message.

> DIXON: Yes, we have gate logs. I'll have them
> ready for you tomorrow.

Audrey frowned. She'd expected the response to be in the negative. Had Dixon forgotten about them? Or had it been a test? So that Celeste knew if they were on the ball or not?

Mei walked in, wearing her pyjamas.

"What are you not watching?" she asked, settling herself into her armchair.

"Uhhh . . . *The Money Pit*, I think. Their house is falling down."

Mei reached across to grab the remote from the arm of the sofa.

"How's the case going?"

"Not bad. No one in the square saw or heard much, but we've got some leads to follow up."

Mei began to flip through the TV guide.

"What's the plan for tomorrow?"

"Meeting Lewis in the morning. Cleaning in the afternoon."

"Interviewing more witnesses?"

"Yes." Audrey wasn't about to tell Mei that she planned to break her promise and visit Paulo Ram's pawnshop. "Any news on the postmortem?"

Mei sighed. "No. I put some pressure on the coroner's office today, so I'm hoping it'll be tomorrow. And . . . I've been talking to Sofia, too, keeping up on the case, that sort of thing."

Audrey looked over at her friend, whose cheeks had gone just a tiny bit pink.

"Detective Larssen?" she said. "Good idea. Not too awkward, I hope?"

"What? Oh, no. Not at all, actually. I hope you don't mind, but I told her about Richard and Paulo Ram. She thought that was a solid lead. She thought it odd Linda didn't mention it."

"Uh, no, I don't mind," Audrey said, although to her surprise found she did a bit.

As Mei gave up searching through the listings and returned to watching Tom Hanks and Shelley Long, Audrey texted Lewis.

> AUDREY BROOKS: Dixon has the logs. We can collect them when we get back from seeing Ram. He's on the police's list now too.

He replied at once.

> FLAT 5 GUY: Shit, really? Wonder how they found out. Good thing we're going tomorrow.

She put her phone away, feeling guilty on two counts. She hated keeping things from Mei, but felt she owed it to Linda to do everything she could. Plus, she didn't trust Lewis and that mouth of his not to get himself in trouble on his own. The last thing they needed was criminals returning to the square.

"You okay?" asked Mei, looking over at her. "You look a bit pale."

"Yes, fine. Just tired. Early night tonight, I think."

"Good idea," said Mei, turning back to the television. "Everything's better after a good night's sleep."

If only.

2929

Lewis

At ten o'clock on Tuesday morning, Lewis and Audrey walked along the wind tunnel that was Oakley Street, an expensive residential area heading north away from the river. Audrey was bundled up in a green woollen coat, a grey scarf tucked around her neck. She had shadows under her eyes, and he wondered if she'd slept badly or if she'd simply stayed up late, like he had, analysing the case.

"I was thinking about the coin last night," she said. "It was definitely recent?"

"Yes." He pulled out his phone and read aloud. "A 2017 Manx Angel. Would be worth a lot if it was gold, but silver . . . about fifty quid."

"So not an antique, and not worth much, either. It must mean something though."

"Possibly. A lucky charm, maybe? Or something he'd won in a poker game?"

A gust of wind barreled up behind them, pushing against their backs. Audrey shivered and tried to sweep her hair from her face.

"Mei hopes the postmortem will be today," she said. "She put some pressure on them yesterday."

"That's good," he said, nodding, partially to reassure himself.

"If it does turn out to be an overdose though, we'll have been wasting our time," she said. "Upsetting people, and turning down work for no reason."

He glanced at her, taking in the downturned mouth and the sad eyes.

"You're forgetting that someone killed Richard Glead too," he said. "If Linda did kill herself, then the police won't be looking too hard for a third person. Celeste didn't just want Linda's killer found, she wanted Linda's name cleared. Maybe we can still give her that. Did you see the news this morning? About the party over in Acton? Three stabbings, one shooting, and four drug arrests. Police've got their hands full."

She looked at him, her gaze serious, but something sparked in her eyes.

"I promised Mei I wouldn't talk to Ram or the other one," she said. "She said it wasn't safe. And after what Manny said about Richard's friends watching Linda . . ."

So that was it. She was frightened.

"You can stay behind, if you like," he offered. "Or I can do the talking? Then you won't technically have broken your promise."

She nodded but didn't speak, and when he looked at her, she was still pale.

They turned onto the King's Road and walked in silence for a while, Lewis enjoying the quiet of the streets. The office and retail workers were all inside, while the tourists hadn't strayed this far. With the pavements empty and the traffic at a low ebb, he found himself appreciating the area in a way he hadn't in years.

"It's just off the King's Road," he told her. "Down a side street." He'd tracked down Ram's shop ages ago, after first reading about it in one of his online groups. He'd hoped that seeing a real-life criminal operation would inspire some clever plot or dynamic character that would break through his block, but the shop had been so inconspicuous and blandly professional-looking that it had inspired nothing at all. As it was no doubt designed to.

"The rents can't be cheap round here," she said. "Richard Glead must have been doing well."

"I doubt it was antiques paying his bills. More likely cleaning cash for Ram and his friends."

As they walked, they discussed the best plan of action, and by the time they reached the turning for Medlar Walk, Lewis was out of breath. He thought he kept himself in reasonable shape, but Audrey walked fast.

"Okay, so we know what we're doing, yeah?"

"Yep," said Audrey. "You'd best put your watch in your pocket. It'll look strange if you take it off your wrist."

Lewis unfastened his watch, and was engulfed by a wave of anxiety. The watch had belonged to his grandfather—a long-service award given to him in 1955—and was one of the few items of value he'd had to pass on to his family. He'd left it to his son, Lewis's father, and before he died, he'd given it to Lewis. He'd been so terrified of losing it, he'd hardly ever worn it, saving it for special occasions.

Of which he had none.

He rubbed his wrist and put the watch into his pocket. They walked down the narrow side street toward Medlar Antiques & Brokers. The shop's small window displayed a ramshackle collection of watches, none of which looked particularly valuable, and some tarnished jewelry, while a couple of joyless, earth-toned portraits hung behind them as a backdrop. A sign on the door read: "Discreet brokerage for watches, jewelry, antiques and precious metals. Ask inside."

Lewis flashed Audrey what he hoped was a reassuring smile, then pushed open the door. A bell jingled quietly, somewhere in the back.

It was dark inside, and small; an oppressive, cluttered cubby of a shop, two walls lined with poorly lit, waist-high cabinets full of jewelry and watches. The space above was hung with musical instruments, gloomy paintings, and old-fashioned clocks, and the whole place smelled of pipe smoke.

Against one wall was a glass display cabinet that acted as the shop counter, topped with a heavy Perspex screen. Bulletproof, no doubt, with a metal grill fixed into the middle for sound, and a drawer at the bottom, for passing things through. There was no one behind the counter, but an internal door stood open at one end, and there were voices beyond. Lewis held his breath, straining to hear, but then a rat-faced man with a scrawny beard and a pipe in his mouth stuck his head through.

"Be with you in a minute," he said, teeth clacking on the pipe, before disappearing again. He was not Paulo Ram.

Lewis's heart sank and he glanced at Audrey, who bit her lip. She looked as anxious as he felt.

Please don't let this be for nothing.

They positioned themselves in front of the counter, glancing down at a motley selection of antique pistols and airguns. A gap in the middle of the display suggested one had been recently sold.

"I don't care what you think!" One of the voices beyond the door got louder. "You owe me and now I need—"

The rat-faced man reappeared, shutting the internal door behind him and blocking off the conversation. He looked them up and down.

"How can I help?"

"Um, right, yes. I was wondering if you could give me a price for this." Lewis reached into his pocket and brought out his watch. He held it up in front of the screen but Rat-Face tapped the drawer in front of him. Lewis placed the watch inside and felt sick as it was pulled through to the other side.

"It's a Patek Philippe Calatrava," he said, watching as Rat-Face turned it over with long, nicotine-stained fingers.

"Got any documentation?" asked the man, screwing in an appraiser's eyeglass.

"At home, yes," said Lewis.

The man gave the watch a brief but thorough examination.

"Five grand," he said. Lewis felt his mouth drop open.

"But it's worth three times that!" This was a line he'd been planning to say no matter what offer was made, but he hadn't been expecting to mean it.

Rat-Face shrugged.

"Then take it to Hatton Garden along with your documentation," he said. "You want cash same day, no documents? It's five grand."

"But . . ."

"It's not worth it," said Audrey, pulling at his arm. "It's your grandfather's watch. I don't need an expensive ring."

"But I want you to have the best," he said, looking from her to Rat-Face with what he hoped was an appropriate amount of dismay. Acting had never been his strong suit.

Rat-Face looked them up and down.

"Engagement, is it?"

"Yes," said Audrey, snuggling into Lewis's side in a way that wasn't entirely unpleasant. "He's a traditionalist. Wants it to be three months' salary."

He put his arm around her.

"I just want your dad to think I'm good enough," he said, which was a line Audrey had fed him but which he thought was overdoing it. He looked at Rat-Face and lowered his voice. "He's not my biggest fan."

"Let me get the boss," said Rat-Face. "Wait there."

They waited, arms awkwardly around each other, as Rat-Face opened the internal door again.

"—know where it fucking came from!" bellowed a voice from the back room, followed by an almighty crash. "But I am not going down for—WHAT NOW?"

They strained to listen, able to just make out Rat-Face speaking quietly but urgently to whoever was shouting. The shouter huffed and swore, then there was the sound of someone standing up.

Rat-Face reappeared at the door, followed by what appeared to be a human potato in a white wig—Paulo Ram. He was average height and muscular beneath a layer of fat, with an undisguisable beer belly sticking out proud from his shirt. The internet said Ram was in his fifties, but the white hair and puffy, weather-beaten skin made him appear older.

"You the young lovers?" he asked, smiling lewdly at Audrey in a way that made Lewis tighten his grip on her. It hadn't occurred to him until just this minute that if Audrey had seen Ram passing through the square on his way to the Gleads', then Ram might have seen her too. If he recognised her, though, he didn't react. "Nice watch you've got there."

"It was my grandfather's," said Lewis, gulping.

Ram picked it up and examined it the way Rat-Face had, holding it close to his dimpled nose.

"You're not wrong that it's worth a bit, but that's with proof of ownership. Tell you what," he said, and his voice was kindly but his eyes were shark-like. "I can offer you six and a half, here and now, or ten if you come back with documentation."

Lewis looked down at Audrey, who shook her head.

"You can't sell it," she said pleadingly, her eyes big and round. "Not for me."

Lewis looked up just in time to see Ram and Rat-Face smirk at each other.

"I'll bring it back," he said firmly. "With documentation."

"You really have it?" said Ram, unable to hide his astonishment. "Then why are you here?"

"Time," said Lewis promptly. "I'm going to Dubai next week, for work. I'll be away for a while and . . ."

"You want to get a ring on it before you leave, eh?" finished Ram.

"Um. Something like that. I was talking to a guy named Glead up on the Pimlico Road, but when I went back, the shop was shut. It's not opened since and I'm running out of time."

The smile dropped from Ram's face at once, his eyes darting through the open internal door and back again.

"The proprietor met with an accident, sorry to say. The shop won't be opening again."

"Oh, I didn't realise." Lewis widened his eyes and tried to sound shocked. "Shit. Poor guy. He seemed nice. Friend of yours?"

"I knew him," said Ram, suddenly guarded. "Good guy. Very sad."

"Pity about the shop." Lewis swallowed, and tried to sound casual. "His wife won't keep it going then?"

Ram narrowed his eyes.

"What do you know about his wife?"

"Oh, he said something about his missus." Lewis shrugged. "I thought maybe it was a family business."

Ram and Rat-Face exchanged glances.

"No. It's not. Why are you so interested?"

"I'm not. Just seems a shame, that's all. I'm into coins actually. Been looking for a Manx Angel for my collection." He looked around the shop. "Don't suppose you've got any?"

Ram shook his head.

"I wish. Scarce, they are."

"Don't I know it. Anyway, thanks for your help. I'll drop by in a few days with the watch and the documents."

"All right then," said Ram, fishing around under the till for a card and putting it in the metal drawer with Lewis's watch. "Give us a call when you find it, and we'll make sure we've got enough cash on the premises."

"Thanks," said Lewis, trying not to snatch the watch back. "Thanks very much."

He ushered Audrey out of the shop, and as he turned to pull the door shut behind him, he saw that Ram and Rat-Face were standing side by side, watching them go.

30

Audrey

"Phew," said Audrey, letting out a long puff of air as they walked away from the pawnshop. "Well done. You handled that very well."

Lewis fastened the watch back onto his wrist, looking relieved to do so.

"Thanks," he said. "Your goo-goo eyes were disturbingly convincing."

She grinned. They turned back onto the King's Road and a rush of cold air hit them as a van sped past. The sky was clouding over but Audrey found the chill cleansing.

"Good idea to ask about the coin," she said. "He didn't react, did he?"

"No. But there was a gun missing from his sales cabinet. Maybe he hired someone, although he'd be a fool to give them a gun from his own shop."

"Do you think that's who he was talking to in the back room?" she asked, putting her hands in her pockets. "The killer? His eyes looked toward the door when you mentioned Richard's name."

"Maybe. Whoever it was, Ram needed a favour from them. One that would stop him going to prison. Shall we grab a coffee? Then I can write everything down before I forget."

"Okay," said Audrey. "But you're buying."

They found a narrow little artisan coffee shop, squeezed between a nail bar and a shop that sold designer wallpaper, and she sat nursing a cup of tasteless English Breakfast tea while Lewis made notes on his phone and took obnoxiously appreciative sips of what he described as "true Italian espresso."

Then, satisfied they'd recorded all the details of their encounter with Paulo Ram, they walked the rest of the way back along the Embankment, where the trees were belatedly shedding their autumn leaves and their feet crunched as they walked along the river, the road thrumming with traffic beside them.

"Why did you ask if Linda was taking over the antiques shop?" she asked.

"Because I had another thought last night," Lewis began, kicking his feet through a small pile of leaves as they passed beneath one of the plane trees. "What if Linda was involved? If her brother-in-law knew who Richard's friends were, it stands to reason Linda did too, and she lied to the police. Killing her only makes sense if she was either running things, or else knew too much to remain alive. And the fact she was killed *after* Richard— so quietly and with no trace—suggests it was planned."

"Which in turns means she had to matter to them," Audrey finished for him. She thought about that. On the one hand, it knocked the whole idea that Linda wasn't worth killing on the head, which she liked. Make Linda a criminal mastermind and suddenly she became important. But on the other hand, she found herself unable to reconcile that with the woman she felt she was starting to know. "But Ram said she wasn't involved."

"He was cagey though, wasn't he? And he said she wasn't involved in the shop but if they had a sideline working for gangsters . . . There's a logic to it, don't you think?"

"Ye-e-es, but I'm not sure it fits. If she'd been the brains of a criminal outfit, would she have stuck with Richard for so long? Perhaps she lied to protect herself. Scared they'd come after her if she incriminated them."

"Or maybe she wanted to blackmail them? Not the ring-leader but not entirely innocent either."

Audrey snorted.

"You really think, after five years trapped in the marriage from hell, she suddenly turned around and decided to blackmail the mob? That doesn't fit either."

"Well, what's your idea then?" he huffed. "I don't hear you coming up with anything."

"I'm not supposed to come up with anything," she said. "We follow where the evidence leads, not the other way around."

He laughed.

"Did you get that from *CSI*?"

She glared at him.

"I've got as much investigative experience as you," she countered. "So you can stop being so patronising."

"But I've researched police procedure," he said. "We have to take the evidence, build a theory around it, then see if it fits."

"What evidence? And I'm telling you, it doesn't fit. She had a glimpse of freedom. Why would she compromise that?"

"For the money!" He spoke as if she were slow. "To set herself up for her fresh start."

"I'm not an idiot," said Audrey tightly, trying not to let her rage get the better of her. "I understand what you're saying, I just don't agree."

"Why don't you agree? It's logical."

"It's only logical if you'd never met Linda," she snapped. "Or ever noticed a damn thing about her. She was free. She was going to pack her bags and leave, that's what she said. Once her escape route was open, she wouldn't do anything to jeopardise that. And certainly not for something so stupid as money."

"You cannot possibly know that!" he half shouted. "You barely knew her either."

"I know more than you think."

Her hostility was so great that even Lewis seemed to sense it was better to keep his mouth shut, and they didn't speak again until they were back at the square, where they said a terse goodbye and parted company.

Audrey had an early lunch before heading back out to clean the newly renovated but perpetually empty house of a Russian businessman in Belgravia. Of all the properties she cleaned, that was the only one that unnerved her, and today, particularly so. The man was a collector and each room was tastefully decorated in white, presumably to better display the art and antiques he never saw. There was something eerie about the pristine white surfaces that had never known anything beyond the touch of her duster and the curtains that had only ever been moved by her vacuum cleaner.

As she wiped imaginary dust from the cases of the antique clocks she wound every week, she wondered what would happen if one day she didn't. Did the smart doorbell alert someone in another country that she'd come to clean? Or did someone come and check her work after she'd gone? She had no reason to think she was being surveilled, but the apparent pointlessness of the task always made her long to do something contrary, just to see if anyone would notice.

But she was thorough, because Audrey was always thorough, so she started at the top, in the master suite, carrying the vacuum cleaner and her cleaning bag up the stairs and then down again, working floor by floor until she reached the wine cellar in the basement. Then she put the vacuum away, set the alarm, and left again, glad to get out of the modern mausoleum and give the next layer of dust time to descend.

As she walked down the front steps, the sensation of the house watching her prickled the back of her neck, and she hurried away, keen to escape the mantle of paranoia she'd draped around herself.

By the time she got home, she found that all she wanted was a shower and an evening on the sofa, so she went upstairs to let the hot water wash the creepy feeling away.

She was just hanging up her damp towel when she heard Mei get home, closing the front door behind her with uncharacteristic carefulness.

"Hiya," called Audrey, coming down the stairs to greet her. "You're home early. How was your day?"

Mei looked tired, her usually lively face grey and drawn.

"Not great," she said, dumping her briefcase on the floor and rubbing the crease between her eyes. "Pathologist's report came back."

Mei's expression told her everything she needed to know, but Audrey held her breath anyway.

"Death by asphyxiation," said Mei. "You were right. Linda was murdered. And now the police know it too."

31

Lewis

Harding stared down at the body of Lindsey Speen, cold and lifeless on the metal slab of the mortuary drawer. Once Ricky's mob connections had been identified, his boss had immediately become obsessed with the who, but Harding felt sure it was the why that was the key to unlocking the case.

Ricky could have been a warning, a message sent to Lindsey. A message she'd ignored and it had got her killed. Who had she been working with, and, more importantly, who had she pissed off enough that there were now two cold lockers labeled "SPEEN" in the morgue?

The more Lewis wrote, the more convinced he'd become that Linda had been involved in something. Perhaps she and Richard were ripping off Paulo and Chaz. Or perhaps she was working with them against Richard. Neither murder had the appearance of a crime of passion, which left only business. Had Linda's murder been a cleanup operation?

Audrey's observation about Linda's final meal had bothered him. Their whole case hinged on the idea that Linda hadn't taken her own life, and therefore, logically, had to have been murdered, but the only indicators for this theory were footsteps no one else had heard, an open front door, and Muffin the stupid dog. Audrey's insistence that Linda wouldn't have phoned her boss to talk about adopting the dog and then sit down to swallow a load of pills was, annoyingly, the only evidence they had regarding Linda's state of mind that night, and unlike Audrey, Lewis simply didn't believe that the prospect of adopting some scruffy mutt was enough to keep a depressed woman from overdosing.

His phone flashed silently, and he reached for it. His heart sped up when he saw it was a text from Audrey. He hoped she wasn't going to start in on the disagreement they'd had earlier. He'd thought about it all afternoon and was still at a loss as to why she'd reacted so weirdly to his theory. He knew he could be clumsy sometimes—he wished he could draft and redraft the spoken word like he could his writing—but he didn't think he'd said anything that wrong.

> THE CLEANER: Postmortem done. Tox panel
> clear. Death by asphyxiation. It's now a double
> murder investigation.

Lewis pushed himself away from the computer and rotated his chair, phone in hand. The room had darkened around him while he'd been writing, and now he stared at the opposite wall through the gloom, considering the implications.

For starters, it meant Celeste had been right, and that he and Audrey hadn't been wasting their time. It also suggested that Linda hadn't killed her husband, although the jury was still out on that one. Linda's murder might have been revenge for Richard's death, assuming anyone liked him enough to avenge him, of course.

Now there was an idea.

> LEWIS MCLENNON: Another possibility:
> Richard had a bit on the side. Linda killed
> Richard, then the girlfriend killed Linda
> in revenge.

He waited, hoping this theory was less offensive than his last.

> THE CLEANER: Possible. If true, then the girlfriend could have killed Richard AND Linda. Or someone else killed Richard and the girlfriend killed Linda out of misplaced revenge.

> LEWIS MCLENNON: What if Linda had a boyfriend? One who killed Ricky because Linda asked him to? Or off his own bat because he thought he was saving her? Then he tells Linda and she rejects him.

> THE CLEANER: Richard, not Ricky. I can't see Linda being the type to cheat, but even if she was, you'd think he'd wait longer than 48 hours to confess.

> LEWIS MCLENNON: People are emotional. It makes them stupid.

He turned back to his computer and read what he'd just written. His plot was too simple, he realised now. He didn't have enough investigative avenues. He needed to list the possible killers for the deaths of Richard and Linda, and see what the motives were.

He pulled up his notes app.

1. Linda killed Richard, Richard's girlfriend (?) killed Linda
2. Linda killed Richard, Paulo/Chaz killed Linda
3. Linda's boyfriend (?) killed Richard, then killed Linda

4. Richard's girlfriend (?) killed Richard, then killed Linda
5. Paulo/Chaz killed Richard, then killed Linda
6. Unknown person killed Richard, then killed Linda
7. Unknown person killed Richard, second unknown person killed Linda

Looking at the list, it was clear the most likely option was still that Linda had killed her husband. Options 6 and 7, meanwhile, he didn't like at all, given the smallness of Linda's life in particular. Someone had to know her to want to kill her, especially once her husband was gone.

No, he decided, deleting the last two from the list. Let the police investigate those avenues and good luck to them. He and Audrey would stick with the people they knew about. For now, at least.

Which left the poker friends as the answer, to either one or both deaths. He reached for his phone again, noticing she hadn't replied.

> LEWIS MCLENNON: I agree that seems the least likely option, but it depends on the motive for the first murder. If Linda was in on Richard's business, then it's probably Paulo or Chaz. If not, then must be a personal reason. We need to find out more about the Gleads.

He returned to his writing, but this time, he went backward, looking for places he could insert extra characters and clues. He moved things around, checking his work over and over, until at one point he had to turn away and close his aching eyes against the glare of the screen.

He checked the time.

Half past seven.

A clang outside made him jump, and he went into the kitchen to look out the window, rubbing his eyes as he went. He had to blink a few times, sleep blurring his vision, but eventually his brain caught up and he registered what he was seeing.

The police had returned to the square.

32

Audrey

Audrey and Mei watched from Mei's bedroom window, the full November moon casting a silvery-grey light across the square and glinting off the windows. A uniformed officer stood near the side gate, the stance suggesting sentry duty. Another stood beside a bench in the courtyard that was loaded up with boxes, while a plainclothes officer with a clipboard appeared to be giving instructions. A couple of people were climbing into paper suits, and Audrey and Mei watched as they took paper overshoes from one of the boxes before climbing the stairs to Flat 10.

"Come back to find whatever evidence they missed the first time," Audrey said through gritted teeth. She felt Mei's eyes on her. "What?"

"I'm worried about you. I think this is raking it all up again."

"I'm fine," she said, not looking at her. "It's the police attitude that bothers me. Richard was shot. And he was probably a criminal. Those things mattered to them. Linda was just a meek, sad woman who lived quietly and died quietly, so they didn't care. Not until the coroner told them to. Just because you live a small life shouldn't mean you don't matter."

She spoke with more conviction than she meant to.

"You don't live a small life, Auds," said Mei softly. "And you do matter."

Audrey kept her eyes on the movement in the square.

"I know I matter," she said, after a moment, "but I didn't used to. Not back then. Not to the police. And I wouldn't now either, if it happened again."

"I'd make damn sure you mattered to them," said Mei, her ferocity making Audrey smile.

"It shouldn't take having a hotshot lawyer in your corner though, should it? It's not fair."

"No. No, it isn't."

They stood in silence for a while, Audrey's head on Mei's shoulder, watching as police officers went up and down the stairs to Flat 10, paper suits glowing in the lamplight. They were just getting ready to go downstairs and make dinner when a knock on the door made them both jump.

"Police?" asked Audrey.

"Probably."

They went downstairs together but when Mei opened the door, it was Lewis standing outside, holding an enormous pizza box and a sheaf of papers.

"Gate logs," he said when he saw Audrey over Mei's shoulder. "And pizza. I saw you both at the window—for ages, actually—and figured you probably hadn't eaten yet. Want to go over them together?"

He looked from her to Mei, whose mouth twitched at the corner.

"Sounds good," said Mei, letting him in. "Very thoughtful of you, Flat Five Guy."

"Was it? Oh. Good." He put the box into Mei's outstretched hands. "Just to be clear," he added, following her through to the kitchen, "I also want some of the pizza."

Audrey grinned at Mei's confused frown. That'd teach her to get ideas.

Audrey took Lewis's coat and hung it up in the hall, while Mei poured three glasses of wine and set out plates and napkins. Lewis accepted the napkin but appeared bemused by the plate, and after grabbing a slice of cheese pizza out of the box, ate it with one hand, elbow resting on the table.

"Could Celeste not have emailed these over?" Mei asked, pushing the papers out of the way to make room.

"That's what I said," said Lewis, with this mouth full. "But it's kind of useful. We can highlight anything suspicious."

"Good idea," said Audrey, fetching some highlighters from the kitchen drawer. She felt a tiny buzz of excitement. She hadn't done any sort of project work since her career change. Except this wasn't a statistical research project for an insurance company, she reminded herself, it was a murder case. Excitement was not appropriate.

Once Audrey and Mei had helped themselves to pizza, they moved the box onto a chair and divided the logs between them. There seemed to be an unspoken agreement that Mei was helping, and Audrey was glad. It would be a good distraction for both of them while the police were poking around in Linda's flat.

"What are we looking for, exactly?" asked Mei, pulling her sheets toward her. "No one can enter without being buzzed in by a flat, right?"

"We're looking for any unusual access or admittances at either the side or front gate between Wednesday the fifth, when Richard was killed, and the early hours of Saturday the eighth, when Linda was killed," said Lewis. "The police don't think anyone could have got in or out without going through one of the two gates, so we're looking at which of the residents either buzzed someone in or entered themselves at a similar time."

"It might not have been a resident," said Audrey quickly, when she saw Mei's expression. "You know how delivery drivers always buzz another flat if they don't get an answer from the one they want. Anyone could have inadvertently let someone in who didn't go out again."

"The end column denotes whether the gate was opened with a key fob or opened remotely from one of the flats," added Lewis. "And also whether it was released by the switch inside the gate, someone letting themselves out. Just highlight anything that stands out."

Armed with a highlighter each, they began to work their way down the lists. Audrey's section started with Bonfire Night, and she diligently highlighted any instance of a gate opening after nine o'clock, regardless of which direction, as that was when Celeste last saw Richard alive.

"This is harder than I thought," she remarked, forty-five minutes later. "It's all right until about seven in the morning on the sixth, but after that, it's just a constant tangle of buzzing. You can only work out who went out by who comes back later."

"Same here," said Lewis, running a hand through his hair. "Anything interesting though?"

"I've got everyone coming home on the evening of the fifth," said Audrey, reviewing her sheets, "including us three. The only exceptions are Celeste and Dixon, who never went out at all, and Roshan, who arrived at eight in the morning and stayed until after the fireworks."

"Nothing else?" asked Lewis.

"One anomaly," said Audrey, circling a number on her sheet. "The side gate's released from the inside at five to ten, just for a few seconds. Looks like someone was leaving, except there isn't anyone *to* leave. With the exception of Richard Glead, all the residents were outside with us. And Lewis, of course."

She paused to look at him, and realised a moment too late that Mei was staring at him too.

"What?" he asked, frowning. "I didn't do it."

"That's what you'd say if you did do it, though," said Mei, taking a bite of now-cold pizza. She sounded like she was only half joking.

"You didn't order food or anything, did you?" asked Audrey, but he shook his head.

"No, I had a microwave thing."

"Okay, let's assume for the moment that Lewis didn't do it," said Audrey, and his mouth dropped open. "I know it was dark, but everyone was chatting and lighting sparklers, and we were handing out mugs of hot chocolate. I feel like I saw everyone, don't you?"

Mei nodded.

"Yes. The fireworks ended at ten, and we all hung about, talking for a bit. I took the rubbish down at ten thirty and Roshan was just letting himself out. There were still people around though. Manny and Joe were messing about with sparklers in the garden, and I thought I heard the Hetheringtons too."

"Which means there must have been someone else in the square with us. Someone who shot Richard Glead and left the square at nine fifty-five while we were listening to the music from the park." Audrey flipped to the last sheet in her pile. "The last release is at ten thirty, when you saw Roshan leave."

"So while we were out having fun," said Mei, "someone with a gun was skulking around in the darkness. That's scary as hell." She shuffled the papers in her pile. "My sheets are from the evening of the sixth to lunchtime on the seventh, and it's just two and a half pages of both gates being opened from the inside. The police, I assume?"

Audrey groaned.

"They had a constable stationed by each one. They were coming and going for hours. What a pain." She looked across the table to Lewis. "How about you?"

"I've got a steady stream of residents coming in and out on the afternoon of the seventh, including Linda returning home at six fifty-two, all via the side gate, which makes sense, as it's nearest the courtyard. Someone buzzed the Hetheringtons at seven thirty, but they didn't let them in. Then someone used the internal gate switch two minutes later. Might be a coincidence or perhaps they went out to see who it was before letting them in? And Mrs. Hildething's fob is used twice from the outside, once at eight at the side gate and again at eleven fifteen at the front gate. Neither gate opens outward in between."

Mei blinked. "She came home twice? How?"

"Don't know. The Flat Nine fob uses the side gate just before eleven—the chef coming home?—but someone else goes out the front an hour later. Emmanuel said he heard voices outside not long after his boyfriend got home. I'm thinking that was Linda's killer."

Audrey let out a breath. Talking about two killers walking around the small, leafy space of their square made the hairs on the back of her neck stand up.

"The only other thing," Lewis went on, "is that the fob for Flat Three comes in the front gate just before midnight, two minutes before our mystery person goes out."

"Victor?" said Mei, glancing at Audrey.

"That explains how he managed to see the light on in Flat 10. But we asked him straight whether he'd been out that night, and he said no. Why would he lie?"

"Maybe he nipped out to dispose of the murder weapon?" suggested Lewis. "Don't look at me like that, it's possible. It's why we're doing this, to figure this stuff out."

"Maybe he'd just been to the pub," said Audrey hopefully. "Or maybe he has a lady friend he didn't want us to know about."

"Or maybe," said Lewis, "he saw something he didn't want to tell us about. All right, so we need to talk to Victor DeFlore and the Hetheringtons again, plus Mrs. Hildebrandt."

"We also need to establish an alibi for Flat Five Guy," added Mei, earning another frown from Lewis.

"She has a point," said Audrey apologetically. "You have to admit, 'I was home alone, with no witnesses' isn't going to cut it with the police."

His cheeks reddened and he ran a hand through his hair.

"If you must know," he huffed, "I was FaceTiming my grandmother."

They looked at him.

"You were what?" demanded Mei. "You have a grand-mother?"

"Why shouldn't I have a grandmother? She's eighty-six and she doesn't sleep very well. Sometimes she calls me. It goes straight through to my headphones, so I don't miss it."

He unlocked his phone and turned it around so they could see the call history.

Nana—Wednesday 5 Nov—Facetime

20:35—Incoming Call—1 hr 23 min

"What?" he snapped. "Why are you smiling?"

Audrey tried to keep her face straight. "No reason."

"We just assumed you hated everyone," said Mei, with a smirk. "Turns out it's just us."

He took his phone back, still glaring at them.

"I don't see why it's weird to mind your own business. You should try it sometime, both of you."

"It's natural to form a bond with your community," said Audrey. "Statistically speaking, when faced with disaster and adversity, people are more likely to survive as a group as opposed to going it alone."

"I don't believe that for a minute. Have you met most people? They're awful. Now, if you're satisfied with my alibi, can we get back to the matter at hand?"

"It's not much of an alibi," said Mei, earning herself yet another outraged look from Lewis. "But I suppose it's better than nothing. What were we talking about?"

"Victor," he said, through gritted teeth.

"We'll have to tread carefully with him," said Audrey. "He wasn't happy talking to us last time."

"I'll head over to the Dogs' Home tomorrow," said Lewis. "See if I can get hold of Nathan Roper or, failing that, his contact details. Turn on the old charm with Pam."

"Val," said Audrey, with a sigh. "We also need to figure out what Richard Glead was up to with Ram. We could check out Glead Antiques tomorrow. Pop along and see what's what."

"Good idea," said Lewis, nodding. "There might be something there to help us. Maybe even something telling us if Linda was involved. That would be a big help."

Audrey and Mei exchanged looks, but neither spoke. They didn't need to. Neither of them wanted Linda to be guilty, of murder or of any other crime, but they couldn't deny the possibility that she might be implicated.

And then there were the other Marchfield residents. How would Celeste feel if they ended up pointing the finger at one of her tenants? And if they were right, would she ever forgive them?

33

Lewis

The following morning, Lewis struck out on his own to find Nathan Roper. An internet search for his home address had proved fruitless, so Lewis's only option was to head over to the Dogs' Home and try to catch Nathan before his shift.

It was a rare day in London, crisp and misty, with a pale sun, more like the picture-book autumns he remembered from childhood than the damp and grey precursor to winter that had dogged the last few weeks. To take advantage of both the weather and the temporary freedom from work that allowed him to be out wandering in the daylight, Lewis had decided to walk, and as he took the shortcut through Battersea Park, he cast his thoughts back to where he'd left off last night: his detective with two murders on his hands and a growing list of shady characters to investigate.

At ten o'clock, the park was almost empty, the only sound the trees rustling overhead and his footsteps on the path. How long had it been since he'd spent any quality time outside? He couldn't even remember. The gardens at Marchfield Square were the only green space he saw these days, and he didn't linger anywhere anymore, keen to get back to his computer for another evening spent staring at a flashing cursor. What was that saying about doing the same thing over and over and expecting a different result?

As he neared the pagoda, he stopped and sniffed the air, the scent of damp grass and unidentified greenery filling his nostrils.

The mist clung to the ground and the surrounding trees in all directions, obscuring any feature more than ten metres away. Lewis appreciated its atmospheric effects.

In a flash of uncharacteristic good humour, he decided to extend his walk and turned right at the pagoda, heading further into the park. He'd never gone this way before and so was surprised when he emerged from the trees into a more formal, open garden. He followed the path, his hands shoved deep in his pockets against the chill of the air. He was just thinking that he'd like a hot drink now when he turned a corner and there, at the side of the path, was a tea and coffee stand, with just one other customer waiting to collect his order.

Lewis bought himself a cappuccino and continued his walk, warm paper cup cradled in his hands, thinking what a travesty it was that not all days could be like this. He should bring Audrey here. She was almost certainly the sort of person who'd like to drink coffee in the park. It took him a full minute, ambling along the path behind the other coffee buyer, to realise that he now considered Audrey a friend. Not that she wasn't a nice person— he could see that she was, even if she was nicer to people who weren't him—but Lewis couldn't remember the last time he'd made a new friend. Now that he thought about it, he couldn't remember when he'd last spoken to an old friend either.

How many years had he lost in the fog of creative depression? Of avoiding conversations about his next book, his next idea? Or as time went on, whether he'd given up entirely? The questions were natural but had felt like punches to the head, rendering him incapable of thinking beyond his failure. His relationship with Audrey was entirely devoid of history, and all the easier for it.

He was so distracted by his thoughts that he was surprised to see the bandstand looming out of the mist ahead of him, an island in a circle of identical trees and identical benches. He stopped and turned around, trying to get his bearings, which was a mistake. Once he'd turned, he had no idea which direction he'd come from.

He decided to follow the other guy with the coffee: a tall black-coated figure walking ahead of him with the casual stride of someone who knew where he was going. As he hadn't turned around and walked back past Lewis, he had to be going in roughly the right direction, and Lewis was in no hurry to get anywhere soon.

Coffee Guy led him down a long avenue lined with trees, the two of them walking in sync but at a distance. Cyclists passed, as did joggers, and once or twice, prompted by some noise or other, Coffee Guy turned around and glanced at Lewis, who was plodding along behind, enjoying his cappuccino.

It took a little while for Lewis to realise that Coffee Guy had sped up, the distance between them lengthening and the black shape only just visible in the mist ahead. Lewis sped up too, trying to keep him in sight until they reached a bit he recognised. Eventually, they rounded a corner and Lewis realised that the boating lake had been on his right the whole time, the density of mist around the water disguising its presence.

Knowing roughly where he was now, Lewis let Coffee Guy out of his sight and slowed his pace again. He followed the carriage drive around the curve of the lake, heading for the entrance on Queen's Circus. The mist thinned as he got closer to the road, and he spotted Coffee Guy up ahead, turning out of the park, heading east. Lewis went in the same direction, emerging onto the busy roundabout full of resentment, as the heavy traffic rushed away his serenity with its noise and fumes.

Coffee Guy continued along in front of him, but paused under the railway bridge, looking backward. Lewis could see the rounded glass building of the Dogs' Home entrance on the other side, but as he neared, Coffee Guy looked right at him, his face a mask of shock and alarm.

"Why are you following me?" he yelled, holding himself ready to run.

"I'm not!" Lewis called back. He put his hands up slowly, so as not to spill his coffee, and took a few steps forward. "I'm just going to the Dogs' Home."

"The Dogs' Home?" Coffee Guy glanced over his shoulder then back to Lewis. "You adopting? It's appointment only, you know."

Lewis inched forward. The man looked to be a bit older than Lewis, pale, with a narrow face and chin-length brown hair swept over in a side parting. He was tall but slight-looking, even while his body was hidden beneath the bulky black pea coat.

"Not adopting, no," said Lewis. "I've just come to talk to someone. You can wait here if you like, and I'll go on ahead. I wasn't following you, I swear." At least, not since the park, he added silently.

The guy's head whipped back and forth between Lewis and the Dogs' Home, then he sighed.

"Sorry," he said, shaking his head. "I'm jittery. The park and the mist . . . I'm going there too."

"Oh?" Lewis began walking again, more slowly. "Do you work there?"

They fell into step beside each other, the shelter coming into view as they cleared the bridge.

"Yes. Well, I volunteer. I help look after the dogs."

"Ah, you must work with . . ." Shit, not again. "Val?" he ventured.

"Yes, that's right," said Coffee Guy, smiling. They arrived at the entrance and Coffee Guy pulled a fob from his pocket. "I normally go in round the back, but I can take you in this way. Who are you going to see?"

"Nathan Roper," said Lewis, and Coffee Guy froze. Lewis sighed inwardly. For fuck's actual sake, he'd been inadvertently tailing the guy for twenty minutes. "Is that you, by any chance?"

"Who wants to know?"

Lewis tried to channel some of Audrey's easy friendliness, holding out his hand and smiling.

"Lewis McLennon. Friend of Linda's."

The guy Lewis was pretty sure was Nathan Roper gasped and did not shake his hand.

"Linda?"

"Linda Glead."

"I know who Linda is," snapped probably-Nathan. "But she didn't have any friends."

"Except you, right?" said Lewis, still smiling. "You *are* Nathan? I'm one of her neighbours."

"Neighbours?"

"I lived downstairs from her." Technically, that was true. "I don't suppose you ever visited her at home?"

Nathan shook his head.

"We only saw each other here. Why do you want to speak to me?"

"I wanted to make sure you knew. About Linda, I mean," said Lewis. "But I see you already heard."

"Yeah." Nathan let out a breath. "Bloody awful."

"I'm sorry."

"We weren't close. Friendly but not friends, you know?"

"Sure. Do you know what happened?"

"No, why would I know?" Nathan was immediately back on the defensive.

"The police think she was murdered."

"Shit. Really? Shit."

Lewis couldn't help but notice that Nathan looked scared rather than shocked.

"That doesn't surprise you," he said. Not a question. A statement of fact.

"Um . . ." Nathan's eyes moved around as he thought. "Well, I . . . her husband was killed, right? On Bonfire Night. Did they—I mean, was it the same person?"

"They don't know yet. You were both on duty that night, weren't you? Because of the fireworks? She mentioned that." Lewis had to talk slowly with the effort of careful wording, to sound like he knew Linda better than he had. "There was that dog she really loved . . . Muffin?" Hah, he remembered that. Stupid name.

"Muffin, yeah." Nathan smiled then. "She loved that dog. Wanted to adopt him and everything."

What was it with dogs? Changed the tone of the conversation every time. He could see why Audrey kept bringing it up.

"Is there anyone else we should tell about Linda?" Lewis asked. "With her husband gone too, we don't know who to contact, to let know, besides her sister, of course. Was she close with anyone else here? Or ever mention other friends?"

"Not to me," said Nathan, shaking his head. "Well, not really."

"You're sure?" Lewis pressed. "Even in passing?"

"I got the impression there was someone. Someone Richard didn't know about. A man."

"Oh? Like a boyfriend?"

"I don't know really," said Nathan, with a shrug. "She said her husband didn't like animals and when I said that must be difficult, she said she talked to her sister and her friend about them instead. Something about the way she said 'friend' made me wonder . . ."

And Audrey had dismissed his theory.

"But no name?"

"No. I think she brought him here once though. To see Muffin. I didn't see him but one of the other volunteers might remember."

"Is there a register or something? A signing-in book?"

"You could try," said Nathan, sounding doubtful. "But if they went in the back way, she probably wouldn't have taken him to reception."

"Okay, well, thanks for your help. Can I give you my number? In case you think of anything?"

Nathan's frown deepened.

"What do you mean, 'think of anything'?"

"About her friends," said Lewis hastily. "Anyone else we should call. Our landlady's trying to take care of everything, help out Linda's sister."

"Oh. Right." Nathan looked unconvinced, but he let Lewis read out his number and typed it into his phone anyway.

"Something's bothering you," said Lewis abruptly. After all, these tactics seemed to work for Audrey. "About Linda."

"Me? No. Nothing. I mean, yes. Obviously. Linda was murdered."

"But it's more than that," Lewis pressed. "What is it?"

Nathan glanced longingly over his shoulder at the building behind him.

"Look," he said. "Linda's husband was a bad guy, working for bad people. I'm sad about Linda, I really am, but it kind of feels . . ." He tailed off and shrugged.

"Inevitable?"

"Yeah."

"How do you know her husband was a bad guy? Did she tell you that?"

But Nathan started to back away.

"Sorry, man, I have to get going. I'm already late for my shift."

"All right," said Lewis. "Thanks for talking to me."

"No problem."

Nathan fumbled with the key fob before letting himself in, pushing the gate closed behind him as though worried Lewis might breach his sanctuary, then breaking into a jog, running through the courtyard and out of sight.

34

Audrey

Audrey was glad to reach the iron gates of the square at half twelve that day. She'd left early for her cleaning job, the air damp and chilly, and the sky heavy with grey clouds, but it hadn't rained a drop all morning. The moment she'd left the Braun residence, however, and stepped out onto the clean, wide slabs of the Mayfair pavements, the heavens had opened. Fat, slow raindrops that splashed onto the street in front of her had quickly turned to a steady shower and now it was hammering down.

Her thin raincoat could do nothing against the driving torrents of water, and her cleaning bag was heavy and unwieldy. She rooted through the clinging fabric of her pockets for her key fob and, after swiping the panel, shouldered the gate and staggered through.

She hurried through the courtyard, hauling her bag up the steps to the balcony, but no sooner had she got her key in the lock than the rain stopped, abruptly and without warning, leaving her gasping at the sudden absence of water.

"Sonofabitch."

She peeled the sodden raincoat off before going inside, and was still shucking off her shoes when someone knocked on the door.

It was Lewis, bone-dry in a new-looking anorak, and smiling at her.

"I saw you get home so thought I'd pop round and see if you were free to go to Glead Antiques? I can fill you in about Nathan Roper on the way."

She stood on the mat in her one waterlogged shoe and stared at him, the damp sock on her other foot squishing beneath her toes. Strands of wet hair stuck to her face and rainwater ran in rivulets down her neck, while her soaked shirt stuck to her body in a transparent, clinging sheath. The raincoat created a steady *drip-drip-drip* onto the floor of the hallway behind her.

It took him almost ten seconds.

"Ah. Shall I . . . come back?"

She sighed, then stepped aside to let him in.

"You can wait in the kitchen," she said, shutting the door behind him before divesting herself of her other shoe. "I need to change before I go anywhere."

She ran upstairs to the bathroom and wriggled out of her wet clothes. Realising that she couldn't get any wetter but was unlikely to get any warmer without one, she took a quick shower and managed to get back downstairs in fresh jeans and a jumper inside ten minutes, only to find Lewis standing at the kitchen window, looking out over the square.

"You could have done that from your place," she said from the doorway.

"You've got a better view," he said, turning around. "Better?"

"Much. Hey, I had a thought while I was cleaning this morning. We haven't tried the church yet. She went there the day she died, and if she was a regular, there might be someone there who knows more about her. She mentioned a priest—Reverend Fitzbride—and said she always felt better after talking to him. Maybe he'd talk to us?"

"That," said Lewis, wagging a finger, "is an excellent idea. Church is like a social club for some people, and especially if you don't have anything or anyone else. We can call in on the way to the antiques shop, if you have time?"

"Sure," said Audrey, pleased he thought it a good idea. Although he'd acted superior at the beginning, she was surprised at how willingly he was sharing the reins. "I've got the rest of today clear. I'll just sort out my things, then we can go."

She dried the hall floor off with a towel, found a cleanish pair of trainers and her warmest coat, and hastily ushered Lewis out onto the balcony. It wasn't that she minded him being there exactly, just that he now fell into an odd gap between friend and not-friend, and showering while he was in the house had felt weird.

She didn't fully relax until they were walking away from the square and Lewis said something annoying.

"You should have put another raincoat on," he remarked, as they turned off Pickering Lane. "It might rain again."

"Who has multiple raincoats?" she said, glad to have something to roll her eyes about. "Besides, they only keep you dry. I'd rather be warm." No need to add that she'd found the coat in a charity shop and it didn't keep her warm either.

They walked up through Glebe Place, a quiet and pretty lane that reminded Audrey of a country village, its Georgian houses well-tended and charming behind their iron railings.

"Tell me about Nathan Roper," she said, as they reached the top of the lane and waited to cross the King's Road. "Was he there?"

"Yes, bit of luck, that. Just turning up for his shift."

"Did you make notes?" she asked, and he nodded. "Read them out then."

He got out his phone.

"Okay, Nathan Roper. White, bit pasty-looking, with long-ish brown hair. Late thirties, about six foot one and skinny with it. Loping gait."

She smiled.

"Um, well, he was nervous because he thought I was following him. Calmed down a bit when he realised why I was there.

Didn't know Linda that well. Said they were 'friendly but not friends.' Knew that Ricky didn't like animals though, and that he was a bad guy."

"Richard," she said.

"Yes, Richard. Nathan also said Linda had a friend. Someone she'd taken to see the dog, that she hadn't told her husband about. I got the impression Nathan thought Linda was seeing him. Like, more than a friend."

They cut through Dovehouse Green, where an old lady sat on a bench watching a flock of pigeons peck the pavement at her feet, and turned onto Sydney Street.

"That doesn't seem like something Linda would do."

"I don't know. The lady at the Dogs' Home said she had a lot of time on her hands. Richard obviously couldn't know everything she got up to."

"You'd be surprised," she said. "Controlling relationships often involve tracking apps and check-in times."

Lewis frowned, and for a moment, Audrey wondered if he was sympathising, or recalibrating his idea of Linda, but then he started typing into his phone. He was taking it down as another idea for his book, she realised with disgust.

"Having a friend doesn't necessarily mean she was having an affair," she said, trying not to let it bother her. "If Richard was jealous, even an innocent friendship could cause her problems."

"I see what you mean. Still, it keeps the theory in play."

St. Luke's Church loomed as they neared, jutting out of its bare, wintry surroundings like a jagged stone knife. They stopped outside, the icy wind whipping Audrey's hair around her face. She took a deep breath.

"All right," she said, tugging a strand of hair out of her eyes. "What are we trying to find out from this priest then?"

35

Lewis

They walked up the drive toward the church. It was big, even by London standards, surrounded by bare trees doing their best to mask the park on one side and children's playing fields on the other. An elderly couple exited as they approached, but otherwise, the grounds were empty.

They climbed the steps, Audrey's boots tip-tapping on the stone. Her cheeks were pink with cold, and her eyes looked grey in the low light. Lewis wondered whether her distant expression was because of their conversation or because she was worried about something.

"We need to find out how much Linda knew about Richard's business," he said, shivering as the wind blew through the columns of the porch. "Whether there's any chance she could have been involved, and whether she really did have a boyfriend."

The last word echoed as they entered the church and Lewis blinked, his eyes adjusting to the gloom.

"Just do like you did before," he said, lowering his voice and looking around. The church seemed even bigger from the inside, the aisles long, like in a cathedral. There were lots of people strolling around, wrapped up in thick coats, looking at the stained-glass windows and the carvings on the walls, while several more sat quietly in the pews. "With the sister and the dog lady, and see where it leads."

"Like I did before?"

"Yeah, y'know . . . with the voice and the chitchat."

"The voice?"

"Yeah, the nice voice. That makes them talk."

She looked at him sidelong.

"But you said I made people cry."

He snorted and began to walk down the nave.

"You're not going to make a priest cry; they see this sort of thing all the time. But I was thinking about it, and actually, people say more when they're all over the place. In my second book, there's this waiter called Brian Brown. He's only got one scene but he's busy and nervy and too distracted to be cagey, and the conversation changes the entire perspective for my detective, and ultimately helps him solve the case. So even the tiniest bit of information could be the key to unlocking this whole thing."

Audrey paused, stopping dead in the middle of the aisle.

"How many books have you written?"

"Three."

"And you remember all your character names? Even the little bit-part people?"

"Of course."

"What do you mean, of course? You forgot my name the other day and I'm a real person!"

"I only forgot the last bit. And I remember them because they have the right name. The right name for the person. You don't just stick any old name down, even if it is a bit part. You give them the exact right name."

"Sorry, are you saying that the reason you can't remember anyone's name is because you didn't get to choose it?"

"Exactly." He nudged her, and pointed to the corner, where a man dressed entirely in black with a white square in his collar sat in the front pew talking to a young couple. "Reckon that's him?" They approached slowly, and as they neared, the couple spotted them.

"I think you're needed, Reverend," said the woman, nodding in their direction. The priest turned and as the couple excused themselves, he stood to greet Audrey and Lewis.

"Hello," he said, smiling and reaching out to shake their hands. He was a tall Black man, greying around the temples, with warm brown eyes and a wide smile. He must have been at least fifty but could probably pass for younger. Handsome, Lewis supposed, if priests were your thing. "I'm Reverend Fitzbride. How can I help?"

"Hi," said Audrey, smiling up at the priest with an expression Lewis hadn't seen before. "I'm Audrey."

"And I'm Lewis," said Lewis.

"Are you here about a wedding?" asked Reverend Fitzbride.

"No—" began Lewis.

"God, no!" said Audrey at the same time.

Lewis paused. He was going to try not to take that personally.

"We're here about Linda Glead," he said.

"Ah," said Reverend Fitzbride sadly. "Poor Linda. May I ask how you knew her?"

"You've heard, then?" asked Audrey. "We weren't sure if anyone had told you. She passed away last Friday night and I know she called in to see you late that afternoon. We thought you'd want to know."

Reverend Fitzbride sank down onto the pew.

"Yes, we heard. We were all very upset. Do they know what happened?"

"We don't know yet," replied Lewis quickly. "The police are still investigating. They might drop by to see you. Ask about Linda's life. If there was anyone who'd want to hurt her, that kind of thing."

He glanced at Audrey, who nodded her approval. First time for everything.

"Oh, dear," said Reverend Fitzbride. "They think she was . . . ? How distressing." He crossed himself and closed his eyes for a moment. "I hope she didn't suffer."

"Did she seem all right when you saw her, Reverend?" asked Audrey. "In herself?"

The priest rubbed his chin, thinking.

"Yes, as well as could be expected. Still rather in shock about the death of her husband, but nothing to give me any concern. Dear, dear."

"One of the neighbours said Linda thought she was being watched," said Lewis. "She was nervous. She didn't say anything to you?"

If a priest could look shifty, Reverend Fitzbride did so now.

"She mentioned it, yes. She thought someone was trying to intimidate her husband. He had some undesirable friends. When I saw her on Friday, she hoped that now he was gone, it would all stop." He sighed. "I'll make sure the police know anything that could help them."

"Did she ever talk about her husband?" asked Lewis, and something flashed in the priest's eyes.

"We were her neighbours, Reverend," Audrey put in. "We all knew. What he was like, I mean."

"Oh." Reverend Fitzbride relaxed a little. "Yes, it was difficult, but Linda was ever hopeful that things would get better. We admired her resolve, but made it clear we'd support her whatever decision she made in the future."

He folded his hands and rested them in his lap, eyes downcast. He was being inconveniently discreet.

Audrey sat down in the pew beside him.

"I wish I'd done more to help her," she said, and Lewis was surprised to see real emotion in her eyes. "We all knew how things were, but with his job and everything . . ."

Reverend Fitzbride nodded.

"Indeed. It's a volatile trade, antiques. Subject to the slings and arrows of outrageous fortune."

"And with the gambling . . ." she added, but he merely nodded again. This was tougher than Lewis had expected.

"Shakespeare," he said absently, and the priest looked up. "Slings and arrows. *Hamlet*, isn't it?"

"That's right," said Reverend Fitzbride, with a smile. "Well done."

"Lewis is a writer," Audrey said suddenly, reaching up to pull Lewis down onto the pew beside her. "He writes novels."

Lewis felt his cheeks heat.

"Oh, really?" Reverend Fitzbride turned to Lewis. "I'm something of a bookworm. What sort?"

"Crime fiction."

"Anything I might know?"

"Um . . ." Lewis flushed again. "*Place a Candle on My Grave*? That did pretty well."

"You wrote that? Goodness. I enjoyed that enormously. Bought a copy for my father for Christmas that year. Nothing since then?"

Oh, the humiliation.

"Nothing you'd have read, I expect." He looked helplessly at Audrey, who widened her eyes and briefly mimed a scribbling action with her hand. More talk about writing. "Um . . . my new one's about art. Art theft and the criminal underworld. I'd been hoping to talk to Linda about antiques, but of course it wasn't the right time, and now . . . well."

"I don't know if Linda would have been the right person to ask anyway," said Reverend Fitzbride after a beat. "She mentioned the shop once or twice, but I'm not sure she was involved with the business. She seemed to have rather a lot of time on her hands, and lonely with it."

"Is there anyone else we should talk to, Reverend?" asked Audrey, using the same tactic Lewis had at the Dogs' Home. "Linda was a private person, but we'd like to let her friends know the sad news, particularly if there was anyone close. The police aren't releasing information yet."

"No one that doesn't attend here, so we've already taken care of that. We passed the news on to our clergy team, and have been remembering her in our service prayers. She will be missed."

They sat in silence for a few minutes, the only sounds the click and tap of footsteps on stone as visitors walked up and down the aisles. Lewis racked his brain for any other way of extending the conversation, but when he looked at Audrey, she was also looking blank. She shrugged.

"We should go," said Lewis, getting to his feet. "Sorry to have taken up your time."

Reverend Fitzbride stood too.

"It was kind of you to think of us," he said, and started walking them toward the door. "Do you know who'll be making arrangements for the funeral?"

"Her sister, Jane, I expect," said Audrey, as they passed someone lighting a candle at one of the votive stands. "But it might be at their local church. In Streatham."

"Ah. There we are then." They neared the end of the aisle, and Reverend Fitzbride stopped. "If you do hear anything about the service, would it be too much to ask you to drop by and let us know? I'm sure several in our community would like to attend."

"Of course, Reverend," said Lewis.

"Or you could send word with Roshan, if that's easier? I don't want to put you out."

There was a pause as the name registered.

"Roshan Jones?" asked Audrey carefully. "Does he come here too?"

"Oh, yes. Every Sunday, and in the week, too, sometimes. It was him who told us about Linda." He shook their hands again. "Bless you both, and thank you for coming. Goodbye."

"Roshan Jones," repeated Lewis as they stopped inside the porch to do their coats up.

"The caretaker at Marchfield," she said, rolling her eyes. "Brown skin, black hair, usually wearing overalls. Worked there five days a week for about a billion years?"

"I know who he is, thank you."

They walked down the drive together, the wind biting their cheeks.

"It doesn't necessarily mean anything," said Audrey, as they turned back onto Sydney Street and started walking. "It is the closest church, after all."

"But it suggests he might have known her better than anyone else at Marchfield, doesn't it? Nathan thought Linda had a special friend, and there aren't many places she could have met someone. I think Roshan Jones just got bumped up the list."

36

Audrey

They walked back the way they'd come and didn't speak again until they reached the King's Road, which was still heavy with traffic and the lunchtime crowd.

"I wonder if the police have spoken to Ram yet," she said, as they navigated the harried retail workers and rain-slick pavements. "Now he's on their suspect list."

"It's not too far from Glead Antiques. Let's do a walk-by and have a look. See if they're about."

All was quiet on Medlar Walk. They strolled along the side street, faces buried in their coats, and passed the pawnshop slowly. It was shuttered and dark, the sign in the window turned to "Closed."

"Perhaps they've taken him in for questioning," said Lewis, speeding up. "Or maybe he's done a runner."

They continued on to the end of the street, then turned right, heading back in the direction they'd come. Pimlico Road was a twenty-minute walk in the opposite direction, but the sun was now filtering through the clouds and as they cut a loop back onto the King's Road, the wet streets glistened before them.

The conversation as they walked was mostly talk of London and its various criminal gangs, including the celebrities within them, half of which seemed to have styled themselves after Hollywood movies, with disturbing nicknames like Concrete Sam and Butcher Braithwaite.

After half a mile or so, they turned down Smith Street, passing the Royal Chelsea Hospital and several groups of red-coated pensioners getting some fresh air and sunshine between rain showers.

"What about that Fixer person you mentioned?" asked Audrey.

"The Fixer's who they bring in to get rid of the bodies, or clean up a crime scene. He's been around a few decades now, so chances are he's getting on a bit. Maybe even old enough to be one of these guys." He nodded ahead to where a Chelsea Pensioner was hobbling up the road with a cane identical to Celeste's. He looked younger than Celeste, but his walk was more laboured, and as they passed, Audrey found herself wondering whether Celeste had a particularly high pain threshold or whether she had this to look forward to.

They crossed at the junction onto Pimlico Road, and within a few hundred yards, they'd already passed a number of antiques shops, interspersed with small, exclusive-looking galleries and designer housewares outlets.

"Good place to hide your dodgy antiques business," said Audrey, watching as a Porsche pulled away from a parking meter and a Silver Shadow Rolls-Royce took its place. "With a load of other antiques businesses."

She'd never had any cause to visit this area before, but it was nice, with a village-like feeling. The streets were wide and clean, and trees stood at intervals along the pavements, screening the high-class shops and cafés from the traffic.

Glead Antiques was on the corner, a discreet black-fronted building opposite a small, tree-lined square containing benches and a statue of Mozart. Metal grills covered the shop window and the signage was so muted—charcoal grey over black—that Audrey would never have noticed it if she hadn't been looking for it.

"Your eyes just sort of slide over it, don't they?" said Lewis, sounding impressed.

They crossed the road and tried to peer through the grills, but it was dark inside, and all they could see was furniture. Cream sofas and mahogany bureaus and dressers filled the space, but not so much that it appeared cluttered. They could see nothing beyond.

"Let's go look round the back," said Lewis. "How do we get in?"

"There." She pointed to a gate, two shops to the left, with an alley beyond. There was a panel of buzzers just inside the wall, indicating that at least half the shops in the row shared the access.

Lewis rattled the gate. "Locked."

She reviewed the list of doorbells and pressed one.

"What are you doing?"

"Gambling."

The intercom remained silent for a moment, then buzzed, long and loud, and the gate lock clunked. Audrey pushed it open.

"Deliveries," she said, as they walked down the passage. "I bet that thing goes off all day."

The alleyway opened out into a narrow yard, which split both left and right and ran behind a handful of shops each way. They turned right, and walked to the end, where a scruffy white door bore a brass nameplate reading "Glead Antiques."

"I was hoping the police might have kicked the door in or something," said Lewis, looking at the door frame. "Then we could have just walked in."

He reached for the handle and she grabbed his wrist.

"What are you doing?"

"Seeing if it's open."

"I didn't think we'd be breaking and entering," she said.

"No breaking," he said, leaning an elbow down on the handle. It swung gently inwards. "But maybe a little entering."

"If it's open, there'll be someone in there!" hissed Audrey, pulling him back. "A member of staff or something." She knocked on the open door, and they leaned into the gap to listen for any noise within.

Except there was nothing.

"Might have been the police," said Lewis. "If they let themselves in to search the place." He knocked this time, louder, and called out, "Hallo? Anyone in?"

More silence.

"Fine," said Audrey, pulling a handful of yellow rubber out of her pockets. "But put these on and make it quick, yeah? If we're caught here, it won't look good."

Lewis looked askance at the marigold gloves before reluctantly putting them on. Her own gloves squeaked as she shut the door behind her, and they stood in the little hall, looking around. There were black scuff marks all over the magnolia walls, from the ground all the way up to shoulder height. The police, brushing up against the walls in their bulky black uniforms? Or perhaps it was from carrying furniture in and out.

Immediately to their right was a tiny cloakroom, functional and grimy, while on their left was an office. Lewis went inside while Audrey remained in the doorway, keeping an ear out for intruders.

Intruders that weren't them, anyway.

The office had an original sash window overlooking the yard and a picture rail running around the top of the walls, supporting a handful of oil paintings of country pursuits. The fireplace had been removed but the chimney breast remained, while the desk was antique, its polish covered in scratches. Marks on the desk suggested that a laptop had been there until recently, and Audrey watched as Lewis tried all the drawers and riffled through them.

"Anything?"

"Nothing."

"What about the backs of the drawers? People sometimes tape stuff underneath."

He pulled a face.

"Maybe on the telly," he said, but began to root around behind the drawers. "In the real world, the police would take the room apart if they were doing a proper search."

"There was a computer here. Did they take it?"

"I expect so. They'd have been looking into Glead's business primarily to see if they could find a motive for his murder, but now they know he was friends with Ram, they'll be back and turning the place upside down, looking for evidence of criminal activity. But Richard would have known his laptop would be the first thing they'd seize if they ever came after him, so he'd be a fool to keep anything incriminating on there."

Audrey looked around the room, trying to think where she'd hide something. There was no filing cabinet, and if there was a safe behind one of the paintings, it would be fixed to the wall, not hanging from the dust-coated picture rail.

Her eyes followed the rail, taking in the fine layer of dust that ran all the way along the top. What she wouldn't give to have a go at that with some detergent, and maybe some white vinegar for the strangely greasy section near the chimney breast . . .

"Can I borrow that chair?" she said, walking over to the corner beside the chimney. Lewis obligingly got up and wheeled it over. She climbed onto it and Lewis did his best to stop it spinning out from beneath her while she reached up to the picture rail.

He craned his neck to look up at her.

"What are you doing?"

"The whole picture rail is dusty. Not so much that you'd really notice, but this bit . . ."—she gripped a section of the rail—"is smeared and greasy. People have been touching it regularly." She pushed it upward and it shifted, so she wiggled it up and down a few times. A small section came away in her hand, revealing a space where a brick had been removed from the wall.

"Bloody hell," said Lewis. "That's genius. What's in there?"

She felt around in the cavity and her gloved hand closed around something.

"A book."

He helped her down from the chair and she put the book down on the desk. It was a small, leather-bound accounting ledger, and as Lewis turned the pages, his rubber-gloved fingertips making the operation clumsy, they could see it was a few pages of names, dates, and cash amounts. The rest of the book was empty.

"It's got to be important if it was hidden like that," said Lewis. "Better take some pictures."

He took off one of his gloves and pulled out his phone. Audrey held the pages while he photographed each one, then she returned the book to its hiding place.

"I wonder if the police will find that," Audrey said as she got down again.

"I'll be impressed if they do," said Lewis, putting his glove back on. "Let's have a look at the shop before we go. There might be something in there."

He went ahead, leading the way through the narrow hall to the showroom at the front. As they'd seen from the street, the room held a collection of unartfully arranged furniture, each piece looking vaguely antique without being striking in any way.

"I don't know why, but I thought there'd be a desk here too," said Audrey. "For customers."

"He must have done everything from the office."

As they turned to leave, Audrey noticed a door in the wall at the back of the showroom, on the same side as the cloak-room, and made a beeline for it. As she opened the door, it met with some resistance, so she leaned her shoulder against it and poked her head through the gap.

It was a kitchen, small and narrow, with grubby cabinets and a kettle no one would want to touch, even with their mari-golds on. There was also something else no one would want to touch.

Audrey withdrew her head from the room.

"How many bodies would you say is a normal amount for a detective to find in the course of one investigation?" she asked, taking her phone out of her pocket.

"Depends," he said, frowning. "One or two, usually. Maybe three, if you're writing about a serial killer. Why?"

"Because our chief suspect is lying on the floor of the kitchen with a hole in his chest. I'll call the police this time, shall I?"

37

Lewis

"That's three bodies you've found now, Mr. McLennon," said DS Larssen, looking from Lewis to Audrey. "That would be enough to give a detective pause, don't you think?"

They were standing in the showroom of Glead Antiques, while the paper-suited Forensics team busied themselves in the kitchen. Discovering the body of Paulo Ram had marshalled a seriously quick reaction, and within half an hour of them phoning it in, the Pimlico Road junction had been blocked off and the building occupied by all manner of personnel, while the little square over the road was full of police vehicles, parked haphazardly across the pavement and between the trees.

"To be fair," said Audrey, "it was me who found this one. And Linda found the first one."

"Yes, be fair. We've only found one each," said Lewis.

"Of course, that's far less suspicious." Larssen's lips twitched at the corner. "This isn't a laughing matter though. What were you doing here in the first place?"

Audrey looked at Lewis, and he could tell from her expression that she had no idea what to say.

"I've been doing my own research," he said after a beat. "I've been inspired to write a new novel, and thought I'd come and take a look at Ricky's office. See how a criminal art trader operated. I asked Audrey to come with me. The door was open when we got here."

Larssen gave him a hard look, then turned to Audrey.

"Is that true?"

"Yes," she confirmed, nodding. "We only meant to look through the window, but then the door opened. We assumed the police had left it open. We may have had a little look around."

Larssen looked pointedly at their hands, still clad in yellow rubber.

"Saw some washing-up that needed doing, did you?"

She was being a lot less hard-nosed suddenly, Lewis realised. Audrey must have won her over somehow. Probably the puppy-eye thing.

"And how long have you been friends?" asked Larssen. "Last week you claimed to not know each other's names."

"Since we started talking about the dead bodies being found in the square," said Audrey.

"And what about Richard Glead, Mr. McLennon? You said you didn't know him." She flicked back a load of pages in her notebook. "You said, and I quote, 'We never really spoke,' but now you're calling him Ricky."

"Oh. Ah." Lewis felt his face get hot. "Well, I'm not good with names. Terrible. Can't seem to help it."

"He really isn't," put in Audrey. "He's been doing it all week. He called Mei 'Maia.'"

Larssen smirked.

"I bet she loved that."

"That was just once!" he said, cheeks burning. He couldn't help it if people had the wrong names; they should take it up with their parents.

"Where's Larssen?" bellowed a male voice from the back of the building, and the smile dropped from Larssen's face.

"In here," she called back, and a few seconds later, DI Banham strode into view, flushed and angry.

"What the bloody hell's going on, Sofia?" he barked. "One minute Ram's the suspect in a double homicide, the next he's been killed with what looks like the same bloody weapon." He noticed Lewis and Audrey, and a vein bulged in his temple. "And what the hell are these two doing here?"

Larssen sighed.

"It seems they've been doing their own research, as Mr. McLennon calls it. It was through them that we found the link between the Gleads and Ram. They stumbled in here this afternoon and discovered the body."

Banham glared at Lewis.

"'Stumbled'?"

"The door was open, sir. Obviously, Ram let himself in and whoever killed him didn't lock it behind them."

"They shouldn't have been here," he growled.

"No," agreed Larssen.

"Have you taken their statements?"

"Yes."

"Then get them out of here." He ignored Audrey but fixed Lewis with his watery eyes, an effect ruined only slightly by his being six inches shorter than him. "McLennon, knock this research on the head. You might think writing a crime novel or two makes you Billy Big-Balls, but if you put one more foot out of line, I'll charge you with obstructing a police investigation so fast, it'll make your head spin."

"We're not obstructing, we're helping!" Lewis protested. "We've already helped." He looked to Larssen for support but she shook her head.

"We don't need your help," said Banham. "Now sling your hook, and stay out of it from now on. Oh. And don't leave town. I've got three murders on my hands now, and the only thing connecting them is you." He jabbed a finger at Lewis. "You're now officially a person of interest."

"We're not staying out of it," said Lewis to Audrey as they walked away. "And what's going on with you and Larssen?"

"Me and Larssen? Nothing. Mei and Larssen? Something, maybe. I'm not sure. I think she's trying to be nice to me though."

Lewis nodded. While it would have been useful for Audrey and Larssen to be friends, he had to admit he preferred that it was Mei instead. They could get the benefit of the connection with no unnecessary complications.

"What did she mean about getting the lead about Ram through us? Was that Mei too?"

"Oh, um. Yes. I've been keeping her up to date and she passed it on. Sorry."

He didn't say anything, too irritated at too many people to organise his thoughts.

"Aren't you worried?" she asked him. "About what Banham said back there?"

"About being a person of interest?" He thought about it. Was he worried? While he knew, logically, that Forensics and everything would exonerate him, he also knew it wasn't impossible that the police could get the wrong man. It had happened before. "No," he lied. "It'll be all right."

They walked quietly back along the Pimlico Road, Lewis lost in thought. These murders weren't the actions of a serial killer, but smacked very much of someone cleaning house.

"Three deaths, all connected," he said out loud, as they threaded their way through shoppers. "Whatever those three were involved in, they either pissed someone off or became a liability. Someone's covering their tracks."

"But if not Ram, then who? Who's his boss?"

"He doesn't really have one, apart from the Fixer, who moves around. He's kind of independent. Like a contractor."

"So it could be anyone?"

"Yeah." He stopped on the pavement, then stepped aside to avoid some pedestrians coming the other way. "Fancy coming to see the other poker friend? Chaz Shaw? We've not spoken to him yet. He's got a bike shop over in Vauxhall. Maybe he can point us in the right direction."

She looked doubtful.

"Why would he talk to us?"

"He might. I could pretend to have a job for Ram or something."

She was silent for a moment, and he wondered if she was going to chicken out.

"All right," she said. "Better sooner than later, I guess, before the killer can strike again. But can we get a bus? I've already walked about 10 kilometers today, and it's a couple more to Vauxhall."

They caught the bus from outside the Royal Hospital, planning their various routes of enquiry along the way, then got off and walked the last couple of streets to Shaw's bike shop, a narrow building on Broadgate Road with an entirely frosted window that had "MOT & Service Centre" in large letters across the front. An archway at the side led to a brick alleyway with a sign on the wall, pointing down toward Shaw's Bikes Workshop.

"Only one way in," said Lewis.

"And one way out," said Audrey, sounding nervous.

"You can wait here if you like," he said. He felt strangely protective, now they were here. But she shook her head.

"Nope, we agreed on a plan. If he's not here, they're more likely to tell me where he is than you."

They walked down the passage, which opened out into a wide, half-covered yard. Motorbikes stood in a neat row beneath a canopy of corrugated plastic, while on their right, a pair of garage doors stood open, revealing the workshop behind.

A thin man in overalls was bending over a bike. He turned around as they approached.

"Hey," he said, walking toward the garage doors. He was middle-aged, with a close-shaved head and a grease mark on his temple. "What can I do you for?"

"Is Chaz in?" Audrey asked.

"No, not this afternoon. Can I help?"

"Sorry, I need to speak to Chaz. Do you know where he is?"

The mechanic looked wary, glancing from her to Lewis.

"It's personal," she added.

"Sorry, can't help you," said the mechanic. "He'll be in tomorrow morning, if you want to come back."

"It's urgent," said Lewis. "Urgent *and* personal."

Audrey glared at him, although he didn't know if that was part of the act or not. It convinced the mechanic anyway, and his eyebrows shot up.

"Try the Red Lion," he said. "Or come back tomorrow."

"Okay, thanks."

They left the way they'd come, and as they emerged onto the pavement, Audrey shivered.

"Ugh," she said, shaking herself out. "Why did you say that? I feel seedy."

"What? All I said was that it was urgent and personal."

She looked at him, the incredulous judgy look back on her face.

"You do know what you were implying, right?"

"What do you mean? I wasn't implying anything."

"Personal and urgent sounds medical, if you catch my drift?"

He shook his head. He did not catch her drift. She sighed. "Oh, never mind. Where's this bloody pub?"

38

Audrey

The Red Lion on Kennington Lane was a classic Victorian ale-house: a long, narrow corridor of a pub with a sweeping mahogany bar on one side and a row of no-frills tables on the other. This was not a pub for gastronomy fans or the after-hours financial crowd, but for people who wanted a simple pint with the same old faces, and who would get their dinner on the way home.

The pub was still quiet, the clock behind the bar striking five as they walked in. The only patrons were a couple of old men sat at the bar, and a young couple looking at their phones at a table in the corner by the window. Looking to the end of the room, Audrey saw a passageway with a sign indicating LOUNGE.

"Might be a long evening," said Lewis. "What can I get you?"

"Oh, thanks. Pint of Guinness, please. And some crisps, if they've got any. I forgot to eat lunch."

They carried their pints and crisps through the bar to the lounge, then pulled up short when they turned the corner and nearly ran into a man Audrey immediately recognised from her internet searches as Chaz Shaw.

"Watch it," growled Chaz, reeling as he tried to support his pint. He was an inch shorter than her, wearing a battered bike jacket over a black sweater and black jeans. His eyes were small and dark, and a black beanie covered his head while a five-o'clock shadow covered his chin. He smelled of beer, and from the way he moved, Audrey guessed he'd been drinking for some time.

"Sorry," said Lewis.

"You didn't spill your drink, did you?" said Audrey, trying to sound concerned. "We'll get you another."

Chaz blinked at her, his face pinched into a scowl as the words took time to sink in. Eventually he grinned.

"Decent," he slurred. "Pint of bitter. Cheers."

By the time Lewis returned with Chaz's pint, Audrey, perched on a stool beside a sticky-looking table, had already watched Chaz down what remained of his original pint. He sprawled in a chair in the corner and cheered when he saw Lewis approach.

"Now THIS," he shouted to anyone listening, "is a gennelman! Cheers, mate."

Lewis sat down on the vacant stool beside Audrey.

"No problem. Sorry about that."

"Your lady friend here bin keeping me comp'ny. As you can see"—Chaz raised his arms and gestured to the room—"I am . . . allalone." He let the last words run together, and scowled around at the other drinkers. A woman with lank white-blonde hair sat nursing a gin and tonic in a booth beside the window. She stared into her glass and didn't look up, unlike the man with a pint sat at the table by the toilet door, who glanced at Chaz then went back to his phone.

"This is Chaz," said Audrey, reminding Lewis that they hadn't yet introduced themselves. "And it's his birthday."

"Shit," said Lewis. "Seriously?"

"Seriously," she said, through gritted teeth.

"Seriously." Chaz leered at them both and raised his glass. "Cheers!"

"Are you . . . waiting for people?" Lewis asked, with a caution Audrey approved of. Something about Chaz's maniacal grin must have made him as uneasy as it made her.

"Do you know," said Chaz, leaning forward, his eyes burning with an intense fire, "I am. I am waitin' for people. I spend my life waitin' for people. But oneofmyfriends . . ."—he paused for a moment—". . . has recently . . . died."

"I'm so sorry," said Audrey at once. "That's awful."

"Yup." Chaz took a slug of his new pint. "And the other . . . is not answerin' 'is phone."

"Why not?" asked Lewis.

"Who knows?!" said Chaz, slapping his hands against his knees. "Who. Knows." He laughed, the sound brittle and dangerous. "Not me!"

Lewis looked at Audrey. Chaz was clearly a loaded gun, and the last thing they wanted was for him to go off.

"Have you tried calling him?" She hoped he couldn't hear how nervous she was.

"Oh, yes," he said, rolling his head from side to side. "But Paulie ain't answering."

"When did you last speak to him?"

"Last night," said Chaz promptly. "He was sat right where you are now." He jabbed his finger toward her stool. "Right. There." He looked up at them sharply. "You not drinkin'?"

They immediately raised their glasses, and Chaz and Lewis both stopped to watch as Audrey drank half a pint in one draught. She put the glass down and wiped the foam off her top lip.

"What?" she said, looking from one to the other. "It's Chaz's birthday. Cheers!"

"Cheers!" said Chaz, enthusiastically lifting his own glass. "She's all right, yor gel." He downed half his own pint, then slammed the glass down on the table and reached for his phone. He looked at it in anger.

"No word?" asked Audrey.

"Fack 'im," said Chaz, tossing the phone back down onto the table. "I've got my two noo buddies, 'ere. What're your names anyway?"

"Uh . . ." she began.

"Anna," said Lewis quickly. Too quickly for her liking. "And Logan."

Chaz roared with laughter.

"Logan!" he shouted, and Audrey giggled. "Like Wolverine!"

Lewis tried to hide his embarrassment by taking another pull on his drink.

"So this friend of yours who died," he began, and she shot him a warning look. Chaz frowned.

"What about 'im?"

"Uh . . . was it recent?"

"Last week," said Chaz, reaching for his phone again. Audrey shook her head at Lewis, trying to convey the message: Do not poke the bear.

"How did he die?" Lewis went on, back to being oblivious.

"Why d'you wanna know, Wolverine?" asked Chaz. Lewis shrugged and lifted his pint.

"Just making conversation."

"Funny conversation."

Chaz, Audrey realised, was not as drunk as he looked. He was uninhibited and acting out, possibly as a form of stress relief, but he still had his wits about him.

"Logan's just a bit insensitive sometimes, aren't you?" she said, laying a hand on Lewis's arm. "He doesn't mean to be."

"Sorry," Lewis mumbled.

"My friend," said Chaz, lowering his voice and looking from side to side, "was shot. By. His. Wife. What d'you think about that, eh?"

"God," said Audrey, gasping. "Why?"

"Who knows?!" Chaz slammed his hands down on the arms of the chair, making her jump. "He might have fooled around once or twice, but that was business! It's no reason to kill 'im!" He eyeballed Audrey, as if she would have an explanation. "I mean, who does that? One minute she's making him dinner, the next, she's shooting him in the head. *Blam!*" Chaz mimed an explosion with his hands and looked sad. "You wouldn't shoot old Wolverine here, would you?"

Audrey had to think about that.

"No," she said, after a beat, which made Lewis frown. "Not even for fooling around."

"That bitch better rot in prison," said Chaz, suddenly nasty. "Fuck, I'm having a shit week. One very shitty week." He picked up what was left of his pint and downed it in one. "Looks like the birthday drinks are on me. What you two havin'?"

"Oh, nothing for me," said Audrey. "We have to go in a minute."

"But you only just got here!"

"Sorry."

"How do you know she shot him in the head?" asked Lewis, apparently desperate to get thumped. Chaz glared at him.

"What d'you mean? How do I know? How d'you think I know?"

"I don't know," said Lewis, and Audrey could hear panic in his voice. "I just meant, was it in the news or something? Or did the police tell you?"

"The cops?" Chaz stood up. "Why would the cops come t' see me? And what's it to do with you anyway, Wolverine? Huh? Coming to my pub on my birthday asking me about my friend who got shot in the head. You got a death wish?"

Yes, she thought.

"No," she said, putting herself in front of Chaz. "He's just insensitive, like I said."

Lewis stood up too, his face red and shiny with sweat.

"Sorry!" he said. "I'm just . . . sorry."

Chaz walked around the table, and although Lewis was taller, Chaz was much more imposing in his leather jacket and black knit hat. His hands curled into fists at his side and now it was Audrey who was panicking.

"We'll just go," she said, raising her hands to try and calm the situation. "Sorry. We'll go."

"Nah," said Chaz, knocking the table to one side and advancing on Lewis. His eyes became smaller, and Audrey could now see that Chaz was a very dangerous man. "Your boy here needs to learn some manners."

"I'm sorry!" Lewis said, backing away. "I didn't mean to upset you."

In the narrow pub, Lewis was up against the wall in seconds. Chaz slammed his left hand into the wall beside Lewis's head, then drew his right hand back, ready to throw a punch. Audrey didn't even have time to think, grabbing Chaz's fist and jerking it back at the wrist, twisting it sharply inwards until Chaz cried out in pain.

"Run!" she yelled, but Lewis was already moving. They bolted through the bar, Audrey knocking into someone as she went. She heard Chaz yell behind her, but they ducked and dived their way through the increasingly busy pub and burst out onto the street.

Lewis grabbed her hand and started to move, pulling her along with him. She heard the pub door slam open behind her and Chaz bellowed after them.

"And don't come back! This is *my* pub!"

They ran until Audrey couldn't run anymore, dodging around pedestrians and cyclists who were starting to fill the pavements at the end of working day.

"Stop," she panted, pulling Lewis into a side street and using the wall for support. "I can't . . . go . . . any further."

He was out of breath too, but looked around the corner to see if anyone was after them.

"I don't think he followed us," he said. "Are you all right?"

She nodded, still trying to get her breath back.

"Sorry. About that," he said. "About me. And thanks. Where did you learn that wrist thing?"

"Self-defence . . . classes." She couldn't get her breathing under control and was shaking so hard, her hand grated against the brickwork.

Breathe, one-two-three, *breathe* . . .

"Are you okay?" He sounded worried. She nodded again, focusing on her breathing, and when she next looked up, Lewis was standing by the side of the road with his arm out. A black cab drew up to the kerb.

"Come on," he said, opening the door and gently taking her arm. "It's all over now. It's over. Let's get you home."

She let him guide her into the cab and collapsed onto the seat without a word.

Breathe, she repeated silently, closing her eyes. Just breathe.

39

Lewis

"What are our next steps, sir?" asked Hughes.

Harding rubbed at the stubble on this chin. He hadn't been home in two days, and was badly in need of a shower and a shave.

"I don't know," he said. "Either one person killed Ricky, Lindsey, and the pawnbroker, or we've got more than one killer. We need to find that gun."

"But where do we start? The pawnbroker was our only lead."

"We go back to the beginning, Hughes. That's the only way. We go back to the beginning and start again."

Lewis swiveled his chair back and round and back again, staring at his clichéd words in frustration. Everything was messy and confusing, and he couldn't think straight. And then there was Audrey. Calm and capable one minute, hyperventilating in the back of a taxi the next. Another puzzle.

He glared at the screen. What were they missing?

Paulo Ram and Chaz Shaw were the two Lewis had been banking on. Both of them violent enough to commit murder, and both could have laid their hands on a gun, but now Paulo was dead and Chaz was out of the frame. Richard Glead and Paulo Ram were apparently killed with the same weapon, suggesting the same person killed them both. But Chaz had made an assumption Richard had been shot in the head, meaning he hadn't seen the body, and he thought Linda was still in police custody. He'd also appeared genuinely bemused that Paulo wasn't returning his calls.

He reached for his phone and pulled up the pictures of Richard Glead's secret ledger. He pinched and zoomed on the images until his eyes hurt, and in the end, resorted to copying out the lists into a notebook. The first was a list of artists, with a date, a set of initials, and an amount beside it. The second was a list of first names, dates, and amounts, while the third was odd. A collection of abbreviations—people, maybe? Businesses?— with amounts and dates beside them.

Lewis began to google. An hour later, he texted Audrey.

> LEWIS MCLENNON: Hope you're feeling better. Pages 1 and 2 of Richard's notebook = leverage trading. 6 of the items listed were stolen in the last 2 years, while another 4 are known to be missing from historic heists.

> THE CLEANER: I've been looking over the second list. See any names you recognise?

Lewis went back to his lists and scanned it.

> LEWIS MCLENNON: No?

> THE CLEANER: Near the top. Bridget H

> LEWIS MCLENNON: Who's that?

> THE CLEANER: Say it out loud.

Lewis huffed, annoyed at having to play games, but did as instructed.

Ah.

LEWIS MCLENNON: Hildebrandt?
THE CLEANER: Her real name is Bridget.
Brigitte was her stage name.

LEWIS MCLENNON: But you said she
was broke.

THE CLEANER: She's one of the first entries,
and it's a LOT of money. Maybe that's
why she's broke? Do you remember I was
surprised Richard didn't have a desk in the
showroom? Mrs. H said she'd seen him sitting
behind one when she was passing by. She
couldn't possibly have done, could she? And
she couldn't have mistaken it. I bet she went
into the office because she had business with
him and got her stories muddled.

THE CLEANER: Also, on the third list, there's
another possibility.

Lewis turned to the third list, the one that was a jumble
with no obvious system. He ran his finger down the page until
something caught his eye.

LEWIS MCLENNON: P&M—Flat 2. £1,000?

THE CLEANER: That's the one. Repeated
several times, decreasing amounts.

He followed the list to its end, and saw that she was right. If
it was Philip and Mekhala Hetherington, then they'd been paying Richard Glead every few months for the last year, but after

three identical payments, the amounts began to decrease. He looked at the rest of the list, which included lines like "Bridger's Finance—£3,000," "Sir Roland—£4,500," and "Cllr Cron—£1,200." All repeated at regular intervals.

> LEWIS MCLENNON: Interesting. Looking at the other entries, I'm thinking blackmail.

> THE CLEANER: Me too. And they were obviously struggling to pay.

Excitement thrummed through Lewis. Another breakthrough. Three potential suspects in the square itself—Mrs. Hildebrandt, the Hetheringtons, and Roshan Jones. The first two victims of Richard Glead, with a strong motive to commit murder; the third an unexpected connection to Linda that needed exploring.

Paulo Ram could have killed Richard and Linda, but then who shot him with what may have been his own weapon? The day in the pawnshop, he'd been guarded and agitated. Shouting at someone. What had he said? That he didn't know where something had come from, but it could lead to prison. Was that to do with the murders or some other facet of his work?

Blackmail was a nasty crime that often turned its victims into killers, but Lewis couldn't quite see either of the Hetheringtons killing Linda, and besides, they had an alibi for the night of Richard's murder. The same went for Brigitte Hildebrandt, but if blackmail was the motive, then the ledger gave them a whole host of other potential suspects.

Then there was Linda. She also had an alibi for Richard's murder, and getting a gun wouldn't have been easy. Was that where Paulo had come in? He could have given her a gun, no problem, but would he? It would be a pretty amateur move, all things considered, to give her a gun from his own shop, but even if he had, would he have helped her kill Richard, who was supposed to be his friend? And even if Linda *had* killed Richard, she couldn't have killed Paulo, so who did that leave?

Chaz said Richard had cheated on Linda more than once, for business. Perhaps Richard had seduced Mrs. Hildebrandt, to get her to part with her cash. But what motive would she have for killing Linda or Ram? Then there was Linda's mystery friend, the one Nathan had mentioned. If Linda had a boyfriend, he might have a motive to kill Richard, but not Linda, and certainly not Ram.

But Lewis couldn't shake the feeling that this was a clean-up operation. A small circle of dodgy people, three of them now dead and the fourth angry and confused. It wasn't a leap to think that Ram might have been involved in Richard's blackmail scheme, but Linda? Was she collateral damage in Richard's comeuppance, or had she been involved in his criminal enterprises from the start?

Maybe their killer was one of the people listed in Richard's ledger, but they still had to find out more about Linda. Her murder just didn't fit. Something had to connect her to the dead criminals in the case—something that went beyond being married to one. They just had to find out what it was.

40

Celeste

Celeste sat up in bed, arranged against the bank of lace-frilled pillows, and waited for Dixon to knock on her door. She'd heard the telephone ring a few minutes ago and had put her book down, waiting for news.

That was the thing about being old. You knew without being told which phone calls were business and which were pleasure, and none of her remaining friends or relatives called late.

"Come in, Dixon," she called when she heard him approach. He knocked anyway, just to be polite.

"That were the police," he said, without preamble. "Forensics have left, so Flat Ten's yours again."

"Good." Celeste nodded. "We'll get Audrey and Lewis in there tomorrow. Will you make the arrangements?"

"Aye."

"I wonder what they'll find."

"Mebbe nothing," said Dixon unhelpfully.

"But maybe something."

"Unlikely to find anything the police have missed. Whatever you think, they'll have done the job thoroughly."

"But the police won't tell us anything," she said. "So Audrey and Lewis may find something that will be useful for solving Linda's murder. I do so hate being kept in the dark."

"You don't mind when the boot's on the other foot."

"That's different," retorted Celeste. "That's out of necessity."

"Do you need anything else?" Dixon picked up her dressing gown from where it lay at the end of her bed.

"No, thank you, Dixon. I've everything I need. Goodnight, dear. Sleep well."

"Goodnight."

Celeste watched as he hung her dressing gown on the back of the door before closing it behind him. The only time he wasn't on duty was after she'd gone to bed, and when Audrey came in to clean, of course. An old-fashioned arrangement, really, like the family had had when she was a girl, but Dixon was too young to remember any of that. She'd have to take more care. It was too easy to take advantage when someone never complained.

She put her reading glasses back on, then picked up her book. She couldn't settle to it though, her mind wandering again to the unfortunate Mrs. Glead and the matter of Flat 10. She wondered if she'd struggle to lease the place, or whether demand would hold up in spite of a double murder.

Of course it would. It was London, after all.

The residents would be rattled of course, and she'd have to improve security for their collective peace of mind. Richard Glead had been a sorry lapse in judgement on her part, made when she was at her most vulnerable. She'd make sure that never happened again.

She closed the book again and returned it to the bedside table, along with her glasses. No more reading tonight. She kissed her fingertip and touched it to the silver-framed photo that stood beside her book.

"Night, Lenny," she said, then turned out the light.

Sleep came surprisingly quickly.

41

Audrey

Audrey slept deeply that night, exhausted by her panic attack and subsequent adrenaline crash. She'd arrived home drained and miserable, and frustrated that Mei had been right. Linda's death was raking up the past, and she could no longer pretend that it wasn't. And then there was the very real possibility that the killer was one of her neighbours. She'd shared Celeste's confidence that such a thing was impossible, but with everything she and Lewis had now discovered, her faith was undeniably shaken. She'd gone to bed feeling sick at the thought, but had fallen asleep quickly, thankfully too tired to dream.

She woke feeling better, however, and after a hot shower and a cup of tea, she curled up on the sofa for a morning of rest, relaxation, and some much-needed self-care.

An hour later, she was deep into a report on using protease enzymes to remove blood from fabric when her phone chirruped with a message, and fifteen minutes later, she was knocking on Lewis's door.

As he opened it, bleary-eyed, wearing a crumpled T-shirt and some baggy pyjama bottoms, she held up a set of keys.

"We're in."

"What?"

"Keys to number ten. Dixon just dropped them off. We're to report back when we're done."

He pushed his hair out of his eyes, immediately more alert.

"Give me ten minutes," he said. "Don't go in without me!"

She grinned and stepped inside. As she went to close the door, a movement in the garden caught her eye and she paused, peering into the shrubbery. Then a breeze rushed through, sending branches and leaves rippling, and she sighed, closing the door. She hated how easily she reverted to being jumpy.

She stood quietly in Lewis's hall, looking around the cramped space. The walls were a grubby magnolia and the corners full of cobwebs, while the floor could have done with a good mop. A jumble of coats hung above a shoe rack piled high with boots and trainers, a single pair of shiny black brogues perched on top. She focused on them. The rest of it made her itch.

Lewis returned in a few minutes, looking much more awake and wearing jeans and a clean, though equally creased T-shirt beneath a thick navy blue cardigan.

"I like your cardy," she said as they climbed the steps up to the Glead residence. Or what had been the Glead residence.

"It's not a cardy!" he said. "It's a . . ."

"A what?"

"A knitted jacket thing. Not a cardy."

They stopped outside and Audrey unlocked it, taking a deep breath before opening the door. They entered the flat, walking down the empty hall and past the lounge to the kitchen.

Although the morning light highlighted different aspects of the room, it was as blank as Audrey remembered. The white table and wooden chairs were in the same place, although the beer bottles, plate, and coin were gone. The kitchen counters were still clear, apart from the kettle and an empty fruit bowl. Had the police taken the fruit away? The window blind was still down a third of the way, and the floor showed no sign of what had occurred there. In fact, the only significant change was the absence of a dead body.

She couldn't help but be a bit regretful at the lack of blood-stains on the floor. The bullet that had killed Richard had been very efficient and tidy. There was dust on absolutely every-thing though, with grey smudges and smears across the surfaces. The window was covered in fingerprints, as were the oven, the kettle, and the fridge-freezer, humming quietly in the corner.

"Does taking fingerprints usually make this much mess?" she asked Lewis, who blinked, then looked around the room again.

"Oh. Those marks are from where they lift the prints off the surfaces. Dusting and then lifting with tape. Anything jumping out at you?"

"No, nothing."

They went through to the living room, and this time Audrey looked around carefully, laying the picture Lewis had painted in his notes over the scene in front of her. She took a deep breath, trying to distance herself from the image, then paused, sniffing.

She could just make out the faintest hint of a familiar fra-grance. An air freshener perhaps? Or aftershave? She sniffed again and a wave of sadness came over her. The lingering scent of Linda's perfume?

"So Linda was there?" She pointed to the end of the black leather sofa, then the little wooden coffee table just in front of it. "And her glass and plate there?"

Lewis read aloud from his phone.

"'Sitting on sofa, upright, head lolling to the right . . . Hands in lap, palms down, fingers curled . . . Knees together, tipping to the right, ankles twisted together . . . shoes left in hall. Sofa and chairs . . . very clean. One velvet cushion on chair. Coffee table—mahogany, shiny. Half a glass of water on a silver coaster, china side plate with pink roses and white crumbs. Handbag on floor next to sofa. Curtains drawn. Lamps on. No sign of rob-bery in living room. Very clean and tidy.'"

She stood on the rug in the centre of the room and rotated, viewing everything in turn. It was dominated by the sofa and the big TV in the corner. On the wall opposite were a couple of ugly paintings of hunting and shooting, similar to the ones in the office at Glead Antiques, that didn't go with the bland décor of the flat at all. Had Richard bought them in bulk? Two black leather easy chairs stood underneath, the arms covered with more fingerprint dust. Against the far wall stood a sideboard, bearing a framed wedding photo, a china figurine, and a lamp.

"This can't be right," she said, turning around. "They were here for, what? Two years? This can't be all the stuff they had. There's no books, no trinkets, no plants. Where's their stuff?"

"The police will have taken some things away," said Lewis, "but this is pretty much how I found it that night. It's like they were ready to do a flit any time."

"Maybe they were."

There weren't many soft furnishings, either. The curtains, made of a draping cream-coloured velvet, and the matching rug in the middle of the room were the only nod to decorating. There weren't even any cushions on the sofa.

"Cushions," she said. "What was your note about cushions?"

"Uh . . . 'One velvet cushion on chair.'"

"'On chair'? Not the sofa?"

"No, it was on the chair over there."

"Who buys one cushion?" she wondered. "You buy two, minimum, for either end of the sofa. What colour was it?"

"Beige. Like the rug. Maybe Linda was sitting on one?"

"Then why isn't it here?"

"Because the police took it away."

"Why would the police take two cushions?"

"Ah." Lewis nodded. "You think she was smothered."

"Maybe," she said. "But if Linda was sitting on one, the killer couldn't have smothered her with it. There should be one left, at least."

"They have to be thorough. Can you sit down? Where Linda was sitting? I'll see if I have to move the table to get to you."

"Um. Okay."

She sat uneasily in the place Lewis indicated while he walked around her, holding an imaginary cushion in his hands. Every now and then, he'd hold it up to her face, then put it down again, change position, and do it again, while she fought the urge to bat his hands away.

"Based on the way her body fell," he said eventually, "I think the killer had to be right in front of her. Standing over her. If I come at you from either side," he held up the imaginary cushion and moved his hands toward her face from her left, "you'll pull at my hands and the cushion, right?"

Audrey put her hands up, and even without a real cushion, she could feel panic rising as he got closer to her face. She grasped his wrists and tried to pull his hands away from her, but he was stronger than she'd anticipated and her breathing grew shallow as she tried to stay put so he could finish his experiment.

"Okay, that's good. Now drop your hands from that position. Straight down."

She did as she was told and her hands fell unevenly, to the left. They enacted it again from the right and her hands fell to the right. Only when he was right in front of her, his leg nudging against the coffee table, did her hands drop into her lap.

"Could the killer have rearranged her?" she asked, standing up the moment he'd dropped his invisible murder weapon. "Afterward?"

"Possibly," said Lewis. "To prevent the police from working out the angle or height of the killer."

"You'd have to have presence of mind for that, wouldn't you? It's not a spur-of-the-moment thing."

"No." He sounded thoughtful. "No, it isn't. And I don't understand why there were no signs of a struggle. She must have fought her killer? Like you just tried to. But her hands and nails looked clean."

"It's almost winter. Everyone's wearing long sleeves. Maybe even gloves."

"Maybe."

They went up the beige-carpeted stairs, discovering the same spare approach to decoration as in the rest of the flat. The landing was a blank canvas, an entirely magnolia space, the only exception the door to the fire escape, which was covered in fingerprints. The beds in both rooms had been stripped of pillows and linen, and the clothing in the wardrobes was disheveled. The police must have gone through every pocket and lining in search of clues.

The bathroom was in the same state as the rest of the flat. Clean, impersonal, and covered in various dusts and adhesive marks. The cabinet was empty, and Audrey assumed the police had taken everything inside away. Even the toilet cistern had been disturbed in their hunt for evidence.

"Now what do we do?" asked Lewis as they reconvened on the landing a few minutes later. "There's nothing here."

"Celeste's paying me to clean," said Audrey, "and she wants their stuff packed away. For Jane and Alf. So you can either help or—well, that's it, actually. I don't want to be alone in the crime scene, so you'll have to stay and help."

She was surprised to hear herself admit that out loud to him and even more surprised when he nodded.

"Okay. Tell me what to do."

42

Lewis

From that moment on, it was all business. They found a couple of suitcases in the cupboard under the stairs and Lewis set to packing up the Gleads' clothes while Audrey began to clean the bathroom. It didn't take her long.

While Lewis filled the suitcases and stacked them on the landing, Audrey dusted and polished the bedrooms to within an inch of their lives. The Gleads' vacuum cleaner was clean, the cylinder presumably emptied by the police, so she set about vacuuming the bedrooms, even convincing Lewis to help her move the wardrobes so she could check behind them.

Then Lewis hauled the suitcases downstairs while Audrey finished vacuuming the spare room before moving on to the landing, wiping all the fingerprint dust marks off the fire door before crouching down to do the small area with the vacuum tools. She turned the machine back on, but as soon as she put the attachment to the carpet, she stopped, slamming her hand down on the switch.

"What is it?" he asked, from halfway up the stairs.

She pointed to the floor. "What do you think this is?"

He sat down on the step.

"What am I looking at?"

She ran her hand over the carpet in front of the fire escape door and held it up. Flecks of brown dirt stuck to her palm.

"Soil?"

They used the torches on their phones to examine the carpet. The dirt wasn't all over, but in two patches going from the door to the top of the stairs, and they had to look closely to see it.

"I think someone's already hoovered it up," she said. "I can see where the carpet's discoloured, but there's barely anything there. It's so dry, though. It'd have been easy to get the rest off."

"The Forensics people might have done it," said Lewis. "They have special tools for sucking up trace material. Not the same as cleaning, I expect."

He stood and looked down on the marks from above, then put his back to the door. He moved forward, following the patches to the stairs and down.

"Footprints," he said, when he reached the bottom step. "When the police came to interview me the second time, DI Banham asked whether I had access to the street from my flat. He mentioned the upstairs fire escapes."

"Ours is the same," said Audrey. "You thinking Linda's killer came in this way?"

"Could be," he said, "but then why risk leaving via the front door? What if it was Richard's killer that came in this way? Everyone was so busy assuming it was Linda who killed him, no one bothered to ask how a different killer could have got in."

They pushed open the fire door and stood on the tiny gantry, looking down. A narrow strip of paving ran behind the building, separated from the street by iron railings and a neat box hedge.

"The spikes on those railings would make climbing over next to impossible," said Audrey. "But someone could have come into the square and snuck round the back. The police are obviously thinking the same—look."

She pointed to the railings, where traces of white powder were once again visible, then went inside to retrieve a different cleaning product and a duster.

When she was done, they followed the footprints down the hall, but instead of stopping at the kitchen, the prints carried on through to the living room.

"Well, this doesn't make any sense," said Lewis.

"They come out again," said Audrey. "They go all the way to the front door."

"Did they come in the front and leave through the fire escape? Or perhaps they're the Gleads' footprints, and not related at all?"

"Linda wouldn't have left them," said Audrey firmly. "They're new, I'm certain."

The marks were so faint, it was hard to tell anything useful, so Audrey vacuumed the stairs before starting in the kitchen. It didn't appear difficult, but to Lewis's eyes, she seemed remarkably diligent, scrutinising every mark and speck of dust before she removed it. He wondered whether the killer had really left no trace or whether the police had taken every scrap of evidence with them.

In the lounge, however, they caught another break. While Lewis was going through the sideboard, looking for anything the police might have left behind, Audrey began to clean the sofa. Lewis didn't think Linda's relatives would want the furniture, but Audrey said she couldn't bear the idea of leaving the forensic marks all over it, the signs of Linda's tragic demise plain for all to see.

She went to work with yet another cleaning product—an antibacterial leather cleaner, apparently—spraying and wiping until all dust and fingerprints were gone. But just when Lewis thought there could be nothing left to clean, she crouched down and began to wipe the bottom of the sofa too.

"Hey," she said, stopping. "Look at this."

He went over at once, dropping down beside her to look at where she was pointing.

Pale pink-brown marks on the front underside edge of the sofa, between the seat and the floor.

"What is it?"

"Not sure." She lay down on the carpet, her nose to the plinth board, and shined her torch onto it. "There's more under here, on the underside of the sofa."

"Just in front of Linda's seat," he said.

"Have you got a knife or something? I'll see if I can get it off."

Lewis went into the kitchen and returned with a small paring knife, which he passed to her along with an old receipt from his pocket. She slid the receipt underneath the sofa and scraped at the marks until little flakes fell onto the it. She slid it out again and put it on the table.

"Paint?" she said, poking it with the knife.

"Looks more like plastic." He stood in front of the sofa again, looking down at his feet. "Shoes. If you were standing in front of Linda, trying to hold her down, the tops of your shoes would be pressed up against the sofa. You might even push them under a little bit, to brace yourself."

She went to stand beside him, and he caught a hint of perfume as she moved to push her trainers beneath the bottom edge of the sofa.

"It's not much," she said, looking down. "But it's something."

He nodded.

"It's something."

43

Audrey

Audrey sat opposite Lewis at Celeste's dining table, Dixon beside her, while Celeste sat at the top, like a head of state. Cake and sandwiches had been laid out, along with two pots of tea, and while Dixon and Audrey were drinking regular breakfast tea, Lewis had poured himself a cup of Celeste's Earl Grey, and was now glaring at it as if it had personally offended him.

"Footprints going from the fire escape to the front door," Celeste repeated, looking thoughtful. "Or the other way around. Large footprints, would you say?"

"Hard to say," said Audrey. "There was barely a trace. But it was easier to see the discolouration on the landing than by the front door."

Celeste glanced at Dixon.

"And the marks on the sofa you think were made by the killer? Someone wearing light brown shoes?"

"It makes sense," said Lewis. "From the position. More sense than the footprints."

"Why do you say that?" asked Dixon.

"The footprints went to the lounge, not the kitchen, which suggests they were from Linda's killer, not Richard's. But the front door was open after Linda died, meaning that if Audrey's right, the killer came in the back and left in a hurry via the front—very risky, and for no obvious reason. If they came in the front and left via the back, then why not shut the front door behind you and reduce the chances of being caught?"

"That is a puzzle," agreed Celeste.

"One other thing," Lewis went on. "You should give the gate logs to the police. Someone could have got into the square and accessed the fire escape that way."

There was a small pause during which Dixon cleared his throat and Celeste took a sip of her tea.

"I think we've already supplied the logs to the police," said Celeste eventually. "Haven't we, Dixon?"

Dixon nodded.

"What?" said Lewis, his annoyance evident. "When? Did it not occur to you to give them to us too? We had to ask."

But Celeste merely shrugged.

"Dixon and I had already looked them over. There was no one on them who shouldn't be, so we assumed the killer had got in another way."

Now it was Audrey's turn to frown.

"But . . . when I was here the morning after they found Richard's body, you said there was no need to worry. That Richard must have invited his killer in himself. Did you know then that the killer had bypassed security?"

"That's rather a strong term, Audrey. And at the time, I was simply supposing. We've never had cause to check the logs before, and I'd quite forgotten until the police asked me."

Audrey looked at Dixon, and from the way Lewis was also watching him, she knew they were thinking the same thing. That Dixon never forgot anything.

"I admit, I wasn't too concerned about the death of Richard Glead," said Celeste, "and so I didn't think too much about it. That was an oversight and I apologise. As you no doubt saw, however, there wasn't anything useful on them."

Lewis opened his mouth to speak, but Audrey quickly kicked him under the table. He glared at her, and she pressed her lips together tightly while keeping her eyes on her tea, trying to tell him to keep his mouth shut. Celeste would be upset if she knew they were looking at the residents. They couldn't tell her that the killer might be one of them. Not yet, anyway.

Lewis scowled but seemed to get the message, stuffing a cheese sandwich in his mouth, which stopped him from saying anything more.

"Tell me what else you've found out," said Celeste brightly. "This third murder rather complicates things, I imagine?"

"Definitely," agreed Audrey, also taking another sandwich. "We think we've eliminated Chaz Shaw, which means we're looking at the possibility of an unknown person." She looked at Lewis. "You thinking the same?"

He nodded.

"We found a ledger in Richard's office. We think he was a blackmailer, which gives us a list of potential suspects. We've got a few leads there, which we're going to follow up. He also seems to have been dealing in leverage art pieces, presumably for criminals, and we have another list, but we don't know what it refers to yet. The other possibility is that there's more than one killer. Linda killed Richard, Paulo killed Linda, and someone else killed Paulo."

Celeste raised an eyebrow.

"That's rather a lot of murderers."

"I don't know what's more likely," he said. "That there are two or more killers, or that there's one person on a killing spree."

Audrey saw Dixon and Celeste exchange another look. Perhaps they were thinking this was more than they'd bargained for when they'd employed her and Lewis to do this.

"Don't worry," she said, to reassure them. "We'll figure it out. I feel like we're getting close to something."

"Good," said Celeste. "I'm determined to have justice for Linda. I feel so sorry for her family, and it quite broke my heart when you told me about that little dog."

Lewis sighed.

"What is it with women and little dogs?"

Audrey was about to respond that it wasn't just women, but men too, when a thought occurred to her.

"Lewis," she said, after a moment. "The dog . . . Do you remember you said Nathan Roper knew about Muffin? That Linda was going to adopt him?"

"Yes?"

"Did he say how he knew?"

"Not specifically," said Lewis, shrugging. "But he worked with her for long enough. Knew the dog."

"But Mei and I were with Linda when she decided. We were talking about the shelter and she said Richard was allergic, so she'd never been able to adopt, and she sort of . . . came to the realisation while we were talking. If Linda only decided to adopt Muffin on Friday evening, and she was dead by midnight, when did she tell Nathan?"

"I . . . don't know." He looked thoughtful. "Pam knew. She said Linda called her that same night. Maybe she told him? He did already know she was dead."

"Val, not Pam, and yeah, could be. But that might be suspicious too. Val said she'd tell Nathan when she saw him on the Wednesday, and you caught him on his way to work. Would she have rung Nathan at home to tell him the news? If it were me, I'd have waited to tell him in person. Wouldn't you?"

Lewis clicked his tongue.

"Ye-e-es. Occam's razor though. The straightforward explanation is most likely the right one."

"I'll call Val anyway," said Audrey, nodding. "Just to be sure. If there's a chance he and Linda were closer than he made out, it would be useful to know."

"Okay," he said. "Nathan was pretty nervy, now that I think about it. Could be suspicious. Good idea."

"Well," said Celeste, putting her napkin on the table, "it sounds like you've got plenty to be getting on with. You've both been working very hard, especially around your other commitments. I'm most appreciative." She got to her feet and began to move away from the table. "I'm off for a little lie-down. As it's Friday tomorrow, Dixon will transfer some money into your bank accounts for the work so far. And if you need any assistance from us, just let us know."

Audrey jumped up and grabbed Celeste's cane, which she'd left propped against the table, and handed it to her with a smile. "Thanks for lunch. It was helpful to talk things out."

"Any time, my dear," said Celeste, beaming at her, all antagonism forgotten. "I do find it helps to speak the problem out loud. Organises one's thoughts. Perhaps you could drop by again on Sunday afternoon? Let me know how things progress."

They were dismissed.

44

Lewis

They took the stairs together quietly, and when they were safely out in the fresh air, Audrey took a deep breath.

"Phew," she said. "That was a bit awkward, wasn't it?"

Lewis was equally relieved to be out of there, but annoyed, too.

"Only because you stopped me from telling her about our suspects. What was that about?"

"Celeste employed us to investigate because she thought the police would only look in the square. If she knew we were doing the same, she might decide to take us off the case."

He opened his mouth, then closed it again. He hadn't thought of that.

"Besides," she went on, "it would upset her. She's convinced no one in the square could have done it. You know how much Richard Glead bothered her. It's her safe haven, as well as ours. If she thought there was more than one monster in Marchfield, she'd be devastated."

Lewis looked around the square, taking in the picture-perfect Georgian mews and the small but immaculate garden. He'd lived there so long, he'd forgotten how he'd felt when he'd first moved in. Lucky, certainly, and more than a little grateful to be given somewhere so nice to retreat to and lick his wounds. He'd been awed, too, unable to believe he was allowed to live in that perfect picture. It *was* a safe haven. When had he started to take it for granted?

Audrey clearly didn't.

"You're right," he said, and she looked surprised. "It was a good call. Although I thought you wanted us to be taken off the case. What changed?"

"I just think we should try to get to the bottom of things before the police do. If Richard was blackmailing people here, then things could get ugly. The last thing Celeste will want is people's dirty linen being hung out in public." She put her hands in her pockets. "Shall we go and find Roshan? He should be working today. Might as well get him ticked off while we're both free."

"All right."

They began to follow the little path that wound its way through the garden.

"We need to talk to Mrs. Hildebrandt and the Hetheringtons about their unusual activity in the gate logs," he said as they walked. "And about their dealings with Richard. It's clear they both have motive, so means and opportunity will be key. Also Victor, about his nighttime excursions."

"Divide and conquer?" she suggested. "You take Philip. Weirdly, I think he likes you. And I'll take Mrs. H. Then we can tackle Victor together."

"All right," said Lewis. "Wait, how do you know Philip likes me? And why 'weirdly'?"

She shrugged.

"How did you meet Celeste? I've been meaning to ask."

He hesitated before answering, unsure how much he wanted to say, and aware that she hadn't answered his second question. It disconcerted him.

"My editor introduced us," he said at last. "I was renting a place in Canary Wharf, everything very modern and clean. But when my third book tanked, I needed to downsize in a hurry, and she suggested I needed a change of scene. Somewhere quieter, more characterful. She and the van Durens were old friends, and Flat Five was standing empty. I didn't think I'd be able to afford it, but the rent was weirdly low. It wasn't until later I found out they kept the rents low on purpose."

"Celeste told DS Larssen that she and Leonard wanted good people, not rich people. Makes you wonder how the Gleads got in, but I suppose everyone makes mistakes."

Lewis stopped dead.

"That's a good point," he said. "Celeste does background checks on all the tenants before agreeing to a lease."

"Does she?" Audrey frowned. "I didn't know that."

"Yes. We should ask her about the Gleads. And about Victor." A gleam came into his eye. "We could ask her about all the residents. Tell her it's to help us exonerate them."

"Calm down, Big Brother," said Audrey. "Celeste won't allow security cameras in the square, and she didn't even volunteer the gate logs. She's hardly going to share that kind of information."

"I don't see why not. Why pay us to find this stuff out when she could just tell us?"

"To protect people's privacy. Besides, if there was anything obvious in there, she wouldn't need to pay us at all. Anyway, go back to you getting the flat."

"You're very nosy for someone who cares about privacy, aren't you?"

"I am, yes. Continue."

He snorted, but continued anyway.

"That's all there is to it. Celeste's very interested in true crime, and we used to have coffee every so often and just talk. She's lived an interesting life. Traveled a lot. She and Leonard couldn't have children, so they kept their lives full of other things. Celeste says they collected people. That's what we are, I think. The residents. People Celeste has collected."

Audrey looked at him for a moment, her head tilted to one side.

"You're right," she said slowly. "What a weird thought."

They walked on in silence.

45

Celeste

Celeste glanced up at Dixon, who was standing beside her at the picture window, then back down to the square, where Audrey and Lewis were taking the long way through the garden. They watched as the pair wound their way down the path that curved through the lawn and flower beds, disappearing behind the shrubbery that concealed the maintenance shed.

"What on earth are they doing?"

"Looking for someone," said Dixon. "Roshan."

"I suppose he's the only one they haven't spoken to yet. What did you make of the substance they found?"

"Don't know. Strange place, bottom of the sofa."

"Yes. A good find."

Down in the square, Audrey and Lewis reemerged, walking past the front gate and following the path around the edge of the garden. The wind blew through the rowan trees and stag's horns, deep in the blazing last throes of autumn, dropping fresh leaves over Roshan's carefully tended garden.

"They were holding back, you know," said Dixon.

"Why should they do that?"

"You know why."

"Because they think it was someone in the square." She nodded. "They're being diligent. I like that."

Dixon snorted.

"Liar."

She smiled in spite of herself.

"Not at all. I'd have been disappointed if they'd taken my word for it. Gratified, but disappointed. I was hoping to avoid them uncovering a few of our residents' . . . quirks, shall we say? But I see now that was a mistake. They must be thorough, and far better them than the police."

"Quirks?" She could hear his raised eyebrow.

"Eccentricities, then. Who knows? Perhaps it will even bring them together."

"Ever the optimist."

"Of course. Pessimism is so dull." Celeste turned away from the window and began to pace, slowly, around her gallery nook. Her physiotherapist had been most insistent that she take it slow. "This Roper person sounds rather suspect, doesn't he?"

"Do you want me to go along? Keep an eye on 'em?"

She thought for a moment.

"No, I don't think so. Based on what happened with Mr. Shaw, I think they can handle it, don't you?"

"Audrey, certainly. Not sure about Lewis."

Celeste chuckled.

"When this is over, you might need to give Lewis a few lessons. For his own good, of course."

"I'll say. No instinct for self-preservation, that one." With one last look at the greying sky, Dixon left the window. "What do you want for your tea?"

"Salmon, I think. Thank you, dear."

Dixon nodded and crossed the room to the kitchen, where he closed the door. A moment later, she heard the faint sound of the radio and smiled. He never had it on too loudly, in case he couldn't hear her call. She really had been blessed when Leonard found Dixon.

After a few more turns about the room, she settled herself back in her armchair and, resisting the urge to take her binoculars from the secret drawer in the tea table, picked up her book and glasses.

She was spending altogether too much time watching her tenants these days, a habit she'd got into while keeping an eye on the deplorable Richard Glead. But there was no need for spying anymore, and the sooner she stopped, the better.

Although, if she'd learned anything over the years, it was that habits are hard to break.

46

Audrey

Roshan Jones was not in Marchfield Square. Audrey and Lewis searched the gardens and in and around the flower beds, the trees, and the shrubbery, then checked that he wasn't holed up in the shed the van Durens had discreetly positioned behind some hedging in the corner of the square, but Roshan was nowhere to be found.

"Now what?" asked Lewis, sitting down on one of the empty benches and looking up at her. The Hetheringtons sat together on the other side of the courtyard, wrapped in blankets and talking quietly, enjoying what remained of the afternoon sunshine.

It was half three in the afternoon, and the grass was already starting to glisten with the damp of an approaching mist. A fresh fall of dry red leaves lay across the lawn and paths, while the tall grasses in the borders whispered incessantly in the wind, soothing with the promise of cosy evenings inside.

"Now we ask Celeste for his address," said Audrey. "If he lives nearby, we can pop over."

As it turned out, they didn't need to ask anyone for help, because as they headed back across the courtyard to ring Celeste's doorbell, they spotted Roshan letting himself out of Captain Gordon's flat, holding his tool bag.

"Oh! Hi, Roshan," said Audrey, making a beeline for him and trying to sound breezy, but one look at him changed her tone. "Are you all right?"

Roshan did not look all right. His face was ashen and his eyes were bloodshot, but he smiled weakly.

"Yes, thank you, Audrey. Are you going to see Celeste? I've just given the Captain's boiler a service."

"No, not Celeste," she said. "We were looking for you."

"Me?" Roshan looked over at Lewis, and seemed surprised to see him, standing with Audrey, in the place they both lived. He closed the door behind him. "Is something wrong?"

"No, nothing like that," said Audrey. "We just wanted to see how you were. After Linda."

Roshan's face did something odd, a sort of half-frown, half-crumpling motion, which he somehow pulled back into a neutral expression.

"How do you mean?" he asked, lips trembling.

"I know you and Linda were friends," she said gently. Roshan looked alarmed, so she added, "You went to church together, right?"

"Oh." He nodded, pressing his lips together tightly for a moment before speaking again. "We knew each other from church, yes. We were friendly. It's very sad, what's happened."

He began to walk away, his shoulders tense and the tool bag knocking against the side of his leg. Audrey rushed to catch up, and Lewis followed.

"Roshan . . ." she said, touching his arm. He stopped and turned around, his face clouded and his eyes full. "Do you think it's true? That Linda killed Richard?"

A flash of fire erupted behind Roshan's eyes.

"No, of course not. She wouldn't hurt a fly."

"Then why would anyone want to kill her?"

Roshan gasped and his lip quivered again, although whether in anger or distress, Audrey couldn't tell.

"Why are you asking me?"

Audrey took a deep breath.

"Because I don't understand it," she said in a rush. She felt they had to come clean with Roshan in a way they hadn't with anyone else. "Linda was kind and gentle, and even if Richard was shady as hell, she wasn't, right? And she was going to get a dog. She told me, on Friday, just before . . . Why would anyone want to hurt her? It doesn't make sense."

Roshan's face softened at once.

"No, it doesn't," he said, dropping the tool bag onto the gravel and sitting down heavily on one of the benches. "She was kind, you're right. My mother's been ill and Linda was always ready to listen. We were friends." His eyes filled with tears, but he wiped an arm across them before continuing. "She took me to see that dog once. Muffin. Said he never got any visitors, and it made him sad. Silly name for a dog, I told her. Imagine shouting it in the park. He'd be embarrassed. But she just laughed at me and said dogs didn't get embarrassed." He shook his head and swallowed. "She was a woman of faith. She would never have hurt anyone."

His voice cracked and he put his head in his hands.

"I'm so sorry," Audrey said, sitting down next to him. "Did you talk to her? After Richard, I mean?"

"I didn't get a chance," he mumbled. "We only spoke here, or at church, but she texted me to say she had been released without charge and was home, safe and sound. I was so relieved. We arranged to talk on Saturday—I came in specially to see her, but . . ."

"Who do you think killed Richard?" asked Lewis. She shot him an annoyed look, but Roshan barely seemed to notice.

"Who's to say?" He shrugged. "He had so many crooked friends. It could have been any of them. And he was swindling people too. Ladies. Perhaps one of them."

Audrey and Lewis exchanged glances.

"Ladies?" Audrey repeated. "Like a scam?"

"Fake investments, I think. Linda was very upset about it. Richard spent lots of time with rich older ladies. One of his friends was involved too. He told her not to be jealous because it was just business, but Linda wasn't jealous. She thought it was cruel to the women, and that he would end up in prison." He pulled a cloth handkerchief from his pocket and wiped his nose. "He should have done."

"Did you report it?" asked Lewis. "To the police, I mean."

"I tried, but they just referred me to the fraud hotline, who said they couldn't do anything if I wasn't the victim."

"Fraud makes up around thirty-six percent of all reported crime," said Audrey, remembering a stat from an old college lecture. "I expect they're quite busy. If Linda wasn't involved, though, it makes no sense for anyone to kill her. They'd have left her alone."

"But there was someone," said Roshan. "Someone Linda thought was watching them. She didn't know who it was or why they were watching, but she was frightened. Richard said she was imagining things. It seems that she was not."

"Watching them where?" asked Audrey.

"In the square, at his shop, all over. The only place she felt safe was at the Dogs' Home. I asked her to go to the police but she wouldn't. Said Richard would kill her."

"Watching her or Richard?" asked Lewis. "Or both?"

Now Roshan noticed him, and he looked up from the bench with narrowed eyes.

"Both, she said. But it was him who was the crook, not Linda. She wasn't like him, or his friends."

"Did she talk about his friends?"

"Not really, except to say that Richard was worse after poker nights. He always lost, you see. She thought he would be better if they weren't around so much." He sat up. "Why are you asking me this? You didn't know Linda, not really. Why do you care?"

Lewis took a step back, but Audrey flushed with embarrassment.

"Celeste," she said, and Lewis looked at her in horror. "Celeste never believed it was suicide, and now she wants us to find out who killed Linda. She wants justice."

Lewis threw his hands up in annoyance, but Roshan seemed strangely reassured.

"Oh, Celeste," he sighed. "She thinks she can right all the world's wrongs. Who does she think killed Linda, then?"

"We don't know," said Lewis, glaring at Audrey, "but we're going to do our best to find out."

47

Lewis

"I just don't see why you felt the need to tell him!" Lewis complained as they watched Roshan walk off down the garden, toward the shed. "Or why you didn't consult me before doing it. He could be the killer and you just told him we were investigating him!"

"Shush," she said, nodding toward the Hetheringtons, on the other side of the lawn. "They'll hear you."

It was starting to get dark, the sky thick with clouds, and tendrils of mist were starting to appear over the grass. He stared at her, still angry, and she sighed. "All right, I'm sorry. But we were giving him the third degree. What was I supposed to say?"

"I don't know. How about literally *anything else?*"

"It doesn't matter anyway," she said. "He's clearly not the killer. He couldn't fake that grief."

"Killers have regret too, you know."

"We all have regrets," she muttered. "Like agreeing to investigate a murder with the most annoying person on the planet."

"I heard that."

They stood in silence, watching as the Hetheringtons got ready to go inside, Philip closing his sketchbook and zipping up his pencil case, while his wife—Mekhala, was it?—folded up his blanket. As they set off toward their flat, they both waved at Audrey and Lewis.

"When are you going to talk to them?" asked Audrey, waving back.

"I don't know. I didn't get anything out of Philip last time, so we need something more concrete to use. What about Mrs. Hildebrandt?"

"Softly, softly with her, I think," said Audrey. "I'm not sure what we've achieved this afternoon, apart from confirming what Manny overheard: that Linda thought someone was watching her."

"You may have ruled Roshan out, but I haven't," said Lewis firmly. "Don't look at me like that—he's a suspect. If he was in love with Linda, he had motive for killing Richard, and if she then rejected him, he had motive for killing her, too."

"Four suspects is worse than three," she pointed out. "And that's not including Richard's other victims. Judging by his ledger, there might be quite a few."

"Then we work on eliminating them. We still have three other suspects to talk to. We can't rule out there being two or even three murderers. It's messy, but possible. There are differences between Richard's murder and Linda's murder—differences in terms of access and entry, choice of weapon . . ."

They stood in silence, watching the sun as it sank behind the London skyline. An idea struck him.

"Hey, fancy a bit of late-night shadowing?"

"Pardon?"

"Shadowing. Following. We'll stake out the square this evening, and the minute we see any of our suspects leave, we follow them. See what we can find out. No one's been honest with us when we've asked, so let's stop asking."

She bit her lip and looked around the square, her gaze coming to rest on Flat 10.

"All right," she said. "I'd have been disappointed if there wasn't a stakeout at some point, and you're right. No one's helping. Let's do it."

They made their plans in the creeping darkness of the garden before parting company and heading home.

A stakeout, Lewis thought, and he couldn't help but smile. Things were getting real now.

48

Audrey

Audrey sat in the living room, her laptop balanced on the arm of the sofa. She hadn't changed into her slobs, and was still wearing her trainers, so she'd be ready to go the minute she got the message. The lights were on low, to make sure she noticed as soon as her phone lit up with a text from Lewis.

She switched to the browser tab she'd been saving about Manx Angels. They were the calling card of a Cold War assassin allegedly responsible for the deaths of at least a dozen people in the sixties and seventies. A silver coin featuring St. Michael slaying the dragon had been left at the scene of each killing, which experts thought signified the assassin's belief that they were a force for good. No one knew who the killer worked for; the victims came from all sides of the Iron Curtain, and all known agencies denied ordering the hits. The only thing appearing to connect the victims, beside their involvement in espionage, was their profiles. Each one was a perpetrator of violence, torture, and other, worse actions against captured enemy agents. The killer had been christened the Avenging Angel because of the coin and the despicability of the victims, but had disappeared without trace in the 1980s and was presumed dead, the calling card never seen at the scene of any crime ever again.

Although not in the league of the Angel's other victims, Richard Glead would fit the profile. The only question was how the Angel would know about him, and why, if it was the same person, would they kill Paulo Ram with the same weapon and not leave their calling card?

Audrey thought through the list of Marchfield residents for possible candidates. Philip and Victor would have been too young for the earliest Angel kills, whereas the Captain would have been just about old enough. Captain Gordon, a former sniper with what now seemed to Audrey to be interrogation skills. Could he have killed Richard Glead and set this whole chain of events in motion? Would he?

Then there was Mrs. Hildebrandt's beau, Fraser. If Mrs. H was one of Richard's scam victims, and Fraser had a track record of murder . . . well, what was one more when it came to the woman you loved?

But, of course, the whole thing could be a misdirection. Someone who'd read about the Angel and thought the coin might put the police off their track.

Her phone lit up.

> MEI CHEN: Home late tonight. Having a drink with Sofia to discuss the case. How's your investigation going?

Audrey smiled. Nice try, Mei.

> AUDREY BROOKS: Slow. No one's talking to us. How's Sofia getting on? I assume if you're meeting, she's got something to report?

She waited while the three dots appeared, then disappeared, then appeared again, then disappeared again. She laughed out loud and put down her phone, wondering how long it would take Mei to come up with an answer.

It was a full two minutes before her phone lit up again, but her grin faded when she realised it was Lewis.

FLAT 5 GUY: Victor's on the move. Side gate.

She slammed her laptop shut, grabbed her phone and the coat she'd left on the end of the sofa, and exited the flat at speed, cursing the time it took to lock the front door behind her. She hurried down the steps into the courtyard, her breath making little clouds in front of her, and saw Lewis waiting by the side gate. He was holding it open, leaning out into the street, no doubt to keep Victor in sight.

She ran along the path, the antique lamps turning the mist into a warm orange smoke. The rustle of leaves overhead blended with the ever-present blare of London traffic. The sound she now recognised as home.

"Hey," she said when she reached him.

"Hey." He kept his voice low. "Just giving Victor a few more paces . . . and we're good."

He slipped through the gate and she followed, pausing to slow the gate closing and silence its telltale clang. She spotted Victor up ahead, walking quickly, and she and Lewis fell into step behind him, trying to keep enough distance between them without losing him in the fog.

"Mei's out with Larssen tonight," she said, trying to speak quietly but loud enough that Lewis could hear her over the steady stream of traffic passing down the road. "I think they're using the case as an excuse to get to know each other."

"Oh?" said Lewis, his eyes still on Victor. "Why doesn't she just ask her out?"

"They had a date, once upon a time, but didn't hit it off. This is a lower-risk strategy for a second attempt."

Victor took a right, heading in the direction of the Embankment, and they hastened after him, waiting at the corner to give him a chance to gain some distance while still remaining in sight.

"Low risk," said Lewis, staring into the fog. "How romantic."

"Romance is just another word for lies," said Audrey. "Better to go in with your eyes open. Then you don't end up married to a man like Richard Glead."

"You think Mei's judgement is as bad as Linda's?"

"No! Just . . . you get burned. You learn what's really important, and it isn't pink roses and Rolls-Royces."

They started walking again, keeping the River Thames on their left. The mist was heaviest over the river, and the golden lights along the banks made Audrey feel instantly Christmassy. Lewis said nothing more, his eyes fixed on the man ahead. She wondered when he'd last been on the dating scene. He was quite nice-looking, when he wasn't frowning or saying something stupid, which was admittedly most of the time, but she was sure he'd have no trouble getting dates if he wanted them.

He must have felt her eyes on him. He glanced at her.

"What?"

"Nothing." She squinted into the gloom. "You're sure that's him, right? I can barely make him out."

"Of course I'm sure," he said, but sped up anyway, and soon Audrey could see that it was indeed Victor and that he was carrying a bag.

They followed him over the Albert Bridge junction, dodging through traffic in their attempt to keep him in view, and on past the Chelsea Church, toward Battersea Bridge, where the bright lights of the queuing traffic blinded them. He turned right at the bridge, heading up Beaufort Street, but now he slowed his pace, and they had to slow too.

"Where on earth is he going?" asked Lewis when they'd been walking for almost fifteen minutes. "We must be close, surely, or he'd have got a bus. Man of his age."

"Maybe he likes the walk," she said. "He's hardly old, and it's not even been a mile yet."

They trailed him all the way up to the Fulham Road, where he turned left and walked past the picture house, but then suddenly, in the time it took them to cross the road without getting run over, Victor vanished.

"What the . . ." Lewis stopped dead. "Where did he go? He was just here!"

They hurried to where Victor had been standing a moment ago, a small stretch of pavement between an estate agent's, a bar, and a burger place with a queue of shivering diners. Lewis ran down the road a few metres but came back shaking his head.

"He must have gone in somewhere. Gone for a burger, do we think? Or for a drink at"—he read the name on the bar—"Proud Maggie's?"

"Can't see Victor in a drag club, can you? I'll check the burger place."

But when she slipped past the queue for Duke's Burgers and had a scout around inside, Victor was nowhere in sight.

"He's not in there. We lost him."

"Damn," said Lewis, sounding truly angry. "I thought we were doing well, but he must have spotted us and given us the slip."

"I hope not," she said as they began to walk back the way they'd come. "It'll make things hellish awkward at the Marchfield Christmas party this year."

They were halfway back down Beaufort Road when Lewis finally piped up.

"What Christmas party?"

49

Lewis

"I've been thinking about the coin," said Audrey, as they walked back along the Embankment. It was still early, and a steady flow of people appeared and disappeared from the mist, while the lights from the traffic reflected off the glistening roads. Sirens echoed in the distance, and the damp, oily scent of the Thames, mixed with smoke and exhaust fumes, filled the air.

"Yeah?" said Lewis, only half listening. As they'd walked back down Beaufort Street, a honk behind them had made him turn, and he'd seen a taxi overtaking a slow-moving car. He hadn't paid it much attention at first, but as they'd progressed down the wide and largely residential street, he'd grown increasingly aware of the steadiness of one set of headlights behind them, the car staying far enough back to remain half-shrouded in the fog but close enough that he could feel its presence. By the time they reached Battersea Bridge, Lewis was sure they were being followed.

"It wasn't an antique," Audrey went on, "so why did he have it? But if it was a calling card, then why was it at Richard's murder but not at Paulo's?"

"Just because they were killed with the same gun, it doesn't necessarily mean they were killed by the same person. I don't think the Angel's got anything to do with it. He's either very old or very dead by now."

They waited at the crossing, and Lewis risked another glance behind. A line of cars waited at the lights to turn left, the fog obscuring all but the front car, while the vehicles in the second lane trundled on over the bridge. As they crossed the road, Lewis caught a glimpse of a silver bonnet waiting to turn but when the lights changed, and the traffic began to flow again, the only cars driving past were taxis and the silver car was nowhere to be seen.

He breathed out, the air puffing in front of him.

"Are you all right?"

She was watching him, her expression one of concern. He considered telling her about the car, then remembered her panic attack the previous day.

"I'm fine. Look, don't worry about the coin. It could have been Richard's lucky poker charm, or else someone gave it to him. It's natural to think everything means something, but people are messy. There will be bits that don't fit."

He was glad when they neared the square, but as they turned onto Pickering Lane, Audrey slowed her pace.

Up ahead, just visible through the fog, a black figure in a motorcycle helmet stood outside the side gate to the square. They stopped walking, instinctively pressing themselves against the wall of a nearby block of flats to avoid being seen.

"Courier, maybe," said Lewis, checking his watch. Half eight. "Or food delivery."

They crept forward a few steps until they were just yards from the railings, but froze when they heard the faint beep of the gate. Then came the familiar clunk of the lock disengaging and the person in the helmet leaned down and reached through.

When the courier withdrew, they were holding a fat cardboard tube about half a metre long. As the gate closed, the courier walked off, cradling the tube like a baby, but instead of getting onto a motorbike, they walked further down the road and got into a car parked on the street. Through the back

window, they could just make out the driver taking off the helmet before starting the car and driving off into the mist.

Lewis looked at Audrey. "Who wears a bike helmet to drive
a car?"

"Someone who doesn't want to be recognised."

"Wonder who they were collecting from."

"Didn't you notice? The way they reached down to accept
the tube? There's only one person it could be."

Philip Hetherington.

"Payment for services rendered, possibly?" He grimaced.
"Looks like I'll need to talk to them sooner rather than later.
You're working all day tomorrow?"

"Afraid so," she said, with a hint of resignation. Was she
starting to prefer their investigation to her cleaning work? "I
had to rearrange Celeste in favour of another client, but I'll
call the Dogs' Home before the end of the day. Check with
Val about Nathan Roper. I'm sure you're right about it being
nothing, but I'd like to cross that niggle off the list before I talk
to Mrs. H."

"All right. I'll see what I can get out of Philip. This doesn't
look good for them, does it? And we should look through Richard's ledger again, see if we can identify any more victims."

"I can do that."

Lewis was relieved to get home and lock the door behind him.
He needed to sit down in his chair and make notes—get it
all out of his head—then he could focus properly on what
came next.

He wrote all night, the fictional case organising his thoughts
on the real one. Richard's complicated criminal life and Linda's
simple innocent one created two jarring lines of enquiry, and he
needed to work out where they intersected.

Harding looked at the board and its neat row of photographs. Four connected people, three of whom were dead
and the other one out of the frame.

It was easy to assume Ricky and Bull were killed by
the same person—same MO, same motives—but something wasn't sitting right. Lindsey's death just didn't fit.

The most logical explanations were that Lindsey had
been killed for her part in the Speen Investment scam, or
else that she'd shot Ricky and been killed as payback by
Bull. But if the former was true, then why wasn't she killed
in the same way? And if the latter was true, then how had
Bull ended up shot with the same weapon?

Had Lindsey planted the weapon on Bull before she
died? It would be a neat way of misdirecting the police to
a likely suspect while also exonerating yourself and taking
control of a lucrative business. Get rid of all the bully boys
who've made your life a misery for years and finally get
what you're owed.

The only other possibility was that there were two different killers with two different motives and Lindsey Speen
had created her own dangerous situation, outside of the
one her husband had involved her in. How likely was that?

Lewis stopped typing, surprised at what he'd written. Had
someone planted the gun at Ram's after Richard's murder? It
wasn't impossible.

LEWIS MCLENNON: Hey, remember the
gun we thought had been sold from Ram's
pawnshop? What if it wasn't taken from
there, but *put* there instead?

THE CLEANER: ???

LEWIS MCLENNON: Supposing the killer
planted the gun in Ram's shop, knowing he'd

be looked at by the police? But Ram spots it
before the police find out about him, and tries
to get rid of it. There was a space in the gun
cabinet and we heard Ram telling someone
he didn't know where "it" came from but he
wasn't going down for it. It's a leap, but it
could explain a few things.

THE CLEANER: That makes a lot of sense!
Might also explain how he ended up killed
with it. Everyone thought Linda killed Richard,
but she was dead and the police had searched
her flat top to bottom, so Ram couldn't plant
the gun there. But hide it in Glead Antiques, and
if the police find it, they'll think Linda stashed it
there when the coast was clear. Maybe the killer
was also searching Glead Antiques, or else
Ram disturbed someone else who shouldn't be
there, and the gun was to hand . . .

LEWIS MCLENNON: I like this idea.

THE CLEANER: You know I don't actually
think Linda stashed it there, right? I still don't
think she killed Richard.

He put his phone down and turned back to the computer.
He disagreed with her about Lindsey. Linda. He'd never seen
a reason to discount her, especially now. Richard was up to his
neck in criminal activity and seeing other women too, and Linda
had known all about it. Just because she was a victim in one way,
didn't mean she couldn't be a perpetrator in another, and in fact,
it would make the whole thing *more* logical, not less. Audrey
would realise it in the end. They just needed more evidence.

He returned to his writing, fingers poised over the keyboard. He was enjoying having someone to bounce ideas off. Once upon a time, he'd been able to talk things through with his agent or his editor, but after his last two books had flopped so spectacularly, he'd become reluctant to talk to anyone, worried they'd be able to see what he couldn't, namely, why it had all gone so horribly wrong.

Audrey was different. He had nothing whatsoever to prove to a cleaner, even if she did have brains, and she thought before she spoke too, which was refreshingly rare. Yes, that's what she was. Refreshing. His life had become stale and he hadn't even noticed. No wonder he hadn't had a decent idea in years.

He cracked his knuckles. Where was he? Ah yes.

He wrote.

50

Audrey

Audrey also stayed up late, examining the pictures Lewis had sent her of Richard Glead's ledger while she waited for Mei to get back from her not-date.

Even with the strange behaviour of Victor and the Hetheringtons, she was sure the killer couldn't be a resident. She looked on them as a family of sorts, bonded by appreciation for the safe space of Marchfield Square, and the debt they owed the van Durens. Victor had left the Merchant Navy with no family, no home and nowhere to go, until his captain had asked Leonard van Duren to help out an old friend. Now he had a home for life. Philip and Mekhala had had to leave their beloved studio in Soho after Philip's forced early retirement meant they couldn't afford it anymore, and were dreading leaving the city after forty years spent in the capital. But then Celeste turned up at their final show at a gallery on Pall Mall, and three months later, a new studio had been made on the ground floor of the big house. She didn't believe any of the residents would risk all that just to get rid of the Gleads, but that had to mean their suspect was someone else from Richard's ledger.

So Audrey turned to the internet and a form of investigation she was good at. Lewis might have his dark-web crime forums, but she had social media and years of practice running her own background checks on potential dates. This was her wheelhouse.

Within an hour, she'd managed to identify almost all Richard's blackmail victims, and then she moved on to the investment scam. These were harder, as Richard had only used first names and a last initial. Clearly, unlike the blackmail list, he preferred not to have any identifying information logged about his scam.

She trawled Richard's socials again, including the ones for Glead Antiques, examining every like and comment anyone had ever made on his feed, but by the time Mei came in, her cheeks flushed and her perfume drowned out by the smell of alcohol, she'd only managed to form a list of four possible victims out of the twenty or so in Richard's book.

"Hey," she said, grinning up at Mei. "Good debrief?"

Mei smirked and threw herself into the armchair, kicking off her work shoes.

"It was fine, thanks."

"Just fine?"

"Just fine."

"Uh-huh. Hey, Mei, who's got black hair, smells of vodka martinis, and lies like a cheap rug?"

Mei laughed.

"All right, Sherlock. It was nice, okay? We talked about Linda, and about the case. And about you and Flat Five Guy. Then we . . . talked about other stuff."

"I'm glad. She seems nice. What did she say about me and Lewis?"

"Her boss still thinks Lewis might be involved." She looked sheepish. "She even asked me if *you* had it in you to kill someone."

"Seriously?"

"I told her no, obviously. Said you'd never hurt anyone, but that if I ever wanted to get rid of a body, you'd be my first call."

"Thanks, hon. What about Lewis though? They don't really think that, do they?"

"A little bit. There's a profile, apparently. Men who commit murders and hang around the crime scene watching, trying to be helpful."

"Ew." Audrey gave a little shudder. "That's not Lewis though. He's writing a book."

"That's what I said, but you have to admit, he has the lamest alibi of anyone here." Mei stretched out her legs and put them up on the coffee table. "I'm so tired. I could murder a . . ." She paused, and smacked her lips, searching for the thing she was craving. "Kebab. If I order one, will you eat half?"

"No way, it's nearly midnight. Have some toast."

Mei groaned but hauled herself to her feet and sloped off to the kitchen, leaving Audrey smiling at her laptop. Tipsy Mei was fun. Audrey couldn't remember the last time they'd been out drinking together. Finances prevented her from having much fun these days, but maybe if she and Lewis could solve the case, the fee Celeste had promised would go some way toward rectifying that situation.

Thinking about Celeste made her stomach twist. She really hoped she'd be able to prove Celeste right, but no matter how much she wanted the Marchfield residents to be innocent, she couldn't exonerate them based solely on how much she liked them. Even she had wished Richard Glead would disappear, and once you'd committed one murder, who knew where it might lead?

She turned back to the computer and the much-neglected Instagram account of Glead Antiques, which had a surprising number of followers considering the feed was a deeply uninspiring selection of pictures of old bureaus, nineteenth-century paintings, and various living room furniture.

Then, a name caught her eye. Not one she initially recognised from the ledger, but one she'd heard before. It could be a coincidence but it was there and the spike of adrenaline she felt when she saw it told her it was something.

On a photograph of a seventeenth-century mahogany armchair, upholstered in gold fabric and trimmed with dark gold brocade, was a comment.

Marion Roper Beautiful chair! Maybe one day I'll be able to afford lovely things like this.

Audrey checked the list. No Marion but a Mari R had given Richard twenty thousand pounds over a year ago. She clicked through to the profile and saw an attractive older woman with a fashionable grey-blonde bob. She clicked through to Marion's list of followers.

It took her a while to scroll through it but there, at the bottom, was the name she'd been looking for.

Nathan Roper.

51

Lewis

Lewis sat on the counter by his kitchen window, breathing in the aroma from his second cup of coffee. It was Friday morning, and he'd been watching for the Hetheringtons since dragging himself out of bed at eight, but so far, no one had left the flat. The temperature had dropped overnight and outside the gardens were white with frost. His breath steamed up the glass as he looked out.

Bored, he looked around at his kitchen, with its off-white tiles and off-white cupboards. He swiped a finger over the sink splashback, frowning at the mark left behind. Maybe they weren't off-white. He barely spent any time in here, but since seeing Audrey clean the Glead place, he was starting to think he probably should do some housework at some point.

He looked back out of the window.

The caretaker emerged from the trees, carrying a bucket and a broom. He made his way down the path, scattering what Lewis presumed to be rock salt over the paths, pausing every few yards to brush it thoroughly over every inch of flagstone. He watched as Roshan worked his way around the square, fastidiously gritting the steps up to the first floors, and going twice over the area outside the Hetherington place, no doubt worried about Philip's wheelchair on the icy stone. Lewis couldn't remember ever seeing anyone so committed to doing a good job.

It was ten when the Hetheringtons finally emerged from the studio. Philip had a blanket and a bundle on his lap, while

Mekhala was wrapped in a shawl and carrying a mug. They crossed the courtyard to the garden, making their way down the path toward the bench Lewis was now starting to think of as theirs.

Philip manoeuvred himself into place beside the bench, while Mekhala put down her mug in order to tuck a blanket around her husband's knees.

Lewis went to get his coat.

It was freezing outside, and as he crunched across the newly salted courtyard over to the Hetheringtons, his breath hung in clouds in the air in front of him.

"Look, Philip," said Mekhala, as he approached. She was an attractive woman, a few years younger than her husband, with a light brown complexion and thick black hair with a single streak of grey. "The young man from Flat Five." Her fingers were clasped around a steaming stoneware cup and Lewis eyed it with envy, blowing on his fingers to warm them.

"This is Lewis, dear," said Philip, looking up from his sketchbook with twinkling eyes. "Lewis, this is my wife, Mekhala. You're becoming quite the social animal, I see."

"Hello," said Lewis.

Mekhala took a sip of her tea, and Lewis caught a hint of something minty and fresh.

"Would you like to sit?" She indicated the bench.

"No, no, thank you. I . . . um . . . I've come to ask you something. It's a bit delicate."

Philip and Mekhala looked at each other, and Philip lowered his sketchbook.

"What do you mean?" asked Philip.

Lewis had already decided honesty was the best policy, especially given the drums of Marchfield had already started beating with his and Audrey's investigation. As he couldn't invoke the police, he invoked the next best thing.

"Celeste has asked me to look into Linda's murder," he said. "Well, me and Audrey. She wants us to find out how the killer got in."

They exchanged glances again.

"What has that to do with us?" asked Mekhala.

"The night of the fireworks. Someone opened the gate at five to ten, either to let someone in or to let themselves out. Did you see or hear anything?"

"Nothing," said Philip. "I already told you."

"Just fireworks," said Mekhala. "We shouldn't hear much if the fireworks were on."

"Then, on the night Linda was killed, someone buzzed your flat at seven thirty. You didn't let them in remotely, did you? You went out to the gate to open it manually."

Philip's eyes narrowed.

"What makes you think that?"

"Because last night, I saw you do it again. Someone came to the side gate and waited for you to answer. You handed them a package, then closed the gate again. They didn't come into the square. Was it the same the night of the fireworks? Who was it that came to the gate?"

"I don't see how that's any of your business," said Philip sharply. "Or Celeste's."

"Because the police have the gate logs too, and they'll be looking at that entry and thinking what we first thought—that it belongs to the killer."

Mekhala took another sip of her tea, but Lewis noticed how she looked at Philip over the rim of her mug, soft brown eyes wide.

"We know that Richard was blackmailing you," Lewis went on, and this time Mekhala gasped. "I think he knew what you were up to and you were paying him to keep quiet. But the money was running out, and that gives you a motive. Maybe the police won't think you did it yourselves, but at the very least, they'll think you let the killer into the square. Maybe it was even money in the tube you handed over last night. Perhaps the second instalment for a job well done. The connection is too easy to make."

"I see," was all Philip said.

There was a pause, and Mekhala's hands trembled around her mug.

"What was Richard blackmailing you about? What's going on with the courier? What was in the tube?"

Mekhala's eyes skitted across to Philip.

"Pip . . ."

Philip said nothing for moment, then sighed.

"We didn't kill anyone, son," he said. "I think you already know that, don't you?"

Lewis nodded, but the truth was, he didn't know it at all. He didn't set much store by intuition or hunches, although they played well when writing fiction, and while he admitted that he didn't *want* the Hetheringtons to be guilty, blackmail was a strong motive and their behaviour was highly suspicious.

"If the police are going to talk to us anyway, then why should we tell you anything?" asked Mekhala.

Lewis hesitated. She had him there.

"The police will find out about the blackmail," he said. "Richard kept records, and they're bound to find them eventually. But the gate logs are circumstantial. There's no CCTV on Pickering Lane, which is why I assume you used the side gate instead of passing whatever it is out of your back windows. It could have been anyone opening the gate. Unless Audrey and I tell them about the courier."

"That sounds a bit like blackmail too, don't you think?"

He had to admit that it did.

"Costs a lot less than a thousand pounds, though."

Perhaps it was referencing the amount Richard had been demanding, or perhaps they just saw the logic of it, but the couple looked at each other and Mekhala nodded.

"Tell him."

"All right," said Philip, handing Mekhala his sketchbook and pencil, and taking the brake off his wheelchair. "But easier to show you, I think. Follow me."

Lewis followed Philip across the courtyard to Flat 2. When he stepped inside, Lewis saw at once that Audrey had been right. The place was huge.

No doubt the conversion of the big house's ground floor had been done specifically with Philip's wheelchair in mind. The hall was spacious and the floors clear of clutter, with widened door frames and wooden flooring throughout. Philip led Lewis through an open-plan living room and kitchen, furnished with an eclectic mix of modern and antique furniture, and painted in neutral colours that showed off the staggering collection of paintings that filled every wall.

"Did you do all these?" Lewis asked, trying to take them all in.

"Some of them," said Philip, crossing the kitchen, which was light and bright from the double-aspect windows, with a low kitchen island and dining table. "Mekki did others. But mainly they're friends' pieces, or bits we've picked up."

A corridor fed off from the kitchen. The first door stood open, showing a wet room beyond, while the two doors on the other side were closed. Bedrooms presumably. Lewis paused, reconsidering the wisdom of being alone in a confined space with a potential murderer. Philip stopped outside the final door.

"Our studio," said Philip, waving Lewis forward. "In you go."

He hesitated, then opened the door and stopped on the threshold. Painted white, with gauzy curtains at the huge window overlooking the courtyard, the space was lighter than he expected, and bright, reminding Lewis of a loft apartment. There were paint splashes on the floor, and the shelves that lined one wall were cluttered with rags, paint tubes, and countless jars of pencils and brushes, while the whole place smelled of turpentine and oil paint. A stack of old paintings leaned haphazardly against the wall beside the door and, standing in the centre of the room, were three easels bearing canvases.

It was the canvases that made Lewis stop.

The first picture was of a small beach landscape Lewis would have sworn was a Monet, while the second easel held an elongated portrait of a young woman in the style of Modigliani. The third canvas was still at the sketch stage, but looked very much like a Matisse.

Not wanting to make assumptions, Lewis walked up to the first picture. At the bottom edge, a fresh-looking signature read: "Monet."

"You're a forger."

"You could call it that."

"What would you call it?"

Philip chuckled.

"*Homage.*"

"That's what the courier was collecting? A painting?"

"Yes. We have a sideline. We need one, you know. My pension isn't much, and we never saved much while we were young."

Lewis examined the pictures. They were good, at least to his untrained eye. He'd never have guessed all three were done by the same hand.

"I don't understand. You can't get away with it in this day and age, surely? They use forensics to test the paint, the wood, the canvas . . . everything. Who's buying these?"

"That's rather complicated, I'm afraid."

"I'd like to hear it."

"All right. Do you know much about organised crime and the art trade?"

"A little. Leverage trading and all that."

"Exactly!" said Philip, impressed. "Precisely that. And what do you think of it?"

Lewis shrugged, confused by the question.

"Well, it's not great, is it?"

"No. It began over in Europe, and with crime being so international now, it's crept over here and now there's quite the demand amongst criminal gangs to get their hands on some Old Masters."

"You're painting these for the mob? Why? So they can swap them with the originals?"

"Not quite." Philip wheeled himself into the room. "A friend of mine—from the old days at art college—is an expert in acquisitions. If you want it, she can get it for you. No matter what. But she started to get an increasing number of requests from less reputable persons for art, specifically with the aim of hiding it away and using it for leverage further down the line. They're not fussy, as long as the artist is famous, so she came up with the idea of supplying fake pieces to them, saying they'd been stolen from private collections. The bigger the collection, the more likely it is to contain pieces of dubious origin, so they aren't surprised when any thefts aren't reported, either. They don't have access to the same forensic analysis as the formal institutions, so they're easier to fool. We use old canvases as a base, for verisimilitude and rudimentary testing. Old paints where we can. Does the trick."

"Really?"

"Yes. Let them squirrel away their Monet, and when it finally comes time to do the deal, let the police discover the fake. Too late for the criminal to do anything about it then, as they're bundled off to prison." He smiled. "Clever, don't you think?"

Lewis wasn't sure about that.

"But what if the criminal sends people after your friend? Or you?"

"It's all done with the greatest care of anonymity," said Philip. "My friend never comes herself, and we've taken all precautions. As you observed, we meet the courier at the gate and avoid CCTV. My friend takes most of the risk, and she never stays in one place long."

"So Richard was threatening to reveal your identity to the mob, rather than to the police?"

Philip's smiled faded.

"Yes. Some deeply unpleasant character known as the Fixer, apparently, who he said he could get word to. Don't get me wrong," he added, "the whole thing is illegal, whether selling fakes to collectors or gangsters, but we were more worried about the criminals than the police."

Lewis didn't know what to say. It made sense, he supposed, although bizarre didn't even begin to describe it. A couple of not-quite-pensioners scamming the bloody mob?

"They're very good, I must say. Lucrative, is it?"

"It's sporadic, and of course, the prices had to be reasonable or the criminals wouldn't bother using a third party but just steal something themselves, but it was, yes. Until Richard worked out what we were doing and put the squeeze on. Drained all our savings over the course of a year."

"How did he find out?"

"Same way you did. Spotted the courier one night, and got suspicious. Broke into the studio when we were out, and saw the paintings. A few weeks later, one of them was offered to him for sale and he realised what was going on. I attempted to bargain with him of course; said I'd put the police onto him in return, but he wasn't worried. Said he'd covered his tracks and the police weren't half as dangerous as this other chap." He looked carefully at Lewis. "You do believe me, don't you? That we had nothing to do with his death? I might have wished him dead, but we didn't lay a finger on him. And we'd never have hurt Linda in a million years."

Lewis was rather disappointed to find he did believe him.

"I do," he said. "Although you'll need to think of a story for when the police come by. And hide the pictures." He considered the paintings. "Richard was involved in sourcing artwork for gangsters himself. I'm surprised he didn't offer you a deal."

"Oh, he did," said Philip. "When the money started to run out, he offered to take paintings instead. That Monet was supposed to be for him." He snorted. "Utterly crass of course. No imagination. As if anyone would believe in an undocumented Monet. Still." He looked proudly at the picture, where sun-dappled waves broke beyond waving clifftop grasses. "It was fun to do. I'll have to find another home for it now."

After promising to tell no one except Audrey what he'd learned, Lewis walked home in a funk. He hadn't wanted the Hetheringtons to be guilty but it would have been rather neat if they had been. As it was, he believed them, especially about Linda. All they were left with now was Mrs. Hildebrandt and Victor, or a load of unknown people from Richard's scam ledger.

Which was the worst plot development Lewis could think of.

52

Audrey

Audrey had to be careful not to rush her work that afternoon. She was paid by the hour, and couldn't leave early without Mrs. Williams noticing and docking her pay accordingly. She was one of those clients who found something to do in every room Audrey cleaned, as she cleaned it, following her around as she worked her way down through the house. Usually, this irritated her, but today she was glad because it forced her to focus and to keep her work steady.

As she left the Williams house, the pink-grey sky darkening with the approaching dusk, her phone pinged. Her stomach lurched when she saw it was a notification from her bank but then she realised it was a deposit notification.

Celeste.

They hadn't discussed the money, Audrey figuring that if it were enough to cover Lewis's recruitment salary, then it would easily cover her cleaning one, but the amount she saw deposited was almost twice her weekly earnings.

She stood in the darkness, cleaning bag in one hand, illuminated phone in the other, and felt almost giddy. It made all the stress and difficulty of dealing with her clients this week worth it. All the tension between her and Mei, worth it. Was that how much Lewis earned every month? How could he hate a job that paid that well?

She hurried home as fast as she could, keen to get back to Marchfield and call Val, to earn the money Celeste had so generously given her. To pay back Mei's loan. Another week or two of this and, combined with her cleaning pay, she'd be almost back at zero. After several years of managing her overdraft on the tightest of margins, even being close to the black would come as a huge relief.

She was so distracted by her thoughts that it took a while for her to register the creeping sensation on the back of her neck, but as she turned from Robinson Street onto Flood Street, she felt it.

She stopped. The sun had dropped below the horizon, and the road was now a steady stream of vans, cars, and taxis as the commuter traffic picked up. There were plenty of people about, none of whom paid her any attention as she stood in the middle of the pavement, looking around. She started walking again, attention focused on her surroundings.

The prickling was still there as she crossed the road, so instead of going home, she took a right turn instead of a left. If someone was following her, the last thing she wanted to do was lead them back to the square. She walked on and on, until she reached the King's Road, where she immediately bumped into Mrs. Hildebrandt, who was waiting on the corner with a load of shopping bags.

"Oh, Audrey, dear," said Mrs. Hildebrandt, moving her bags from one arm to the other. She was wearing her fur hat again, strawberry-blonde hair flicking out from underneath. "I don't suppose you've seen Fraser on your travels? He's supposed to be picking me up. He drives a Rolls-Royce."

Audrey tried not to roll her eyes. Everyone in the square had heard about Fraser's car.

"No, sorry, Mrs. H. I can help carry your bags back if you'd like?"

"Oh, no, darling, we were going on to an early dinner, that's all. Very sweet of you though."

"That's a lot of shopping," said Audrey, nodding to the bags. "Have you had a good day?"

"I've had a wonderful day," gushed Mrs. Hildebrandt. "Fraser is so generous, and what girl doesn't love to be treated? I can't believe how lucky I am."

Audrey could easily believe how lucky she was. Beautiful women, even those in their sixties, often landed on their feet.

"It is nice to be treated," she agreed. "Special occasion?"

"No, not really. I've had a little run of bad luck lately, but Fraser's been determined to cheer me up, bless his heart. Where are you off to?" Mrs. Hildebrandt looked down at Audrey's cleaning bag. "Surely not to work at this hour?"

"No, just on my way back actually. Took the long way home." It was then that Audrey realised the creeping sensation was gone. She looked around. The pavements were increasingly busy and the traffic now steady, but couldn't see anyone or anything suspicious. She breathed a sigh of relief and smiled at Mrs. Hildebrandt.

"Mrs. H . . ." she began, deciding to take the bull by the horns. "Can I ask you something?"

"Of course! Although not if it's for my chocolate cake recipe. I've told you, that's a family secret."

"No, it's not that. It's about Richard Glead."

The effect was immediate. Mrs. Hildebrandt stiffened and pursed her lips.

"What about him?"

"I recently found out . . . that is to say, someone I know found out, that Richard had a bit of a sideline in investment opportunities." She thought quickly, trying not to use the word *scam*. "Some people lost their money. I just thought perhaps you'd invested some money with him. I know things have been tough for you recently."

She blushed as Mrs. Hildebrandt stared at her, and had to fight the urge to say "Never mind" and run off. But then suddenly, Mrs. Hildebrandt's lip quivered and tears began to run down her cheeks.

"Oh, darling, you're so sensitive, aren't you?" She gripped Audrey's hand. "How on earth did you guess?"

Audrey felt her face burn with shame.

"Well, after what you just said about bad luck . . ."

"Goodness, I do let my mouth run away with me, don't I? I'm such an open book." Mrs. Hildebrandt shuffled her shopping bags again, so she could root in her handbag for a tissue. "You're quite right, I let that awful man dupe me. Not long after they moved in—you know, before things started to go wrong—I was on the King's Road, looking in a shop window at a pair of shoes I couldn't afford, and he passed by and stopped for a chat. He was positively charming. I explained how I came to be at Marchfield, my tragic little story, and he said if I had any savings, he knew a man who could double them in two years, and triple them in three."

She sniffed and pressed her nose into the tissue.

"You had no reason to doubt him," said Audrey. "I'd have done the same thing, I'm sure."

"That's kind, dear," said Mrs. Hildebrandt. "But I'm sure you wouldn't be so silly. I believed him because I wanted to, I suppose. He took me to meet his broker, a very smart-seeming man, expensive suit and all that. I gave them all the savings I had. I thought I could scrape by for a few years, and then things would get easier. And he was so very charming and solicitous. Except of course, after a year, I started to see what sort of man he really was, and felt uneasy about the whole thing. I tried to ask for my money back but he was most unpleasant. Said if I were to pull out now, I'd get back less than I put in. So I stuck with it.

"Then a man came to see me. Told me one of his relatives had been seduced by Richard, and persuaded to invest all her money in his scam. He was committed to bringing Richard down, and had somehow discovered I was one of the other investors and wanted to warn me. I was utterly humiliated."

"You poor thing," said Audrey, full of sympathy. She knew what it was to lose everything, but to be scammed like that out of your life savings? It made her blood boil.

Fresh tears appeared in Mrs. Hildebrandt's eyes.

"I went straight to Richard's office, told him I knew it was a scam, and demanded my money back, but he refused. Stuck with the story that it was a genuine investment, and said I had to wait it out for the full three years. Said women shouldn't dabble in speculation if they couldn't handle the uncertainty. Virtually threw me out of his shop. I'd never been treated like that in my life, and I knew then I'd been swindled. I felt such a fool, Audrey, I can't tell you."

"I'm so sorry, Mrs. H," she said, putting her arm around Mrs. Hildebrandt's shoulder. "That's truly awful. Does Fraser know?"

Mrs. Hildebrandt smiled and dabbed at her eyes, trying not to ruin her mascara.

"Oh, yes, he knows, and he's been wonderful. He's simply the most wonderful man, and some days I even wonder if it wasn't all worth it. I'd never have met him otherwise."

"Did Linda know, do you think?" asked Audrey, trying to work her way up to the real matter in hand, namely, how to ask Mrs. Hildebrandt if she'd killed three people. She almost wished Lewis were here, to just blurt it out.

"No," said Mrs. Hildebrandt, the fur hat bouncing as she shook her head. "I'm sure she didn't. She wasn't the brightest spark, was she? And too frightened of him to ask any questions. She only cared about animals."

"Yes, she spent all her free time at the dog shelter. She was going to adopt one you know, after Richard died?"

Mrs. Hildebrandt smiled weakly.

"Yes, I had heard. One with a silly name. Sweet girl. No, I held no grudge toward Linda, if that's what you're thinking."

Audrey relaxed. Of course Mrs. H wouldn't have hurt Linda. She didn't really think she could hurt anyone.

"Who was the man?" she asked. "The one who told you Richard was a con man?"

Mrs. Hildebrandt opened her mouth to answer but a discreet toot made them turn, and a silver car turned the corner, the street lights glinting off the curves of its bonnet. It pulled sedately up to the kerb and Fraser leapt from the driver's side, running around to Mrs. Hildebrandt.

"So sorry." He took the bags from her. "Traffic's already terrible. Hello, Audrey." He opened the boot and dumped the shopping inside.

"Careful, darling," said Mrs. Hildebrandt. She waited for Fraser to open the passenger door for her, then sat down on the seat, lifting her feet, clad in a pair of new Gucci heels, into the footwell as gracefully as any Golden Age movie star. No more scratched nude pumps. "Could we give Audrey a lift? We're passing the square, aren't we?"

"Of course," said Fraser, smiling. He opened the rear door. "Hop in."

Audrey slid self-consciously onto the back seat, all cream leather and plush carpeting, keeping her cleaning bag on her lap in case it left a mark. She fastened the seat belt and Fraser pulled out into traffic, the other vehicles seeming to drift apart to make room for him.

Two minutes later, Fraser turned onto March Street and drew up outside the front gate. Audrey already had her hand on the door handle when he jumped out and opened the door for her.

She tried to be as graceful as Mrs. Hildebrandt, failing miserably as she scuffed her bag against the inside of the door. "Thank you. Are you going somewhere nice for dinner?"

"La Maison Lafayette," he replied, shutting the door gently behind her. She wondered then, whether he just hadn't trusted her not to slam it.

"Lovely." She stepped away from the car. "Have a good evening, both. Thanks for the lift."

"Any time."

She watched as they drove away, heading for the exclusive Belgravia bistro and for the first time, it occurred to her to wonder who Fraser Townsend actually was, and just how well Brigitte Hildebrandt had landed. It took more than money to get a reservation at La Maison Lafayette.

Audrey let herself in via the front gate, and walked down the path through the garden. Mist was beginning to rise over the lawn, and the orange glow of the lamps made it eerie and beautiful. Celeste's picture window looked down at her from above, the draped curtains silhouetted by the light beyond, warm and reassuring.

She felt more relief than usual when she finally got home. She checked the time. Four forty-five. Her detour had cost her.

She called the Dogs' Home and after waiting in a phone queue for five minutes, asked for Valerie James, only to be told by the harassed-sounding receptionist that Valerie was with the dogs and that she'd have to leave a message. She guessed that

Val wouldn't get back to her until tomorrow now, and cursed herself for her paranoia.

Mei was right that the case was raking it all up again, but then she'd never really been able to leave it behind in the first place. What had happened to her, she'd come to realise, had been a formative experience. She just had to live with that. And other stuff had come from it, too, things that weren't all bad. The self-defence classes, the flat in Marchfield Square, her cleaning business. It wasn't where she'd planned to be, but probably most people felt like that. At least sometimes.

And if she could help to solve Linda's murder, that would also be a good thing. Even if that was the only important thing she did in her life—getting justice for Linda—then that was more than most people could say.

She could live with that.

53

Lewis

Lewis stood outside the door of Flat 7 and waited for Audrey to answer. He'd figured she must be home by now and couldn't wait any longer to discuss the latest revelations with her.

He put his ear to the door, listening. He heard footsteps, then a pause, and then the door opened.

Audrey stood in the hall, wearing green dungarees over a vest and some thick pink socks. She looked flustered to see him, quickly gathering her hair into a knot and tying it up.

"Hey," she said. "What's up?"

"I thought I'd fill you in on my day," he said. "Have you got a minute?"

"Yes, sure."

She let him in and he went through to the kitchen, where all the lights were on. The air smelled of cleaning products and when he looked around, he saw a spray bottle and cloth on the countertop. She entered the room a minute later, pulling a cardigan on.

"Were you cleaning?" he asked, bemused.

"Only a wipe-down." She went over to the counter and wiped it over, then threw the cloth into the sink and put the bottle away underneath. "Coffee?"

"Thanks." He seated himself on one of the stools. He was starting to feel a bit more relaxed in her presence now, although from the stiff way she was standing, filling the kettle, the feeling wasn't yet mutual. "You got home from a day's cleaning and immediately started more cleaning?"

"Just decompressing."

A decompress clean. Was that a thing?

"Everything okay?"

"Yes." She flicked the kettle on before turning around. "What happened then? Did you speak to Philip?"

"Not half," he said. He was going to enjoy this. "Get this. The Hetheringtons are forgers."

"What?"

"They're art forgers. They've been faking Old Masters so people like Glead can acquire them for leverage trading. They're scamming the gangs of London."

Her mouth dropped open.

"You're kidding me?"

"Nope. He showed me the paintings. They're bloody good. Anyway, Glead found out and started blackmailing them. When they couldn't pay, he made them paint for him instead."

"So he was also scamming gangsters?"

"Looks like. Which means there could be others who wanted to kill him."

Audrey groaned and leaned back against the counter.

"Of course there are. I'm starting to wonder how Richard Glead stayed un-murdered for as long as he did."

Lewis grinned.

"Did you call the dog lady?"

"Val. Yes, but I had to leave a message. I bumped into Mrs. H so was late getting home."

"You spoke to her?"

"Yes. She admitted investing in Richard's scam shortly after the Gleads moved in, when he was still doing his Mr. Charming act. Gave him all her savings. She started to get the heebie-jeebies about it, but when she wanted to back out, he told her she'd lose everything." She took some cups out of the cupboard. "Then a man came to see her. Told her one of his relatives had been scammed by Richard too. That's why she went to see him that day in the shop."

"Who was the man?" Lewis watched as she spooned the horrible instant coffee into a mug. "Sounds like a good suspect to me."

"Me too, but Fraser arrived before she could tell me. I'll pop round and ask her tomorrow."

He nodded.

"Good to know we were right, though. How did she seem? Angry? Happy? Vengeful?"

"Embarrassed," said Audrey. "Humiliated. She didn't blame Linda though. Said she was sweet and not too bright. But Fraser knows all about it and is splashing the cash on her, so she's recovering." The kettle clicked off and she reached for it. "I think we should look into Fraser, by the way."

"Really? Why? He's only been around a few months, hasn't he?"

"Yes, but I think there's more to him than meets the eye. He's obviously very wealthy, with his Rolls and his town house, and his gifts for Mrs. H. But he also managed to get a table at La Maison Lafayette for tonight, and last I heard, the waiting list for a reservation there was longer than for a Birkin bag."

"I don't know what that means."

"It means the wait is months. That guy from the *Avengers* did an online review last week—said he'd waited five months to get a table—but a couple of pensioners can get in on a Friday night? Fraser must have some clout with someone." She put the mug down in front of him. "Sorry, instant again." She sighed.

"What?"

"It's just so complicated," she said. "I really thought by now we'd have narrowed it down to a single motive or one strong suspect, but it seems just about anyone who ever met Richard could have a reason to kill him, which puts Linda in the firing line too."

"I know. But we are getting closer. We must be." He slurped his coffee and winced.

"Snob," she said, although she didn't sound annoyed.

"Sorry. It is horrible though." He pushed the mug across to her. "Taste it."

"I don't need to, I know it's horrible."

"Then why do you keep giving it to me?"

"To be polite."

"You're making me terrible coffee to be polite?"

"I keep forgetting to get the ground stuff, and you keep showing up unannounced. It's rude not to offer a drink, so you get horrible coffee." She lifted her tea and her eyes were twinkling at him over her mug. "That's on you."

"You are a very strange person."

"I know." She sipped her tea. "I have another lead by the way. Nathan Roper."

"What about him?"

"Someone in his family invested in Richard's scam too. Twenty thousand pounds."

"Shit, that is a good lead. How do you know?"

"Glead Antiques Instagram account." She got out her phone and began to swipe through it. "About a year ago, someone named Marion Roper commented on one of their pictures. There's a Mari R in Richard's ledger, so I clicked through to her account and checked her followers. Nathan Roper is one." She tapped the phone a few more times, then turned it to face him. "Same guy?"

The picture on the screen showed Nathan Roper standing on a beach with an older woman, his shoulder-length dark hair windswept and a broad smile on his face. The post was captioned, "Day at the beach with mum."

"That's him." He took another slug of bitter coffee. "So that's two suspects off, and two suspects on. Nathan and whoever it was who told Mrs. H about the scam. They could even be the same person. Maybe he tried to stop others falling victim like his mother had."

"And don't forget Victor. We still haven't ruled him out. And the other people in the scam ledger."

"I've been thinking about that," he said. "Killing Richard seems a terrible way to get your money back. Following him, yes. Gathering evidence for a case against him, yes. Killing him? That achieves nothing. It doesn't make sense for one of them to kill him."

"I see what you mean," she said. "But is murder logical like that? If you thought you were never getting your money back, revenge might be the motive. Or prevention. Stop them doing the same thing to someone else, like the man who tried to warn Mrs. H."

"Murder as a public service?" He almost laughed. "I hardly think so."

"Do you think he could be the one who was following Linda?"

"It would make sense."

"Although . . ." She hesitated, as if she was still working it out. "What if one of those victims decided to build a relationship with Richard's wife? A friendship. Away from the husband. She's kind. Caring. Goes to church. With the husband gone, once you tell her what he's done, she's bound to give the money back. Assuming she can find it."

He stared at her, impressed and furious at the same time. Impressed that she'd thought of it, and furious that he hadn't. It was perfect.

A man like Richard Glead would never give back his ill-gotten gains. Even if you took drastic measures, he had too many dangerous friends; you'd never get away with it. But the wife? She's an easy target.

Spend a few months laying the groundwork during your shifts at the Dogs' Home, building up trust, talking about animals. Then shoot the husband, wait a respectable amount of time to pay your condolences, and drop the bombshell. Your husband ruined my family, and if you happen to come across some money you can't account for . . . From what Lewis knew about Linda, she'd be a soft touch, all right.

"When you speak to Val, can you ask her how long Nathan's worked at the shelter?" he asked out loud, when his thoughts slowed enough for him to talk. His fingers were starting to itch with the need to write it all down.

"Sure," she said. "You think he arranged it? Specifically asked for the same shifts as Linda?"

"I'd be surprised if he hadn't."

She nodded.

"No one's what they seem, are they?" she said, after a pause.

"Everyone's hiding something," he said. "But they can't hide forever. We're getting closer, I know it."

Lewis left ten minutes later, keen to get home and start writing, but as he trotted down the steps from Audrey's flat, tugging his coat around him, something caught his eye and he stopped. It wasn't even six yet but it was dark and misty. The temperature had dropped and the garden was already glittering with another frost, while the trees rustled softly overhead, and Lewis's breath huffed out in little clouds in front of him. There was no one around. He started walking again, but by the time he'd crossed the courtyard, he felt the urge to stop again.

"Hello?" he called into the darkness beyond the street lamps. The trees continued their endless waving, creating a flickering dance of shadows, and Lewis stared into their depths, wondering if there really was someone there.

Paranoid, he told himself, when he finally locked the front door behind him. The case is making you paranoid. But nevertheless, as he went to draw the curtains before settling down at the computer, he checked the locks on every window.

Better safe than sorry.

54

Audrey

Audrey and Mei ate pasta at the dining table that night, talking about work and how the case was progressing, as well as Audrey's windfall.

"At least something good's come out of this," said Mei, lifting her wine glass. "And you do seem to be a bit good at detecting, don't you think? That's impressive work at the crime scene."

Audrey grinned.

"I'm certainly annoying Lewis, which suggests you're not entirely wrong."

The doorbell rang.

"Who the hell is that?" said Audrey, and Mei flushed, immediately putting her on the alert. "Is that Sofia? Do you have a date?"

"It is Sofia," said Mei, making for the door. "But no, I don't have a date."

Audrey waited at the table while Mei answered the door. A minute later, she was back, ushering Larssen into the kitchen.

"Thanks for coming," Mei said to Sofia, and Audrey frowned. "Glass of wine?"

"No thanks," said Sofia, standing awkwardly in the doorway. "I'm technically on duty."

"Tea then?"

"That'd be great, thanks."

Mei busied herself making tea, while Audrey pulled out another chair.

"Take a seat, DS Larssen," she said, forcing a smile.

"Sofia, please," she said. "No need to be formal."

Audrey nodded and sat down again, squeezing her nails into her palm to stop her hands from shaking. What was this about?

"You look surprised to see me," said Sofia. "I hope you don't mind. Mei said you'd picked up some useful information and I was keen to hear it, so she invited me round for a chat."

They both turned to look at Mei, who had the good grace to look embarrassed.

"I just thought it was easier than exchanging information through me. It would help Sofia to understand what's going on, Auds."

"So, what is going on?" asked Sofia, turning back to Audrey, blonde hair swishing against her shoulders and giving off waves of apple-scented shampoo. "Why are you investigating this yourself?"

Audrey was going to kill Mei.

"Celeste. She was angry that you didn't believe Linda had been murdered, so she asked Lewis and me to see what we could find out. Before the trail went cold."

"I admit we were slow to respond to that," said Sofia, "but when you have a gated community like this, the most logical answer is usually the right one. And thanks for your earlier tip-off about Paulo Ram, by the way. We should have discovered that sooner."

"No problem."

The little black notebook appeared on the table in front of Sofia.

"Do you mind if we go back to the beginning? You and Mei spoke to Linda the day she died?"

"Yes. She talked about volunteering at the animal shelter, and said she was going to get a dog. She was a bit shell-shocked, but looking to the future. Then she went to church."

"St. Luke's, yes?" said Larssen. "And Mei said you spoke to her sister? You and Lewis McLennon?"

Audrey knew she'd promised to report whatever she and Lewis found to the police, but now that she was faced with this amenable version of DS Larssen, she suddenly didn't want to.

"Yes. We wanted to pay our respects. Let her know we were thinking of her."

"That was kind. What did you talk about?"

"Jane and Alf were pretty devastated. Both of them. They practically raised Linda, by the sound of it. Hated Richard. Worried about his friends. They were adamant she hadn't killed him, and didn't believe she'd end her own life. She was religious, and always believed he'd change. The lack of a note bothered them more than anything. They didn't believe she'd have done that to them."

"Seems you talked quite a lot," said Larssen, sounding almost impressed. "They weren't so forthcoming with us."

Damn it, thought Audrey. She should have said less. She'd just assumed Jane would tell the police the same thing.

"I've got one of those faces," said Audrey. "People just tell me stuff. You won't tell them I told you, will you? I don't want them to think I'm a *snitch* or anything." She looked over at Mei, but Mei just pulled a face at her and continued filling the teapot. Teapot? Since when did they use teapots?

"Don't worry. Who else did you and McLennon talk to?"

Lewis was going to be so pissed when he found out.

"Chaz Shaw. We bumped into him after we found Paulo's body, but he was under the impression Richard had been shot in the head, didn't seem to know Linda was dead, and was upset because Paulo wasn't returning his calls."

"'Bumped into,' eh?" Sofia raised an eyebrow. "We also spoke to Chaz, and he has an alibi for both Richard and Paulo.

We're not ruling him out for Linda, but it seems unlikely. What about Lewis McLennon?"

"What about him?"

"How well did you know him before you started investigating for Mrs. van Duren?"

"Not at all. We'd never spoken."

"And how does he seem to you?"

"What do you mean?"

The detective tipped her head to one side, as if considering how to phrase the next question.

"Is he friendly? He was the only resident not at the fireworks, I'm told."

Shit. This was about alibis.

Audrey turned her head slowly toward Mei, who brought over the teapot and a mug for Sofia, then went back for the milk, the plastic bottle ruining the charming effect she was clearly going for. "Excuse the bottle," she said, avoiding Audrey's eyes.

Sofia smiled warmly at Mei before turning back to Audrey. "Lewis?" she prompted.

"No, he wasn't at the fireworks. Manny invited him but he forgot. He's not big on socialising. He was home, talking to his grandmother."

"Yes, so he said. But the only residents not there were Lewis and the Gleads?"

"Yes."

Sofia flipped to another page of her notebook. "Mei says you and she were together on Friday night as well, but what about Tuesday night? When Ram was killed?"

"Tuesday?" Audrey sighed with relief. "We were all here, weren't we, Mei? You, me, and Lewis."

"Oh?" Sofia looked to Mei for confirmation, who nodded. "Well. That's good."

"You can't seriously think Lewis killed anyone?" said Audrey. "What would be the motive?"

"You'd be surprised," said Sofia, "what people will do for artistic inspiration. He wouldn't be the first crime writer to kill, you know. And you have to admit, he's a little bit odd."

"That's a terrible reason to suspect someone!"

"Not when combined with the discovery of three bodies, and no alibi for two of the murders. But his call log checks out, and the coroner thinks Ram was killed on Tuesday evening, sometime between eight and midnight, so at least he has an alibi for that."

Audrey was horrified. She couldn't argue that she knew Lewis well, or that he wasn't a bit odd, but he wasn't so odd that he'd murder three people for no reason and then take money to investigate his own crime.

Although that would be a good plot for a book.

"We spoke to Reverend Fitzbride at St. Luke's," she blurted out, attempting to redirect the detective. "Linda confided in him. Said she thought she and Richard were being watched."

"Watched?" Sofia sat up. "By who?"

"She didn't know. But possibly . . ." Audrey hesitated, wondering whether to mention the ledger. Something in her gut was screaming at her not to tell Sofia any more, and she'd learned the hard way what happened when she ignored her instincts. Plus, Lewis had promised the Hetheringtons, and Mrs. H didn't need any more stress. "Someone involved in Richard's business?"

"Financials looked into Glead Antiques but it was squeaky clean. Suspiciously so, they said, for an antiques business. We're assuming Glead was working for Ram or one of his associates. Perhaps Linda knew something about the business, something that got her killed. Or perhaps she tried to blackmail Ram in exchange for her silence."

Not this again.

"Linda wasn't like that," said Audrey.

"I thought you didn't know her well."

"Just because she was a victim doesn't make her stupid," said Audrey, not bothering to hide her frustration. "Someone was spying on them, and Linda was frightened. If she knew her husband had mob connections, she'd almost certainly know what blackmailing them would do, and a frightened woman wouldn't choose to jump from the frying pan into the fire."

Sofia held her gaze for a moment, and Audrey waited for her to argue, like Lewis had.

"You're probably right," she said, instead, "but finding out what Linda knew could be relevant. And important."

"Motive," said Mei.

"Exactly." Sofia's eyes sparkled. "It's a good lead though, and one no one's mentioned until now. You must have a way with people."

Audrey shrugged. What could she say to that?

"Was that why you were at Glead Antiques?" Sofia asked. "That didn't look good, you know. DI Banham's still raging about you getting there before us. He thinks it's too much of a coincidence."

"We figured Linda's death must have something to do with Richard's business and we knew you'd already looked there, so we thought we'd have a peek and see if anything jumped out."

"Something we'd missed, you mean?" Sofia was smiling but her eyes were sharp. Audrey had no intention of falling into that trap.

"No, but you'd hardly share information with us, would you? Not like we are with you."

"No, I suppose we wouldn't."

Sofia looked down at her notebook. "This has been really useful. We've got a lot on our plates right now, but a triple homicide involving Paulo Ram is the priority."

"It wasn't a priority before?" Audrey asked, unable to stop herself. "Two people killed in their own home?"

Sofia flushed and glanced at Mei.

"It's a matter of triage. Like I said, we've got a lot on our plates."

But instead of being angry, like Audrey had heard her before when ranting about the Met's priorities, Mei simply shrugged.

"We get it, Sofia," she said. "You're doing the best you can."

Sofia broke into a smile that Audrey felt was much bigger than the statement warranted.

"Thanks," she said, eyes fixed on Mei's. "Not many people understand."

Audrey was too annoyed with Mei to enjoy the ridiculous scene in front of her.

"Do you have any more questions for me?" she asked the detective, standing up. "I think I'm going to have an early night."

Mei looked up guiltily. Good.

"Oh, um . . . no, I don't think so," said Sofia, obviously used to being the one doing the leaving. "Is there anything else you know or have heard? Anything else that might be relevant?"

Audrey paused, thinking again about the shoe marks on the sofa, and the secret ledger hidden in Richard's office.

"Nope," she said, shaking her head. "Nothing at all."

55

Lewis

The following morning, before he'd even opened his curtains, Lewis read back what he'd written last night, gripped by his latest idea. He'd stayed up until almost one, typing furiously and breaking only to heat up a microwave meal before returning to the screen.

Harding looked at the collection of photographs on the board. On either side of the picture of Lindsey were those of her two friends: the gardener and her fellow volunteer at the animal shelter. The one who had lied. Had he been in touch with Lindsey the night she died?

The final picture on the board was that of a shadow no-man, the generic picture the police used when they didn't know who a suspect was. Who was the person who'd been watching the Speens? To what end had they been stalking them, and who else had they shared their information with?

It all seemed to hold up in the cold light of day, and brought those niggling questions to the fore. Was Nathan Mrs. H's informant? Or had whoever it was talked to Nathan too? It would make sense. If Audrey had found him easily, then so could someone else. Then he remembered what Audrey had said about Fraser Townsend and switched to his web browser. Now there was someone with the right name. It suited him right down to the ground, from the way he looked and the way he spoke, to everything they knew about him: rich, handsome, privileged.

Unfortunately, Lewis could find nothing on Fraser at all. No socials, no professional profiles, no newspaper articles. Not exactly unusual for a man of his age, but for a man of his means, Lewis had expected at least some fleeting mention in the business pages, if nothing else.

The only search results were on Companies House, under Personal Appointments. The name Fraser Townsend was associated with two active businesses and three dissolved ones, each with a lifespan of under four years. After looking up the business addresses and filed accounts of all five companies, Lewis was pretty sure that the dissolved ones were shell companies, while the two active ones were so healthy, yet so carefully flat in their numbers, that they didn't appear any more legitimate. Audrey was right. There was more to Fraser than met the eye.

Not that that made him a killer of course. Plenty of rich people used shell companies to avoid tax; they just tended to use them abroad.

He then turned to his crime forums.

~CrimeWriter159~ Doing some research into Paulo
Ram's recent demise. Known associates?

While he waited for one of his fellow true crime fans to respond, he kept digging. Ram's business interests went back thirty years, the only two still in operation were the pawnbroker and a share in Chaz Shaw's bike shop. Yet there were large gaps in the timeline, and given his age and contacts, Lewis had to assume there were other interests, perhaps registered under other names.

His phone lit up in the gloom and as his eyes left the computer screen, he blinked before picking it up.

THE CLEANER: Larssen came over last night.

LEWIS MCLENNON: What? Why?

THE CLEANER: Mei invited her. She wanted to know what we'd found.

LEWIS MCLENNON: What did you tell her?

THE CLEANER: As little as possible. But Banham is suspicious of us. Larssen checked our alibis for all three murders. Luckily, Ram was killed on Tuesday evening, when we were all together, but your alibis for the Gleads aren't great. We need to track down Nathan. I think he's the priority now.

LEWIS MCLENNON: Agreed. Nathan, then Victor. I'll drop round in a bit.

He put the phone down and tapped his fingers on the desk. The alibi thing was annoying when the video call would so easily prove his whereabouts, but the police clearly hadn't even bothered to check it with his nana yet. A single person, living alone, not going to stupid neighbour fireworks things, and suddenly you were a murder suspect.

That and finding three dead bodies.

He knocked on Audrey's door a few minutes later but it was Mei who answered.

"Oh. Hi." She sounded annoyed. "Come in."

"Thanks." He stepped inside, feeling uncomfortable. Why did he feel like he was in the doghouse? He held up the bag of coffee he'd brought with him and tried to sound cheerful. "I brought coffee."

Audrey appeared, her expression unreadable. The atmosphere was decidedly frosty.

"We're going out," she said.

"Uh, what?" Lewis lowered the bag. "But—"

"Come on, I need some fresh air." She grabbed her coat from its hook and pushed him out the door.

He hurried to keep pace as she stomped down the steps to the garden, feet crunching on the grit the caretaker had laid the day before. Even at ten in the morning, the air was cold and crisp, and Lewis's breath clouded in front of him.

"What's going on?" he asked, stuffing the bag of coffee into his pocket as he followed her down the path past the Captain's flat, heading toward the side gate. "Is this about Larssen?"

"Mei and I are fighting," she said, pulling up short beside the gate, where a broom leaned against the wall beside a bucket of gritting salt. "About her cornering me with Sofia last night. I didn't have time to think and I didn't know what Mei had already told her, so I don't think we came across very well."

"Oh." There was a pause as he caught up. "When you say *we* . . ."

"I had to tell her about Jane," she said, picking up the bucket. "And about Shaw, and about talking to Reverend Fitzbride. I didn't tell her about Nathan or Roshan, or about the shoe marks in the Glead place. Or about the ledger. I didn't want to set her onto the residents."

She began to walk backward, scattering grit along the path from the gate to the courtyard.

"That doesn't sound too bad. Stop a minute, will you? What are you doing?"

"Gritting." She stopped and took a deep breath. "Sorry. I'm wound up."

"No kidding. Look, don't worry about Mei or the police. We knew we'd have to share with them eventually, and you didn't tell them the good stuff so we might still be ahead of them. Just . . . calm down."

The look she gave him was pure daggers but she took another deep breath, and let it out in little cloudy puffs.

"I'm perfectly calm," she said, glaring at him. "Grab that broom and make yourself useful. I'm going to give the Dogs' Home a call. See if Nathan's in, or maybe Val. No point schlepping over there if he's not even in."

While she looked up the number, Lewis began to sweep the grit around, the *swish-swish-swish* of bristle against stone filling the air. He had to admit, in spite of being a highly emotional person, Audrey was also pragmatic. He'd been surprised at her detachment in analysing the crime scene, and especially dealing with Chaz Shaw in the pub. He wondered if Celeste had known about Audrey's self-defence skills when she'd put her on the case.

"Hello," said Audrey into the phone. "Could I speak to Val James, please?"

There was a moment's pause.

"Of course, I should have realised. I'll try her tomorrow then. Or perhaps I could speak to Nathan? Nathan Roper?"

Another, much longer pause.

"All right, sorry to bother you. I'll ring back then." She disconnected the call and Lewis stopped brushing. "Neither of them's in today. Val's in tomorrow but Nathan's next shift isn't until Wednesday."

"You should have asked for his address."

She rolled her eyes.

"They won't just give that out, you goon. There'll be rules."

"You could at least—Did you just call me a goon?"

"Yes. I'll have to wait and speak to Val, see if I can wangle the address out of her. She might not give it, though."

Lewis leaned on the broom, thinking.

"I could always hang around outside the Dogs' Home on Wednesday. Follow him home."

"That's five days away, though," she said. "Not to mention, a bit sinister."

Across the square, a door slammed and they both looked over to see Captain Gordon walking away from his front door, a bright red poppy pinned to his blazer. He spotted them standing in the courtyard and held up a hand in greeting and they both waved back.

"What do you suggest, then?" asked Lewis, turning back to Audrey. "How else can we get it?"

But Audrey wasn't looking at him. Her gaze was still on the Captain, who ambled down the path toward the side gate.

"Don't know," she said, breaking into a smile. "But I know a man who might."

56

Audrey

After waylaying Captain Gordon on his way out of the square, Audrey, amidst much huffing and scowling from Lewis, explained their problem. He'd listened with an expression akin to delight, then turned right around to return home, inviting them inside his flat, which was as clean and tidy a space as Audrey had ever seen, with green damask wallpaper, polished wooden furniture, and not a cobweb or speck of dust in sight. The Captain clearly ran a tight ship.

He knew a chap, apparently, who would be able to get them Nathan's address if they could give him just one other piece of information to go with it: date of birth, a phone number, a car registration. Unfazed to discover they knew none of these details, he took it upon himself to find out.

Now, she and Lewis sat side by side on the Chesterfield sofa, facing the Captain in his armchair. He held the phone in front of him, on speakerphone, so they could all hear the conversation.

"Good morning," he began, all plummy grandfatherliness, "May I speak to Nathan Roper, please? I understand he's one of your volunteers."

"Nathan isn't in today," said the young man on the other end of the phone, with a sigh.

"Then may I speak to your Human Resources department?"

"I'm sorry, they don't work weekends. You'll need to call back on Monday."

"I'm afraid that will be too late, young man," said the Captain, his voice creaking with overemphasised old age. "Far too late. You see, my brother-in-law recently came back from overseas but he's very sick and probably not long for this world. A few days at most."

"I'm so sorry to hear that," said the nice young man. "But—"

"Now, my brother-in-law doesn't have any children but he does have two sisters—that's rather obvious, isn't it? As I'm calling you? Now my wife and I haven't been blessed, but my sister-in-law, Marion, has. Now she's Nathan's mother, you understand. We've become estranged, I'm sorry to say, but my brother-in-law—that's Nathan's Uncle Geoffrey . . ."

An extraordinarily convoluted story then followed, during which the Captain talked about family rifts, hospital visits, long-lost heirlooms, and, finally, the insurance levels of the Dogs' Home, a query which thoroughly baffled the poor receptionist until the Captain explained that he'd be sending the aforementioned heirlooms to the Dogs' Home for Nathan Roper to collect when he was next in, and could they guarantee appropriate security levels for the items until his next shift?

Three minutes later, the receptionist had given up, the Captain had Nathan's mobile number, and, after phoning his friend, a man named Denzil, they had their answer.

"Eleven Granville Gardens, SW11," said the Captain triumphantly, putting the phone back into its cradle. "Nothing to it."

Lewis point-blank refused to let Audrey come over to his place, claiming first that he had no food and then that it wasn't in a fit state for visitors so, much to her annoyance, they traipsed back up to Flat 7 to have lunch before heading out to find Nathan Roper.

Mei was in the kitchen when they arrived, standing in front of the sink and looking out of the window. The taps were running to fill the washing-up bowl, steam misting up the window. A sandwich sat on a plate on the counter, beside the usual sandwich-making accoutrements.

"I saw you gritting the courtyard," she said, turning off the taps. "You needn't have bothered, though, Roshan's just arrived."

She wiped a hand across the window to clear the steam. Audrey made a silent note to clean the smears off later.

"How was I to know he'd be in?" she replied. "He doesn't usually work weekends."

"I wasn't having a dig," said Mei softly, and Audrey paused, wondering whether their row was over. Then she remembered it was her that had been angry and she sighed, smiling apologetically. She hated fighting with Mei.

"I know."

Mei looked as relieved as Audrey felt, while Lewis, who'd been standing awkwardly beside her, relaxed and took a seat at the counter, placing his bag of coffee in front of him while looking enviously at Mei's cheese sandwich.

"Where have you two just come from, anyway?" asked Mei. "Looked like you came out of the Captain's flat."

"We did. He got us a suspect's address and phone number."

"The Captain did?" Mei looked astonished. "How?"

"I'm not entirely sure," she said. "Some sort of conversational witchcraft. He always says he was a sniper in the army, but it was clearly more than that."

Mei took two more plates out of the cupboard, putting one down in front of Lewis. She nodded to the bread, butter, and cheese already laid out.

"Help yourself," she said, then looked at the bag of coffee. "I'll put the kettle on, shall I?"

If Lewis noticed Mei rolling her eyes, he ignored it, and started to make himself a sandwich. Mei returned to the sink to fill the kettle, then glanced out through the partially steamed-up window again.

She froze, kettle in hand, then shoved it to one side and wiped her hand over the entirety of the window.

"What is it?" asked Audrey, walking around the counter to join her at the window.

"The police," said Mei, and she sounded shocked. "They're back."

57

Lewis

Blue lights flashed steadily from the direction of Pickering Lane. Lewis watched, squeezed in alongside Audrey and Mei, from their kitchen window as two police officers in bulky armoured vests entered the square via the side gate, guns trained in front of them. Two other people, also in armoured vests but carrying smaller guns, were with them. They were followed by someone short, his face indistinct, and someone tall, her long blonde hair shining in spite of the clouded, grey sky. Banham and Larssen. The group crossed to the little courtyard, the armed officers in front, and began to walk purposefully up the path through the centre of the garden.

"They're searching for something," said Lewis. "Or someone."

Had the police solved the case already? Even with the adrenaline flooding his system, he couldn't help but feel disappointed. But then, the police had resources he couldn't hope to have. He shouldn't be surprised.

The police moved about the square, up and down the paths and in and out of Lewis's line of sight.

"I can't see properly," he said, leaving the window. "I'm going outside."

"But they've got guns!" protested Audrey as he crossed the kitchen at speed. "They must think it's dangerous."

He ignored her, walking out to the hall and opening the front door. A few seconds later, he was joined first by Audrey, then by Mei, and they stood together on the balcony, shivering and looking down into the square.

One by one, the pretence of discretion left the other residents too. Manny and Joe emerged from their flat to watch from their own balcony, while Captain Gordon appeared and joined the Hetheringtons in the courtyard, his expression grim as they watched the proceedings. Only Mrs. Hildebrandt and Victor were missing, but Lewis could see Mrs. H at her kitchen window, staring out at the scene.

"Get back inside!" roared DI Banham, trying to wave them back inside. "For your own safety!"

But before anyone could react, another cry went up from the other end of the garden, and as one, they all turned to where Roshan Jones had appeared, tool bag in hand, and was now frozen to the spot as four armed police officers trained their weapons on him.

"Drop the bag!" yelled Banham. "On your knees. Hands where we can see them."

Looking terrified, Roshan did as he was told, kneeling down in the middle of the path. Banham and Larssen walked quickly toward him, tasers drawn.

When they reached him, Larssen holstered her weapon, then patted Roshan down. Banham hauled him to his feet and marched him over to one of the benches, pressing down on his shoulder to make him sit. Larssen began to speak, but Lewis couldn't hear what she said. Roshan didn't say much in return, nodding or shaking his head and barely moving his lips at all. Then suddenly he leapt to his feet, causing the armed officers to raise their guns again. He began to wave his hands about, talking urgently, pointing first to the gate and then to Linda's flat, and then back again. Lewis strained to hear but couldn't make out any words.

Larssen held her hands out in the universal gesture for calm, and pressed Roshan back down onto the bench, while Banham went over to the gate. A few seconds later, more police officers poured into the square, this time carrying tools.

Lewis had already seen the police search the square once, beating bushes and shining lights into trees, but this was different. This was focused.

He watched as they walked up and down the garden, swinging a metal detector over Roshan's neat flower beds.

"What on earth's going on?" said Audrey, her face white. "They can't seriously think Roshan killed anyone."

"They're looking for the gun," said Lewis. "They've had a tip-off."

"How could you possibly know that?" asked Mei at once, sounding accusatory.

"The metal detector," he said.

They all watched from their opposite sides as the police targeted every patch of soil.

It didn't take them long to find it.

A shout went up from deep in the gardens, near to Jones's shed and the front gates, and the other police officers stopped, turning their heads in that direction. A minute later, a female officer marched down the centre path, a plastic bag held triumphantly aloft. She carried it over to the bench and handed it to Banham.

Roshan stared in desperation at the detectives, turning from one to the other then back again. Banham nodded at Larssen, who reached for her handcuffs.

Roshan stood stock-still while she cuffed him, his eyes wide with horror. Larssen turned him round to face her and began to speak, presumably reading him his rights. When she'd finished, she waited, looking at the caretaker, whose chest was rising and falling quickly. Eventually he nodded, and after a brief word with the two armed officers, Banham and Larssen took an arm each and marched Roshan Jones out of the square.

Lewis stared after them. He and Audrey hadn't ruled Roshan out entirely; there was a chance he'd killed Richard to protect Linda, and a much slimmer chance that he'd killed Linda, but what possible motive could he have had for killing Paulo Ram?

What the hell had they missed?

58

Celeste

"I won't stand for it," said Celeste, as Dixon paced up and down behind her armchair. "It's utter nonsense, I don't know what the police think they're doing."

"They don't arrest people for no reason," said Dixon, with infuriating calmness.

"But why would he do it, Dixon?" she asked, lowering her binoculars. "There's simply no motive."

"Maybe there is and you just don't know what it is."

"Don't be absurd."

Celeste was raging. Roshan Jones had been a loyal employee for over fifteen years. The idea that he should suddenly take it into his head to start murdering her tenants was bordering on laughable.

"You always said he was sweet on her."

"Fond. I said he was fond of her. He's a kind and generous soul; of course he'd worry about her, given what she'd been through, but that's no reason to arrest him. And even less reason for him to kill her. What was he doing here on a Saturday anyway? Did you call him?"

Dixon stopped his pacing.

"No. Look, no matter how good them binoculars are, you don't know what goes on inside their 'eads, or what they get up to when they leave. People aren't always who they seem to be."

"Well, why would he kill that other fellow? Ram?"

"I don't know. But they found a gun buried in the garden."

"*A* gun? Or *the* gun? In any case, someone else must have put it there. It's a fit-up. Or a frame-up, whatever you call it. Maybe it's an old one. Everyone used to shoot in the old days. My great-great-grandfather was always fighting duels. Perhaps it was one of his?"

"I don't think so."

"Pfft."

She stared, unseeing, out of the window.

She refused to believe the killer was one of her people. She'd made a single lapse in judgement with tenancy applications— one, in fifty years!—but that had been after Lenny had died, when she wasn't thinking straight. She stood firmly by the rest. She knew them. Knew their histories, their backgrounds. They were all here for a reason. Richard Glead had been the only exception.

She was affronted that the police thought her capable of employing a murderer, and offended that Dixon should think she was losing her touch. And worst of all, she was disappointed that DS Larssen, whom she'd thought rather well of, could make such a colossal mistake.

"I won't stand for it," she said again.

"What can you do?"

She got up and went to stand beside the window.

"We'll send Mei Chen over, for a start."

"And if she won't do it?"

"Why on earth wouldn't she?"

"She has strong feelings about men who hurt women, remember?"

"But Roshan didn't do it, she must know that. You ask her, Dixon. I'll cover all the costs. And if she won't help, get Peterson onto it. He'll do anything for a price."

Dixon nodded, then melted away to make his phone calls, leaving Celeste standing in front of her window, tugging the pearls at her throat.

Larssen wasn't the only one who'd made a mistake. Some-one had breached the sanctity of her beloved square and framed one of her people, and when Celeste found out who it was, she was going to make them regret it.

No one crossed Celeste van Duren and got away with it.

No one.

59

Audrey

Audrey watched from the sofa as Lewis paced up and down in the living room. Mei was on the phone to Dixon, and had shut herself in the kitchen for some privacy.

"They must have had a tip-off," Lewis repeated, aggrieved. "How else could they have figured it out so quickly?"

"They are the police, Lewis," said Audrey. "I expect they found out all sorts of things we didn't."

"I mean, Roshan was on our suspect list." He carried on as if she hadn't spoken. "We hadn't ruled him out, but what's the motive? Richard, yes, if he was trying to protect Linda, but why kill her too? And how does Ram fit in?"

"I don't know. Maybe Paulo Ram killed Linda, thinking *she*'d shot Richard, then Roshan killed him too?"

He was on his third lap of the room when Mei returned.

"Celeste wants me to represent Roshan," she said, sitting down. She looked pained. "Dixon was very persuasive. Said Celeste was adamant Roshan was innocent and had been framed." She turned to Audrey, elbows on her knees. "I told Dixon I'd call him back with an answer, but I just don't know what to think." She fixed her brown eyes on Audrey's. "Tell me honestly, is there anything you left out when you were talking to Sofia? I know I've made it difficult for you to talk to me about this, but I also know you've been holding back. Is there anything you've discovered that might suggest Roshan could have done this?"

Audrey glanced up at Lewis, who shrugged. She let out a long breath.

"Well, for starters, I . . . um . . . kind of broke my promise to you. We went to see Paulo Ram at his pawnbroker shop, before he was killed, and Richard's death seemed to be a bit of a shock to him. And after we found Paulo's body at Richard's shop, we went to see Chaz Shaw. He was drunk and sad—confused because Ram wasn't returning his calls, and upset because Richard was dead. He thought Linda had shot him because he cheated."

"Okay," said Mei, through gritted teeth. "We will very much come back to you breaking your promise, but not right now. What else?"

"Richard was a blackmailer, and he was running some sort of investment scam too. Mrs. H is one of his victims, although you mustn't let on I told you, she'd be mortified. And a woman called Marion Roper. Her son, Nathan Roper, volunteered at the shelter with Linda. He told Lewis they weren't close, but he knew about Linda's plan to adopt Muffin before anyone died. We're thinking he might have wormed his way into Linda's life somehow in hopes of getting the money back. It's just a theory, but it might give him a motive to kill Richard. We're working on it."

"That seems like a lot, actually," said Mei, sounding impressed despite herself. "You've really done a lot of work."

"There is one other thing . . ." began Audrey, wondering what Mei would say when she told her. "Nathan at the shelter said that Linda had taken a friend to see Muffin, the dog, then Reverend Fitzbride said Roshan used to talk to Linda at church, so we put two and two together and asked Roshan if he was the friend. He admitted he was, but that it was never any more than that."

Mei's eyebrows shot up.

"And you believed him?"

"Yes. And for what it's worth, I still believe him. He said Linda confided in him about Richard scamming people, and it was him and the priest who told us the Gleads were being watched. Roshan said Richard wouldn't take it seriously, but that Linda was frightened."

"Why didn't you tell Sofia it was Roshan who told you?"

"I don't know really." Audrey shrugged. "He was so upset about Linda and I didn't want to send the police barreling in to upset him any further. Plus . . . I didn't want her to get the wrong idea."

"Well, that backfired, didn't it?"

Lewis snorted.

"If you hadn't ambushed Audrey with Larssen, maybe they wouldn't have found out about St. Luke's or looked at Roshan at all."

Audrey looked at him aghast.

"You're saying it's my fault?"

"You'd have to have told the police sooner or later," said Mei, folding her arms. "Withholding evidence is a crime."

"We weren't withholding evidence," Lewis retorted. "We were withholding hearsay."

They glared at each other.

"Anyway," said Audrey, trying not to think about her part in Roshan's arrest. "We've not identified Linda's stalker yet, and we need to talk to Victor too. There must be a reason he lied about going out the night of Linda's murder."

"If we can find out where he went, maybe we'll have leverage for that conversation," said Lewis. "Maybe he knew it was Roshan all along, and it was him that tipped off the police."

Mei looked at him.

"You really think the police had an informant?"

"They came with a metal detector, meaning they had reason to think it was buried in the grounds. Whether the gun was planted or Roshan really had it, someone else must have known."

"What about the man who warned Mrs. H?" asked Audrey. "He was watching both the Gleads. He could have seen both murders."

Lewis nodded, looking thoughtful.

"You know . . . there's a missing person in all this," he said, starting to pace again, and Audrey found herself looking at the carpet for signs he was treading in any dirt. "Someone who knows about Richard's scam, and the blackmail, and about Linda's friendship with Roshan. I know we said it was possible but it feels like Nathan and Linda's stalker have to be one and the same."

"I know what you mean." Audrey sighed. "Let's talk to Mrs. H again, see if her guardian angel gave her his name. Why would the killer—whoever it is—want to frame Roshan though? They're clearly ahead of the police."

"It's tidy," said Lewis. "You remember I told you about the Fixer who worked with Ram? That's the sort of thing he does. Ties up loose ends and leaves them all in a neat little package for the police to find. Then the police stop looking. I've had a feeling from the start that someone's cleaning house. Maybe planting the gun in Marchfield is an attempt to do that."

Mei sat back and looked from one to the other with a curious expression. "You really are good at this detective thing," she said. "Maybe you should consider a change of career."

Lewis looked pleased but Audrey just laughed.

"Hardly," she said. "But as a side hustle, it's pretty interesting, and the extra money from Celeste will be a huge help." She sobered at once. "Are you going to help Roshan?"

Mei sighed.

"Based on what you've said, it doesn't seem likely he did it. I'll go along to the station today, and see what he says in his interview but if he killed Linda . . . I won't defend him, Auds."

"I know," said Audrey. "I'll be here when you get back. Will you tell us what he says?"

"No can do, little buddy." Mei smiled ruefully. "If Roshan wants to share, then that's up to him, but I can't tell you anything without his permission." Lewis opened his mouth to speak but she cut him off. "I can't even tell Celeste, and she's paying my bills."

Lewis's shoulders sagged with disappointment but he didn't argue.

"Okay," said Audrey. "We understand. I really hope this is just a mistake."

"Me too." Mei rolled her shoulders, then rubbed the back of her neck. "What will you two do next?"

"We need to talk to Mrs. H," said Lewis, not looking thrilled at the prospect. "Find out who this bloody stalker was. He's our prime suspect. And we need to track down Nathan Roper, too, find out what he was really up to."

"Well, good luck." Mei got to her feet. "I think we're all going to need it."

60

Lewis

The heavy cloud of the morning had finally begun to thin and a pale sun broke through and made the grass glitter with frost. As they stood outside the door of Flat 6, Lewis noticed Audrey put her hands in her pockets and squeeze her arms to her sides. The sound of traffic and aeroplanes filled the air, and the smell of freshly dug earth reminded him of the police.

"Oh, hello, Audrey," said Mrs. Hildebrandt, when she opened the door. She was wearing a silk print tunic over leggings, and a pair of black loafers with a pair of interlocking letter Cs on them. Was that Chanel? A chunky crystal pendant hung around her neck, giving her a fashionable, bohemian look. She looked at Lewis with distaste. "And Lewis again. To what do I owe this pleasure?"

She sounded breezy but Lewis could see at once the nervousness in her eyes, as they flitted from him to Audrey.

"Hi, Mrs. H," said Audrey, smiling. "I'm sorry to bother you."

"No bother, although I'm expecting Fraser any moment. Do you want to come in?"

She saw them inside, and as they stood in her living room, all fringed lamps and cream furniture, and decorated with glamour shots of the actress in her heyday, Lewis could sense her discomfort. She must really not like him.

"Tea?" asked Mrs. Hildebrandt with faux brightness, but she couldn't hide her relief when they declined.

"We'll make it quick, Mrs. H," said Audrey. She'd insisted on taking the lead, in case Lewis somehow offended the woman. "I don't know if you heard, but Celeste asked me and Lewis to look into Linda's death. When the police still thought it was suicide."

Mrs. H put a hand to her crystal pendant.

"I heard. No offence, darling, but I hardly think you're qualified."

Lewis opened his mouth and Audrey shot him a warning look. He closed it again.

"No, well, that's as may be. But after what you told me the other day . . . well, I was wondering who it was who came to speak to you about Richard."

Mrs. Hildebrandt's shoulders dropped.

"Ah. I wondered if you'd told him."

So that was it. She was embarrassed about what she'd told Audrey about falling for Richard Glead's scam, and hadn't wanted Lewis to know.

"Just the top line," Audrey said, her voice gentle. "But now the police have arrested Roshan, we need to find who else might have had a motive for killing Richard and Linda. I was wondering if he gave you a name. The man who came to see you."

"You can't think the police have got it wrong, surely?" said Mrs. Hildebrandt, frowning. "They found the gun and everything."

"No, we just want to be thorough. What was his name, Mrs. H? We just want to go and ask him who else might have . . ."—she paused, searching for the right word—"had dealings with Richard Glead or his broker, so to speak."

Mrs. Hildebrandt fiddled with her necklace.

"It feels rather a breach of trust, Audrey, darling. I don't know if I ought."

"Please?" said Audrey, and there were the big eyes again. "If Roshan is innocent, we have to try and help him."

There was silence for a moment, then Mrs. Hildebrandt shrugged.

"Oh, all right, although I think you're barking up the wrong tree. His name was Roper. Nathan Roper. But don't ask me for any more details, because I simply don't know."

Lewis could have punched the air. Finally, a break. Nathan Roper and Linda's stalker *were* one and the same. That narrowed the field even further, with the added bonus of proving he'd been right.

"Thank you," said Audrey. "We really do appreciate it."

Another statement belatedly registered with Lewis. "What broker?"

"What?" said Mrs. Hildebrandt, and Lewis looked at Audrey.

"You didn't mention a broker."

"Oh. Didn't I?" She glanced at Mrs. Hildebrandt, who looked a little mortified. "There was another man, wasn't there, Mrs. H? Involved in Richard's . . ." She trailed off, clearly unwilling to use the word "scam" but not knowing what to replace it with.

"You can say it," said Mrs. Hildebrandt, sighing. "Richard's swindle. Yes, there was a man. I looked him up on the internet after we met and he had a website but it's gone now. I assume he was an actor of some sort."

"What was his name?" Lewis demanded. "What did he look like?"

Mrs. Hildebrandt flushed, and Audrey nudged Lewis to take it easy.

"Jonathan Smythe," she said, and Audrey gave her a supportive smile. "He was in his sixties, I'd guess. White hair. Quite rotund. A rather puffy face."

"Looked like a potato in a wig?" asked Lewis.

"Oh. Um, yes, I suppose he did rather. But in a terribly nice suit."

"Paulo Ram," said Lewis to Audrey. "He was running the scam with Richard. Maybe even the blackmail."

"Blackmail?" Mrs. Hildebrandt looked alarmed. "No one said anything about blackmail."

"Richard was up to all sorts, Mrs. H," said Audrey. "He was an awful man."

Mrs. Hildebrandt nodded.

"Are we done here?" she asked, looking from one to the other. "Only Fraser . . ."

"Of course," said Audrey. "Thanks for speaking to us. Hopefully this will be an end to it."

"I do hope so," said Mrs. Hildebrandt, seeing them to the door. "I can hardly bear to think about it. Oh, here's Fraser now."

As they stepped out onto the path, they saw Fraser coming toward them. He smiled when he saw them.

"Hello again," he said, blue eyes twinkling. "What's going on here then?"

"Morning, darling," said Mrs. Hildebrandt, kissing him on the cheek. "Audrey and Lewis stopped by for a chat. They're just leaving."

"How did you get in?" asked Lewis, by way of greeting. "We didn't hear the buzzer go."

The smile dropped from Fraser's face and Audrey let out the audible puff of a sigh. What was her problem now?

"Fraser has my spare fob," said Mrs. Hildebrandt, looking equally annoyed. "It's perfectly within the rules. Come on in, darling," she said. "We'll let these two go about their business, shall we?"

"Good idea," said Fraser. "Nice to see you both."

Mrs. Hildebrandt didn't exactly slam the door but she couldn't have shut it any faster.

"That was useful," said Lewis. "I wish you'd told me about the broker sooner. That gives Nathan-the-stalker a definite motive for killing Paulo as well as Richard. He was involved in the scam!"

"I forgot," she said defensively. "And now we know how Mrs. H managed to come in twice the night Linda was killed. The second one must have been Fraser."

"Yes, that's very helpful." Lewis paused for a moment, thinking. "You were right about him. I think we need to do a bit more digging into Fraser Townsend."

"Once we've tracked down Nathan."

"I think you need to call Val first," he said, mind ticking over as they headed back across the square. "Nathan's now top of our suspect list and we need to know just how much luck was involved in him getting to know Linda, and whether Val told him about Linda's murder or if, as we suspect, he already knew. Come on, let's go back to yours. I never finished making my sandwich."

While Audrey phoned the Dogs' Home and left another message for Val, Lewis made them both a very late lunch and they sat at her dining table to eat, the plates and breadcrumbs reminding him of Linda's last sad meal.

"Another suspect," said Audrey, picking up a crumb from the wooden tabletop and dropping it carefully onto her plate. "Roshan and Nathan for definite, and maybe Victor and Fraser now too. Whenever we cross one off, another two pop up in their place."

"Yes, Fraser is ringing some alarm bells," agreed Lewis. "The only fly in the ointment is Linda. Richard and Paulo are connected—anyone connected to Richard's victims would have motive to kill them both—but killing Linda still doesn't make sense unless she was in on it, and there was nothing in either the flat or the shop to suggest she was."

Audrey fell silent, chewing on her lip.

"What?" he asked. "What's bothering you?"

"I don't know. I don't want the murderer to be someone from Marchfield but something's bugging me. I think I've seen something recently. Something important."

"What kind of thing?"

She shook her head and closed her eyes.

"I don't know. It feels stronger now. I keep trying to picture it, but every time I get close, it slips away."

"Something in the square? Something to do with Fraser and Mrs. Hildebrandt?"

"Maybe," she said slowly, then sighed. "I didn't tell you this, but I thought I was followed yesterday."

Lewis sat up at once.

"When?"

"On the way back from work. I took a detour and ran into Mrs. H. She and Fraser gave me a lift back."

"That's a coincidence," he said. "The night we were following Victor, I was sure a silver car was following us."

"Really?" She shivered, and picked up another crumb. "That's not good. I'd hoped I was just being paranoid."

For a moment, he considered telling her about the sensation he'd had the previous night, of being watched in the square, but then decided against it. She was fixated on Marchfield being a safe place, in spite of all the recent evidence to the contrary. No need to make her any more paranoid than she already was.

"That's probably all it was," he said, shrugging. "Thinking about Linda being watched. It gets inside your head."

"Yes. It does."

Something Audrey had said earlier resurfaced in his memory.

"Your idea that there might be two killers . . . that would fit, you know. If the police are right, and Roshan did shoot Richard Glead and Paulo Ram, Linda's killer could still be one of our other suspects."

Audrey's phone chirruped and she pulled it out of her pocket and frowned.

"Looks like we'll find out soon enough. Mei's on her way home."

61

Audrey

"How did it go?" Audrey asked Mei, the moment she walked through the door an hour later. "What's happening with Roshan? Can you tell us?"

Mei sighed, taking off her coat and draping it over one of the stools before answering. She looked drawn and wrung out.

"Against my advice, Roshan wants me to tell you and Celeste everything. He knows Celeste believes in him, and he thinks you will too. Said he knew you were acting on Celeste's behalf for Linda."

"Good," said Lewis.

"You won't be saying that when you've heard the case against him," said Mei, pulling out a chair and joining them at the table. "I don't even know where to begin."

Audrey reached for her hand and squeezed it.

"Just tell us straight. What did Sofia say, first of all?"

Mei took a deep breath.

"She said she got an anonymous tip-off on Friday night, after she got back to the station. Someone called in and asked for her by name. Said Linda had been having an affair, and that Paulo Ram had been blackmailing her over it. Sofia went to the Dogs' Home, and then the church, to talk to the priest you mentioned, Auds. Roshan's name came up pretty quickly."

Audrey's blood ran cold. Lewis had been right. This was all her fault.

"Prime suspect is now the gardener, so they requested permission to search the grounds at Marchfield again. When they spoke to Roshan, he denied it but, of course, they found the gun straight away, and arrested him."

"What was he even doing here?" Lewis asked.

"He claimed someone put a note from Celeste through his door, saying her lift was broken and asking him to come in. He hadn't kept it though, and Dixon denied leaving it.

"The gun meant they were able to get a warrant to search his flat, at which point Sofia found a cushion matching one of Linda's in his lounge, among a load of other cushions. Hiding in plain sight, she said. Roshan claimed he didn't recognise it. Shortly after that, they found some pictures of Linda taped to the back of his bedside cabinet."

"What kind of pictures?" asked Audrey, and Mei sighed again, rubbing the crease between her eyes.

"Creepy ones," she said flatly. "Photos of Linda in her flat, taken through the window with a long lens. Photos of her talking to a priest outside the church. Of her in a coffee shop, and outside the animal shelter. Walking up the path of her sister's house. Everywhere she went, he was there, snapping away with his camera."

There was silence as they took this in, and Audrey's stomach twisted.

"An anonymous tip-off?" said Lewis, his tone contemptuous. "If that's not suspicious, I don't know what is. Linda knew him. How could he have stalked her without her knowing it was him? Without anyone here noticing him sneaking around, taking pictures?"

"Because he's the bloody gardener," growled Audrey. "No one notices him because he's always here, working. No one likes to look at other people working. They like to imagine it's magic and that no one has to get their hands dirty. Just like no one looked too closely at Linda, because we didn't like what we saw when we did. That made her invisible too."

She thought she might throw up. This was so much worse than anything she'd imagined. Even when she'd considered Roshan a suspect, she'd been imagining a crime of passion. Not this seedy, dirty crime born of terrifying obsession.

"Anyway," Mei went on, "the cushion is in the lab and they expect to find Linda's DNA on it. So now they have both murder weapons—one found in Roshan's flat, one found in the garden—plus evidence that he was stalking her. The traces of soil on the carpet in the Glead flat match the soil from the garden here, and Roshan's handprint is on the bottom of the rail to the fire escape."

"Anyone in Marchfield could have got soil on the carpet," said Lewis. "Including the Gleads. They must have found soil when they emptied the vacuum cleaner, for crying out loud! And if his print was only at the bottom, then he could have touched the rail when he was sweeping the path or trimming the hedge."

"If I was defending, I'd be making that case too," said Mei. "But you can't dismiss the rest."

"Are his prints on the gun? Or the cushion?"

"No, but then he'd have worn gloves."

"Even with the cushion?" Lewis turned to Audrey for support. "This can't be right. It's too neat, like we said. It has to be a setup. Are they sure it's the same gun?"

"Yep," said Mei. "They put a rush on ballistics. They're saying he killed Richard out of jealousy, killed Linda out of rage at being rejected, and killed Ram because he knew too much. Roshan's denying everything, but they've got a good case."

Lewis looked at Audrey again, as if hoping she'd also speak up for Roshan, but she couldn't. She knew what it was like to be on the other side of that window, to feel watched every minute of the day, to be too frightened to go out, or even open the curtains. She felt full of impotent rage, horrified that it had been happening under her nose and sick at what it had led to. And worse, she felt ashamed, because she should have recognised a stalker when one was right in front of her. She might have been older but she was clearly no wiser.

"He sat and listened to Linda tell him how frightened she was," she said, hot fury building inside her. "When all the time, he was the one frightening her. She thought she was being stalked because of Richard, but it was about her all along, and Roshan was comforting her, advising her."

"This has to be a setup," said Lewis, ignoring what was right in front of him. "Someone planted that stuff in his flat. Why would he take the cushion? Why would he *keep* the cushion and put it on display? He'd have to be a psychopath."

"Don't you see?" said Audrey, "he *is* a psychopath. It wasn't about Linda, it was about him. She was just an object he fixated on. Stalkers think their victims belong to them. They want to control them. They want to win. Richard was in the way, so he had to go, but when Linda wouldn't submit, she had to go too. The cushion was a trophy. It's sick, but it fits."

Lewis stared at her, then turned to Mei, who was suddenly at Audrey's side, offering silent support.

"This is demented," he said. "You were both defending him this morning."

"The evidence is clear," said Mei. "He's not the man we thought he was."

But Lewis shook his head and rounded on Audrey.

"When it was logical that Linda killed her husband, you refused to believe it because it didn't fit her character. Refused point-blank, regardless of what the evidence said. Roshan's character hasn't changed since this morning, but you're accepting this nonsense wholesale!"

"You were the one who kept him on the suspect list," retorted Audrey. "Now there's all this evidence and you're changing your mind? Why? Because it's too obvious? Not clever enough for your books?"

"Psychopathy is a hidden condition," said Mei, sounding tired. "They're often very charming to the people around them. No one knows the truth except the victims."

"Do you not think—"

"You should leave now, Lewis," said Audrey abruptly, and she had to turn away from his dumbstruck face. "Mei's exhausted and I am too. We can talk about it tomorrow."

"But—"

"Sorry," said Mei, ushering him out into the hall. "It's been a hell of a day but it'll seem better in the morning."

"For who?" demanded Lewis.

"For everyone," said Mei firmly, and Audrey heard her opening the front door. Mei's voice dropped for a moment, so low that Audrey barely caught the tail end of their goodbyes. ". . . okay? Just give her tonight."

The door closed and Audrey heard the keys turning in the lock.

"What did you say to him?" she asked, when Mei returned to the kitchen, and a faint blush coloured her cheeks.

"I just told him you were tired and needed to rest," she said. "Don't look at me like that, Auds, I didn't tell him anything, I promise."

Audrey spent the rest of the afternoon curled up under a blanket on the sofa in the lounge, her head pounding and her stomach churning. She felt as though she'd been punched in the chest.

That evening, they watched a terrible straight-to-TV film on the Christmas channel, but as the predictable plot played out in front of them, Audrey's mind was on one thought and one thought only.

Roshan Jones. And how on earth she could have got it so wrong.

62

Lewis

Lewis nearly slipped as he stomped down the steps from Audrey's place, already glistening with frost. That made him think of Roshan, so carefully salting the area outside Celeste's house. As much as it annoyed him when Audrey discounted people simply for being nice, now that he was faced with it, he couldn't see a man like that, so concerned for the well-being of others, being a triple murderer.

The sky had clouded over again and in spite of the hour, the square was as dark as if it were dusk. The street lamps had just come on and the air was damp and chilly, making Lewis shiver in his coat.

As he neared the courtyard, however, a movement near the side gate caught his eye and he turned just in time to see someone disappearing through it. He didn't know who it was, but his agitation was so high that he didn't care. He jogged up to the gate and opened it, looking both ways to see who had just left.

Victor was hurrying away down the road, bag swinging in his hand. Lewis watched him go. Four o'clock on a Saturday afternoon didn't tally with Victor's previous nighttime excursions, but perhaps he should follow him anyway. At the very least he could prove he wasn't as useless at following someone as his previous attempt had suggested. He slipped through the gate.

With it not being so dark, Lewis easily kept Victor in sight this time. He followed as he turned right onto the Embankment, and as he crossed the Albert Bridge junction, Lewis's excitement rose.

He trailed Victor to Battersea Bridge, quietly muttering, "Please turn right, please turn right," to himself. When he did turn right, Lewis silently cheered. Victor was taking the same route as the other night.

On the Fulham Road, Lewis began to close the gap between them, determined not to lose his quarry again. As they neared Duke's Burgers, his eyes hurt with the effort of keeping Victor in view, but when he stopped outside a plain black door beside the entrance to the bar, Lewis halted, and darted to the side.

He watched as Victor pressed a button set into the wall, and waited. The door opened and in he went, and the moment it closed, Lewis ran over to it. The mystery was about to be solved.

Except that it wasn't. The door was unmarked and the buzzer at the side simply labeled: ARTISTES ONLY.

Lewis stood back and looked at the building. The bar beside it—Proud Maggie's—was a drag club, and now that Lewis wasn't staring at Victor's back, he spotted the sandwich board outside proclaiming: "Saturday Cabaret, 5 p.m.–11 p.m." He paused. Surely not?

He looked at the door and considered, then sighed and pressed the button. He was done being subtle.

A little old man opened the door.

"Yes?"

"I've come to see Victor," said Lewis. "Victor DeFlore."

He waited for some pushback, to be asked more questions, or to show ID, but the man just stepped aside and waved him through.

"Come on in. Down the corridor, third room on the right."

Increasingly baffled, Lewis walked down the hall, which was painted a grubby mustard yellow and lined with framed photo upon framed photo of spectacular-looking drag queens. The first door stood open to a large room filled with mirrored dressing tables, each surrounded by light bulbs and supporting more makeup than Lewis had ever seen before. Two of the chairs were already occupied by artists in hairnets, the first dabbing foundation on her face with a sponge, the second painting bright blue eyeshadow onto her eyelids.

The second room was empty of people but full of clothes—the walls lined with racks of feathery dresses, sequinned jumpsuits and unidentifiable items in leopard print—while the third room held yet more mirrored dressing tables and a dozen wigs on stands.

And Victor.

"You're a bit early, my darling," said Victor, pinning up a sweep of hair on a blonde wig before standing back to take a look. "I've only just start—" He caught sight of Lewis in the mirror and froze, turning slowly to look at him.

"Hi, Victor," said Lewis, sheepishly raising his hand.

"Did you follow me?" asked Victor, his tone sharp and his eyes narrowed.

"Yes."

Victor barked a short laugh.

"Least you're honest. Can I ask why?"

"Suspicious behaviour in the gate logs," said Lewis. "Coincided with Linda's murder. We had to look into it."

"That's the police's job," said Victor, sitting down in one of the salon chairs. "I told them I was here all night, and they spoke to Maggie and the girls to confirm it. Besides, they've arrested someone now."

"The police may have the wrong man," said Lewis. He looked around the room. "You do hair and makeup then?"

Victor sighed.

"No makeup. I'm a hair technician. Learned in the navy."

"What?"

"The crew was always putting on entertainment, getting dressed up, putting on a show. I'm not much of a performer but I like the wigs. You have to be clever creating a hairpiece, see? How it's structured, how it's balanced. So you can dance and move about without it falling off. And those boys could dance, man. I do three evenings a week here, plus the weekend cabaret. Gets me out of the house, meeting new people." He looked at Lewis, who could see his own puzzled face in the mirror. "What did you think I was doing?"

"Well . . . I don't know." Lewis shrugged. "Something a bit criminal, to be honest. You were pretty shady about it."

Victor smiled.

"I'm not ashamed, but I'm also not brave enough to tell people I work in a drag club. My generation . . . they can be less accepting about these things."

"I understand. Look, I'm sorry I followed you. I won't tell anyone if you don't want me to."

"Not even Audrey?"

"Maybe Audrey," Lewis admitted.

"You might be wrong about Roshan," said Victor, after a moment, looking uncomfortable.

"Oh? Why?"

"I thought nothing of it at the time," he said, "but the night Linda died . . . I'd just come through the front gate and was passing the maintenance shed when I thought I saw something. Just a quick flash of white, behind the hedge. I went back, but there was nothing there, so I went home and forgot about it."

"What did you think it was?"

"I thought it was a bird, maybe, or my eyes. I'm not getting any younger, am I? But now . . ."

"Now you think it was Roshan. Leaving with the murder weapon."

"Yesterday, I'd have said it was impossible. But the police know their business. You should leave it alone."

Lewis sighed. Anyone with access to the square could have been hanging around the maintenance shed in the dark, but it was always kept locked. And then there was the missing cushion found in Roshan's house. The missing *beige* cushion.

Victor brightened up. "You can stay for the show if you like? I have free tickets and I never use them."

"Oh. Sorry, I can't tonight," said Lewis, feeling guilty when he saw Victor's disappointed face. "But perhaps next week? I could bring Audrey. I mean, I could ask Audrey. She might like to come."

"Any time," said Victor, shrugging. "Just let me know."

He left Victor to his wigs, emerging from the black door back onto the Fulham Road. That made one less suspect, and he'd done it without the cleaner or without going around the houses, at least the metaphorical ones. Just Nathan and Fraser to go.

As he reached the Embankment, he looked out over the river, where ribbons of mist were beginning to form over the grey water. The back of his neck prickled and he turned without thinking, catching a glimpse of a silver car as it turned a corner out of sight.

The case was getting to him too now, he realised, as he let himself back into the square. He glanced up at Audrey's as he crossed to his flat. All this talk about being watched, and strangers getting in unseen had clearly made her uneasy, and now it was starting to rub off on him. He was used to being oblivious. He *liked* being oblivious. Finding he suddenly had someone to worry about was an unwelcome and uncomfortable feeling.

That evening, he dug his headphones out.

63

Audrey

Audrey was still in bed when her phone rang at ten o'clock on Sunday morning. She'd tossed and turned until the small hours, and when she'd finally dropped off, she'd dreamed of a hand around her throat and had woken an hour later, her duvet wrapped tightly around her.

She reluctantly stuck an arm outside the covers and reached for the phone. It took her two tries to jab the green button before pressing it to her ear.

"Hello?" she mumbled.

"Hello, is that Audrey? It's Val. Valerie James."

"Oh, hi, Val," said Audrey, wriggling up into a sitting position and rubbing her eyes. In all the horror, she'd forgotten she was expecting a call.

"I had some messages to call you? Sorry it's taken so long. We've had the police in, and all sorts this week, so I'm behind. Sunday's supposed to be my day in the kennels. What can I do for you?"

"It's about Nathan Roper," she said. "Bit of a strange question, but when we met last week, you said you'd let Nathan know about Linda. Did you call him at home?"

"I wouldn't do that. I waited until he came in for his shift, but I needn't have bothered. He already knew. Saw it in the news. Why?"

"No reason. Just . . . uh . . . trying to help Linda's sister get a list together for the funeral. Wanted to make sure Nathan knew."

She pulled a face. That was clumsy. Val didn't seem to notice though.

"A couple of detectives came in to speak to us yesterday," she said, and Audrey heard papers rustling in the background. "Told us it wasn't suicide after all."

"We heard that too. What did they want to know?"

"Wanted to know who Linda worked with, who her friends were, whether she ever brought her husband here. They spoke to everyone."

"Including Nathan? What did he say?"

"Not much. Said Linda had brought a chap here once, to see Muffin. Somebody Jones, I think it was. And that Linda went to church. I didn't know that." She sounded sad.

Audrey's breath caught in her throat. Nathan had been the one to put the police onto Roshan, not Reverend Fitzbride. Nathan, who'd claimed not to know the name of Linda's friend.

"Has Nathan been volunteering with you long then?" she asked.

"About six months, I think. He'd have had his training before that though, which takes a few weeks. Plus, he could only do certain shifts."

"Were he and Linda on all the same shifts? Together?"

There was a pause as Val thought.

"Pretty much. Why?" Her tone became suspicious. "Why are you asking me all this? You don't think he's involved in Linda's death, do you?"

"No, nothing like that," said Audrey hurriedly. "Just Linda's sister was wondering whether to invite him to the service too. If they were friends."

"Oh."

"One last thing," she said. "Did you tell Nathan that Linda wanted to adopt Muffin?"

"No. Didn't occur to me. Now was that all? Only I've got a lot to do before I head out to the kennels."

"Sorry. Yes, that's all. Thanks for your help."

"No problem," Val said, then sighed. "Sorry for snapping. The police have got me on edge, and I've not been able to fill Linda's slots yet."

"Happy to help if you need it," said Audrey, then added wickedly, "Lewis too."

"Thanks, love, but you need to go through the training. You take care now, and let me know about that service for Linda."

"Will do, Val. Thanks again. Bye."

She hung up and threw the phone down onto her bed, wrapping her arms around her knees.

Nathan Roper was a liar.

Linda's death hadn't been in the news. It had pissed Manny off, and she'd checked herself. Not a word about it, so Nathan had lied to Val about that. He'd told Lewis he didn't know who Linda's friend was, then a few days later, had named Roshan to the police.

She took a deep breath, trying to get her thoughts in order. Roshan could still have done all the things he was accused of. She knew only too well that people weren't always what they seemed. He had means and motive, and the gun had been found in Marchfield. He was still the most likely culprit.

But Nathan Roper had a grudge against the Gleads, had spent months cosying up to Linda and lied about it, then put Roshan well and truly in the frame. There was only one reason Audrey could think of for that.

To get himself out of it.

64

Lewis

Lewis was asleep when a knock at his door woke him up. He was still in his chair and blinked, confused, then checked the time. Not even eleven yet. Were the police coming to interview him again?

He shambled through to the hall, yawning so widely his jaw cracked.

He opened the door and found Audrey standing outside. She was wearing an oversized sweater and jeans, her hair in a messy knot on top her head, while the shadows under her eyes told him she hadn't slept well either.

"Um, hello," he said, hastily combing his fingers through his unruly mop of hair. Why hadn't she texted him? He was still in yesterday's clothes and, more importantly, yesterday's deodorant. "What's going on?"

"I'm here to clean."

"What?"

She held up a bag, stuffed with dusters and cleaning products, and smiled.

"You said your place was filthy, so I'm here to clean it."

"No, no no no." He couldn't let her clean his disgusting hovel. "No way. Besides, I can't pay you."

"It's a freebie." She sighed. "Look, you were right, okay? About Roshan. Possibly, anyway. Possibly right. He might have been framed."

Lewis folded his arms.

"What changed your mind?"

"Val called me this morning. Nathan Roper started volunteering a few months after Linda. Specifically requested a particular set of shifts too. And by the time Val spoke to him on Wednesday, Nathan already knew that Linda was dead, and Val didn't tell him about Muffin either."

"Damn."

"One more thing. She said that when the police came back to talk to them, it was Nathan who told the police about Roshan. He specifically named him as being the man Linda brought to the Dogs' Home."

"But he told me he didn't know who it was!"

"Exactly. He's a liar."

They looked at each other for a moment. It was big of her to come over and say she'd been wrong.

"I have news too," he said, making his own peace offering. "I followed Victor again last night. I know why he was so cagey about his nighttime excursion."

"Oh?"

"That drag club on the Fulham Road. Proud Maggie's. He works there."

Audrey blinked.

"Excuse me?"

"He's a hair technician, works on wigs and stuff. Learned in the navy, apparently. Anyway, he saw something in the garden when he got home, the night of Linda's murder. A flash of white, near the shed. Could have been someone running off with the murder weapon, or else hiding it."

"And only Roshan uses the shed so we still can't rule him out." There was a pause as she absorbed this new information, then suddenly she grinned. "Victor really does wigs? For drag artists?"

"Yep."

"Reckon he could get us tickets?"

He laughed.

"He's already offered." He looked at the cleaning bag hanging by her side. "Why the cleaning?"

"I need to think and cleaning helps me think." She craned around him, trying to see past him into the flat. "Now let the dog see the rabbit."

He held fast to the door, barring entry.

"Absolutely not."

They glared at each other for a moment, then she held a spray bottle up to his face.

"This is a highly caustic cleaning solution. I have twisted the nozzle precisely forty-five degrees, meaning this bottle is locked and loaded. You do not want to be in the way when this bad boy goes off."

"You could just . . . twist the nozzle back again?"

Her green eyes fixed on his in a way he found alarming. The plastic trigger creaked beneath her fingers.

"Fine," he sighed, standing back to let her in. "But I want it noted that I find this weird." She barged past him and through the hall, heading straight for the kitchen. "Very weird!"

"So noted!" she called back. He heard a thump as the bag of cleaning supplies hit the floor.

He closed the door and followed her through. What was he supposed to do now?

"Do you want a cup of coffee or anything?" he asked, hovering by the kitchen door. Was that what people usually did for their cleaners?

"God, no, you don't want to be ingesting anything while I'm using this stuff. In fact, you should probably open some windows." She opened the oven and looked inside, her face breaking into a delighted smile. "Things are about to get noxious."

65

Audrey

Audrey pulled her sponge through the loose, foam-topped grease, and the gleam of clean enamel made her smile behind her mask. She rinsed the sponge in the washing-up bowl she'd placed on the floor and soon, the inside of the oven was sparkling clean.

After hovering behind her for an uncomfortable few minutes, Lewis had gone off to have a shower. He'd apparently slept in his chair last night, and said he needed a wash and a change of clothes.

It felt good to get stuck into a challenging clean. It was therapeutic and distracting. Her brain worked better while she was busy, and she had a lot to think about.

"Hey," said Lewis, reappearing at the kitchen door, his hair wet and a clean T-shirt clinging to his damp torso. Audrey had assumed that underneath the coats and fisherman sweaters, Lewis would probably be a bit doughy, but that did not in fact appear to be the case.

"Hi," she said, pulling down her mask and moving aside so he could see her good work. "Look at this."

"Wow," he said. "I didn't know it could be that shiny."

"It's a thing of beauty," she said happily, climbing to her feet. She poured the filthy water from the bowl down the drain.

"Thanks for doing that," he said. "How does it help with thinking, though?"

"Just helps me organise my thoughts. I'll do the stove-top next."

"Before you fill the room with chemicals again, do you want a coffee?" He edged into the small room. "I don't have tea, but I could do you a latte?"

"Thanks, that'd be nice."

She pulled off her gloves and rinsed her hands, then squeezed past him and into the lounge. While the first-floor maisonettes had two storeys, with two bedrooms and a bathroom on the second floor, the single-storey ground-floor flats were still a good size. There was room for a sofa and armchair in Lewis's living room, plus a coffee table, an enormous TV, and a desk in the corner by the street-side window with the biggest, most luxurious leather wheelie chair Audrey had ever seen.

When Lewis came in carrying the coffees, he found her nestled in the desk chair and pulled up short.

"This chair is amazing," she said. "I can see how you fell asleep in it."

"Yeah, it's comfortable." He handed her a mug, then sat down in the armchair. "What were you thinking about? While you cleaned?"

"Nathan Roper. He has to be the killer, right?" Lewis nodded. "But how did he do it? He had to get in and out of Marchfield at least three times: once to kill Richard, once to kill Linda, and again to frame Roshan. He also had to break into Roshan's house to plant the incriminating photos. And he was at the shelter on Bonfire Night."

"I was thinking about that in the shower," said Lewis. "What if he wasn't? What if he snuck out of the shelter, knowing Linda was out of the way, then nipped over to Marchfield and did the deed? It'd be ten minutes in a cab at that time of night, and it only takes a few seconds to shoot someone. He could have slipped in behind someone else, maybe, when everyone was distracted."

"Risky though," said Audrey. "How could he be sure he'd even get in? And why kill Linda? Her murder seems more spontaneous than premeditated—perhaps his plan to persuade her to give the money back didn't work and he snapped? But he had the presence of mind to avoid buzzing the flat and then again after the fact to take the cushion with him? That seems . . . odd."

"It does," he admitted. "Unless you were a professional. But it is possible. Once he realises what he's done, self-preservation kicks in and he starts to clean up. But the doors still bother me. If he'd knocked on Linda's door, she'd have let him in, so why the business with the fire escape? And if you came in through the fire escape, why not leave the same way? The more time that elapsed between him leaving and the body being found, the harder it would be for the police, so why leave the front door open? It's like a deliberate trick to mislead us."

"Maybe it was," she said, taking a sip of coffee. "Maybe he's cleverer than we're giving him credit for. What about Ram?"

"I don't know," he said. "Maybe he'd always planned to kill Ram for his part in the scam, or maybe he arranged to meet him and threatened him. A final attempt to get the money back. Ram refused, so he shot him. But now you've killed all the suspects in the case. There's only you left. What do you do?"

"You need another plan," she said, picking up the thread. "You can't let the police figure it out themselves, because they'll end up back at you, but if you can set up someone else, you're off the hook. You know about Linda's friend, Roshan, and maybe she's told you he works in Marchfield . . . Ram's a bit of a sticking point, but if you can nudge the police into thinking Linda was having an affair, blackmail's not a huge stretch."

"Exactly." Lewis nodded. "You've lost all chance of getting your mum's money back, but at least you're not going down for three murders."

They looked at each other, and Audrey couldn't help but smile. They'd actually solved the murders! She was about to ask what they did next, when Lewis opened his mouth.

"Can I ask you a question?" His expression was odd and it put her on edge at once.

"Okay."

"The way you reacted to the idea of Roshan being the stalker. Something happened to you, didn't it?"

She felt herself flush and took another sip of coffee. She swiveled the chair away from him.

"It's all right," he said. "You don't have to tell me. But something did, didn't it?"

She didn't reply for a minute, the silence heavy between them.

"Mei and I met at university," she said eventually. "She was doing law, I was doing statistics. After graduation, I landed an internship at this huge insurance firm in Manchester, doing analysis. First step on the ladder, kind of thing. They had this huge open-plan office, all pods and booths and endless carpet.

"One of the bosses—Ross Farmer—was young, handsome, charming. He'd bring in pastries in the morning, pay for pizza when we stayed late, got us all work phones so we could keep work and home separate, or so he said. Everyone liked him but . . . I don't know. I found him a bit intense. Then one night, a group of us were working late and he made a pass at me. I was flattered but told him I wanted to keep things professional. He said he understood.

"But on the way home, I saw him standing on the street near my house. It was dark and I was tired, so I thought I was probably mistaken, but over the following weeks, I started seeing him everywhere. Outside my local coffee shop, outside my hairdresser's, outside the house at night. He never spoke, just stood there, watching. At work though, he was totally normal. It went on for months, until I genuinely started to think I was going mad.

"I talked to Mei and she was on the first train up from London to stay. She started collecting me from work every evening, making sure I was never alone. One night, he sat in his car outside the house for three hours and Mei called the police.

"By the time they got there though, he'd disappeared. They kept asking me what I'd said or done to give him the wrong impression. Implied I'd led him on or flirted for advancement. They didn't take it seriously.

"Then Mei started wondering how he always knew where I was. We found an app on my work phone, one that pinged him my location. I went to HR, informally. I didn't want to ruin my chances at the company. The woman said that unless I made a formal complaint, there wasn't much they could do but if I liked, she could have a quiet word with him. He admitted to asking me out but said I'd overreacted. But he did stop. Stopped following me, stopped hanging around the house. It was like it never happened. I still felt him watching me sometimes, but I convinced myself I was overreacting, like he said, and tried to get on with things.

"But one night, just before a big presentation, I got an email from his assistant saying everyone was working late and could I pick up some food. It happened so often, I didn't think to question it, just went out, bought some sandwiches, and went back to the office. But when I got to the conference room, there was no one else there. Just him.

"He told me the internships were coming to an end but that he could make a permanent position for me, if I wanted. I just needed to stop resisting the 'chemistry' between us. I said no, accused him of stalking me, and tried to leave, but he pushed me down onto the table and started choking me."

She heard the change in Lewis's breathing but she didn't stop. She had to get it all out.

"I grabbed the conference phone off the table. Clobbered him over the head with it, and ran. Left him on the floor of the conference room, bleeding. One of the cleaners saw me running. She took me to the police station, but he'd already called an ambulance and said he'd been assaulted. Said I'd gone crazy and hit him, and that he'd had to put his hand on my throat to stop me hitting him again. The marks on my neck were nothing compared to his skull fracture, but he said he'd drop the charges if I dropped mine and 'sought help for my disorder.'

"So I dropped the charges and left Manchester. My land-lord said if he could rent the house out quickly, he'd let me off the rest of the lease, but when he went to inspect it, it'd been trashed. Completely and utterly trashed. Furniture smashed up, graffiti on the walls, paint on the carpets . . . Ross must have broken in and destroyed the place. I lost my deposit and had to keep paying the rent while the landlord fixed everything.

"I crashed with Mei while I tried to get another job, but he had contacts everywhere and left a tombstone reference on my file so I couldn't get another job in the industry. I ended up sign-ing with a cleaning agency but most of their work was cleaning offices—after-hours, evenings, and weekends—and I just felt unsafe the entire time. So now I do private houses. The pay is terrible, I can barely afford my rent, and I can't clear any of my debts, but it could be worse. At least I'm doing something I like."

Lewis was silent for a moment and she couldn't bring her-self to look at him. She didn't know if he'd be sympathetic and pity her, or whether he'd be dismissive, and tell her she should have got over it by now.

As it was, he did none of those things.

"I'm sorry that happened to you," he said, his voice tight and angry. "He should have been locked up."

She shrugged, discomfited by the emotion in his reaction.

"I'm a bit sensitive still, I guess."

"I can see why. You never heard from Ross Farmer again?"

"Do you know, it's the weirdest thing. Not long after I moved to London, I was still seeing him. Mei and I were flat hunting—I had to get a loan for the deposit—and he'd just appear, like a phantom, in the strangest places. Even when we had our interview with Celeste, I thought I saw him outside. I panicked that he'd somehow ruin our chances to get the flat, and ended up telling her the whole story. You know Celeste, she was so sympathetic and understanding, asked lots of questions. She offered us the flat there and then. Told me I'd be safe in Marchfield Square and I believed her. After that, I never saw him again."

She rotated the chair from side to side, keeping her eyes on the floor, hoping he wasn't about to say something nice. She didn't trust herself not to cry if he did. After a few minutes, however, she looked up and saw him typing on his phone.

"Are you making *notes*?" she shrieked, and he jumped a mile in his seat.

"Just a few," he said, flushing beetroot red and shoving the phone away. "You should have killed that guy, and when I write it, you will. Might need to use a paperweight, though. I expect a conference phone is too light to do the job."

She tried not to laugh but failed spectacularly, which at least gave her a reason to wipe her eyes.

"So what do we do next?" she asked. "About Nathan? Tell the police?"

He shook his head.

"We need hard evidence. I say we confront him. Corner him in his flat, and record it. He'll probably deny everything but if we can force him to make another move, now Roshan's in custody, he might trip himself up."

She tried to ignore the lump forming in her throat.

"Confront him."

"Yes. We know he's got rid of the gun now, and they're too hard to come by for him to have another." He sounded confident but looked worried. "Not you though. You should stay here and if I don't come back, you can tell the police everything."

"Don't be stupid," she said, strangely touched by the offer. He might do a good impression of a socially inept goon, but there was some empathy in there. "We're both going. Although," she added, biting her lip, "I will leave a note for Mei. Just in case."

66

Lewis

They caught the bus to Battersea, skipping lunch, but neither of them seemed to notice. It was cold and grey as they walked from the bus stop, the air damp and smelling of petrol fumes. The wind was bitter against their cheeks, and Lewis was glad he'd invested in a good winter coat. Audrey's was too thin, and she pressed her arms into her sides in an attempt to stay warm.

Granville Gardens was on Granville Street, which was made up entirely of apartment buildings. After walking the length of the street, which included a brand-new development advertising over a hundred new "luxury" apartments, they were relieved to discover that the smallest, shabbiest-looking block at the end was Granville Gardens.

Lewis stopped at the entrance, examining the buzzers, then took a few steps back and looked up at the building.

"We need a plan," he said, scanning the windows and counting. "We need to get inside first, make sure he can't run."

"How do we do that?"

"I'm taking a leaf out of your book," he said, pressing one of the buzzers. "And gambling. Let's see . . ."

She frowned but said nothing, watching as he pressed the buttons for Flats 6 and 7, then waited, his heart thudding against his ribs.

"What?" barked a female voice over the intercom. "I'm trying to get the baby down."

"Package," said Lewis into the speaker. "I can leave it in the hall?"

"Okay, thanks."

The door buzzed and he pushed it open, grinning.

"How did you know which flat to buzz?" she asked, astonished.

"Kid's pictures stuck to one of the windows of the second floor. Four flats each floor. Lucky they were in."

They entered the building. It was less shabby inside than it was out, but gloomy, with no natural light and dark fire doors at every turn. They took the stairs to the third floor as quickly and as quietly as they could, lest either of the flats Lewis had buzzed came out to check for packages.

They stopped outside number eleven, and Lewis heard Audrey take a deep breath.

He knocked on the door.

For a long moment, Lewis thought no one was home. He put his ear to the flat door and heard nothing within. He looked at Audrey.

"Shit," she murmured, and he saw her shoulders drop as she relaxed. "He's not in."

But before Lewis could respond, the door was wrenched open and Nathan Roper stood in the doorway, frowning. He was wearing a faded black hoodie and cargo pants, and his hair was scraped back into a short ponytail.

The colour drained out of his face as he looked from Audrey to Lewis, recognition making his eyes widen in alarm. "What the . . . ?"

"We just want to talk," said Lewis, holding up his hands.

"Talk about what?" asked Nathan.

"Your mother. Marion," said Audrey. "And Linda Glead."

He looked from Audrey to Lewis and back again, and for a moment Lewis thought he was going to charge them.

"We know everything, Nathan," he said, putting his foot firmly against the door jamb. "The police know Roshan Jones didn't kill anyone. They have Richard's accounts, and when they find out about your mother, they'll trace the pictures back to you. If you talk to us, we'll give you a head start."

Nathan's eyes nearly popped out of his head.

"Wh—why would I need a head start?"

"For killing Richard and Linda Glead, and Paulo Ram."

"What?! I didn't kill them! I didn't kill anyone!" He balled his fists. "You tell the police that, and I'll sue you!"

"Let's have the whole story, shall we, Nathan?" said Audrey. "Can we come in? We shouldn't have this conversation in the hall."

Nathan reluctantly stood aside, closing the door behind them with shaking hands. He directed them into the lounge, a messy, cluttered room with posters of sports cars on the wall and piles of damp-smelling clothes on the sofa. Audrey perched beside Lewis on the edge of her seat, her elbows tucked into her body, as if afraid to touch anything.

"You don't have any pets then?" she said, once Nathan had sat down opposite them. She sounded mean and sarcastic. "You've not adopted any from the shelter?"

Nathan turned red.

"Landlord doesn't allow pets."

Lewis understood Audrey's hostility. This was the man who'd pretended to be Linda's animal-loving friend, but had instead added to her fear and misery. Who'd held a pillow over her face until she'd stopped breathing. He slipped his hand into his shirt pocket and turned on his phone's voice recorder.

"Shall we start by telling you what we know, Nathan?" began Audrey, her tone hard. "Then you can jump in whenever you like."

Lewis frowned but said nothing. He'd imagined he'd take the lead, but he had the feeling she needed to get this out. Nathan was breathing heavily, thick brows furrowed, his nostrils flaring.

"Richard Glead scammed your mother out of her life savings. Twenty thousand pounds, to be exact. You went to his shop and threatened him with the police, but he laughed at you. That was his style. So you started spying on him. Him and Linda. Following them, taking pictures, tracking their movements. You hoped you'd find out what Richard did with the money, where he hid it, where it had gone, because it certainly wasn't in any investment scheme.

"But Richard wasn't that obvious. You realised pretty quickly that Linda was terrified of him, but you figured maybe she was the answer. You'd been stalking them both for weeks by then, and knew she volunteered at the Dogs' Home, so you signed up, did the training, then got yourself the same shift pattern as Linda.

"You chatted while you worked with the dogs, digging into her private life and making her think you were a *friend*, even while you continued to spy on her. Do you know, she told Roshan that the only time she felt safe was when she was at the shelter? That's because it was the one place you didn't need to spy on her."

Nathan squirmed in his chair and looked at his feet.

"You started recognising the people they came into contact with," said Lewis, not wanting to be left out. "Like Paulo Ram, aka the broker Jonathan Smythe, and Brigitte Hildebrandt. And Roshan, Linda's only friend. Besides you, of course. Eventually, you realised she genuinely knew nothing about Richard's business. She only cared about dogs. So you had to come up with a different plan."

"If you could just get Richard Glead out of the way, then your friend, Linda, would get everything," said Audrey. "You knew she was a good person. She was bound to give the money back, once she knew what Richard had done. So on Bonfire Night, when she was busy with the dogs, you sneak away and break into Marchfield, and shoot Richard Glead."

"I never—" he began, but Audrey didn't stop.

"Linda's taken in for questioning but as soon as she's released, you go to see her. She tells you about her hopes for the future and her plan to adopt Muffin. She still thinks you're her friend. Then you tell her about your mother and Richard's scam, and ask if she'll return the money, except she doesn't know anything about it. She doesn't know where the money is or what Richard has done with it. You've committed murder and she doesn't know anything. You lose your temper and smother her with a pillow."

Lewis heard the crack in her voice and took over. He could see from Nathan's trembling hands and horrified expression that it was working.

"But now you're screwed," said Lewis. "The police can easily connect you to Linda, and Brigitte Hildebrandt can connect you to Richard. It's only a matter of time before they bring you in.

"You panic. You have to make it look like Linda's been killed by a stranger, so you open the fire escape and leave muddy footprints to suggest someone came in that way. You take the cushion because you don't know if you've left any DNA on it.

"Now you're trying to clean up," he continued. "You break into Glead Antiques, looking for Richard's accounts, but you can't find them. You call Paulo Ram, threatening to tell the police about the scam and get him to meet you. But he won't hand over the accounts either. You shoot him and now you've killed three people. There's no one else to blame but you.

"But you've got the gun, you've got some photos of Linda, you can set someone up. Roshan isn't just the perfect candidate, he's the only candidate left. You sneak back into Marchfield on Friday night and bury the gun in the flower bed, then on Saturday, you post a note through his door asking him to come in to work. While he's out, you break into his house, plant the cushion and the photos, and get rid of the rest. All you have to do now is call in an anonymous tip, confirm to the police that Roshan and Linda were friends, and that's that. Goodbye, Roshan Jones."

They stared at the sweating Nathan Roper, Audrey wearing a grim, if uneasy, smile. There were a few things the story didn't take into account, like the shoe marks on the sofa, or exactly how Nathan had managed to sneak into Marchfield undetected so many times, but maybe he'd stolen Linda's keys when he killed her. Apart from that detail, they had a very strong case.

"I . . ." began Nathan. "I didn't . . . I mean, I couldn't."

"Couldn't what?" asked Lewis. "You can't seriously be saying we got anything wrong?"

"Yes!" shouted Nathan, leaping to his feet and making them both jump. "It's true I was following the Gleads, and I did join the Dogs' Home to get close to Linda, but just to find out more about Richard, that's all. And I was at the shelter the entire time on Bonfire Night, I swear. There's like, six people who can vouch for me. I cared about Linda. I'd never hurt her."

"What about Ram?"

"I never called him! I've never even met him! I didn't even know he was dead until you just said!" Now he was pleading with them. "I never killed anyone. And I never framed anyone either. I swear I'm telling you the truth."

Lewis glanced at Audrey. If looks could kill, Nathan Roper would have dropped dead on the spot.

"Bullshit," she said. "Your photos of Linda were found in Roshan's house. How did they get there if you didn't plant them? And how the hell did you know about Muffin?"

"I . . . Muffin? What do you mean?"

"You knew Linda was going to adopt Muffin."

"So?"

"So Linda didn't decide that until Friday evening and she was dead by midnight. If you didn't see her on Friday, how did you know she was going to adopt the dog?"

"Oh." Nathan looked relieved. "Well, that's easy. That was Bridget."

"Bridget?"

"She told me about Muffin. When she told me Linda was dead."

67

Audrey

The stunned silence that followed seemed to last for an eternity. Audrey felt the room start to spin and she gripped the arm of the chair. Lewis cleared his throat.

"What?"

"Bridget called," said Nathan, sitting back down in his chair. "Asked me to meet on Tuesday. She told me Linda was dead—murdered, possibly—and that people might think I'd done it. She told me to get rid of all the evidence."

"Wait, wait, wait," said Lewis. "Back up. When did she call you?"

"Monday, I think." Nathan fumbled with his phone. "Yes, see?" He held up the screen so they could see the call log. Two calls from Bridget H. "Monday night."

"And you met her on Tuesday? How did she know about your evidence?"

"Because I showed her. When I met her the first time. I showed her all the names and statements from the other victims. All the photos. Glead was still doing it, you see. Meeting women. Swindling them. Sleeping with some of them. But Bridget said, in light of Linda's death, that I'd better get rid of it all."

"And did you?"

"Kind of."

"What does that mean?"

Nathan looked uncomfortable.

"Well . . . I didn't want to just dump it. I thought, once it had all settled down, that maybe I'd take it to the police. Maybe they could get some of the money back. So I gave it to her for safekeeping."

"With the photos?" said Audrey. "You gave the photos of Linda to Brigitte Hildebrandt?"

"Yes." Nathan looked from one to the other. "I didn't know that was her name though—Hildebrandt. She never told me. She said she'd keep them safe until the investigation was over. I swear, I never planted anything on anyone. I've never even held a gun!"

Audrey felt Lewis's eyes on her, and when she turned, his shocked face must have mirrored her own.

"It's one of them," she murmured. "Mrs. Hildebrandt or Fraser. One's been covering up for the other."

"It's perfect." Lewis sounded awestruck. "The perfect setup with the perfect backup. If anything goes wrong with Roshan, they have another fall guy ready and waiting."

They both looked at Nathan.

"Me?" he said, taken aback. "Bridget's setting me up?"

"Not yet," said Lewis, jumping to his feet. "But once we prove it wasn't Roshan, you're next on the list. Come on." He grabbed Audrey's hand and hauled her to her feet. "We have to get back to Marchfield."

"What about me?" called Nathan, as they headed out the door. "What should I do?"

"Get to a police station," Lewis yelled back. "And stay there. You're not safe here."

"I don't understand," said Audrey, as they hurtled down the stairs and out of Granville Gardens. "Why is Nathan not safe?"

"Because Fraser's been following us," said Lewis, dragging her down the street by the hand. "He'll know that we've just spoken to Nathan, and he'll be looking to clean up again."

"The silver car."

"He's been following us in a brand-new sodding Rolls-Royce and presumably one of his other cars Mrs. H was falling over herself to mention." He shook his head in admiration. "I can't believe it."

"Wait, slow down." She pulled him to a stop at the end of the road, her heart racing. "What's the plan here? We know where Mrs. H lives, why are we running?"

"Because they'll clear out. Look, if Fraser is who I think he is, then he's good. Really good. But in those circles, when things don't go your way, you don't stick around, you disappear."

"Who do you think he is?"

"The Fixer. I don't think he killed Richard. If he'd wanted to get Mrs. H's money back from Richard, he could have. Easily. I think Mrs. H killed Richard and Fraser tidied up, and he's been tidying up ever since. Linda, Paulo . . . they must have both known about Mrs. H, and Fraser's been making sure they couldn't tell anyone."

For the briefest of moments, Audrey felt just a tiny bit envious of Brigitte Hildebrandt. Finding a man who loved her enough to kill two people for her, in spite of her ancient fur hat and scuffed shoes.

The shoes. *Oh my god.*

She gripped Lewis's arms.

"The shoes! The marks on the bottom of the sofa. It wasn't Fraser who killed Linda, it was Brigitte."

"She has light brown shoes?"

"No, she has *nude* shoes." She almost laughed at his baffled face. "Nude shoes! Pinky-brown, supposed to be neutral, depending on your skin tone. Go with anything. She's been wearing the same pair for years because they're designer, but when I saw her after Linda was killed, they were scuffed." She groaned. "Fraser just bought her a new pair. And the perfume. I smelled perfume in Linda's house but it was so faint, I didn't recognise it. I'm an idiot!"

They started walking again, their eyes on the traffic as they searched for a taxi, and this time Audrey didn't notice the cold, damp air or the sound of the traffic thundering down the road.

"Okay," said Lewis, thinking out loud, "Mrs. H killed Richard, then killed Linda because she wouldn't tell her where the money was. She calls Fraser—he's on the gate logs that night with her second fob, coming in at eleven fifteen—and he takes the cushion and leaves the footprints to confuse the police. He plants the gun at the pawnshop. There are other guns there already, it's possible no one will even notice, but if they do, Ram's an excellent patsy; connected to Richard and dodgy as hell. But Ram spots the gun and knows he's being set up, so Fraser kills him instead, then uses Nathan's pictures to frame Roshan, knowing they can just as easily point the police in Nathan's direction should anything go wrong."

"Two things," said Audrey. "Why kill Ram? You said Ram and the Fixer were friends."

"I don't know," said Lewis, still scanning the road. "Maybe because he was part of the scam? Maybe Ram had come to clean out Richard's hiding place and refused to hand over the ledger? Fraser's doing anything to protect Mrs. H at this point. Why is there never a cab when you need one?"

"But they didn't get the ledger, we know that."

"Look, we can't know everything. What's the second thing?"

"The second thing is, once the police did find the ledger, they'd talk to Nathan again. Wouldn't he tell them everything he just told us? About giving Mrs. H the pictures?"

Lewis looked grim. "Something tells me Nathan Roper wouldn't be found alive to ask."

They drew to a halt at the bus stop.

"I think we should call the police," said Audrey after a beat. "I think it's time."

"Agreed," said Lewis. "I don't fancy facing Fraser Townsend without backup. Can you call Mei? See if she can meet us at the square with DS Larssen?"

"On it," she said, pulling out her phone, then noticed him reaching for his. "What are you doing?"

"Trying to get the last piece of evidence," he said. "I think we're going to need it."

The bus arrived and they got on, swiping their cards and finding a seat near the doors. Audrey's cheek grazed Lewis's shoulder as she watched him type.

"The Fixer runs out of Paulo Ram's shop," he explained. "Has done for years, but no one knows his name. No one except Ram. Ram's had his fingers in lots of pies over the last couple of decades, has lots of connections."

"How does that help us?"

"Unless you're born into a crime family, most people start out legitimate. Their real names exist somewhere. These gangs have long histories and longer memories. There'll be someone who knows something. I just need a springboard, which is why I asked the experts. Aha."

He handed her his phone, an old-school-style message board on the screen.

~CrimeWriter159~ Doing some research into Paulo Ram's recent demise. Known associates?

~TruCrimeFan99~ Chaz Shaw, Peter Guest, Mama Jack, Neil Leonard, Ray Ricketts, Frank Tapper, Mikey Willmont.

~**LilNarco**~ Neil Leonard's dead. Fished out of the Thames down in Gravesend. Ray Ricketts went down for running a dodgy tax scheme eight years ago, implicated a load of people at his trial, and died in prison. Rumour has it Guest's in Spain, but Willmont and Tapper are still around, if you know where to look. Heard Mama used Tapper a few years back for a problem with one of her boys.

~**CasualAlien1983**~ I heard that too. He was using the name Toser back then.

"Fixer candidates?" she asked, handing back the phone.

"Possibly. Willmont's unlikely though. Too high profile. Frank Tapper, though."

"Who's he?"

"No idea, but he has the same initials as Fraser."

"Tapper to Toser to Townsend?"

"I'd be willing to bet on that," said Lewis. "It's the perfect name. But we need a picture to be sure. Let's hope LilNarco can help."

Lewis took his phone back and while Audrey typed out a long and detailed message to Mei, he typed out his own message.

~**CrimeWriter159**~ Frank Tapper. What's his line?

~**LilNarco**~ Troubleshooter. When you know, you know.

~**CrimeWriter159**~ Any photos online?

By the time they were off the bus and walking back toward the square, the fog was growing thicker and Audrey had to steer

Lewis so he didn't walk into people while he hit the refresh
button six times a minute. They'd almost reached the front gate
when LilNarco came up trumps.

~LilNarco~ LES. 17th April 2004.

"What's that?" asked Audrey, as Lewis clicked the link.
"*London Evening Standard*. Archives."
He leaned against the railings and Audrey pressed in close
to read the article.

"Gang of hoods" leader convicted in absentia

The leader of a criminal gang in East Peckton was
today sentenced to ten years imprisonment after a trial
in absentia that lasted two weeks. Noddy Broning, who
absconded from custody before his trial, was convicted
of armed robbery and running what Judge Markham
described as a "gang of hoods" out of an abandoned air-
craft hangar in East Peckton.

There were two accompanying pictures, a mugshot of the
aforementioned Noddy Broning, and a photo of him enjoying a
day at the races, surrounded by a group of other men, all looking at the camera.

"Ho-ly shit," Audrey breathed, when she saw the second
picture.

There, standing at the back of the be-suited group, was the
man they knew as Fraser Townsend, taller than the others, and
younger than he was now, but unmistakeable nonetheless.

"It's him," she said in amazement. "Twenty years younger,
but it's him. You were right."

"*We* were right."

"And what," said a voice from behind them, "is it you think
you're right about?"

68

Lewis

Lewis heard Audrey gasp as Fraser loomed out of the fog. He was wearing an overcoat and appeared broader than before, while the twinkle in his eyes had disappeared, leaving nothing but a cold blue that pinned Lewis to the spot.

"Hi, Fraser," said Audrey, her voice breathy with forced brightness. "You made me jump."

"Did I?" he said mildly, looking from one to the other. "You must have been distracted. I was standing there for several minutes."

Lewis's body temperature dropped several degrees, and he stepped closer to Audrey. He fumbled in his pocket for his keys.

"Hands where I can see them, please," said Fraser, a gun appearing in his hand. "Let's not do anything silly."

"Wh—What's going on?" asked Audrey, and Lewis admired her ability to act under pressure. He was too busy staring at the gun, a small-calibre Sig, by the look of it. With a silencer. "Why do you have a gun?"

"Don't play dumb, Audrey," said Fraser, his tone disapproving. "It doesn't become you."

A noise behind Fraser made him tilt his head. The soft thunk of a car door. Footsteps.

"Get back in the car, Brigitte," called Fraser into the fog, but the footsteps only paused, then continued again.

"What on earth are you doing, darling?" said Mrs. Hildebrandt, when she emerged, wearing her fur hat and a trench coat. She noticed Audrey and Lewis standing in front of the gates. "Oh, hello, Audrey. Lewis."

"Hi, Mrs. H," said Audrey.

"Why are we all standing around?" said Mrs. Hildebrandt, turning to Fraser. "What . . ." Her eyes fell on the gun and her face turned ashen. "Oh, Fraser. What are you doing?"

"Protecting you, darling. Now get back in the car, please."

Mrs. Hildebrandt began to tremble.

"But you can't . . ." she said. "It's Audrey."

Lewis's spine turned to ice at the exclusion. Is that what going to neighbourhood fireworks parties got you? *Not* murdered by a gun-toting gangster?

"Doesn't matter who it is," said Fraser. "I'm doing what needs to be done. Get back in the car, please."

"Fraser, darling . . ." Mrs. Hildebrandt put a hand on his arm. "There must be another way."

"There isn't," he said, with conviction. "Now get. In. The car."

Mrs. Hildebrandt hovered uncertainly between them for a moment, then dipped her head and stepped aside. At the same time, Audrey took a small but quick sidestep toward the gate post. Lewis heard the lock disengage with a muted clank. Cheap coats had their advantages.

As one, they pushed backward through the gate but they'd barely got a yard inside when Fraser charged through after them and grabbed hold of Audrey. She yelped as he hauled her toward him, spinning her round and throwing an arm around her neck. He held her against him and lifted the gun to her temple.

Lewis froze. He held his hands up.

"Please," he said. "There's no need for this."

"I think there is," said Fraser, and although his eyes were glittering with menace, his voice remained calm. How many times had he done this?

"You can get away," said Lewis, trying to match Fraser's reasonable tone. "If you go now, you'll have plenty of time to leave the country." He nodded to Mrs. Hildebrandt, who was now standing beneath one of the trees that overhung the gate, her eyes wide and terrified. "Both of you. New place, new names."

"Oh, we're leaving," said Fraser, "don't worry about that. But the new identities pose rather a problem when one of you is a film star."

"But . . ." Lewis began, and he saw Audrey look alarmed. "She's not *really* a film star anymore, is she? Would anyone recognise her now?"

He could tell from the way Audrey closed her eyes that he'd said the wrong thing, even before Fraser's expression became angry.

"I recognised her," he snarled. "Anyone with an ounce of taste and culture would."

"Yes," said Lewis quickly, "yes, of course. I just meant . . ."

"I suggest you stop talking," said Fraser. He pointed the gun at Lewis. "Now turn around and start moving."

Confused, Lewis turned and began walking into the mist. He tried to remember what was in this corner of the square, between the hedges, the trees, and the path, but he was almost upon it when he realised. The caretaker's shed was so well screened by densely planted shrubbery that with the fog rising heavily from the ground, it would be a miracle if anyone spotted them going in.

"What's the plan here?" Lewis asked, heart hammering in his chest. "Roshan's in custody—there's no way anyone will think he killed us."

"They'll be looking for us within hours," added Audrey.

"Correct on both counts," said Fraser, putting the gun back to Audrey's head. "But the police have already searched his shed. They won't be coming back here. Gives me time to figure out what to do with the bodies."

"Nathan's heading for the police station as we speak," said Lewis, clenching his fists to try and stop his hands shaking. "You can't pin it on him."

Fraser's gaze was hard and unflinching.

"How inconvenient," he said. "I thought I'd set that up rather nicely. Still, always have a Plan C. A few text messages to Celeste, and this one's flatmate"—he tightened his hold on Audrey—"sent from your phones, should convince them you're off chasing a lead somewhere. Couple of amateurs, getting themselves into trouble. Could take the police weeks to track you down." He smiled a shark's smile. "Or should I say it *will* take them weeks?"

"Fraser, darling," quavered Mrs. Hildebrandt, making him start. "You must stop this. This isn't right."

"Right? Brigitte, you've killed two people. What's two more?"

"But that was different," she said pleadingly. "I lost control with Linda, I didn't know what I was doing, and killing Ram was an accident. If he hadn't brought the gun, it would never have happened. This is different, you must see that."

Lewis and Audrey reacted at the same time. Paulo Ram had brought the gun to Glead Antiques?

"Brigitte," said Fraser, with inexplicable patience, "I'm a problem-solver, this is what I do. Please stop arguing and make yourself useful. Open the shed."

Lewis saw Audrey stiffen in Fraser's hold and had to resist the urge to lunge at him. If the gun went off, it would be Audrey that caught the bullet. At least, right now it would.

Mrs. Hildebrandt scurried over to the shed and began fumbling at the door.

"It's locked," she said, sounding scared. "With a padlock."

"Four—eight—zero—seven," said Fraser. He smirked at Lewis. "I pay attention."

"Could you loose your hold a little bit?" asked Lewis, nodding toward Audrey, who looked like she might start hyperventilating. "Before she passes out."

"Might be better if she did," said Fraser, but he relaxed his grip and Audrey gasped, taking in gulps of air. Behind him, Lewis heard the rattle of the shed door as Mrs. Hildebrandt opened the padlock and realised that he needed to keep Fraser talking. As soon as they were inside the shed, they'd be fish in the proverbial barrel. If he could keep them outside, keep Fraser looking at him, then at least Audrey might have a chance to get away.

"So you didn't kill Richard Glead then?" he called to Mrs. Hildebrandt, as the shed door creaked open. She returned to Fraser's side, her eyes wide.

"Of course I didn't," she said, as offended as if she hadn't killed anyone at all. "That was Ram."

"Ram?" said Lewis. "Why?"

"Who knows?" said Mrs. Hildebrandt. "No honour among thieves, I suppose."

"Paulo denied it, Brigitte," said Fraser. "He said Linda planted the gun in his shop to incriminate him. She wasn't an innocent, she knew exactly what she was doing." He pointed the gun at Lewis and then the shed. "In you go."

Lewis took a few steps, then stopped, addressing Mrs. Hildebrandt again.

"Was that why you killed Linda? Because you thought she was in on it?"

Mrs. Hildebrandt's hand fluttered to her throat.

"No! I . . . I went up to give her my condolences, and to ask about Richard's investments. See if there was any of my money left. But she kept saying she didn't know anything. She said she was sorry if her husband had cheated me, but that we were the same, she and I. Me! The same as that pathetic little mouse." Mrs. Hildebrandt's eyes began darting around, and Lewis could see a flicker of the frenzy she must have been in that night, enraged at Linda's ignorance. "She rabbited on with platitudes about learning from our mistakes and God having a plan, and then started talking about dogs, of all things! Saying she was going to adopt some mutt from the shelter.

"The next thing I knew, I was standing over her holding the pillow and . . ." She put her hand to her mouth. "I must have had some sort of breakdown. I didn't know what I was doing. I've never hurt anyone before in my life."

Lewis frowned. She was convincing, he admitted, but then she was an actress.

"Then you panicked and called Fraser, didn't you? He came over to tidy up, removing any signs of a struggle, taking the cushion, and staging the footprints to confuse the police. He got you to go and talk to Nathan, put the wind up him about Linda's death and the police, and hand over the files. He didn't know your full name, so if push came to shove, you could deny ever meeting him. All you had to do was get Richard's accounts, and you could destroy it all and be in the clear. Until you killed Ram as well."

Mrs. Hildebrandt let out a strangled whimper.

"He was hiding the gun in the antique shop when I . . ." She stopped abruptly and swallowed. "I heard a noise, so I hid in the kitchen but then in he walked with the gun. I recognised him as Jonathan Smythe—Richard's fake broker—and he recognised me. We had a . . . disagreement, and the gun went off."

"It was Fraser," said Audrey, squirming beneath his arm. "That day in the pawnshop. Paulo was asking you to get rid of the gun for him."

"It was," said Fraser. "Imagine my surprise, sitting in Paulo's back room, when I heard your voices out front. I couldn't figure it out at first, but then I heard you asking the residents questions and realised you were trying to investigate. I thought it would be amusing to watch, but you turned out to be rather better at playing detective than I thought."

"Why was Ram planting the gun at Glead Antiques then?" asked Lewis.

"Because I rather had my hands full," said Fraser, glancing toward Mrs. Hildebrandt. "Paulo was the least of my worries."

"Until Brigitte called you again, and you had to clean up a second time. That must have cost you. Even if he was a swindler, Paulo was still your friend."

"It did cost me," said Fraser quietly, and Mrs. Hildebrandt gazed up at him lovingly, seemingly oblivious to Audrey's frightened face pressed into the crook of his arm. "But it was worth it. Which is why dealing with the pair of you won't lose me a minute's sleep." He advanced, dragging Audrey with him, and jabbed the gun at Lewis. "Get in there. Now."

Lewis looked at Audrey, and her eyes fixed on his.

"This is your fault," she said, and he blinked.

"What?"

"I told you this was a stupid idea, that we'd be in over our heads, but you ignored me."

"Now hang on—"

"And now I'm going to get shot and left in a shed. In a *shed*, Lewis."

"I'm going to get shot too. And be fair, it was Celeste's idea."

"But you agreed. I said it was stupid but you didn't listen. Just typical of you."

"Enough," barked Fraser. "Move."

But Lewis didn't move.

"What's that supposed to mean?" he demanded.

"You're so arrogant," said Audrey. "So convinced you're the cleverest person in the room. And now look at you."

"You could have backed out any time you liked."

"And left you unsupervised? Fat chance."

"Oh, because your supervision has worked out brilliantly, I suppose?"

"I said, enough!" barked Fraser, taking another step forward, shifting Audrey fractionally to the side in order to jab the gun at Lewis. It was all they needed.

Lewis launched himself at Fraser. He kept low, going in for a rugby tackle, while Audrey ducked and twisted at the same time, bringing her knee up to Fraser's groin just as Lewis made contact with his knees. The gun went off, not the bang Lewis had expected, but a muted crack; the effect of the silencer. Mrs. Hildebrandt screamed as she leapt away and the rest of them went down together, scrabbling around on the cold, wet ground.

"Audrey?!" yelled Lewis. He fought to get hold of Fraser's wrist, trying to get the gun away from him.

"I'm okay," she panted, as they wrestled with the man on the ground, who was bucking and punching in his attempts to get free. Lewis was vaguely aware of Audrey getting up and then Fraser cried out. Out of the corner of his eye, he saw Audrey's foot pressing down on Fraser's wrist, then a second shoe came into view as she kicked the gun out of his hand and into the bushes, while Lewis managed to bring himself up to a sitting position, pinning Fraser beneath him.

"Armed police!" shouted a voice from somewhere in the fog. "Nobody move. Everyone get down on the ground and place your hands where we can see them. We have you surrounded."

69

Audrey

Audrey froze and put her hands up, looking down at Lewis who scrambled away from Fraser and got to his knees, putting his hands behind his head. Fraser, however, simply relaxed onto the damp ground and laughed.

"Unbelievable," he said.

DS Larssen emerged from the fog, holding a taser, wearing a stab vest under her blazer. Audrey peered around for the other officers but could see none. Mrs. Hildebrandt stood quivering near the gates, tears running down her cheeks, and Audrey found herself wanting to go over and comfort her.

What was *wrong* with her?

Larssen took in the scene, then glanced at Audrey.

"You okay?"

"I'm fine," she said. "Thank you."

"You can stand, Mr. McLennon," said Larssen to Lewis. "And, Mr. Tapper, sit up please and put your hands behind your back."

"Tapper?" murmured Mrs. Hildebrandt.

"I don't think I will, if it's all the same to you, Detective," said Fraser, getting to his feet with surprising speed. He was at Mrs. Hildebrandt's side in an instant, putting his arms around her protectively.

"Stand away, Mr. Tapper," commanded Larssen, pointing her taser at him. "Hands where I can see them."

He ignored her, his mouth to Mrs. Hildebrandt's ear, reassuring her. Lewis stood up and went over to Audrey. He smelled of damp grass and had soil marks on his face. His coat was covered in mud.

"Mr. Tapper, I won't tell you again."

"It's Townsend," said Fraser, releasing Mrs. Hildebrandt and stepping away with his hands up. "No need for the taser, I am unarmed."

"His gun's there," said Lewis, pointing to where the weapon had landed in a bush a few feet away, but Larssen kept her sights trained on Fraser.

"Turn around and put your hands behind your back," shouted Larssen, not lowering the taser. They watched as Fraser did as he was told, Larssen quickly holstering her weapon before handcuffing him, then turning to Mrs. Hildebrandt, who was shaking like a leaf.

"You too," said Larssen, pulling a second set of cuffs from her pocket. "Turn around and put your hands behind your back. I'm arresting you both on suspicion of murder and conspiring to pervert the course of justice."

Mrs. Hildebrandt looked at Fraser, whose eyes flashed with anger even as he nodded.

"Do as she says, Brigitte."

Trembling, Mrs. Hildebrandt turned around. Larssen put the cuffs on her, then began to caution them.

"Where are the other police?" whispered Lewis to Audrey. "Was she bluffing?"

"I don't know," said Audrey. "There's someone there though, look."

A shadow was moving in the garden, deep in the fog, and Audrey peered into the gloom. What were they doing?

When Larssen had finished cautioning Fraser and Mrs. H, she pulled an evidence bag and a glove from her pocket and backed up to where Fraser's gun lay in the grass, never taking her eyes off them. As she sealed the gun into the bag, Fraser began to laugh again.

"Dear God," he said, rolling his eyes. "You're entirely alone, aren't you?" He glanced at Mrs. Hildebrandt and shook his head. "The things we do for love."

Then the sound of sirens filled the air, distant at first, but rapidly becoming louder and more urgent, and within a minute, the fog strobed with flashing blue lights. As she turned to look, a figure came out of the mist toward Audrey, and her heart lurched in fear.

"Mei!" she gasped, clutching her chest. "You scared the shit out of me! What are you doing here?"

"You asked me to meet you and bring Sofia," said Mei, "so I did. She told me to hang back until it was safe. Are you okay?"

"I'm fine."

Mei stared at Mrs. Hildebrandt, who was standing on the path with her hands behind her back, weeping.

"Was it really her?" she asked. "Linda and the pawnbroker?"

"It was," said Audrey. "I can hardly believe it myself."

"Mr. McLennon," called Larssen, her eyes never leaving Fraser and Mrs. Hildebrandt. "Would you open the gates, please?"

Audrey and Mei watched as Lewis disappeared into the fog and a moment later, a stream of police poured into the garden. Sofia took Fraser by the arm and walked him down the path toward the gate, followed by another officer escorting Mrs. Hildebrandt away, the fog so thick that they vanished in just a few paces.

"I think you'd all better go inside," said Larssen, when she returned. "It'll take us a while to clear the square in this bloody fog. It would be useful if you could stay in one place, then I'll come and take your statements." She looked pointedly at Audrey. "Your full statements, this time."

"All right," said Mei. "Our place?"

"No," said Audrey, glancing at Lewis. "Celeste's. This is her investigation, and she wants to hear the truth. We'll go to Celeste's."

70

Lewis

"So let me get this straight," began DS Larssen, looking from Audrey to Lewis with an exhausted look on her face. It was late, and Audrey, Mei, and Lewis had waited with Celeste until the police had finally arrived a few hours later. They were sitting around the dining table in Celeste's apartment, Celeste at the head of the table with Dixon behind her shoulder, while Larssen sat opposite them, her notebook open in front of her. DI Banham paced up and down behind her with a face like thunder, pausing occasionally to glare at everyone before resuming his pacing again. "The day you found Paulo Ram's body, you also found the ledger, took photos, and put it back."

"Yes," said Lewis.

"Why didn't you tell us?"

"We thought we'd be in more trouble than we already were," said Audrey. "Lewis was sure you'd find it."

"Of course we found it," growled Banham, stopping to glare at them both. "We know how to do our job."

"How did you find out who Mari R was?" asked Larssen.

"Glead Antiques social media. I saw Marion Roper on there and recognised the surname. Nathan shared all of Linda's shifts."

"Yes, we didn't go back to the Dogs' Home until we got the tip-off about Linda's friend," said Larssen.

Celeste smiled with what Lewis considered to be a bit too much satisfaction. "You didn't think Linda had been murdered."

"We spoke to Mrs. Hildebrandt," said Lewis, "who said that Nathan had been the one to tell her about the scam. That he had photos, interviews. We thought he'd done it."

"And rather than telling us, you popped over to Battersea to confront a suspected triple murderer yourselves," said Banham, froggy eyes bulging. "Explain that."

Audrey shrank back in her seat, but Lewis just shrugged.

"We didn't have any evidence," he said. "So we thought we'd stir things up, see what he said. We recorded the interview."

Larssen closed her eyes for a second and took a deep breath.

"That was *not* an interview," barked Banham.

"Send me that recording please, Mr. McLennon," said Larssen when she opened her eyes again. "But it was foolhardy to say the least."

"He said he didn't do it," said Audrey. "We didn't believe him at first, because he knew about Muffin, you see. But then he said it was Mrs. H who'd told him. That's when we knew."

"Muffin?" said Larssen, confused.

"The dog," said Mei, sighing, as if she also thought the whole Muffin thing was ridiculous. "On Friday evening, Linda decided to adopt a dog called Muffin from the shelter. But in spite of her being killed only a few hours later, a surprising number of people knew about it."

"A dog," repeated Larssen faintly. "I see."

"Linda had told Mrs. H when she'd gone up to see her that night," explained Lewis, "and Mrs. H told Nathan when she went to warn him. Told him he might be a suspect and offered to hide the evidence he'd collected. Then, when he realised we were still investigating, Fraser decided to frame Roshan. He buried the gun in the garden, then faked a note from Celeste, asking him to come in on Saturday. He waited for Roshan to go out, then broke into his house and framed him as the stalker."

"Which you fell for, hook, line, and sinker," said Celeste, getting to her feet. She walked over to the picture window in the centre of the room, and stared out into the darkness. Lewis wondered if she was sad about Brigitte Hildebrandt. The woman had lived in the square for years. Celeste probably considered her a friend.

"Perhaps," said Banham, stopping his pacing, "if your amateurs had been up front with us about what they'd found, we'd have had more reason to doubt the case against Jones."

"To be fair, it was a good case," said Larssen. "Jones never told us about his friendship with Linda, and the whole thing fitted the profile of an obsessive."

"The Fixer is good at what he does," said Lewis.

"Yes, how did you identify him?" asked Banham, suddenly less hostile. "Tapper's been missing for years, with not a whisper on any of our networks."

"I asked around, did a bit of googling. Found an old newspaper report with a picture. Just got lucky."

He felt everyone's eyes on him.

"A bit of googling," repeated Banham. "You expect me to believe that?"

Lewis said nothing, but he noticed Audrey smiling.

"Mrs. H said she didn't kill Richard," said Lewis. "She thought it was Paulo Ram."

"It's possible," said Larssen, nodding. "If Roper was about to report their scam to the police, that could have made things difficult for Ram. In their line of work, you sometimes have to get rid of a liability. We'll keep digging, though."

"What will happen to Mrs. H?" asked Audrey. "I really don't think she planned to kill anyone."

"That's for a court to decide," said Banham, back to scowling.

"If she makes a full confession, it'll help," said Larssen. "And it means you won't have to give testimony in court. But I heard part of your conversation in the garden before I arrested her, and Nathan Roper made a full statement when he presented himself at Lavender Hill Station earlier today. We should have enough to go to trial. We're still searching her flat, but no sign of the evidence file you mentioned yet."

"Fraser wouldn't be that stupid," said Lewis.

"No, I don't suppose he would. We have found a pair of shoes that match the marks you found on the sofa, though."

"I'll pay for Brigitte's lawyer," said Celeste, turning away from the window and walking back to the table. "The woman obviously lost her head, and I blame myself." Her cheeks coloured slightly. "For allowing the Gleads into the square, I mean. I take full responsibility for the events that transpired. She must pay her dues, of course, but she should be properly represented at trial."

Banham and Larssen exchanged a look, their frowns suggesting they considered this beyond eccentricity. But as the residents knew, this was par for the course with Celeste van Duren.

Once they'd emailed Larssen their pictures and recordings, the police got up to leave, Banham still radiating fury and insisting they make full statements at the police station the next day. Larssen however, smiled and shook their hands, and Lewis could have sworn he heard her whisper "Good job" to Audrey before she left.

"Sofia was right," said Mei, as Dixon saw the detectives out. "You did an amazing job."

"Thanks," said Lewis.

"I hope we don't have to go to trial," said Audrey. "I'd hate to testify against Mrs. H."

"She killed Linda though," said Mei.

"She did," said Celeste. "Nevertheless, it won't be easy. I'm very proud of you both. And now you're free to go back to your regular jobs."

"Oh," said Lewis, disappointed, thinking of his book. He grinned at Audrey. "We should have taken longer."

"Nonsense!" said Celeste, as Dixon returned from the hall. "I said I'd pay you for the month, and I will. I admit, I thought it would take you a little longer, but one shouldn't be penalised for efficiency."

Lewis looked at Dixon, feeling guilty about taking Celeste's money, but Dixon nodded.

"Take it," he said. "You've earned it."

Audrey's face turned pink again. That money would make a lot of difference to her, Lewis knew.

"Shall we have coffee, Dixon?" asked Celeste, walking over to the sideboard. "Perhaps a little nightcap?"

"All right," said Dixon with a smile. "Just the one, mind."

"Celeste!" exclaimed Audrey suddenly. "Your hip! You're not using your cane anymore."

Dixon paused, looking at Celeste as if this was a surprise to him too.

"Oh." Celeste appeared momentarily flustered and looked around for her walking stick, which was leaning against her armchair by the window. "Yes, it's much better now. Good as new. Well, it is new, of course."

"You had your hip replacement surgery?" Audrey looked astonished. "When?"

"A few months ago. When we were in Switzerland."

"I thought that was a holiday. You never said."

"Didn't I? I thought I had." She smiled at them all. "I must have had a senior moment."

Lewis was surprised Celeste hadn't mentioned her operation, but Audrey seemed particularly puzzled. The frown remained on her face for some time, even as she sipped the whisky Dixon handed round, as if she were thinking something through, and as they left 1 Marchfield Square a little while later, stepping into the freezing fog, she stopped beneath one of the street lamps.

"You know, we never considered Celeste as a suspect for Richard's murder," she said, "because of her trouble with stairs. But she could have got up to the first floor after all."

Lewis thought about it.

"I guess," he said. "But then why did she pay us to investigate?"

"I know." She shrugged. "It just occurred to me, that's all."

"You've solved the case," said Mei, glancing over to Mrs. Hildebrandt's flat, where bright lights and dark figures moving in the fog told them the police were still busy. "You got justice for Linda, like you wanted."

"We never proved for sure the coin was Richard's." He laughed. "Maybe Celeste's the Angel!"

"You're hilarious," said Audrey, rolling her eyes. "I was just saying."

The effects of the whisky were starting to wear off and Lewis shivered.

"It's cold," he said, sticking his hands in his pockets. "I'm going home. I've got less than three weeks to get a first draft down before I have to go back to work. Need to get back to it."

He'd only taken a few steps when he heard Audrey's voice behind him.

"I'll be over tomorrow afternoon," she called, and when he turned, he could barely see her in the mist.

"What for?"

"Coffee, of course." Her voice got fainter as she walked away. "And maybe I'll tackle the hall while I'm there."

The hall? he thought, as he let himself into his flat. What was wrong with his hall?

But as he settled down in front of the computer and opened his novel, he found the idea of a coffee break quite a pleasant one. Breaks were good, he told himself. Everyone needed breaks.

He cracked his knuckles and looked at the words on the screen.

He wrote.

71

Celeste

Celeste and Dixon sat beside each other in their armchairs by the picture window. Between the fog and the hour, it was almost pitch-black outside, but the faint rectangles of orange light told Celeste that her residents were all inside their homes, and Marchfield Square was safe once again.

"You might as well get it off your chest," she said to Dixon, who hadn't spoken a word since the children had left.

"If you hadn't killed Richard, Linda might still be alive."

"You think I don't know that?" she said. "How was I to know Brigitte had given Richard all her money? How could I have known?"

"I warned yer that you didn't know everything about them," said Dixon, his accent more pronounced in his agitation. "It was arrogant to think yer did. Arrogant to think you were the only one who'd think of the fire escape, and arrogant to leave the coin."

"I know that now. Although I've never left a footprint in my life."

"I blame myself as well," he went on. "I thought the plan to frame Ram was a good one—two criminal birds, one stone—but if I hadn't put the gun in his shop, he wouldn't have taken it to Glead Antiques and Brigitte would only be going down for one murder instead of two."

"He had no business carrying it around with him," said Celeste shortly, who felt not one iota of guilt about Paulo Ram's death. "Serves him right for trying to frame Linda."

"You got lucky there. If he'd succeeded, Linda would have been blamed for Richard's murder, alibi or no alibi. As it is, they can still pin it on Ram. They'd never have made that stick to Brigitte Hildebrandt, with everyone in the square as her alibi."

"As it was meant to be," said Celeste. "I waited for Bonfire Night for that very reason, knowing Linda would be at the shelter and everyone else would be together. But yes, that was fortunate." She sighed. "If I'm honest, Dixon, I don't feel too guilty about Brigitte. She smothered Linda with a cushion, for goodness' sake. All this time, I'd been thinking the Gleads were the only problem we had. I can't believe Lenny and I could be so wrong. But then he always did have a soft spot for women in trouble."

"As do you."

Celeste pursed her lips. One of the traits she admired most in Dixon was his wisdom, but she deplored it when he applied it to her.

"The world is better off without the likes of Ross Farmer," she said. "Even you have to admit that Audrey is a dream, and quite come out of herself with this terrible business. She's brought Lewis out too, which I consider a small triumph."

"She was nearly onto you. When she realised about your hip. I could see it in her eyes."

"I know. I found it rather exciting."

They fell silent, but she could practically hear Dixon brooding beside her.

"You've got plans for them, haven't you?" he said eventually and this time she smiled.

"Perhaps, perhaps not. But I shall think things through thoroughly next time, don't you worry. Up, down, left, right and inside out."

"Then go ahead and do it anyway."

Celeste van Duren smiled into the darkness beyond the gallery window.

"I never could stand a quiet life, Dixon," she said. "Never could stand it."

Acknowledgments

The road to publication is a long and difficult one, and I'm grateful that I haven't had to travel it alone. To the friends made through competitions, to the writing community I found online, to the publishing teams at Union Square & Co. and Bloomsbury Raven, I've been very lucky to have met and worked with some wonderful people.

First, thanks to Claire Wachtel and my brilliant US publisher, Union Square & Co., for taking the plunge on this book. Huge thanks especially to Juliana Nador, for your enthusiasm, kindness, and patience throughout. Thanks to my UK editor, Thérèse Keating, for loving *Marchfield* and for helping me make this story so much better, and to Alison Skrabek, Alison Kerr Miller, and Barbara Berger, for your editorial wisdom and attention to detail. Apologies for all the weird little Britishisms you had to check! Also, huge thanks to designer Patrick Sullivan for such a bold and classy cover, and Jared Oriel, Kevin Ullrich, and Sandy Noman for producing such a stunning book. I'm very lucky indeed.

Thank you to my family, for their unending faith and encouragement. To Andrew, for supporting this dream years before I ever let you read a word and for being pleasantly surprised when you did, and to Mia, for not being surprised at all. I love you.

Mum, thanks for the bedtime stories. This all started with you. I know crime novels aren't really your thing, but well done for not skipping to the end. Ed, you'll probably never read this, but if you do, think of this as an easter egg. Dad, you shaped my reading from the very beginning, and I wish so much you could have seen this. We miss you every day. And to my little sister, Sam. I've been telling you stories for the whole of your life and somehow, you're still not bored. Thank you all for everything, forever.

David H. Evans, thanks for your support over the years and for reading literally all the drafts (and half-drafts). Sorry to abuse your speed-reading skills so much. I'd like to say I won't do it again but we both know I'd be lying. To Kirsty Fitzpatrick and Simone Greenwood, thanks for the love, laughter, and magic you bring to my days; and to my friends, Fiona Noble, Paul Henderson, Helen Baker, Jon Woolcott, and Jenny Coombes, thank you for your love and support, and for understanding what this means to me. I'm so very lucky to have you all in my life. Thanks also to Iain Martin, Beth Archer, and Fiona Whitworth for just getting it, and to George Walkley for having excellent timing.

Thanks to Anna Barrett, who helped me shape that first draft of *Marchfield Square*, and to all the amazing writers I met online in 2020 and beyond, who have continued to be the best cheerleaders anyone could have. There are so many, but in particular: Vikki Marshall, Teara Newall, Butterfly Hartley, Charlett Goretzka, Annaliese Avery, the Write Magic crew, and the GEA team. Thank you, my lovely friends. To my CWIP group: Gemma Tizzard, Niloufar Lamakan, Silvia Saunders, Veronika Dapunt, Christina Carty, Jo Waldron, and Fiona Cooper; and my Cheshire Novel group: Rachael Dunlop, Jane Lomas, Elaine Chiew, and Mel Carvalho, thank you for all your support and encouragement, and particular thanks to Farrah Yusuf for your time and generous advice. And to Claire Quinn, thank you for your friendship, your wisdom, and for not letting me forget how amazing it all is.

And of course, huge thanks to Jason Bartholomew, without whom none of this would have happened; and to Joanna Kaliszewska, for making it happen again in new places. You are the definition of a dream team. Thank you for everything.

Book Discussion Guide

1. Marchfield Square is Celeste van Duren's safe haven, a planned community in a well-to-do area of London with a foot in the past as well as the present. What do you think makes it feel so safe for the residents? The location? The security? Or is it something else?

2. Why do you think Celeste van Duren has gathered all the residents around her? Is it noble and altruistic, or self-serving? Does she like the power she holds over them, or is that simply a side effect of her generosity?

3. In spite of being frustrated by Lewis's lack of consideration and occasional rudeness, Audrey appreciates his honesty and lack of guile in a way many of the other residents don't. Why do you think this is? Does the conflict between them bring out the worst in her? Or does Lewis's bluntness allow Audrey more freedom in her own reactions?

4. How did your understanding of the other Marchfield residents evolve as the book went on? Were there any clues that might suggest why Celeste has brought these particular people together? How might this community evolve in the future?

5. Audrey and Mei have a deep and caring friendship, but due to their differing circumstances, there could easily be an uncomfortable power dynamic. It's clear that Audrey is

aware of this, but do you think Mei is conscious of it too? How do you think the two women avoid it becoming a problem? And can any friendship survive long-term in those circumstances?

6. Audrey and Lewis end up working well together as team. Is this in spite of their differences, or because of them? Which attributes does each contribute to the investigation process, and how valuable are they? Could either of them have solved it alone?

7. Toward the end of the book, Audrey reveals why she left her chosen career and became a cleaner. Can you understand why she might have made that decision? Do you agree with it? Do you think she's hiding from the world at work as well as at home? Or has she found her true calling?

8. One of the themes in the book is the value of unlikely friendships. Which relationships between the residents can you see developing further? And what benefits will they bring to the individuals concerned?

About the Author

NICOLA WHYTE studied Drama at Aberystwyth University and spent many happy years as a bookseller before becoming a web developer. She now co-owns a digital agency in the West Country. She's been writing since she was very young, and her work has been listed for the Comedy Women in Print Prize, the BPA First Novel Award, the Cheshire Novel Prize, and the Daily Mail First Novel Competition. She lives near Stonehenge in Wiltshire with her family.